A Nation Divided

VOLUME ONE

Storms Gather

A Nation Divided

VOLUME ONE
Storms Gather

ROBERT MARCUM

Covenant Communications, Inc.

Cover images: *Sailors Ancient Kit* © Irina Tischenko, *Confederate Flag* © Aydin Buyuktas, *Aged America* © littleclie.

Cover design copyright © 2012 by Covenant Communications, Inc.
Published by Covenant Communications, Inc.
American Fork, Utah

Printed in Canada
First Printing: October 2012

20 19 18 17 16 15 14 13 12   10 9 8 7 6 5 4 3 2 1

ISBN 978-1-62108-182-1

To my parents, who celebrated their seventieth anniversary
this year and who have always believed in me.

And to my wife, my greatest advocate and the one who makes life a joy.
We're at forty-five years, and eternity will never be long enough!

Preface

I WISH TO THANK MY wife, Janene, for her honest suggestions and editing. And to Kathryn Gordon and the Covenant family, I thank you for believing I had the ability to write about such an important time in our history. This is a hard story to tell—there were so many rights and so many wrongs on both sides of the issue. The fact that we survived such a conflagration as a nation is both humbling and amazing.

Nearly 660,000 men lost their lives fighting for what they believed. All of us should acknowledge such a sacrifice. But we should also remember—remember what pride and a rush to war can really cost. If we do not learn the lessons such a war can teach us, we are bound to repeat the same mistakes. Pride is the one true evil. If we learn anything from the Civil War, it is to be a humble people.

Chapter 1

RANDOLPH HUDSON DROPPED TO THE hard ground, a bullet streaking through the air where his head had been. Confused and shaking with fear, he tried to force his body even closer to the earth as another bullet whizzed above him. Then another.

Then they stopped, the night suddenly eerily quiet and foreboding. His fear was paralyzing, so strong that he could not move, could hardly breathe. He tried to calm his racing heart as his tears wet the already rain-soaked ground.

Suddenly a strong hand grabbed him by the coat collar, roughly picking him up and half dragging, half carrying him over the soaked earth. He fought, but the grip was so firm and his shoes so slippery that it did no good. Wet mud splattered his face, and a firm palm in his chest pinned him against the rough-hewn boards of a nearby wall.

"Shhh!" The noise was hard and demanding. Rand caught and held his breath, choking down both air and words as he recognized the face that was just an inch away from his own.

His father turned away, peered into the night, and listened. Rand still held his breath. Then his father turned back and spoke quietly.

"Are you all right?"

Rand nodded quickly. Large for the young age of twelve, he frantically swiped at his tears, lest his father think him a coward.

"What is in your head, son? I told you, under no circumstances . . ." Rand winced at his father's anger and frustration. "You could have been killed."

"I . . . I just wanted . . . I didn't know . . ." He forced the words, his fear still heavy against his chest.

Baker Hudson was watching the street. Voices, more shooting, and angry screams pierced the air from several directions.

"You should not have come up here, Randolph. I told you to stay home, take care of your mother and Lizzy!"

"Mother said . . . she needed you . . ." He choked on his own tears.

Baker's eyes softened, and he took a deep breath. "All right, all right. Calm down. I need you to settle down so we can get out of here."

Rand finally got his racing heart under control and stared out from behind the wall past his father into the dimly lit street. The full moon revealed no movement; his father took his hand and pulled him up and into the street. There was a sudden flare and explosion. Rand's scream split the air, and—

Rand sat straight up with a jolt, his eyes wide, anger and fear gripping his heart with tight fists once more. As always, it took several deep breaths to wrest control from this recurring nightmare. He was covered with sweat and immediately threw off the covers. The last embers from the fire in his room gave enough light for him to stumble to the cabinet. Leaning against it, he lowered his head and took several more deep breaths then stood erect, poured water from the pitcher into a basin, and doused his face with it.

The dream was always the same, and it was always just as real as when he had actually lived it. It was the last time he had seen his father alive.

Grabbing a towel, he dried his thin face and dark hair. At nearly six feet tall, Rand had dark eyes that glinted when he smiled and pierced to the soul when he was determined. Like his father, he had thick, black hair and he wore no beard, though he had to shave at least once a day to prevent it. His shoulders were broad but his muscles elongated, quick and powerful when called upon, and he had a sharp mind with an uncanny ability to see solutions that most other men grasped for but never found.

He lit a lamp and glanced at the picture of his father on the end table. Baker Hudson stood tall and somber, his musket slung across his shoulder. He had died that night.

Sitting in the chair in front of the hearth, Rand put his head in his hands, wondering if the dreams would ever stop, ever quit haunting his nights. He picked up a second picture of both his father and mother from the reading table next to his chair and let his thoughts drift back.

As part of the Nauvoo Legion, Baker Hudson had helped protect the city against mobs, violence, and even friends who had turned enemies. He was well thought of, even loved by the leaders of the Church, and had been asked to lead a company of Saints west when that trek began. But all that had changed when Baker Hudson was killed just a few days before they were to leave.

The Hudson home had been in turmoil after the deaths of Joseph and Hyrum Smith at Carthage. Rand didn't know why then, and wasn't completely sure why even now, but his parents had carried on hushed arguments about what would happen, where they should go, and whether they would follow Brother Brigham. When attacks from mobs resumed and the less firm in the faith began to leave the Church, his mother also seemed ready to leave it, while his father remained steadfast. But his mother had stayed by his side, even supported his decision, and all of them had been planning on making the trip west. But after his father's death at the hands of the mob, she became adamant. They would not go.

Packing up her children and her servants, she had moved them and all they owned south to St. Louis, telling them only that she'd had enough of the trials of a new religion and the sorrows it seemed to bring. Her seeming bitterness for the price her family paid had changed Rand's life forever.

At the time, Rand had hated her for it and swore to her that he would run away. But he had not. He could not, not with his father's last words to him haunting his thoughts. He had promised to take care of his mother and Lizzy, and he could not break that promise.

He looked at the picture of his parents, taken at their baptism. Now they were both gone.

He felt exhausted but knew he would not sleep. He never did after one of these nightmares. He got up and put on his wool robe and his slippers. Lighting a small lamp, he left his room and went down the wide staircase to the main floor, then to his mother's library. He entered, lit several lamps, and poked the embers in the fireplace before throwing on some kindling. When the flames were high, he added larger split quarters. He warmed his hands and then turned to glance around the room.

This had been his mother's domain—the place where she and Rand had spent endless hours during the last sixteen years discussing everything from business to women, though not always in that order. Papers, books, reports, and ledgers, all stacked high across the large cherrywood desk, seemed to await her return. Though she had been gone for more than a week, he could not bring himself to go through any of it yet.

But then there really wasn't any need.

He felt the tears welling once more and forced them away; going to her desk, he sat in his usual chair across from hers. Few people knew that Mary Hudson had been the silent power behind his father's highly successful business ventures. Intelligent and well educated for a woman of her day,

Mary Hudson had a knack for seeing advantage where others saw only ruin. She had counseled her husband privately to buy and sell properties that others regarded as liabilities. Her counsel had paid off in large profits, which his father and mother had used to build a small fortune. Of course, few men knew of his mother's involvement in those early successes in New York state and of her shrewd dealings with money after coming to St. Louis.

Though much of the Hudsons' early fortune had been spent moving to Nauvoo, building a home and business there, and making contributions to the building of the temple and the city, there had still been enough left to get a new start in St. Louis. The city was a boomtown with opportunities waiting on every corner if one had the ability to see them. Mary Hudson had possessed that ability and had used it to very quickly rebuild their fortune and take it to new levels. Hudson Company's manufacturing and shipping businesses were the biggest in the state and well known across the country. They stood now as a monument to Mary Hudson.

Rand took a deep breath and forced himself out of his chair to hers. Lighting the lamp on the desk, he began perusing the papers. It was time. Though his mother's assets had already been transferred to him and Lizzy, there were papers here that needed filing.

The sun was giving light to the room by the time Rand had the desk materials organized. He moved to the drawers, only to find the top left drawer locked. Removing a key from the middle drawer, he unlocked it to find a handcrafted walnut box inside. Though it was obviously worn from use, he could not remember ever having seen it before. Removing it from the drawer, he placed it on the desk, raised the lid, and looked inside. The book he found was familiar, though he had not seen it in years. With reverence he lifted it from the box and turned back the front cover, where his mother's signature graced the top in her beautiful hand, along with what Rand knew to be her baptismal date.

There was a knock at the door, then it opened slightly and his sister's head appeared. "Are you all right?" she asked.

He sat back, nodding. "Yes, fine," he said softly. "What time is it?"

She slipped inside the room and looked at the clock on the mantel. Apparently it was easier to ask than to look. "Six A.M."

Rand nodded, his eyes on his sister. She looked so much like their mother, her long blond hair hanging past her shoulders and setting off her thin features and large brown eyes. At five feet eight inches in height, she was taller than most women, and her thin form hid a physical ability and strength few women possessed. Smart, quick, and more energetic than most men, Lizzy was created in her mother's image. She lowered herself into the chair opposite him, her usually bright eyes filled with concern. "I heard you cry out. I . . ."

"I'm fine, Lizzy, really. Just the dream."

It was no surprise to Lizzy. She understood that from the time their father was killed, Rand blamed himself, though she and their mother had both tried to help him understand it was not his fault. He had finally come to a tentative peace about it during daylight hours, but the dreams continued.

"Did I wake Andrew?" Rand asked.

She shook her head in the negative. Andrew was Rand's best friend from the academy and had come to attend his mother's funeral. Andrew's room was three doors down from Rand's at the far end of the upper hall.

"When was the last time this happened?" Lizzy asked.

"Too long ago to remember," Rand answered. He didn't tell her he'd awakened early this time. The ending was the worst part, and he was glad to have been spared this time. The two men who had threatened to kill him after killing his father had not made it into this dream. He was grateful.

Lizzy looked around the room. Neither she nor Rand had been in it since their mother's death. So many memories. She felt the tears well up in the corners of her eyes and blinked in an effort to force them away.

"Have you seen this lately?" he asked, his eyes on the book as he thumbed through it.

She leaned toward him, grateful for the diversion. As she saw what it was, she drew in a soft breath. "It has been years. Where was it?"

"In this box."

Lizzy glanced at it. "The one Dad gave her when they got married. I remember."

Rand nodded. "The pages are more worn than I recall."

Lizzy took the offered book and thumbed through the pages. "Her notations. There seem to be even more."

"She studied for endless hours, hardly able to put it down. She'd even read as she worked so we could hear it. "

"Then she would discuss it with us at dinner," Lizzy said with a smile.

"It was her very strong witness about this book that gave life to my own testimony," Rand said.

"And mine." Lizzy took a deep breath, sadness in her eyes. "And then she just walked away."

"And everything about the Church became suddenly taboo," Rand said with some frustration.

"And we finally quit bringing it up."

"It just didn't seem worth it after a while," Rand said.

Both of them sat in silence, thinking, once more pondering the past.

"Do you remember sneaking off to church with me, at least at first?" Lizzy asked with a sudden smile.

He chuckled. "We told her we were going for a Sunday morning ride. We would take the horses up in the hills, then cut across the country and work our way into the city to the hall where the branch was meeting at the time." He shook his head as the memories returned. "There were lots of immigrants in those meetings. I couldn't believe some of their stories. The losses to disease and the horrible conditions where they lived in England and Ireland." He paused, a slight smile on his lips as he remembered. "I nearly went west with one of them."

"Christine. The green-eyed girl with blazing red hair." Lizzy laughed. "You had a horrible crush on her."

"Yes, well, you weren't without a few of your own. "The convert from France. You fell for him the first time you saw him."

She smiled. "It was the accent. Then I found out he was married." She played with a wayward strand of hair. "Do you ever wonder how our lives would be different if we had gone west?"

"I did at first." He shrugged. "But then things changed. They closed the branch when the Church started bringing converts through New York, and there was no place to go anymore. I started to find other interests on the Sabbath."

"But you kept reading, didn't you?" she asked as she handed their mother's book back to him.

"For a while, then just off and on, when a crisis or something happened." He fingered the cover of his mother's book. "I hate to admit it, but I stopped altogether five or six years ago. And you?"

"I still read almost every day, and I write letters to a few friends still, but most have stopped replying," she said wistfully. "They're married now, and I am sure they just don't have time." Lizzy was nearly twenty-four. Most girls were married by twenty, but not Lizzy. It wasn't that she had not had opportunity. But most . . . well, she wanted someone about whom she was passionate—someone who would more than just provide and protect, someone who made her go soft in the knees. There simply hadn't been any of those. At least not until now. She pushed aside the thought to prevent a flush to her face and tried to remember what it was she had been saying. "I . . . I feel just as strongly as I ever did about the Church, Rand, maybe even more so. It is so wonderful to know what we know. I hope you will start reading again. I really do."

He laid the book aside. "I still believe, Lizzy. What I know has prevented me from picking up horrible habits like spitting at spittoons and potbellied stoves. That must be worth something."

Lizzy chuckled. "Yes, it's worth a great deal." Her eyes went to her feet with a sudden thought. "Do you . . . do you ever tell others?" She looked up.

He avoided her eyes. "Not since we first moved here. You?"

"I stopped when plural marriage was announced." She paused. It hurt to think about. After moving to St. Louis she had told her closest friends about her faith. They had thought it unusual, a curiosity, and a good secret. Until the Church had announced plural marriage. Then everything had changed. "We are such hypocrites, aren't we?" She leaned forward, her eyes sad again.

"Yes, we are," he replied softly.

There was a knock at the door, and one of the servants announced that breakfast would be ready in twenty minutes. Lizzy glanced at the clock. She still had to dress and shoved aside her sadness before getting up from her chair. "Then I suppose the question is, what are we going to do about it?" She stepped around the desk and leaned down and gave him a kiss on the cheek, then stared into his eyes. "We must talk more about this, Rand. I don't like being a hypocrite, and I am tired of being alone when it comes to our beliefs."

Standing straight, she turned toward the door. "Don't forget, you have to take Andrew to catch his steamship this morning." She closed the door behind her.

Rand smiled. Lizzy was strong willed, and he could expect to hear about it all again, like it or not. But he found himself looking forward to it. His mother's death had caused more turmoil for him than he had thought possible. Though he was an adult of an independent nature, having both his mother and father gone was more frightful than he had expected. He had finally cried for relief through prayer. Possibly this was at least part of his answer.

His gaze went to his mother's book even as he wondered where his own Book of Mormon was. It wasn't that he hadn't seen it over the years—

he had—but he always just shoved it back in the drawer or closet or put it on a shelf and left it alone. He determined to locate it.

He put the wooden box back in the drawer and locked it as another knock sounded on the door and Lydijah entered. A large, round black woman with a deep voice that soothed as well as commanded, Lydijah was the head housekeeper and ran the place with a tight hand. Her husband, Mose, of similar size and nature, ran the farm. Rand loved them both nearly as much as he loved his own parents, and now they were all that remained of their Nauvoo family.

"Mista Ran', Mista Clay be leavin' soon. Breakfast be ready shortly. You best be gettin' ready." She glanced at the desk that had been cleaned and organized. "'Bout time you done it," she said. "Time to get on with things 'round here."

Rand smiled as she closed the door. Upon the death of his mother from something the doctors had never been able to pinpoint with any clarity, no one had cried harder or longer than Lydijah. It had been the same when his father had died. It was Lydijah who had most helped Rand deal with his loss—not just the loss of his father but the loss of his Nauvoo home, friends, and religion. Had it not been for Lydijah, Rand knew he would have drifted away far more quickly, and probably more completely, than he had.

The door opened again. "I means what I says, Mista Ran'. Now you get movin', ya here? You been mopin' 'round here long enough, and Miss Mary wouldn't like it none. Mista Benjamin has business wi'd you, and you hain't been in de office fo' days, and all dem steamers probably rotting in deys docks. Now get goin', 'fore I gets my whip and makes you do it."

The door slammed shut, punctuating her words and forcing a smile to Rand's lips. She was right; he hadn't left the house for more than a week, hadn't even thought of work, but he hadn't spent the entire time moping either. War was coming, and he had spent a good deal of time looking over possible places to take his steamers when it did. Missouri could go over to the South, and he wasn't about to lose his ships in the chaos. As one of the country's largest steamer companies, Hudson Company would lose millions if that happened—and as president of the company, Rand wasn't about to let it. He'd pored over maps for hours, written letters, and sent out inquiries about alternate ports. Being home had given him the chance to do so without the disturbance of everyday business and without raising suspicion with his uncle Benjamin, whom Rand wanted to keep out of these dealings.

Benjamin was his mother's brother and had been a constant thorn in her side—and now in Rand's. The man was horrible with money and accumulated debt like high mountains accumulated snow in winter. He had managed one of their companies into the ground, and something had to be done. To make matters worse, Benjamin had recently purchased a small foundry and gun works on credit; Rand had no idea how he intended to pay for it without the help of Hudson Company, but Rand was certainly reluctant to give it. It would be like pouring money into a raging river and expecting a full recovery.

He left the library and hurried upstairs to his room, shaving and dressing as quickly as he could.

Grabbing his valise and filling it with necessary papers, he blew out the lamps and left the room, meeting Lizzy as she stepped into the hall from her own room.

"Andrew's things have been taken to the carriage. May I accompany you to the docks?" Lizzy asked.

"Of course," he said with a forced smile as they started down the steps. The amount of time Lizzy had spent with Andrew made Rand a bit nervous.

To this day Rand found it amazing that he and Andrew Clay had ever become friends at all. Andrew had been spoon-fed Southern pride, states' rights, and slaves as human property since he was knee high to a spider. Whether he admitted it or not—and even though he had privately told Rand he hated slavery—he was as stuck in those arguments as the strict Southern-rights and slave-holding father he had sworn he would never be like. He was a Southern gentleman, born and bred, and any personal dislike he had for slavery was simply swallowed up by the greater Southern family into which he was born.

Rand hated the idea but knew that if war really did come, he and Andrew would almost certainly be fighting on opposite sides. There would be dozens of others he had served with at the academy fighting for the South as well. It gave him chills to think about.

"You are going to work," Lizzy said with a pleased smile. At times Rand admired the way Lizzy could hide her feelings. During the day it was if nothing happened, but at night, behind closed doors, he knew the tears flowed.

"Lydijah's orders," Rand said.

She smiled. "Good for Lydijah. You have been . . . well, hiding in that room of yours far too much."

"Yes, but with good purpose."

She glanced at him curiously. "And what purpose would that be?"

They had arrived at the dining room, where Andrew sat waiting. He rose to greet them, and Rand smiled at Lizzy. "We'll talk later."

Andrew, in full military uniform, placed his hat on a nearby chair. His sandy hair was short and, like Rand, he had no beard. He was of average height and weight, with blue eyes that glinted with mischief from a face that always seemed tanned. Most women found no imperfections in Andrew Clay. Rand had learned in their training at the academy that his friend was deceptively quick, agile, and strong, and that behind those clear blue eyes was a sharp, quick mind of above-average intelligence. With his smooth charm, he was never left wanting as far as women were concerned—a trait that caused Rand to worry a bit for Lizzy.

Rand greeted him with a smile and a "Good morning." Lizzy added her greeting with a bit of a blush that caused Rand to wince.

They all sat as breakfast was put before them under Lydijah's watchful eye.

"Eat hearty, Andrew," Rand said. "It is a long way to South Carolina."

"Your steamers have fine kitchens, Randolph. My greatest fear is that I will return overweight and very indolent. Your hospitality, and that of Elizabeth, has spoiled me."

Rand noted the glance between his friend and sister and once more felt a twinge of relief that Andrew's visit was over.

They talked of simple things, avoided politics as usual, and were soon finished. Gathering their coats, the three of them were soon in the carriage. Rand had forgotten his valise, and after returning to retrieve it, found himself sitting opposite Andrew and Lizzy. From Rand's perspective, they sat much too close to one another, and for a brief moment he was tempted to sit between them. He resisted, knowing Lizzy would throw him from the carriage for it. Still, it was a temptation.

The ride to the docks took only about fifteen minutes.

"I am sorry that I haven't been very good company, Andrew, but . . ." Rand started to say.

"It is quite all right. Lizzy has done her very best to pick up the slack," Andrew said with a glint in his eye aimed at Lizzy, who seemed to blush a bit.

Rand was not amused. "How are things at home, Andrew?" he began.

"Fine," Andrew said with a slight smile.

"And your father, is he still involved in politics?"

"My father will always be involved in politics," Andrew said flatly.

"I assume he supports Breckinridge," Rand said.

From southern Kentucky, John C. Breckinridge was a slaveholder. When Stephen A. Douglas had refused to support a proslavery agenda, the Democratic party had split and the slave states held their own convention, electing Breckinridge as their candidate.

"Yes, Father supports him. He feels Breckinridge will protect the South if elected."

"And continue to allow slavery," Rand said. "Breckinridge will not be elected, Andrew, and we all know it," he added. "The Southern states nominated him to send a message. They want a president who will protect slavery, and if we in the North don't give it to them, they will secede. Breckinridge is an attempt to blackmail the rest of us into submission. As I have said before, it is not a *solution* your father and other Southerners want, Andrew. It is a *continuation*, and we cannot, will not, give it to you."

Andrew glanced at Lizzy, "So I have heard."

"He just doesn't listen very well, I'm afraid," Lizzy said with a wry smile.

Rand and Lizzy had learned as children about the evils of slavery. Their father's father had held slaves, and Baker Hudson had learned to abhor it, setting free the slaves he inherited. From the time they were old enough to sit up straight, their father had taught Lizzy and Rand the inhumanity of the practice. Having Lydijah, Mose, and other freedmen as near relations helped them see them as real people instead of the beasts of burden for which some used them.

"Between the two of you, I have spent most of the last six years of my life hearing about the evils of slavery," Andrew said. "What neither of you seem to accept is that I was already a convert before I met you, but as I have told you endless times, it is not easy to set free nearly two hundred slaves without them immediately starving to death," Andrew said.

"Now, now, dear boy, aren't you being a little bit dramatic?" Lizzy said. "We have discussed at length how such a thing has been done on other plantations and it can work at the Meadowlands as well."

"Other plantations do not have my father to deal with," Andrew said with some frustration.

"That's true enough," Rand said. "A tyrant if there ever was one, Elizabeth."

"Yes, so you have both told *me* . . ." she pretended to count on her fingers, ". . . twenty-eight times. The only thing I cannot understand is how such a tyrant could possibly produce such a handsome man as this one." She leaned into Andrew and put her arm through his, pulling in close.

"It was his mother," Rand said, a bit disgruntled at his sister's show of fondness of Andrew.

"Yes, my mother," Andrew said, enjoying her sudden attention.

"Well, then, I must meet her sometime," Lizzy said with some allure.

"I will see if it can be arranged if you like," Andrew replied.

Rand caught the smile that transpired between them and wished he had not left them alone as much as he had. Though he and Andrew were best of friends he did not relish the idea of Andrew using his charm on Lizzy. Though Lizzy hated slavery even more than Rand did, love changed minds as well as hearts.

He was about to speak when they arrived at the dock and their carriage came to a halt. Rand pulled his watch from his pocket and gave it a hard look. It would be an hour before the steamer would leave.

"I fear to leave you two alone, but I am afraid I must. Uncle Benjamin has someone he wishes me to meet with this morning, and—"

"We are not in love, Rand . . ." Lizzy said with a sly smile.

Rand's relief at this bold admission was instantly dashed by her completion of the sentence.

"At least not yet." She smiled mischieviously. "Andrew knows that I would never marry a man who holds slaves, don't you, Andrew?"

"Unfortunately, yes," he said. "But, I shall continue to rely on my exceptional good looks and wealth to sway you somehow. Is it possible?"

"Highly unlikely," Lizzy said. "My hand is not so easily won, Mr. Clay. You should know that by now,"

"Yes, unfortunately, I do." He smiled. "But, I shall perservere in hopes that someday . . ."

"How gallant of you," Lizzy said wryly. She leaned over to Rand from where she sat and gave him a peck on the cheek. "Have a wonderful day, dear. Now boys, be off with you. I have shopping to do."

"Shopping? But I thought we . . ." Andrew was completely surprised at this sudden development.

Lizzy turned to him and gave him a full kiss on the lips. "I'm sorry, darling, but your steamer leaves, your plantation awaits, and life goes on."

He fumbled for his watch and quickly glanced at it. "Not for twenty minutes. We . . ."

"But I am sure you two boys have things to talk about. Now out of my carriage before I have Elliot give the boot to both of you. Go on. Scoot."

Rand and Andrew both scrambled from the carriage, received Andrew's luggage from Elliot, and watched the carriage pull away. Andrew was quite stunned, Rand amused.

"Charming, isn't she?" Rand said with a chuckle.

"Most of the time," Andrew said. "Why do I have the feeling I have just been struck by . . . by . . . lightning?"

Rand put his arm around his friend's shoulder. "You should actually take it as a good sign."

"And why would that be?"

"Because Lizzy likes you, more than I care to have her like you. That's just her way of leaving you . . . shall we say . . . wanting more?"

Andrew grinned. "Well, it worked."

"How does it feel to get a little of your own medicine?"

"Horrible," Andrew said.

"Then good for Lizzy," Rand grinned.

Rand picked up one of the two suitcases and waited while Andrew quit staring after the carriage and picked up the other. They started walking toward the steamer, *The Sam Houston*, one of Hudson Company's finest passenger vessels.

"She'll never marry you, Andrew," Rand said.

"Who said I would ask?"

"It's written all over your face. It is a look I have seen once before," Rand said.

Andrew had fallen in love once. She was a beautiful but very poor girl whom his father wouldn't let him marry.

"Yes, well, I fear that I feel even more strongly this time. What can I do to convince her?"

"Selling your slaves would be a good start."

"Umm. And if I did, would you give your consent as well?" Andrew asked.

"Of course, but we both know it will never happen. Your father—"

"Yes, once again, my father." They walked in silence until they reached the plank breaching the water between dock and steamer. "Lizzy is just what my father needs, you know."

"But your father isn't what Lizzy needs, is he?" Rand asked matter-of-factly.

The whistle blew and Rand looked up to see the captain. He waved and received one in return, then extended his hand. "I hope we see each other again, Andrew, but I fear that war will come and you and I—"

"You shouldn't. There will be no war. It will be settled before we get to that, you will see."

"Umm. I hope you are right, but I suppose having a war would have a silver lining," Rand said.

Andrew gave him a quizzical look.

"It will free all slaves and Lizzy might consider marriage, once she gets past how homely you really are."

Andrew chuckled. "I had forgotten how sharp your tongue can be."

"Then just another reminder. If you hurt Lizzy, I will take it very personally and you won't like the result."

Andrew could see he was very serious. "Yes, I know. Good-bye, Rand. I only hope you will let Lizzy decide for herself." With that he picked up both suitcases and boarded the steamer. Rand watched the boarding ramp be pulled aboard and the lines withdraw; he finally waved to Andrew, now at the rail on the second deck with other pasengers, as the steamer pulled away. He turned toward his office.

When he and Andrew first met, Rand thought they were poles apart when it came to slavery, but as time went on and they had private discussions—discussions where other Southerners were not present to influence Andrew—Rand found that Andrew personally and privately hated slavery, mostly for what it had done to his father. But in public he continued to defend it, helping Rand reach the conclusion that Andrew Clay would never publicly turn away from Southern views no matter the cost to him personally. It was the major reason he was concerned about Lizzy's interest in him.

He took a deep breath, shaking off the dark, hard feelings that such thoughts seemed to always bring. Possibly he should have said more when he first saw Lizzy's interest in Andrew growing, but he knew then, even as he knew now, it would do no good. Lizzy was her own woman and to try to drive a wedge between her and Andrew would only drive them together.

The sun seemed to disappear, and Rand pulled his coat up around his ears, his thoughts on Andrew's last words. Lizzy was also a smart woman with strong instincts—often stronger even than his own. He must trust that she would not let her heart control her good sense, because in the end it really did have to be her decision.

Chapter 2

Rand climbed the stairs to his offices and greeted his clerks as they busied themselves with the day's business while debating the pros and cons of the election. Two of the clerks were engaged in an argument. Rand was not surprised: one was a Douglas Democrat, the other a Lincoln supporter. The room quieted as he entered, and the argument stopped abruptly. The Douglas Democrat, Pete Hicks, turned to Rand, who had always maintained an approachable attitude toward the people who worked for him.

"Sir," he said with a wrinkle of concern in his brow. "You have met Lincoln, visited with him at length. Will he compromise? Surely he must, in order to prevent war."

A former Douglas Democrat himself, Rand had been intrigued with Lincoln's views and had traveled to Springfield, Illinois, to sit down with the "railsplitter" and hear his views personally. He had come away determined to sustain Lincoln in his bid for the presidency. His shift from Douglas had caused him grief from other businessmen in St. Louis who favored the South, and though he had stayed adamant, his views had cost him several friendships.

"Though Douglas might hold the Union together, he will only prolong and even increase the pain that will be required to end Southern intransigence," Rand said. "I am tired of being blackmailed by Southerners with the threat of secession every election. It has to end, and if that means war, I believe Lincoln has the strength, born of his past and what he has personally suffered and learned, to get the country through it."

The office was quiet, and Rand realized he had said the words with vexation.

Taking a deep breath, he finished in a more calm voice. "It is not Lincoln who will refuse to reach out to the South, Pete, it is the South that will refuse to reach out to Lincoln." He smiled, reminded them all that they had a business to run, and entered the door to his own office. The discussion continued, though somewhat more muted.

He removed his coat and hung it up before glancing at his desk, where a stack of papers demanded his attention. He took another deep breath and then turned to the window.

Democrats south of the Potomac River had declared Lincoln a "relentless, dogged, free-soil border ruffian . . . a vulgar mobocrat and a Southern hater." With endless statements like these and worse, they had talked themselves into the corner of hate, and only war would allow them to escape with their false but considerable pride still intact. To believe that Andrew, like so many others in the South, knew that the defense of slavery under the guise of Southern rights was wrong at its core was as frustrating as anything Rand had ever dealt with. But that pride was real, and Rand knew in his heart it would bring war.

He ran his hand through his heavy black hair. He knew he must not let the subject distract him at the moment. He had a business to manage and would begin to put his plans in place today.

He pulled several maps from his valise and spread them out, then withdrew a list of his steamers and possible ports he had researched in the North and upper Mississippi/Missouri drainage. He knew the size, hull depth, and ability of each of the steamers and painstakingly began to pick places for them to be sent when war broke out. Two hours later he was just about finished when a knock came at the door. Rolling up his maps and putting away his papers, he called, "Come in."

The door opened, and his head clerk, William Dickson, stuck in his head. "Your uncle is here, and he has three others with him. One of them is David Atchison."

Rand's brow furrowed. Atchison, a former Missouri senator, was an outspoken proponent of slavery and other Southern views and was not a bit shy about strong-arming others into agreeing with him. Rand was not pleased that his uncle had brought him here and knew it was a bad sign of just how desperate Benjamin may have become.

Benjamin Siddell loved money but had no knack for acquiring it. Of light complexion and handsome features, he was thin and tall and had sandy-colored hair that he was losing quickly. Rand's mother was his older sister and had done her best to keep him from becoming a total failure, but even she had finally given up trying to cover every debt and bad decision. Rand knew this visit was about money, and if it involved Atchison it meant his uncle was beyond desperate.

"See them in, William," Rand replied.

William ushered his uncle and the others into the office. Atchison and another were dressed for business, the third in frontier gear that included a sloppy-brimmed hat atop long, greasy, blond hair. The heavy beard hid his features and the hat his eyes, but Rand knew the man as well as he knew Atchison.

"Mr. Atchison," he said as evenly as he could to a man he disliked so much. Atchison was no longer a senator because of his fanaticism and direct involvement in the border wars between slaveholders and abolitionists of Missouri and Kansas. Men had died in raids he either led or encouraged in an attempt to ram slavery down the throats of Kansas settlers.

But the work of Atchison and his border ruffians had not discouraged antislavery settlement, and as that element grew in the state, Atchison continued to encourage raids and ambushes by his Missouri supporters. The antislave element fought back and atrocities increased, turning both states into chaos and literally bleeding Kansas for years.

But fate had a way of balancing some scales. While Atchison and the Missouri proslavery element were off bludgeoning Kansas's anti-slavery Northerners, immigrants from Germany and Ireland had moved into Missouri's large cities, especially St. Louis and its surrounding county. They quickly became a strong voice in her politics, and by the time the situation had finally settled in Kansas and Atchison and his proslavery friends had taken a good look at their own state, abolitionists outnumbered slaveholders in Missouri. Since then Atchison and his pro-slavery element had been fighting to keep their home state in pro-slavery hands, and it wasn't going well. The state was split between Little Dixie, including the Missouri River shores clear to Independence, and St. Louis; St. Louis was winning. Now Atchison and his friends, including Governor-elect Claiborne Jackson, were in a desperate battle to keep the state from falling into Northern hands, and Rand knew that Lincoln's election would make them even more desperate. They wanted Missouri in the South, and they would beat the state into submission if they could.

"Mr. Hudson," the senator said, grasping Rand's hand with a seemingly delighted smile. Atchison was tall, dark-haired, and self-confident. He had powerful arms and shoulders, and his dark eyes carried a hint of both arrogance and warning. Rand would not underestimate the man behind the smile. Though David Atchison had lost some power with the change of the political wind in Missouri, he was still a dangerous man in much of the state.

Atchison turned to one sitting next to him. "I assume you know Mr. Shelby."

Rand nodded, shaking the extended hand of a competitor in the shipping and steamboat business. Joseph Shelby lived along the Missouri River at Waverly and was the owner of small steamboats that worked from St. Louis into Nebraska and clear to the Dakota Territory. As a pro-slave advocate, he was involved with the border ruffians, and most knew it was his steamers that were used to import illegal slaves into Missouri and Kansas.

"Mr. Shelby," Rand said calmly. He then glanced over at the third man sitting on the couch, his muddy boots already resting on Rand's work table and a burned-out cigar clenched between teeth that were barely visible through his thick, unkempt beard.

"Mr. Ridges, your boots are not welcome on my table. Remove them," Rand said stiffly.

Ridges glanced up, the cold, dark eyes taking in Rand. He didn't move his boots.

"Mr. Hudson is right, Ridges. Get your boots down," Atchison said.

"This is a waste of time," Ridges said coldly. "We know where this black Republican stands."

"Mr. Ridges is as unwelcome here as his boots, Mr. Atchison, and if he doesn't take his tick-infested carcass out that door, I'll take the time to drive him out, and you and I will have nothing further to discuss," Rand said coldly.

Sam Ridges was the worst of this lot. Land owner in Little Dixie, border ruffian, gun for hire, murderer, and slave pen owner, he had been in Missouri since before statehood and was involved in both legal and illegal slave trading. Rumor had it he had been at Haun's Mill when a mob attacked Mormons and butchered more than a dozen. Slaves were no better than horses or mules to Ridges, and beating them to get more out of them before he buried them endeared him and his brother Castle to Atchison. But Rand had a particular distaste for Ridges. Ridges and Castle had murdered one of Rand's freedmen, who had tried to intervene in the whipping of a slave. Rand had sent the man on business to Independence and had regretted it ever since. Though Rand had been successful in getting Ridges arrested and tried, a pro-slavery court in that county had freed him.

Atchison raised his brow. "It seems you two gentlemen have a history." He motioned a thumb toward the door. It was meant for Ridges. "Wait for us outside, Sam."

Ridges got up slowly, a sneer on his face, but he left the room and slammed the door behind him, rattling its hinges.

"We come as friends, Mr. Hudson. If I had known . . ." Atchison waved his hand dismissively. "May we sit?"

Rand didn't answer, but the three men still standing found three wooden chairs and dragged them to face Rand, who had moved behind his desk. Atchison was obviously the talking head of this little group and cleared his throat to press his purpose. Rand's uncle Ben had already turned pale and was doing everything he could to avoid eye contact with Rand, knowing that if looks could kill he would be a dead man.

Atchison continued. "As I was saying, if I had known you and Mr. Ridges had personal differences, I would have left him behind."

Rand wanted to tell Atchison that he disliked him nearly as much as he did Ridges but he bit his tongue. "It is probably a good idea to get to the point, Mr. Atchison. I am sure you and Mr. Shelby are nearly as busy as I am and do not wish to waste time."

Atchison forced a smile. He clearly did not like being put on the defensive. Rand thought it might be a good place to keep him.

"We wish to hire your ships," he said.

Rand leaned forward, placing his hands on his desk. "I don't run illegal slaves, and you know it."

"Nor do we," Atchison said stiffly. "It pains me to say this, but in a few days it seems that an illiterate farm boy from Illinois will probably win the national election for president." He said the words with such arrogance and conceit that Rand's hair bristled.

"Kentucky," Rand said.

Atchison blinked as if he didn't understand.

"Lincoln was born and raised in Kentucky," Rand corrected.

Atchison bit on his cigar with force.

"But you're right, Lincoln will win. What is your point?" Rand asked impatiently.

"If he does, all Hades will break loose. It will be war, Mr. Hudson, war! And we who have Southern blood in us do not intend to give one inch." He sat back, fuming. Rand had heard of his quick temper, and now he had a front-row seat. "Our intent is to hire enough steamers to move a large body of men out of Missouri and Kansas to fight for the South. If we are to defend that blessed part of this unholy nation, we will need to move quickly. We want your steamers, Mr. Hudson, and we will pay you handsomely."

"It is a lot of money, Randolph," Benjamin added anxiously. "Strictly a business deal, one that could keep us financially stable during this entire conflagration. They do not care about your politics. I strongly advise—"

Rand gave him a cold stare that shut him up and then looked back at Atchison. "My uncle seems to think I should listen. Please continue."

Atchison gave him a patronizing smile. "Your uncle is right. We need those steamers, and we call on you as a Missourian with the largest and fastest flotilla for help. Whether you believe in the institution of slavery or not, you can surely see that we cannot let Lincoln and his Northern Johnnies take away our rights as citizens. We must all fight for them. We ask only that you work with us to protect and defend our liberties as citizens of the United States."

"You're not on the stump here, Mr. Atchison, so let me be clear. Secession is treason, nothing more, nothing less. Traitors have no rights, and therefore there is nothing to protect and defend." Rand's anger toward his uncle gave him the worst kind of burning in his stomach. Benjamin knew where he stood on slavery and secession and should never have brought these men through his office door. "Now, if you don't mind, I have work to do." He leaned forward, taking some papers in hand as if to end the conversation. The men stood their ground, though Benjamin, visibly sweating, removed a handkerchief to wipe his forehead.

Atchison leaned forward and looked at Rand with hard, cold eyes. "It is unfortunate that you feel as you do. Your uncle thought—" He smiled hard at Benjamin. "He told us you were a freedom-loving man—that you understood our right to defend our lives and institutions."

"Uncle Benjamin was right, but the institution I will protect and fight for is the Constitution of the United States and the freedom from the tyranny that slaves and even non-slave holders must endure under the hands of men like you and Mr. Shelby here."

Atchison grew red in the face, and Shelby seemed to think it prudent to intercede with some pressure of his own. "We had hoped for your cooperation, Randolph, but we will have your ships one way or another." He removed a letter from his pocket. "This letter is from Governor-elect Jackson asking for your cooperation. You will also read that if the state votes to support the South, which it surely will, he will requisition your ships and use them whether you like it or not." He sat back for effect, his face hardened by controlled anger. "You're a smart businessman, Randolph. Take the money or receive nothing at all. It should be an easy choice for you."

Governor-elect Jackson would take office early in January. He had run a coy conditional unionist campaign, even though he was a slaveholder and Southern sympathizer.

"You are a bit overconfident, Mr. Shelby. The state legislature has already voted for conditional unionism. It will keep us neutral, and Mr. Jackson, timid coward that he is, won't dare touch my steamers." He lifted the letter. "This is nothing more than an obvious attempt at intimidation, and you can stuff it back in your pocket and remove it and yourselves from my office before I lose my patience and throw you out."

Atchison scowled. "Mr. Hudson, there may be those who would think of you as a hero for not allowing us to use your steamers, but there are also many, many men who would look upon your reluctance as that of an enemy. If you are not with us, you are against us, and we cannot stand idle and let the Union use your vessels instead."

Rand stood. "Then I am against you. Now get out of my office before I begin the war here and now."

Benjamin's face had turned the color of his white shirt, and his eyes were wide. Shelby was already moving toward the door, and Atchison, his long face burning, stood and faced Rand for one last word.

"You, sir, have made a serious miscalculation. I will see that you lose everything!"

"I would rather lose it than aid the Confederacy, but you, sir, should understand I will not lose it without a fight. And if someone should come here to take it from me, including Mr. Ridges, whom I am sure was brought here as a part of your plan to intimidate me, I will find you, and you will pay at least as dearly as I. Now, get out!"

Atchison left in a huff, and Rand called for William, who, because the office walls were thin and he had heard everything, was pale as a ghost. "Get every captain in here immediately, and tell them to arm their men. I want our docks and ships covered with an army before nightfall!" He made sure the words were loud enough for Atchison to hear even though he was halfway down the entrance steps.

The clerk nodded mutely and left the office. Rand heard his rapid footfalls on the steps and counted twice that he nearly fell. Hoping William wouldn't hurt himself, he smiled and turned back to his uncle, closing the door.

The smile turned to a frown. "You are a fool, Uncle."

Benjamin was obviously frightened and confused; things had not turned out as he had hoped. He could not speak immediately, but by the time Rand returned to his desk, he had managed to work up enough saliva to spit out a whispered reply.

"They will burn everything."

"I meant what I said, Uncle, and they know it. They will be cautious, and that will give me time enough to secure the safety of our steamers." He did not tell Benjamin that he was in the final stages of setting forth that plan. It was obvious his uncle could not be trusted with such information. He leaned forward. "You didn't really think they were going to pay us for them, did you? Not in real money."

Benjamin looked confused. "Of . . . of course. Senator Atchison . . . he . . . he is a . . ."

"He is a man who has lost his way. I know his reputation, Uncle. Men like that will take what they want and stomp on every man who opposes them. Have you forgotten the border wars?" He stood straight again. "At the very best they would give us some sort of promissory note to be drawn on the Confederacy, whose money will be worth about as much as their purpose. We would never see a dime."

"It is not I who is the fool, Randolph—it is you," his uncle said bitterly. He stood, and his back stiffened. "I know what they will do. I convinced them to approach you, to try to convince you . . ." he spluttered. "I tried to save your steamers! I can do no more! I—"

"Sit down, Uncle. You did no such thing. How much did they promise you if I agreed?" Rand asked evenly.

Benjamin lifted his chin proudly. "There was no money involved. I . . ."

"Then what else *did* they promise you, Uncle?"

Benjamin flinched. "They did not promise, but the foundry and gun works . . . I am to have contracts for producing Confederate armament in the entire western front."

Rand sighed. "And you believed them even though you haven't got a single mold for making weapons, you haven't got a consistent supplier of the kind of iron or any other metal they need, and you haven't got room for even the smallest expansion."

"I can get all of those things once I have the contracts," Benjamin insisted.

Rand thought a moment. "How much do you owe on the foundry?"

Benjamin told him, and Rand winced inwardly.

"How are you going to pay it?"

"The loan is not due for a year. By then I will be quite profitable."

"If you get those contracts."

"I will get them."

Rand only shook his head. "Did you ever stop to think that Missouri might not secede, and if she remains in the North, Atchison will have no influence over contracts?"

"She will not. Governor Jackson—"

"Who sold you the foundry?"

"A friend of the governor's. He was in over his head and—"

"Didn't it occur to you that if Jackson could really deliver on his promise that his friend would surely want to keep his business?"

Benjamin went pale. "There were . . . other reasons . . . his health, and . . ."

"Who made you the loan?"

"Some of Senator Atchison's friends, but the Senator arranged it."

"Stop referring to him as *senator* in my presence. It sullies the very word." He took a deep breath. "Atchison arranged it. And now you are in his debt and the debt of his friends. You are a bigger fool than I thought, Uncle."

Benjamin's jaw hardened. "I assure you that they have been quite considerate, and if I need more time to repay—"

"I hope you are right, Uncle, because if you are not and you do come to me, I tell you now I will not pay the debt."

Benjamin's face went pale again, and he brushed his handkerchief against his sweating brow. It was obvious he had not thought things through, and now his eyes were being opened to new, unpleasant possibilities. But he was a stubborn, prideful man and his jaw hardened. "You are wrong," he said forcefully.

"You had better be right, because you will be finished here if you are not. Now, if we understand each other, Uncle, I have work to do," Rand said.

Benjamin got stiffly to his feet, firmly straightened his suit coat, and turned to leave. He hesitated for a moment as if about to say something and then bit it off and left the office, closing the door. He was obviously more than a little worried. He should be. His stupidity might end up costing him what little he had left.

Rand turned and went to the windows that looked out on the street below. He watched his uncle leave the building and wait while a carriage pulled away from its parked position and approached. Someone inside opened the door and leaned forward, offering a glimpse of a man in frontier wear and a floppy hat covering greasy, shoulder-length hair. It was Sam Ridges. Uncle Benjamin was playing with fire.

Chapter 3

NEWTON DAINES WATCHED AS THE ship glided around a bend in the river and the city known as St. Louis came into view. The deck erupted into celebration as a small band of homemade instruments struck up an English jig, and the immigrants began dancing about the deck as the captain announced they would soon dock. Passengers quickly dispersed and disappeared below decks, but Newton waited until most came up with their meager belongings before going after his own.

After finally going into the hold and gathering his possessions, he took one last look around the tight quarters in the belly of the ship. The place made him shudder. People had died here, their dreams coming to a sudden end. The thought that he had survived while so many had not invoked a feeling of gratitude. Then guilt. He was alive; they were not. How did God pick and choose, and why had He chosen to let him live a little longer? Why was he among the lucky ones?

Or was he? He shoved aside the melancholy thought. What was simply was, and there was no rhyme nor reason to it. The sickness had come; some had been taken but most had not. He would count his luck and let it be. And then, as a good Catholic, he crossed himself, just in case.

He left the hold and was climbing the steep stairs to the main deck when the hurrah echoed off the sails and timbers of the ship.

"At last! Praise the Lord!" cried one woman.

"What now, Ma?" asked a child near her skirts.

Newton was cheered by the thought that the excitement felt at the first of the journey seemed to have returned despite the losses at sea. Life simply went on. He managed a spot at the rail as the ship eased into the docks, where endless steamers stood. The bustle up and down the waterfront was chaotic but exciting. He was in America. A new beginning. For the first time in his life, Newton Daines felt really free.

The gangway was in place now, and Newton got in line to leave the steamer.

"What you gonna do now, Massa Daines?"

Newton turned around to find Felix behind him. Felix Coulon was the personal steward of the ship's captain. The two men had met the first day Newton had boarded in Liverpool, England. Felix was a former slave, a freedman as Felix made clear, working at sea in order to earn the money to free his mother and sister. Such devotion was no small thing in the mind of Newton Daines, and he respected Felix for it—especially since he had been at it ten long years and had survived at least two cholera epidemics on board.

But it was Felix's own life that had intrigued Newton most. The stories he shared about American slavery when both men were free of onboard duties held Newton's attention as no others in his life. Slavery reminded Newton of the serfdom in his own country of Ireland, and it was therefore to be hated on its face. He had come to America to escape such horrors, and to learn he had not was a revelation to Newton. He firmly intended to be this evil's adversary.

"Fin' tha' housin' ya tol' me abou'," Newton said in his Irish brogue. "Ya 'ave yer muny now, and ya'll be goin' after yer mum and sis, I suspect."

Felix gave a wide grin. "Fo' sho, Massa Newton. I has my pass, and I be goin'." He patted a leather pouch hung around his neck with a strong leather shoulder strap.

Felix had told him that in most of America, but particularly in states that still practiced slavery, freed blacks must have passes in order to travel. To Newton this was a sham. A man was either free or he wasn't, but Felix had only shrugged the matter off. It was the way it was, and he saw little value in discussing why it should be something else. He said he had little control of decisions about his so-called freedom, so fussing about what he didn't have only spoiled enjoying what he did.

When they disembarked, they walked up the docks going north until they reached a main thoroughfare called Biddle Street that headed into the heart of the city, where Felix began educating Newton regarding what lay ahead.

"Four blocks, Massa Newton, turn no'th and go to Mulanphy Street. Dey boards Irish immigrants for a few days, or dey knows what places does more long-term stayin'. Dey calls dat area de Kerry Patch—cause them folks is from Ireland somewheres."

"County Kerry," Newton said. "It's a place hit hard by the famines o' ten years ago. Immigrants cum 'ere in droves."

"And dey's still here. Plenty boardin' houses in dat place, but take care now, it be a place of bad folks and crim'nals. You doan trus' nobody, Massa Newt. They's jes soon cut your throat as look at you."

Newton embraced his friend and expressed his thanks. "Ere y' sure ya doan need me help? I could be goin' wi' ya, keep ya outta tru'ble."

"I thank ya kindly, Massa Newton, but I be fine," Felix said. "I been cross dis land lookin' fer m' family afore, an' I knows what ta do. Now y' be gettin' on. Soon as I has 'em free I'll be findin' a house, and then I fin' you and we'll be celebratin'. Go on, Massa Newt. You got worries a yer own."

Newton knew Felix was anxious to get out of the city before sundown, so they shook hands and he let Felix go while watching him dodge through endless wagons and men on horseback. He crossed one street and disappeared down another after one final wave.

Now alone, Newton felt his stomach churn. The city was busy, crowded, noisy, and unfamiliar; the streets were filled with carriages, wagons, horsemen, and the low-slung, sturdy drays crammed with goods meant for the docks. As he watched them all maneuver around one another, he wondered how there weren't accidents happening moment to moment. For a man or woman to cross from one side to another seemed to be flirting with death, yet he had seen Felix and a dozen others manage it. He supposed it wasn't so much different from Dublin or Liverpool; like those cities, despite a rushing pace, there seemed to be a sort of reckless order to it all.

Taking a deep breath and checking both ways, Newton darted across the cobblestone road to the boardwalk of Biddle Street. It was lined with shops, businesses, and dozens of people about their evening routine, and he was immediately grateful that the boardwalk was wide, it being nearly as hard to dodge folks as it was to dodge drays and carriages in the middle of the street. However, he soon discovered the latter the more risky as he was forced to step into the street by the congestion of both men and women, distracted with their animated conversations and haughty approach to others. A dray missed him by inches, and he felt the wind of the driver's whip slap near his ear, accompanied by a curse in some foreign tongue that still burned his ears though he couldn't understand a word. Moving to the inside of the boardwalk, he found progress easier until he collided with a man stepping rather forcefully from the door of a business.

"Watch where you're going, Irish," the man said with an angry and arrogant tone.

Newton wondered if someone had written the word "Irish" across his forehead.

"You scum all look alike," the man added with a sneer.

"An' your scum, does it all loo' alike as well?" Newton responded in a sarcastic tone.

The man cursed him again as he rushed into the street, dodging left and right to cross it. Newton had the notion that it would probably be no great loss if the man did not make it but then retracted his thought as a dray nearly granted his wish.

Reaching the corner where he was to turn north, Newton looked back the way he had come. It was sunset and decidedly a pretty picture as the steamboats and sea ships moved along the wide river and in and out of the docks below. As congested as the harbor was, it looked much more peaceful than the streets, and he wondered if his experience aboard the ship from Liverpool could get him a job in that less hectic world. But then, Felix had said that the best-paying jobs were on the docks, not aboard steamships, and as his savings wouldn't last more than a month or two, he needed the best job he could find.

As he turned his attention back to land, his eye caught hold on the goods in the window of the nearby shop and he drew closer, barely missing two ladies who swept past as if he were a bug on the wall. He was beginning to see that America was not really much different from Dublin or Liverpool, where class distinction that bred pride and haughtiness were alive and well.

The clothes in the window were finely made and were definitely those of a gentleman. It struck him that now that he was in America, he could actually think about having such finery someday and wondered at their cost. Never shy about such things, he opened the door and stepped inside to ask.

Several men, women, and even children, all finely dressed, threw an unwelcome gaze at him, which he accepted with a tip of his cloth hat and a smile just to irritate them as much as their uppity ways irritated him. A man in an apron stood behind a counter, a pair of pince nez glasses hanging on the end of his nose. He looked at Newton over the top of them and gave him a genuine smile. "Good afternoon, sir, how can we help you?"

The other patrons resumed their browsing, though their whispers and haughty expressions continued. "'Tis a fine set of clothes ya 'ave in tha' winda'. I be wonderin' 'ow much they migh' be costin'."

The clerk smiled. "Would ye be wantin' th' 'ole set, then?"

Newton smiled. "Ya be Irish."

"I am, but I been here long enough that the brogue is mostly a thing o' the past. County Cork me place o' birth." He extended a hand and they shook.

"An' mine be Kerry, tho' I be most recent from Dublin."

"Just off the ship from the looks o' ya." The clerk smiled. He scanned Newton's ragged coat and britches, the cloth tote in one hand and his wooden toolbox in the other. At five feet ten inches and about one hundred and seventy-five pounds, Newton was not a small man, and the extra size would probably cost extra money for such fine cloth.

Newton nodded while ignoring the once-over the clerk was making of him. "An' lookin' fer work."

The man looked more carefully at the toolbox Newton was carrying. "You 'ave a skill with hammer and plane?"

"I do. I worked makin' fine furniture in Dublin and then in th' shipyards in Liverpool, England, fer a bi'. Ship's cook as well t' earn me passage."

"Skills will help, but the Germans control most of the good jobs," the clerk said, lowering his voice a bit. "The docks will have some work fer ya t' start. Check with a Mr. Fitz on the dock worker's office south of Biddle on Front Street. He knows what's available, and if'n there is need of a good Irish carpenter, he'll know it as well."

"I be thankin' ya fer tha.' An' how much be them duds in the winda'?"

The clerk smiled again. "A good carpenter be making three dollars a day, six days a week—seven if he skips mass. That set'll cost you a month's wages."

Newton whistled. "Blessed day of St. Patrick, now tha's a fair penny."

The clerk chuckled. "That one's just fer display, but we 'ave cheaper cloth and our tailor is quite reasonable. I'm thinking you'll be back soon t' make a choice."

"Tha' I will. Could I buther ye fer a name of a goo' place fer a man to lay 'is 'ead til he gits on 'is fee'? I hear of the Mulanphy boardin' house for immigrants but I ha' the muny for somethin' more long-term."

"The least expensive is along 9th Street, but 'tis a dangerous place to be livin.' The best place outside of there, and at a good price, would be with a Bridget by the name of O'Grady, who runs a house in O'Fallon Street. Still a rough and rowdy place, but they won't murder you for a cross look. Tell Mrs. O'Grady that Peter McGrath sent you."

"Peter McGrath, yer a gentleman, an' I than' ya. I be Newton Daines." He extended his hand, and they shook again.

McGrath gave him directions to O'Fallon Street and the house of Mrs. O'Grady, then leaned across the counter and whispered one last warning.

"'Tis a tough place. Best watch your back."

"I than' ya fer the warnin'," Newton said.

A customer called to the clerk, and Newton said his good-bye and promised to return.

Newton left the store and walked north, noting that the farther he went the shabbier his surroundings became. Cobbled streets turned into mud roads, and boardwalks and buildings were increasingly in need of repair and a good whitewash. The appearance of the people went from gentry to middle class to poor, and the street itself narrowed and grew steeper. He found O'Fallon Street running east and west and immediately felt as if he had returned to his old street in the middle of Dublin's saloon row. The sounds of Irish piano and gruff male singing flowed out of a dozen doors, and drunks stumbled along muddy streets looking for their next glass of cheap whiskey. As Newton walked along the rotting boardwalk, he was offered the comfort of a half dozen women and dodged one drunk thrown out the doors of a saloon into the muddy street, where he lay until another drunk stumbling through the same doors picked him up. Crossing the street and talking incoherently, they tripped up another set of stairs and entered another saloon. Seconds later they were ejected again, cursed the bouncer, and then held one another up as they stumbled toward a third establishment.

Moving more quickly, Newton passed to the next block, where he heard the sound of sharp yelling and immediately recognized a boxing match down the alley he had just crossed. Backing up, he saw torches against the growing darkness of evening held high above a crowd of rowdies; no doubt inside that circle there were two men beating each other's brains out for money. He kept walking.

He passed out of the saloon district and found Mrs. O'Grady's boardinghouse in the middle of the block just above the docks along the river. A lantern hung from a post near the door, and a large lady in a greasy apron leaned against the wall, her ample arms folded across her chest. She was talking to an old gentleman who was sitting on the steps smoking a pipe. From the sound of his speech, he was toothless and non-Irish. A large, flop-eared, brown and black dog lay at his feet, its head flat on the boardwalk between extended paws.

"'Tis Mrs. O'Grady then," Newton said, looking at the woman with a smile. She was missing at least two teeth on the right side of her mouth, but even in the half-light of the lantern, there was a glint in her eye and a smile.

"'Tis so," she said, "and from th' look o' ye, 'nother ship has brung some Irish from the land 'o death and despair. How be the king o' England and 'is gentry, may God take their souls."

"They be robbin' the goo' folks as always."

She smiled. "An' ye be?"

"Newton Daines, come fro' County Kerry by wa' o' Dublin and Liverpool," he answered.

"'Tis an 'ard way," she said. "An' ye cum fer a room?"

"Peter McGrath sends me, and love for the lady o' 'is 'eart. Mrs. O'Grady ha' the bes' to offer at a goo' price, he says."

"Ah, me boy, Peter. A goo' ma' that. Cum in me house, Newton Daines. We ha' a spot fer ye, but taint nothin' fancy like ye git on tha' ship wha' brung ye 'ere. Cost ye three dollar a munth. Ye pay th' firs' now or we ha' no more to spea' of."

Newton removed coins from his pocket and handed them to her.

"Goo'," she said with satisfaction.

A man came out through the door dressed in a gambler's waistcoat and wool pants, a rounded derby hat on his head. For a moment Newton's breath caught. He knew this man, and this man knew him. He looked away from the lamplight as the man greeted Mrs. O'Grady with a smile and a word of thanks.

"If ye be don' with it, git on yer way, O'Shay," she said. Her words were firm and cold. Newton had the strong impression that this woman did not like Mickey O'Shay any more than he did.

"Ah now, Mrs. O'Grady, ya kno' I don' like t'cum to yer 'ouse fer such business, bu' Mr. O'Brien needs the muny owed, and Patrick left us no choice."

"If ye messed up me 'ouse I be breakin' yer nose, O'Shay," Mrs. O'Grady said.

"Will ye now?" O'Shay's voice turned cold. "I think no', me Bridget. An' if ye don' trea' meself more like th' gentleman I am, I be takin' it to me 'eart. Ye don' wan' me to take it to me 'eart, do ye, Mrs. G?"

"Be gone wid ye," Mrs. O'Grady said. "I go' better to do tha' sit abou' an' jaw wid the likes a' ye." She opened the door and started inside, calling to Newton as she did. "Mr. Daines, cum alon' now and let's be gettin' ya settled."

O'Shay was already past Newton when he heard the name and turned back. He could not see Newton's face because Newton kept his head down as he walked up the steps and followed Mrs. O'Grady inside. Newton doubted if he would have recognized him anyway. He hadn't shaved, and his beard and shoulder-length hair would have changed his appearance considerably since leaving Dublin.

In Dublin, Mickey O'Shay had been in the fight business in a messy sort of way. He was a collector, muscle without a heart, who worked for the Dublin fighting syndicate for which Newton had been a boxer. O'Shay had put his steel knuckles into many a face of gamblers who welched on their bets, disfiguring some and giving brain damage to others. When a boxer got out of line, it was Mickey O'Shay and three or more like him who made the man reconsider. O'Shay and Newton had crossed swords, and O'Shay had come away the worse for it and would like nothing better than to use those steel knuckles on Newton Daines's face. Newton vowed to try to stay out of O'Shay's way. He didn't want trouble, and O'Shay walked in it like the mud on O'Fallon Street. But if O'Shay did come around looking to bust heads, Newton wouldn't run again. He'd done enough of that in his young life.

Inside, things were quieter. Several men sat about visiting in a small sitting room, while others sat in the dining area at a long table eating bread and soup. Mrs. O'Grady told Newton that food was an extra charge and gave the prices. He figured he could eat here cheap as anywhere, and his stomach rumbled at the thought of a home-cooked meal. They climbed the stairs, where several men were gathered around a door; a man's cursing and a woman's firm but comforting voice came from inside. As Mrs. O'Grady stepped up, the men moved aside. Her size left only a small space through which Newton could see a man sitting in a chair with his head back, a bloodied rag pressed against his nose by a woman dressed in a linen dress of faded gray.

Mrs. O'Grady shook her head and told the man in no uncertain terms that he'd best either come up with the money owed or leave town. If he didn't, he'd be floating the Mississippi downstream to the Gulf of Mexico. The woman pulled away the rag, and Newton saw that his nose was mangled and his face cut. O'Shay's work, that was sure.

"Gambler, tha' one. Goo' at i' too, but not goo' enuf to bea' O'Brien's cheaters," Mrs. O'Grady said in a voice low enough that those inside wouldn't hear. Seeing that Newton was watching the woman, she added a bit more.

"The gambler is Patrick Sweeney. He visits 'ere to see Mary. Thin's she belongs to 'im. He owns a gun an' 'as bee' known to use it, so don' mess with 'er unless ye be lookin' fer trouble."

"He looks like he's busy enuf protectin' 'is own carcass without lookin' after me own," Newton said. But his eyes did not leave Mary McConnell.

She was a pretty enough lass, but there was something special in the look of her that made his eye linger.

Mrs. O'Grady laughed. "Tha' be true, and Mary don't like 'im much anyway."

Mrs. O'Grady left the doorway and led Newton to the end of the hall, where she knocked on another door and then opened it with an announcement that she was walking in. With the door open, Newton scanned the room and the half dozen men inside. He recognized no faces from his past and relaxed for the moment.

Most of the men were sitting or lying in two sets of three tiers of bunks on each side of the room, much like his quarters aboard the ship. The top bunk on the left seemed empty, though its height made it difficult to know for sure. Mrs. O'Grady put his curiosity to rest when she pointed at the bunk and told him his pillow and blanket awaited him. Explaining the general location of the outhouse and the washroom, she closed the door and the men went back to either sleeping or reading, not really caring who he was, which was fine with Newton. He searched the room for a place to set his bag and its meager contents and noticed a cabinet on his right with six different cupboards. He opened the first to find it occupied, also the second and so on through the fifth. The sixth was empty, and he quickly emptied his belongings into it before shutting the door. Like every man in the room, he had little in the way of possessions, but what he had he intended on keeping. Locks were expensive and were replaced with the threat of a busted jaw or worse if one man stole from another.

"Irish," the man in the lower left bunk said. "Can't say as we like you Micks trippin' off them boats all the time tryin' to take our jobs."

Each man looked up from what he was doing. There was not a weak back in the bunch, and none looked less than five foot six and one hundred and fifty pounds. If they did decide against him, they could toss him out the second-floor window without much trouble. But never a shy lad about asserting his right to free speech and his fair share of space, he figured that if such an attempt came, and he thought it might, two of them would precede him in the effort.

"Ye mus' be of the bloody English," Newton said.

"American, born and bred," the man said.

"A mystery then. Me though' only th' English were stupi' 'nuf t' offen' an Irishman."

The man came out of his bed with fight written all over him, but Newton moved quickly to put a fist on the end of his nose and knocked him back into his bed, unconscious, in the process. He shook his hand, wondering if it was broken. The man had a face of steel.

Two others came out of their beds while the last two chose to wait their turn. "'Tis a donnybrook ya seek then," Newton said. "Gla' to oblige, but it be best t' se' th' rules ahead don' ye think? If'n I be the winner o' this 'ere donnybrook, ye le' me be. If'n I don', I be movin' on to other quarters. Bu' I tell ye now I inten' to be stayin.'"

"Yer a cocky 'n," said one of the men with a wry grin.

"'Tis a good fighter who knows 'is possibles," Newton said. The man took a swing that Newton easily ducked while the man's friend prepared to deliver a second, and the donnybrook began.

* * *

Mary McConnell heard the ruckus, and it was no surprise to her. She had heard the noise of men fighting since she was a child living on a street a few blocks from here. Her father and her brothers were all Irishmen who enjoyed the fight nearly as much as they enjoyed the drink; they brought both of them home enough that Mary had moved out as soon as she could make her own living.

At ten years but looking fourteen, she began as a maid in an affluent home in East St. Louis. She was there only a month before the master of the house took a liking to her and tried to lay his bloody hands on what he liked. She fought back, raking his face with her nails and nearly putting out his eye, and was fired for it. After that she was a maid for a widow in another house for three years; she was grateful. But then the widow died and Mary was tossed into the street again. Unable to find another house needing a maid, she worked as a dancer and entertainer in the saloons along O'Fallon Street until she could no longer look herself in the mirror. That was when Mrs. O'Grady offered her work at the boardinghouse. Though even some men tried to lay their hands on her here, a fist or club to their chin gave them quick discouragement. Her dislike for such things became well known, and few were fool enough to make advances anymore.

Mary walked smartly down the hall, picked up her oak club, and went to the door where the ruckus was taking place. Just as she was about to enter, she heard one last thud and then only silence. Opening the door she peered in to find several men laying about the floor and two spread-eagled in their bunks. Only one was still standing, though he was barely able because of the fairly substantial bruising he had taken.

She set the club aside and propped him up but was unsure where to put him. Finally she helped him from the room and leaned him against the wall, where he melted to the floor. Stepping to the washroom, she retrieved a wet rag, returning to stoop down and wipe the blood from his nose and mouth. One eye was already beginning to close and would probably be completely shut before morning.

"Well now, ya mus' be the new lad just off the ship. Didn't yer mother teach ya 'ow t' make friends then?"

The man smiled. "Nah, taugh' me boxin' though. A lad ha' to know 'ow to survive where I be growin' up. The name's Newton, by the way. Newton Daines."

Mary nodded. "Well, Mr. Daines, from the looks o' the mess ya made in there she taught ya well."

"The' say the' don' like Micks."

She smiled. "They must 'ave a 'ard time lookin' in the mirror. Micks one and all. Probably jes testin' yer grit."

"Well then, maybe we'll git along jes fine." He looked at his knuckles, scraped and bloody. "I though' their 'ead's were a bi' hard nah t'be Irish."

Newton looked at her dress and realized she was the woman who had been tending to the man Mrs. O'Grady called Patrick. "Ye be th' gambler's girlfrien' then," he said. "Mary, is it?"

"Mary McConnell. Mrs. O'Grady tell ya tha' abou' Patrick?"

"Sai' t' watch out fer 'im. Carries a gun."

"I ain't nobody's girl but me own. The gambler likes someone on 'is sleeve when he marches into them saloons. Says it 'elps 'is image. For a cut o' 'is take 'tis worth it."

"An' does tha' cut include wha' he owes O'Brien then?" Newton asked.

She stopped wiping the blood away, then started again. "His debt is 'is own. You'll be havin' a bath soon, I hope," she said. "The smell of fish is such that even the most tolerant cannot stand it."

"Had me a ba' a few weeks ago."

"Then yer due another. Two streets east a 'ere ya be findin' a bathhouse. Costs a few pennies, an' they be throw in washing yer clothes. I suggest ya visit there tomorra 'fore lookin' fer work. Not many men 'ill be able t' stomach yer presence long enuf t' hire ya."

Newton smiled despite himself. "Yer a cold-hearted lass, tha's sure, but I'll be takin' yer advice. Seem's rightly enuf gi'en."

Mary was a looker even though life's hard knocks showed in the dark rings around her eyes and the wrinkles in her face. Her blond hair was long and fell past her neck to just above her chest, which was largely uncovered. She stood up, and Newton thought she was about his same height but couldn't tell from his present position. Struggling to his feet, he found out that his estimation was close. "Yer Irish, bu' . . ."

"I don' soun' like you?" she said without a smile. "You'll find tha' anyone who has been 'ere long has lost some of the old language. Another generation an' we'll all be speakin' like bloody rich folks."

Newton could hear moaning and groaning coming from his room and glanced in to see his five assailants coming back to life.

"Five against one. Ya must 'ave a hard fist," Mary said.

"Aye, an' it's quick as well." He smiled. "Bu' they were kin' enuf to cum jes two a' a time."

"Ah, I see. That is nice," Mary said with some sarcasm. "I don' know if Mrs. O'Grady told ya, but I 'elp 'er run this place. She'll expect payment if anythin' is broken."

Newton looked inside the room. He had tried to be careful, but it looked like the cabinet was tipped over and would need some repairs. "I'll be fixin' the cabinet. Ha' me own tools fer such work."

"You're a carpenter then?"

"Tha' I am, gla' t' do wha' I kin if ye or Mrs. G. be needin' somethin' dune," Newton answered.

"We'll pay ya fair, but it'll 'ave to be in food, not in money. But that does not include the cabinet in there. Ya fix that for breakin' it."

"Fair enuf," he said.

She picked up her club and turned to go back down the hall. "Now ye be washin' up," she said again. "And tomorrow 'tis the bath or the river fer ya, or you'll be lookin' at the fat end o' this club. We run a clean place around 'ere an' tha' includes any gentlemen who infest it with their Irish pride."

Newton watched her turn to go down the stairs. She was certainly not one to be messed with, and pretty too. For Newton it was a good combination.

He headed back into his room, where everyone was sitting on the edge of the lower bunks, nursing sore jaws and cracked noses. Two of the men would have eyes swollen shut by morning.

"Well now, we ha' a deal. I 'ope yer goo' Irish gentleme' an' will be keepin' it," Newton said, closing the door behind him.

"We'll be keepin' it," said the man who had first attacked him. "My name's Liam, an' tha' one is Sean," he said, pointing to the man next to him.

Newton shook hands as the third man sitting on that bed stood. "Name is Clancy, and those two over there are Owen and Tory."

Newton could see why the one was called Tory. The name meant "rock," and though the man had a glass jaw, his body was hard as granite. "Ye be foolin' me abou' th' land a yer birth," Newton said.

Liam smiled. "Jes' needin' a little o' the exercise."

"And t' test yer mettle," Clancy added, also smiling. "Yer fists made o' steel?"

Newton laughed. "Nah, jes learned boxin' a' a young age."

"Wha' yer name?" asked Tory.

"Newton. Newton Daines from County Kerry," he replied. "An' I jes as soo' ya keep it an' this lil donnybrook betwee' us. Don' much care fer th' figh', and people cum lookin' to put ye into it if'n' they hear ye ha' a strong fist."

They all nodded. None of the men looked anxious for word to get around that one man had bollixed the five of them.

Newton turned back to the door. "Mary McConnell says I be needin' to wash up a bit. You gents fee' free t' do th' same. Smells like a pigsty in summer."

They smiled at each other and followed him out the door. By the time they had finished washing up, Newton had learned more about his new friends and what they did. Most worked making bricks for new buildings. They said there was always work for another strong back, but the pay wasn't the best. If he had carpentry skills, what McGrath had told him was correct—he needed to see Pitts down on the docks. Good skills brought good wages.

Liam moved his jaw from side to side as he looked in the wavy old mirror over the basins. "We regre' testin' ye, but a man needs t' know who 'e can count on 'round here. We'll be at yer side if ye need us and hope you'll do th' same."

"I don' go lookin' fer trouble, but if yer life be in danger ya kin coun' on me," Newton said.

They shook hands and returned to their room. Clancy opened the window for a bit of fresh air, and each man climbed into his bunk. Newton lay awake for only a few minutes even though he was sore from head to toe, especially around his stomach, back, and face, where his new roommates had gotten in their fair share of licks. His lip was swollen, as was one eye, but he'd dealt with such injuries before and knew that they usually cleared up quickly. Finally, exhausted, he drifted off to sleep.

Chapter 4

THE NEXT MORNING THE BOARDINGHOUSE was a beehive of activity as men dressed and left either to go to work or to find it. They stopped by the dining room long enough to gulp down oatmeal, bread, and coffee at a long table surrounded by benches. Some picked up a lunch from Mary McConnell on their way, giving her the necessary coins that Newton figured amounted to two pence. He did not know what a meal might cost out on the street but figured he could go without until dinner if he needed to.

Newton, with his only other set of clothing tucked under his arm, walked past Mary, who reminded him of the baths and noted that they opened early. He gave her a fine smile and a tip of the hat in return.

Walking the two blocks to the baths in the chill of the morning, he was glad he had a decent jacket. Finding the baths, he went inside and, feeling the warm humid air, realized how much he was looking forward to a hot tub—until he read the prices. Turning around and heading back outside, he figured he'd need a good job to bathe there even once a month and a really good one to bathe every week and still save money for his dreams. For now he would use the river.

Going back to the house, he retrieved his beat-up rag of a towel and his straight-edged razor from his cabinet before leaving the building and heading down O'Fallon Street to the river. He walked along the bank some distance before finding a path through the trees to a natural inlet that was protected on three sides by undergrowth while the water brush on the riverside blocked any view. Voices from the shoreline revealed that he wasn't the only one who could not afford the public baths, but he was not one to bathe with others and decided to walk upstream. The fresh air filled his lungs, and he decided to keep walking and follow the stream up the hill. Time passed quickly, and before he knew it he stood on a hill high above the city, the small stream in a ravine some fifty yards below him. It was a clear morning with no breeze, and chimney smoke hung over the city and river like a blanket. But above the smog line a number of houses glinted in the morning sun. It was then that he noticed a small pond in the stream below and up from where he stood and decided it would be the best place to bathe. He found a small animal trail that went down the side of the ravine to the pond, where a thin mist of steam softly rose from the surface. He stooped down and felt the water for temperature. Cold, but no worse than the streams of Ireland where he had bathed most of his life. Stripping down he dove in and felt the exhilaration of the water against his hot skin, bringing a smile. It felt good, refreshing, and he determined that if the water didn't get any colder, it would be a weekly routine.

After washing as thoroughly as he could, he trimmed his beard with scissors and blade before setting them on his clothes and lying back in the water to float a bit, trying to relax while keeping a sharp eye on the spot where he'd stashed his clothes. All alone, he felt comfortable—even peaceful. He let the feeling settle over him, closing his eyes as the quiet eased the pain in his sore muscles.

It was hard to believe he was really in America, but so it was. He had come a far way since leaving County Kerry after the death of his grandfather, the one who had raised him after both is parents had died of cholera. A far way indeed.

He thought he had found his place in Dublin. He had actually enjoyed the fight at first, and then the constant use of his head for a boxing pummel had begun to scatter his brains and he had decided to get out. Of course, it wasn't as easy getting out as it was getting in. The man who had championed him didn't like the idea of an undefeated boxer leaving him in a lurch and had sent Mickey O'Shay to pass along the message. O'Shay, of hard build himself, had been overconfident, coming alone. Newton had laid him out cold after only a few punches, packed his belongings, and left the city. He was sure O'Shay would be looking to get even.

He used the soap to wash his hair, his thoughts turning to Mary McConnell. He wondered if she meant what she said about the gambler; wondered if she was as free as she thought. Men like the gambler got rather possessive about a woman like Mary. Even in Newton's mind, a lass like her shouldn't be running free, and it was something he intended to look into.

He thought of another lass, long years ago when he was still in Kerry. They had nearly married, then her father had pushed her into another man's arms for a better dowry. It was one of the reasons he left for Dublin.

The other reason was the death of his grandfather. They'd lived as tenants, scraping out just enough to keep from starving while the two of them worked as carpenters for the landowner. His grandfather had finally just worn out. Newton decided he wasn't going to follow that path. He wanted more, and he left to find it.

It was several moments before he realized that there were voices nearby, and he quickly went to his stash, withdrew fresh clothes, dressed, and then shoved his old clothes in his cloth bag. Just as he finished, someone came through the trees nearby, saw him, and spoke.

"Sir, this is a private pond," the man said haughtily. "Trash, no matter their color, are not welcome here. Get off our land before I bury you in it."

Newton did not like being ordered about like some house dog and decided to hold his ground. "I suppose you'll be showin' me some sort o' paper declarin' this to be yer lan.'"

The man flushed hot. "I need no paper." He raised a shotgun that had been cradled in his arm just as two other men joined him from behind.

"Tha' there goon is a bit unfriendly, mister," Newton said. "If I was you, I'd—"

The man sighted the weapon and fired across the pond at Newton, who ducked left and felt pellets rake his hip. He scrambled to his feet and ran into the trees just as another weapon fired, then a third, ripping branches off trees around him. Bolting up the steep path, he was quickly out of range and over the ridge of the hill, his legs carrying him as quickly as they could through unfamiliar forest.

It was then he heard the dogs.

Chapter 5

November 7, 1860

"LINCOLN ELECTED!" WAS BLAZONED ACROSS the top of Rand's morning newspaper. He read the article half a dozen times looking for some hope that the South would be conciliatory after the vote was in. He found none. The article was filled with quotes that threatened riots in large Southern cities and with abusive language that made his hair stand on end.

Secession was coming, and there was little to be done about it. War would surely follow. He wondered what Andrew would think now.

"Good morning," Lizzy said from behind him. She went directly to the stove to pour herself some coffee. Rand knew she hadn't slept well the last couple of nights, but he had left it alone. Dressed in riding pants, blouse, and wool sweater, she had already prepared herself for the day.

"And to you," Rand said as she joined him at the table. He slid the paper across to her. She glanced at it, then smiled. "I suppose you voted for him," she said. The election had taken place only two days earlier, and he had watched her carriage come to the polling place as his left.

"So did you, and we both know it," Rand teased.

"Umm, but don't tell Andrew," she said with a wry smile. "He so wanted me to vote for Breckinridge."

"Andrew's father must be in mourning," Rand said.

"And Andrew," Lizzy replied. "But not for the same reasons. Andrew wants to end the war before it begins. He is afraid, Rand. I hope you understand that."

"Afraid?"

"Of losing everything, of what will happen to his family, and even to the slaves. He and I have talked a good deal about it. He has tried many times to talk some sense into his father, but as you can imagine he isn't having much success."

"Yes, I can imagine." Rand knew Andrew had tried—and had given up long ago. No one could change Horatio Clay's views on slavery.

Rand sat straight as the cook placed his breakfast of eggs and sausage in front of him along with fresh rolls, butter, and a small dish of honey. He put fork to mouth as he watched his sister's eyes. Clear blue and always easy to read. He saw concern as she continued down the page, then anger, and finally horror.

She folded the paper and slammed it on the table but said nothing. Rand knew the articles, had read them half a dozen times. South Carolina had already declared her intent to secede, Tennessee was ready to follow, and Kentucky was warning that she would reconsider her neutrality if any hostile action was taken against any of her Southern sisters.

"South Carolina will vote on it before Christmas," Rand said between bites. "By the end of January, the rest of the deep South will follow. The real fanatics will push hard now. They have to. Southern pride is at stake."

"They're fools."

"Agreed, but they have stated that they want out, and they've created a frenzied anti-Lincoln, antiabolitionist environment that leaves them no choice. They cannot threaten to leave and then change their minds. They must see it through now. They'll go after Maryland, Kentucky, Virginia, and even Missouri to join them. If they succeed, there will be no more Union, and the few Northern states that are left will be in a box that forces them to allow slavery forever just to save the Union. The Southerners know exactly what they are doing. It is just another attempt to continue to force slavery down all our throats."

At Lydijah's direction, a servant placed a dish of oatmeal and cream in front of Lizzy, along with fresh-squeezed orange juice in a large glass.

"Virginia will not secede, Rand," she said. "Andrew knows many important people and is a personal friend of the governor's son. He has learned that the governor is actually going to ask for a peace conference next month to work this all out. They will try to stop this . . . this lunacy. At the very least they will remain neutral."

Rand felt his breath catch. He dabbed his lips with his napkin and sat back. "Who was it just a few weeks ago who declared neutrality an impossibility, Liz?"

Lizzy blushed. "I was speaking of Missouri. Virginia is different," she said defensively.

"Is it? And what makes it so different?"

She did not answer, so Rand went on. "Neutrality is just as impossible for Virginia as it is for Missouri, Liz—in fact, even more so. War between North and South will call for an invasion of Virginia by one side or the other just because of its location. The state will be forced to take sides just like everybody else. As you so aptly put it on several ocassions, this will not be some tug-of-war where some jump to the ropes while others stand on the sidelines wishing everyone well."

He saw Lizzy's face pale a bit, and she stood and went to the window. Finally she turned around and returned to her chair, a familiar look in her eyes that meant a question was coming and he probably wasn't going to like what it was.

"You have been to Andrew's home, Rand. What is it like? And I want the truth."

"Do you?" He smiled. "Or are you looking for some justification to accept Andrew without accepting slavery, just as I did?"

She threw him a dark look, and he took another deep breath.

"Being Andrew's friend is a constant challenge. He is a remarkable person in many ways; very likable, interesting—and, as you are becoming personally aware, filled with enough Southern charm to put even the most ornery abolitionist in a conciliatory mood. I knew only one man, or woman, who did not like Andrew Clay, and that person was such a hard-nose he had not a single friend in this world." He leaned forward and touched Lizzy's hand. "But these likeable qualities do not change the fact that Andrew is complicit in his father's practice of slavery and will remain so because he will never walk away from his inheritance and his Southern heritage, even for love. So if you have some interest in Andrew that might include becoming his wife, you will hold slaves, Lizzy, whether you like it or not." Rand took a breath. "Frankly, Andrew spends a good deal of his life living as two people. There is the kind, charming, happy man who would throw a beggar his coat in a moment, and the slaveholder who denies others their freedoms and will even use a whip to keep them under control."

Lizzy looked at her plate. "Andrew hates his father for what he does to control his slaves. He would never whip them."

"Yes, he hates it, but he doesn't stop it and he doesn't leave it. A man can only live like that so long before it changes him. His father was in that same position when he inherited the Meadowlands, and the result is not a pretty picture."

"But I thought his father always agreed with slavery," Lizzy said, a bit shocked.

"A man does not always agree with slavery, Lizzy. It is against our very nature. We know it is wrong at our very core, but it is a seductive and seemingly easy solution to our desire to have wealth and success—and like the forbidden fruit, when men eat of it, it changes their very being, seducing them first and then, if they aren't careful, poisoning their very existence. Some can resist becoming vile in its practice, but none can resist its ease and the wealth to which it leads. Some soothe their conscience by being kind and telling themselves that they are the answer to a black man's prayers. After all, they clothe them, feed them, and house them. For this they feel quite benevolent." He paused. "But with rare exceptions, even the best men, when threatened by the loss of a system that gives them power and wealth, will turn to harsh means to prevent that loss. As they do, their souls canker and they become quite different men." He took a deep breath. "It is true that Andrew hates slavery, Lizzy, but it is in large part because of how it has changed his father—what it has made of a man who once was quite different—but he will also fight for it. His family's position, his Southern roots, will leave him no choice." He leaned forward. "And eventually, if slavery is not denied him, Andrew will hold on to it and hate himself for it everyday of his life."

"If Andrew left there, if—"

"He won't. He is the only son, and he will inherit everything once his father is gone. To leave it would be to walk into poverty."

"We could help him. We—"

"Do you really think Andrew's pride would allow him to give up nearly a thousand acres of prime land, an inheritance that is valued in the hundreds of thousands of dollars, to take a handout from us?"

She did not answer, but the look on her face said she did not. She took a deep breath.

"Then maybe his father can change."

Rand could not help but laugh. "Now that, dear sister, would be as monumental as you or I walking on water."

He saw the disappointment in her eyes and regretted his reaction. He squeezed her hand to soften the blow. "Dearest Lizzy, I suppose if there is one person in this world who could change Horatio Clay, it would be you, but believe me when I say it really would take a miracle."

She smiled at him, confusion in her eyes. "Oh Rand, what am I going to do?"

Rand felt her ache and knew there was really only one solution. He felt his heart thump soundly against his chest at a pace he thought would surely cause it to burst. He was taking a horrible chance but saw no other way. "Andrew wants you to come to Virginia. You should go."

Lizzy's surprise showed on her face. "You would allow it?"

Rand smiled. "We both know that I haven't had a thing to say about your life, especially when it involves men, for at least five years, but that isn't why I say you should go." He leaned down and placed his palms on the table, leaning toward her. "Your heart is involved now, and you are beginning to wonder if you can find a way to give it to Andrew. It is a question that can only be answered at the Meadowlands, not here."

She sat back in her chair, thinking. "I suppose you're right," she finally said.

"Then write to Andrew and see if it's possible," Rand said, forcing a smile.

"You mean there is some doubt?"

"Horatio will decide if you can visit his home, Lizzy, not Andrew." He smiled. He could see that Lizzy really didn't understand how much control Horatio Clay had over his son. Rand knew that Andrew Clay was no more free to do what he wanted than the slaves his father purchased for his plantation. Horatio Clay had determined that Andrew needed the status that a military background would give him and had arranged for his position at the academy and then saw to it that he received his position at Sumter. Horatio determined who Andrew's friends were—with the exception of Rand—and Horatio would determine who Andrew would marry. He had already done it once.

But Rand decided he shouldn't say any of those things. Lizzy would find out soon enough. He turned and retrieved his coat. "Time to get to work," he said.

"I saw Ann yesterday," she said. "She—"

Rand put up his hand up, fending off the rest of the sentence. "No matchmaking today, please."

Lizzy pushed on. "She is twenty-one, and her uncle is your friend, and—"

"And he wants his niece married. I know, he has told me so. Frank is under pressure from his wife. Another good reason to stay single."

"*And,*" Lizzy said, trying to finish her comment, "there is not another woman in this world who could put up with you and make you happy. I warn you, Randolph Hudson, if you pass Ann by, you will regret it."

He put on his riding hat instead of responding. He actually liked Ann very much, but he was not about to reveal that to Lizzy. He would make up his own mind in time.

She glanced down at the book half hidden by a page of newspaper. She stood, leaned across the table, and retrieved it.

"Then you are reading it," she said with a good deal of satisfaction.

"Until I can find my own." Setting aside his riding gloves, he picked it up and thumbed through the pages to the one he wanted. "Remember how Mother used to put dates by scriptures she found important to something she needed at that particular time? There are dates in this book as late as just a few days before she died."

"She was reading again," Lizzy said softly. "Why would she keep it a secret from us?"

"Guilt . . . fear . . . maybe pride. She was angry when she left the Church behind, remember? Whatever it was that drove her away was probably still gnawing at her."

Lizzy only nodded, her eyes misty. "It's never too late. If there is one doctrine in our faith that I know to be true, it is *that* one." She paused before going on. "She is all right, Rand. I know it." Tears burst from the corners of her eyes, and she quickly stood as Rand took her in his arms and let her cry. The funeral and even Andrew had kept her so busy she really hadn't had time to properly grieve, and now the emotion poured out. He remembered his own moments of sorrow, and there were not just a few. Minutes later she finally pulled back and smiled at the soaking she had given his shirt. He remembered another time, when their father had died. They had both nearly drowned in their tears then as well, but he had had an even harder time adjusting then. He supposed that was just the way it was between fathers and sons, mothers and daughters.

"My, my," Rand said. "Now I know how Noah felt when the rains came."

She laughed softly while retrieving a hanky from her pocket and dabbing at her eyes. "I miss her horribly. Every morning when I wake up, I catch myself thinking I need to talk to her about this or that. These are not the first tears I have shed, I assure you."

"That's curious," he said with a playful smile.

"Curious?"

"That the house is not afloat. Between the two of us it surely should be."

She chuckled again. "You? Hard-nosed, mister businessman, Randolph Hudson? I do not believe it."

"You know better. Which of us always cried at the death of a puppy or kitten, or even when we had to shoot a deer for food? My leaky tear ducts have always been an embarrassment."

He picked up the book again. "I had forgotten how much this used to mean to me, how comfortable it made me feel."

Lizzy smiled gratefully. "And have you decided what you are going to do about it?"

Rand returned the smile, their conversation in the library fresh in his memory. "For now, just keep reading. I am not as sure as I once was." He paused. "Now I have a question for you. Does Andrew know about the secret life of Elizabeth Hudson?"

She looked sheepish.

"You know it will matter, don't you?"

"It shouldn't," she said, the tears gone and the old independent Lizzy returning.

"It will, especially to his father, whom I have heard speak of the need to 'annihilate the Mormons and their abominable religion.' Ironic, isn't it? He practices the abomination of slavery and yet considers our religion even worse. A nice way of soothing his conscience, I suppose."

Lizzy stiffened. "It isn't that I want to move west, or . . . I just want to keep my beliefs. Surely Andrew or anyone else, including his father, can understand that."

"There is always an excuse, Liz, but I promise you this: If I decide to practice my religion again, you and I are going to have to go public about it. No more hiding. Until then we both have some soul searching to do about our past faith. But I can tell you one thing for sure: If you tell Andrew that you are a Mormon, it will not set well with him, and especially not with his father."

He stood and put on his leather riding jacket. Then he nodded at the book. "Put that back in Mother's desk, will you? It goes inside the ornate wooden box."

As Rand finished buttoning his coat, Lizzy looked out the window and saw his beautiful black horse, Samson, being brought past the window, saddled and ready. She stood to give him a peck on the cheek, her mind extremely unsettled.

He kissed her on the forehead, walked through the kitchen door, and mounted his horse. From the window she watched him leave, then stepped to the front porch as he galloped the black down the lane until he exited the front gate and disappeared behind the high wall that fronted their property. She took a deep breath of the morning air and looked at the sky. There might be a chilly rain today and a cold night.

Rubbing at the goose bumps exploding on her arms, Lizzy turned back inside and called for one of the servants, whom she instructed to add wood to the fireplaces and stock the wood boxes completely. Returning to the kitchen, she found Lydijah removing the dishes from the table. Lizzy sat and sipped her juice while thinking about her mother, then picked up her Book of Mormon and thumbed through it.

She hadn't hidden her religion from her friends at first. In fact, she had relished telling them about it until her friends' parents had said she couldn't come around anymore. Feeling the loss deeply, she had been thankful that her family had moved from their Uncle Benjamin's neighborhood to a new neighborhood where she could start over again. Since that time—and it now shamed her to think of it—she had said little to nothing.

But she hadn't stop believing, even after her father's death, and when she heard that there were members meeting at a local hall, she found a way to sneak away and meet with them. During these meetings she had found peace and relished the teachings the missionaries gave them. She had nearly run away to the Salt Lake Valley twice. There were so many young women just like her passing through from England that it would be easy to tag along and go west. But the guilt of leaving her mother and Rand behind kept her from doing so until she had grown accustomed to living as a "private" believer, her every physical need being met as their mother's businesses exploded in profits. She felt the guilt of it now—she really had sold out for money.

"Liddy, when did mother start showing interest in this book again?" Lizzy asked as she thumbed through the pages. Lydijah turned, squinted through her poor eyesight, and then smiled.

"Been long times since I seen dat book. My, my, yes, Miss Lizzy, a long time." She came to the table, sat, and reached for the book. "Kin I?" Lyidjah's dark eyes danced above the round cheeks of her face, and her smile caused the creases around her eyes and in her forehead to deepen. Lizzy knew no other woman who had kinder, wiser eyes that Lydijah. Not one.

"Of course," Lizzy said, handing her the book.

Lydijah straightened the headcloth wrapped around her hair, wiped her hands on her apron almost reverently, then took the book and thumbed through it. "Jes' like de one she gave me dat long time 'go." Her face grew sad. "When we all left Nauvoo, she said we wasn't to be discussin' dis an' de Church with you and Massa Rand. No sirree, na'tall. Never understood why she turned so 'gainst it. She was strong once—strongest of 'em all." Lydijah shook her head slowly. "Nevah thought I'd see de day when she would leave it. Nevah."

"Why didn't you go west, Liddy? You were baptized and so was Mose. Coming away with us—"

"Brigham Young," Liddy said. "He's da reason why, Miss Lizzy. Mose went to Brother Brigham afta yo' pa's death, and Brother Brigham said we should stick with yo' momma. God would understand. We done it, an' here we is." She got up and went back to the sink. "We been prayin for yo' momma ever since. Me and Mose, we worry 'bout her soul, we do." Lizzy felt the sadness in Lydijah's voice. She got to her feet, went to her lifelong friend, and picked up a dishtowel to dry the dishes.

"Do you and Mose still read?" Lizzy asked, eyeing her mother's book.

Lydijah kept at her task. "Mose, he reads good, and he make sure t' read evah night." She paused. "Me, I nevah learned much readin' so it hard fo me. Mose, though, he read to me, and I knows dat book front to back."

"Have you ever *wanted* to go west, to be with the Saints?"

"Sometimes me an' Mose, we talk, but we's old, Miss Lizzy. Too old for Injuns and walkin' all dat way. Mose, he writes to Brother Brigham and gets a letter now and again, but tha's all."

"And what does Brother Brigham say?"

"Tha' we's always welcome, and he asks 'bout yo' momma, and you and Mr. Rand. Hadn't heard from him in a long time, though. He a busy man with all that settling and immigratin' and such." She looked out the back window. "Dat's Mose bringin yo' horse to de barn. You best be gettin' on with it, Miss Lizzy. Go on now, get your coat and be gone with you. Scoot now!"

Lizzy could not help but give Lydijah a hug before running off like a child told to do some chore. As she slipped upstairs and grabbed her heavy coat lined with lamb's wool, she thought how strange it was that for all these years she and Liddy had stayed close to their old faith but never talked about it once. For the first time she realized how much her mother's anger and stubbornness had truly cost them. The threat of upsetting Mrs. Hudson had always hung over the house like a thick cloud, and for what purpose? What had it accomplished except that they had all learned to live a lie or to simply give up their feelings and blend in with hers?

As she left the house and headed for the barns, these thoughts made Lizzy angry. All those years could have been filled with so much more if God had been allowed in their home, but her mother had banished Him.

"Why, Mother? Why would you do such a thing?"

"What's dat, Miss Lizzy?"

Lizzy didn't realize she had spoken out loud until Mose's words broke her out of her thoughts. He stood a few feet away with a pail of oats in his hand.

"Nothing, Mose," she said, forcing a smile. "Just thinking out loud."

Lydijah's husband managed the Hudsons' land, barns, and animals. He had a half dozen others to help him with this work—all freedmen earning a fair wage. She greeted each man by name when she happened upon him as they worked with the dozens of horses, cows, and other animals owned by the Hudsons. She knew who was married and to whom, along with how many children each had. Most lived in small but comfortable homes built for them on the property and all were as loyal to Lizzy and Rand as they had been to the late Mrs. Hudson.

"Then I bid you a good mornin', missus," Mose said with a wide grin and deep bass voice that seemed to shake the leaves off trees. His black hair was gray now and, like Lydijah, his girth had increased a good deal but also like Lydijah, his eyes were filled with care and concern and even love. He had become the only real father figure for Rand and Lizzy after their father's death, and Lizzy couldn't imagine life without him and Lydijah. She reached out and took the partially filled bucket of oats she fed to her beautiful mare every morning, and Mose touched her hand.

"You all right, Missy?" he asked.

She nodded. Now was not the time for a long discussion about things she wasn't even sure about. "Fine," she smiled.

He gave her a smile and turned back to his work as she turned toward the stall where her mare waited. "Good morning, Rose," she said to the mare as she lifted the bucket and let the animal get a mouthful. She rubbed the mare's neck with her free hand. Feeling the soft, slick hair and the warmth underneath was always comforting to Lizzy, and she stroked Rose until she had finished her oats.

A few moments later, Mose and Lydijah's son Elliot brought several cubes of sugar in a cup. Elliot had grown up as a good friend of Lizzy's. "Good morning, Elliot," she said, pleased to see him.

Elliot tipped his hat slightly, "Ma'am, tain't the best day fo' ridin', so's you be careful now." He smiled and continued on to the barn.

When the oats were gone, Mose handed her the riding blanket, then the English saddle, and finally the reins. When all were in place, Mose gave her a leg up and she put her feet in the stirrups. Lizzy clicked her tongue, and the mare walked from the saddling area of the barn onto the grass and dirt road that led to the far reaches of the five-hundred-acre farm her mother had purchased a few years earlier. She loved these morning gallops and the invigorating start they always gave to her day, especially on crisp autumn mornings like this one. After the mare stretched out a bit, Lizzy nudged the horse with the heels of her boots and they went to a gallop. The overcast sky and the leaves that had fallen from the trees muffled the sound of the mare's hooves, giving a quiet to the forest around Lizzy that she relished.

Mary Hudson had been a wonderful mother, and Lizzy felt a bit guilty for feeling angry. Surely there were good reasons for what her mother had done, reasons that were too painful to share—or overcome. But oh how she wished she hadn't let her mother bury matters like she had; how she wished they had talked about all of it! If she had just been more forceful and refused to let her mother put her off, things surely could have been different.

But she hadn't, and neither had Rand. Mary Hudson was the most forceful, stubborn woman Lizzy had ever known, and it was just easier to let the matter go rather than deal with the conflict it caused. And in the end, the past was the past: gone. And though regrets remained, she knew she must move on. Rand was painfully right; she had been hiding her beliefs. The question was, would she continue to do so? Was she still so committed to her old faith, or was it just a passing notion—a way to rebel against her mother's stubbornness? She did not like that thought and did not think it true, but why then had she hidden her beliefs so long and so completely?

Suddenly she thought of her father. What would he think of her actions? A man she had never seen lose his temper once in her entire life, Baker Hudson could show his disappointment with a single glance that melted her into a change of heart and action. Would he be disappointed in her now?

She pushed the thoughts aside. They were painful, and she needed to pay more attention to the trail. As the mare came to her stride, Lizzy tried to let the feel and exhilaration of the fresh cool air dissipate her feelings.

And then it happened.

Chapter 6

NEWTON WAS IN GOOD SHAPE, but the hurried climb up the hillside to evade his pursuers had tired him; he stopped running for a moment, leaning against a tree. He pulled up his shirt to find several spots where lead shot had sunk deep into his skin and he was bleeding. Though he'd bled more from the cut of his eye in a boxing match, it was enough to cause him concern and a good deal of anger.

The distant sound of the dogs behind him was barely a sound at all, but he started running again. He was just off the ship, Irish, and a man who had no idea what penalties there were for trespassing in the United States. If caught, he was afraid they would send him back. Worse still was the fear of dying at the hands of madmen who would just as soon shoot a man as look at him.

After another mile, he could no longer hear the dogs but kept going just to make sure. He had seen several houses and tried to steer clear of them, running in a direction he thought would take him deeper into the woods. Suddenly the hill turned sharply downward and the thick trees and brush blinded him as the force of his momentum tossed him into them. A sudden rustling and movement behind him revealed a deer leaping out of the bushes and disappearing through thick trees. He fell to the ground exhausted, listening, wondering if he had lost his pursuers. Then the sound of a horse in panic and a woman's scream forced him back to his feet and in the direction the deer had taken. Someone was in worse trouble than he.

* * *

Lizzy saw the deer bolt from the woods. Rose reacted with a hard lurch to the left, which made Lizzy scream with fear. The unexpected lunge caught

Lizzy off guard, and she realized she was losing her balance then falling. She grabbed for Rose's neck, missed, and tumbled to the hard ground, hitting her shoulder and then rolling. Surprisingly, she felt no serious pain until her feet flipped over her head and the left one slammed down on a large rock at the side of the trail. She screamed a second time at the sudden pain and realization that something was seriously damaged.

She came to rest on her back, looking up at the sky. The pain shot up her leg, making her grimace and grit her teeth against the moans that she simply could not help. After a moment she looked around to see Rose standing a few yards away, one leg off the ground, her head hanging in obvious discomfort. Lizzy was not the only one hurt.

As the pain began to subside and Lizzy tried to maneuver into a better position so she could remove her boot and check her ankle, she heard the rustling of leaves in the forest to her left. She glanced over to see a bedraggled man exiting the timber, an old bag clutched to his chest by one arm. He jumped the rock wall and ran quickly to her side.

"Seems ye'r in a bi' 'o truble," the man said.

In too much pain to be wary of a stranger, Lizzy nodded. "A deer came over the wall without warning and . . ." she grimaced. "The mare—"

"My fault then," the man said, glancing over at the mare and then back to Lizzy. He had obviously been running and seemed tired for it. He was a handsome man, even with long, wet hair clinging to his face and neck. It was his eyes, she thought. Their green color was quite stunning.

"'Tis your foot, then," he said.

"My ankle. You're Irish," she commented as he ran his hand down her boot to her ankle. The touch caused an immediate jolt of pain, and she took a deep breath while gritting her teeth once more against her discomfort.

"'Tis so. Just stepped off th' boat yesterday. Was tol' of a place t' bathe bu' was run off by men who doan take kindly t' such things in a place they say was theirs, though I believe God owned it firs'," he said.

Lizzy noticed the red stain on his shirt and pants. "You're hurt," she said.

"A bit, but nah somethin' t' worry a lady like yerself. 'Tis yer foot abou' which we mus' be concerned. I fear tha' I'll be havin' t' remove yer fine leather boot wi' me knife . . . that is if ye'r agreeable."

She nodded. "My foot is not bleeding, but your wound—"

"Pellets from the man's shotgun. Stings a bit, bleeds a little, bu' nothin' to concern yerself abou'." He removed his knife from his pocket and carefully cut away her boot as if skinning a rabbit, doing his best to cause her as little pain as possible. Still, she grimaced. The sock came next, and she was suddenly embarrassed that he was looking at her foot. She had horrible-looking feet—at least she thought so, and she had always kept them carefully hidden for fear that anyone who saw them would surely flee in utter disgust. The Irishman didn't seem to notice.

Gently probing her ankle, he finally spoke. "Probably a ba' sprain, nah broken. Such injuries usually 'urt like th' dickens though." He laid her foot carefully on the grass, glancing over at her mare. "Th' mare 'as nah been so lucky." He went to the horse, reached down while speaking gentle words, and lifted the leg. "Her leg is bad damaged, possibly ev'n broken," he said.

"No, it can't be. It was a small slip. She . . ." Lizzy felt tears rise in her eyes.

The Irishman was already removing the saddle and bridle, placing them on the rock fence. He rubbed Rose's neck gently, soothing her. "She'll 'ave t' fend for 'erself while I get ya back t' where'er ya cum from."

"About a mile back. Our home . . ."

He left the mare at ease and came to her side. Then, extending his hand to her as if to shake it, he quickly hoisted her up over his shoulder. Before she could utter a word of protest, he had adjusted her weight for the carry, picked up his cloth bag with his free hand, and started walking.

"This is not necessary! I am sure I can walk," she squealed in protest.

"'Tis a light load ya are, and if'n ya try t' walk 'twill only make it worse. I'll be carryin' ya if ya doan mind." His stride was lacking any real jolt that made her uncomfortable, so she reluctantly settled herself.

"And you are?"

"Daines. Newton Daines."

"And from what part of Ireland did you come?"

"Most recent from Dublin."

They walked a good half mile without talking before she noticed the blood splotch had grown on his shirt and pants. "You are bleeding in earnest now. Please, at least let me look at your wound. Possibly I could bandage it or—"

"'Tis nice of ya t' offer, an' I am a bi' tired." He stopped, looked about, and finally placed her gently down next to a large tree where the ground was covered with fall leaves. He sat beside her, removed his jacket, and lifted his shirt. She could see where the pellets were already causing the wounds to turn red and would cause infection if not removed.

"Your knife," she said, extending her hand.

He removed it from his pocket and handed it to her. It was very sharp, with a point that was as good as a needle.

"This will hurt a bit," she said, frowning.

He stiffened as she deftly slipped the point into the wound and under the pellet before popping it out. Six others followed, one quite deep and from which most of the blood had flowed. She then removed her own coat and was about to untuck her shirt to rip off a bandage when he spoke.

"That'll nah be necessary, miss. I . . ."

She quickly finished the untucking and ripped off a wide piece of the shirt to use for a bandage before putting her coat back on. She felt the throb in her ankle, but concentrating on his wounds helped her ignore it. "Remove your shirt, Mr. Daines," she said firmly.

Sheepishly he did as he was told as she repositioned herself so that she could wrap the cloth around his wounds. Thankfully there was just enough material for her to wrap it tightly.

"That will at least keep you from bleeding to death until we can get you better care," she said. "Could you describe the men who did this? The police—"

"Doan want to involve no police. An Irishman jus' off th' boat . . ."

"I understand," she replied, though she felt a burst of anger toward the men who had so callously inflicted this injury. "Well, let's at least get you back to the house."

"'Tis a wonder," he said, as he took her extended hand and lifted her up to his shoulder a second time.

"What is a wonder?"

"That a fine an' pretty woman cares at all abou' a poor Irish lad like meself," he answered.

She blushed slightly but admired his direct manner and willingness to pay the compliment.

"You think it an uncommon act?"

"Most ladies of such a fine upbringin' would nah concern themselves wi' me 'ealth, Miss . . ."

"Hudson. Elizabeth Hudson." Lizzy knew he was right. Her so-called class was given to big acts of charity where their money could vouch for them, but very few would give a man such as Newton Daines the time of day if confronted by him on the street. In fact, many would only turn up their noses.

"I caused yer misery an' ya 'ardly thought twice abou' it. Tha' is nah the way of most fine ladies."

"I will accept that as a compliment, but you do not strike me as a man who would harm a woman, no matter her standing."

"I be thankin' ya for sayin' so," he said. He stopped briefly to take her from his shoulders and carry her in his arms. This was more comfortable, and Lizzy thanked him. She looked at his strong face and asked a question. "I suppose you have plans to go west?"

"Free land is bein' offered. A man o' my past standin' canno' refuse such a thing," he said. "Bu', it will take sum time. I'll be needin' work t' provide meself wi' a wagon an' team, an' tools fer farmin'."

"Then you are a farmer," she said.

He laughed lightly. "Everyone who lives in Ireland is a farmer, Miss Hoodson. Survival depends on it, bu' me trade is with 'ammer and plane."

"A carpenter then," she said.

"And one of the good Lord's finest." He smiled.

"And a humble one I see," she teased.

He chuckled and looked at her. It was then she noticed that his face was bruised, his lid and socket swollen, and his lip slightly cut. She reached up and touched the swelling around the eye gently. "Did your attackers . . . ?"

He smiled. "No, 'tis from a hearty welcome I received at the boardin' house of Mrs. O'Grady last evenin'. A few o' the Irish testin' me mettle."

"A few?"

"Enough to make it interestin'." Newton had never felt so comfortable with a woman. She was pretty as anyone he'd ever seen, and though he hadn't spoken to many ladies like her, he knew there were surely none as genuine.

"Well, I fear that a man who knows the fight will be in great demand in Missouri. With Lincoln as our new president . . ."

"War will come, then," he said matter-of-factly.

"You know about our politics," she said.

"I purchased sev'ral newspapers in New Orleans, an' i' was th' talk o' everyone on the steamer 't St. Louis." He paused, adjusting his hold on her a bit. She was light, easy to carry, and . . . soft. It was all he could do to keep his mind properly focused.

"I do nah know where a woman of yer standin' falls wi' slavery, bu' I consider it an evil o' the worst kind."

"Then we are agreed," she said. "Not all households in the United States hold slaves, Mr. Daines—least of all my own."

"Then I'll be apologizin' to ye for presumin' so," he said. "But on the steamer, most seemed t' favor the holdin' o' slaves an' fightin' fer the South. They say Missouri will surely be of the same opinion."

"Missouri will not side with the Confederacy, though many men who live here wish it to be so and will probably go south anyway. But there are also many who will fight tooth and nail for the Union."

"Then 'tis the Union who will be winnin'. God will make it so."

"I hope you are right," she said.

He walked a good distance without further discussion. Lizzy could tell he was getting tired and asked him to put her down once more and take a rest. He did not argue.

She sat back against one tree while Newton rested his back against another.

"It isn't far now," she said. "I can probably walk with a little help."

"'Tis not necessary, Miss Hoodson," he replied quickly. "I am strong enuf." He looked over at her and added, "'Tis a mean business, slavery. How d' men justify such a thing?"

Lizzy thought of Andrew. They had talked often, and his arguments had been the usual secessionist line and, it seemed to her, given more because he was a Southerner than a believer. When she had taken them on point by point, he had always used his charm to change the subject and had even finally agreed that it was a practice that must be ended. But for Andrew there was still the delicate matter of timing.

"I could give you their arguments, Mr. Daines, but believe me when I say that all of them hold about as much water as a bucket with no bottom."

Newton laughed. "Aye, tha's sure, at least the ones I hear." He paused. "I had a friend, a freed slave, aboard th' ship from England. He taugh' me a goo' deal abou' slavery. He has worked ten years now t' save the money t' purchase 'is mother an' sister an' has gone into a place he called Little Dixie t' locate 'em. I doan know a better man."

"He is to be admired." She paused, thinking before deciding to go on. She would speak with caution. "Whites will not usually sell to black freedmen—he knows that doesn't he?"

Newton nodded. "Once he locates 'em, he intends t' find a lawyer who can 'elp."

"There is an organization, the American Anti-Slavery Society. I am a member. If . . . when he returns, bring him to me. I can help."

Lizzy's involvement in the society was not well known, and she hoped to keep it that way. Not because she was afraid or ashamed but because she simply preferred to do her work in anonymity. She had seen how public knowledge of a person's involvement in the Society caused them to spend most of their time fending off attacks instead of moving the work forward, and she wanted nothing to do with such distractions. Worse, she was not orthodox in her personal approach, and she wanted no one to discover just how far her work really went.

He glanced at her. "I'll be doin' so, and thankin' ye fer yer kindness as well."

"My involvement is not common knowledge, so if you could keep it between you and your friend, I would be thankful."

He looked at her a bit curiously but only nodded before getting up and offering her a hand. "'Tis safe wi' me, tha's sure." He once more picked her up in his arms, and they started the last leg of their journey.

"The papers in New Orleans do nah 'ave a high opinion o' such organizations as yers."

She laughed. "No, I don't suppose they do. They have tried several times to crush us legislatively and with violence." She sobered. "Several have died defending it, but we must not give up."

"And what does Mr. Hoodson think o' yer work?"

She was confused for a moment before she realized he was talking about a possible husband. She laughed. "The only Mr. Hudson in my life is my brother, and he is quite agreeable."

"Then yer bruther is involved in this Society of which ya speak," Newton said.

"Not in the Society itself but in other ways. Important ones," she said.

Newton stopped moving. "Ah, 'tis a pretty sight," he said as he looked toward barns and a large house. "An' it seems yer servants 'ave seen us cumin an' ere ready t' receive ya." Several men were making a mad dash in their direction, a small cart in tow.

"Nah a bit too soon," he went on. "Though ye be ligh' an' quite pleasant t' carry, I be a bi' worn out in the knees. Not as strong as I thought, bu' then most men let ego get in th' way o' reality." He stopped and went to one knee to put her down. She looked up into those green eyes and saw a man she could be friends with. It was a strange thought but there was mirth and intelligence and a good deal of gentleness hidden behind that bedraggled exterior and it pleased her to think of him in such a way.

Newton seemed to read her thoughts as he spoke. "If ya doan mind, I'll consider ya me friend, Miss Hoodsun. Our views seem to require it and I'd be pleased ta…"

Seeing his discomfort at being so forward, she quickly spoke. "And I as well, Mr. Daines," she said.

Mose approached and Newton stood and explained the mare's where-abouts while Lizzy watched, thinking of how she might help Mr. Newton Daines. As Mose jumped to action, shouting orders for the horse to be found quickly and brought to the barn, Newton once more lifted Lizzy and placed her in the back of the waiting cart.

"I want a vet sent for immediately, Mose," Lizzy said. "The mare is not to be put down unless there is no other choice."

"Yes'm," Mose replied. He then picked up the arms of the cart and began the trek toward the house while barking at a house servant standing in the distance to send for the doctor.

"Mr. Daines, you must come to the house and have your wounds tended to properly," Lizzy said.

Newton wanted very much to accept the invitation but knew it would not be wise. "I'll be goin' back to me place, Miss Hoodsun," he said. "Yer bandage 'as worked wonders."

Realizing Newton was not going to follow her, Lizzy told Mose to stop as an idea suddenly came to mind. "My brother hires carpenters to work on our steamers," she said to Newton. She gave him the address of Rand's office. "I will send him a message and tell him you are coming and that you should be hired. Will you go?"

Newton grinned. "I am Irish bu' I am nah a fool. I'll be acceptin' yer offer, Miss Hoodsun, and thankin' y' for it. But it is not necessary because of me help."

Lizzy gave him a friendly smile. "We are friends, aren't we, Mr. Daines, and friends help one another. Now, I expect you to see my brother."

Newton grinned. "Friends we are, Miss Hoodsun, and I'll be thankin' the good Lord for it."

Mose started moving again, and Lizzy quickly added another thought. "And don't forget, if your friend needs help once he finds his mother and sister. . ."

"I'll remember."

"Good. Mose, have Mr. Daines delivered to town by carriage immediately, will you?"

"Yes'm," Mose said with a wry smile. He had known Lizzy all his life, and he knew when she was fond of someone, but this one . . . well, it was a bit unexpected.

"And Mr. Daines," Lizzy said, "stay out of forests and private ponds. Next time they might not miss."

Newton grinned, bowed slightly, and watched as Mose took Lizzy away to the house. "God bless, Miss Hoodsun. I am sure th' doctor will fix ya up nicely."

As the cart bounced gently across the uneven path, Lizzy contemplated Newton Daines; he was a curious one, even intriguing, and she really did want to be friends. She watched the carriage pull up and Newton get inside before the carriage lurched toward the city. How strange, she thought, that such feelings could come so easily between two people with such varying backgrounds. And it was even stranger to her that there seemed to be no romantic inclinations.

"Do you know him from someplace, Missy?" Mose asked.

She shook her head. "It seems like I have known him all my life," she answered softly.

"And will these feelings be love, Miss Lizzy?" Mose asked with an air of teasing.

She laughed lightly. "No, Mose, but I think we will be the best of friends."

Mose only nodded as Lydijah came down the steps and started giving orders and asking questions and making a fuss. Lizzy was lifted from the cart in such a way that she could see the carriage leave through their front gate. "Yes," she said, softly. "The very best of friends."

Chapter 7

THE CARRIAGE DID NOT WANDER onto O'Fallon Street; instead, it let Newton out several blocks away. Such a carriage would not be safe in the Kerry Patch, and Newton had no desire to put Miss Elizabeth Hudson in any trouble.

When he was back at the boardinghouse, he found Mary McConnell in the kitchen. When he asked if there was someplace he could wash his clothes, she simply pointed to the back door. Outside he found several large barrels filled with semiclean water. Soap sat on a table next to them, and he quickly scrubbed out the dirty shirt he had removed before bathing that morning. He then removed his bloodied shirt and pants and did his best on them before hanging them all out to dry and pulling on his old, dirty pants. They'd have to do until the others dried. The sun was out, but it was cool and it might take a while. He untied the bandage Lizzy had put around his wound and checked it. He'd need some salve and a new bandage. He went inside and was about to ask when Mary saw the wound and frowned. "Sit," she said pointing at the stool.

He looked at her quizzically.

She retrieved a bottle of ointment and a clean rag from a cupboard and told him to sit a second time.

"An' th' cos' will be . . . ?" Newton asked.

She smiled. "No cost this time—double next."

"A bargain fer sure," he said with a wry smile, but he sat down and allowed her to inspect the small pellet holes that were already staunched by clotted blood. "Fine doin's," she said impatiently. "Ya haven't been in St. Lou' fer twenty-four hours an' already ya got yerself shot. At tha' rate you'll be dead by week's end."

"Only if I go swimmin' in a fool's private pond again."

She smiled. "Went up creek, did ya?"

"Crowded next t' the river," he answered.

"But no one shoots ya fer swimmin' there," she replied. She cleaned the blood from around the wound and then applied the salve to the holes.

"You ever hear of Hoodsun Company?"

Mary hesitated in attending his injuries then spoke. "One of the best businesses in St. Louis. Mrs. Hudson jus' passed away, an' her son an' daughter run the business. An uncle is involved as well, but he's a clinger."

"A clinger?"

"A parasite—greedy one at that. Why d' ya ask?"

"I met the sister. She's offered me a job."

Mary stopped working altogether, a disbelieving look on her lightly freckled face. Newton explained what had happened.

When he had finished, she shook her head, causing her long, curly hair to bounce around her shoulders. "The luck o' the Irish. 'Tis a good day fer ya, Mr. Daines. Hudson pays top wages, an' if you do well, he'll reward ya fer it." She finished wrapping his wound and tying it off.

"Ye seem t' be knowin' wha' yer doin," he said as he looked at the bandage. "Course, the gambler probably gives ya plenty o' practice."

She drove him out the kitchen door with a bit of an Irish curse, and Newton ran upstairs to wash up. When he got back downstairs, Mary McConnell was waiting, his wet shirt now dried and ironed.

"How much do I be owin' ya?" he asked.

"A dime, though with connections like yers it shou' probably be a dollar."

He removed a coin from his pocket and handed it to her. "I ha'n't got th' job yet, so le's stick wi' th' dime."

She folded her arms across her waist as she watched him put the garment on. He was an attractive man, there was no mistaking that—his arms and torso were muscled, even powerful. She shook off the thought long enough to give him directions.

"The fastest way t' the office o' Hudson Company is t' go t' the river an' follow the docks back t' where the tracks're being built fer the new railroad. Go one more street t' the south an' turn uphill. Mr. Hudson's office is abou' halfway up the block. Name on the window."

Newton nodded, but his gaze lingered on Mary. She was a bit heavier and shorter than Elizabeth Hudson, but her form was well proportioned, her eyes were as blue as any he'd ever seen, and she had dimples in her cheeks that deepened when she smiled.

"Then I'll be needin' me tools," he said turning back upstairs. When he returned she was gone, and he quickly left the building while shoving aside his disappointment. He found the office just about the time dark clouds, heavy with rain, had begun to block out the sun over the city. He hoped Mary McConnell would be kind enough to bring in his clothes and find a warm place for them, or they'd not dry for days.

He climbed the stairs to the office and asked for Randolph Hudson.

"And who's askin'?'" inquired the clerk at the first desk, looking him over.

"Newton Daines."

"Ah, Mr. Daines, we've been expecting you," the man replied with a smile. "Mr. Hudson isn't here but has instructed us to find you work. What are yer skills, an' where are ya from?"

"A carpenter cum from County Kerry t' find me fortune," Newton said with a bold smile and an extended hand. The clerk shook it with a raised brow.

"Kerry's full of thieves n' butchers," he said, giving Newton a hard look. "From the look a yer face, I think ya be one of these."

"Never stole a penny or hurt a man who didn't deserve it," Newton said.

The clerk's expression softened and he extended his hand once more. "I be pullin' yer leg. The name's Norman Pitts. Always glad t' welcome one of the Irish. Not enough a us in this town. County Kerry, eh, the blessed heart of the good Irish folk. I lived in Killorglin as a boy." He looked down at Newton's tools. "Miss Hudson says yer good with hammer and plane."

Newton shared his background.

Pitts had flaming red hair bursting out from under a plain woolen cap with a small bill protruding at its front. His eyesbrows were as thick as haystacks and kept his brown eyes shaded. "You'll be findin' tha' most skilled jobs are taken by the Germans, who control most o' the workforce in the city. But Mr. Hudson is not one to look at the heritage of a man but at his skills and reputation. You come with the very best recommendation, so you'll be treated kindly unless ya show us your skill is mostly in your head an' not in your hands. Understood?"

Newton nodded.

"Good, kin ye use pen and paper?"

Newton nodded his head in the affirmative and was handed both. One was a work form asking for information. He wrote down Mrs. O'Grady's name and the address on O'Fallon Street along with his full name, past employment, and skills as a carpenter. Pitts took the form and gave it the once-over.

"Ah, an' a pretty hand it is. Kin ye do figures as well?"

"Me mother taugh' me such when I was just a lad, an' the abacus as well," Newton replied.

"'Tis a goo' thing. I kin pu' ye to work on th' docks day after tomorra."

Newton felt relief course down his spine. "I do nah wan' to be ungrateful to ya boss, bu' wha' will the wage be?"

"Ah, the wage, yes, 'tis small to be startin'. Dock workers be gettin' a dollar and twenty five cents a day."

Newton tried to keep a straight face. That was more than he'd expected.

Pitts smiled. "'Tis nah a fancy wage for thi' city. Ditch diggers ge' as much as tha', but if ye be lookin' ahead, you'll be havin' better. Now you be reportin' to the docks day after tomorra. Find Conrad Dieter and gi' 'im this note. He'll be puttin' ye t' work until we 'ave need for yer carpenter skills. Will that suit ya for now?"

Newton nodded and took the note. After shaking Pitts's hardened hand, he left, his tools in tow as he stepped into a drenching, cold rain. His inclination was to do a little Irish jig, but he thought it best to get out of the rain quickly. A saloon just down the street caught his eye; perhaps he might just celebrate his good fortune. He wiped his hand over the back of his lips. He had a thirst for whiskey. Trouble was, when he started he couldn't stop, so he'd made up his mind years ago to avoid it altogether before it ruined him or killed him like it had so many others, including his father. Besides, he had a job, a future, and now was no time to take a chance on renewing his friendship with the devil's fire.

The air was cold and the streets quite empty, except for the occasional carriage and a few folks rushing in and out of buildings to keep from getting soaked. He ran for the covered porch of a nearby business and stood there while pulling his coat tightly around his shivering frame, his toolbox hanging heavy in one hand. He decided he'd best get the tools home and cleaned and dried or they would rust.

Retracing his steps to the boardinghouse, he found the place nearly empty of humankind except for Mrs. O'Grady, Mary McConnell, and the gambler, whose face was now bandaged. They were in the kitchen drinking coffee. The gambler, who was eating eggs and grits, glanced up at Newton, frowned, and turned back to his food.

Mrs. O'Grady had strung a line along one side of the room, and Newton's clothes, along with those of others, were dripping onto the floor. A mop stood close by to clean up the water as it pooled.

"I thank ye fer bringin' in me clothes," Newton said from the doorway between the kitchen and entry. He was soaked and shivering; the smell of coffee was strong and enticing, but food was money, and he quickly left the door and started up the stairs.

"I'll 'ave you a cup of coffee when ya come down t' dry yerself by the fire," Mary called after him. He looked down to find her in the doorway of the kitchen and gave her a smile and nod.

"An' 'ow did it go?" she asked.

"I star' on th' docks day after tomorra," he replied. "Hoodson's clerk, man name o' Pitts, says better will cum soo'."

"Good." She smiled as she disappeared back into the kitchen.

He put away his tools and dried his hair, face, and whiskers with the still-wet towel he had used that morning. A small potbellied stove sat in one corner of the room, and he supposed it went unfired unless one either cut and hauled his own wood or paid for what he needed. The room was chilled enough that he wondered if one blanket would be enough for sleeping tonight, but he wasn't about to spend his money on wood either. He'd just make do.

Returning downstairs to the sitting room, he stood in front of the fire to dry his clothes and warm himself. The chill in his bones slowly dissipated and was nearly gone when Mary brought him a cup of coffee and told him to pull a chair up to the fire before returning to the kitchen. He could hear the harsh tones of a discussion coming from the next room but could not understand the words; moments later the gambler fumed out of the kitchen and went upstairs, the slam of his door echoing throughout the boardinghouse. Mary came back into the sitting room and pulled up a chair of her own.

"Yer beau seems a bit outa sorts with ya," Newton said, watching the fire.

"I told you, he ain't my beau," she said sternly.

"Then i' mus' be th' coffee tha' upsets 'im, though I don' see why. It's a goo' cup."

"Patrick needs money and thinks I 'ave some 'id up. E'en if I do, I wouldn't be givin' it to the likes o' 'im," she said.

"An' if this boss that Mr. O'Shay works for 'bout kills 'm for it, 'ow will ye feel, Mary McConnell?"

"O'Brien won't kill 'im. He might break both 'is arms, bu' 'e won't kill 'im. Patrick's daddy 'as power an' money an' would bring the roof down on O'Brien," she said.

Newton tensed. "O'Brien, ya say?"

"McKinnon O'Brien. He controls most gambling, boxing, an' other such vices in the Patch."

Newton felt his heart sink but didn't let on. "Then why doesn't Patrick go t' 'is father. If O'Brien jus' wants 'is muny, he won' be particular abou' wha' pocket it cums from."

"He will, eventually, an' O'Brien knows it. He's just applying pressure to move things along," Mary said.

"I don' like Mr. O'Brien, tha's sure. I dealt wi' 'is kind in Dublin, an' they be a vicious lot," Newton said.

"O'Brien is Dublin bred an' born. Has a brother there still," Mary said.

"Matthew O'Brien, boss of the nor'side," Newton said matter-of-factly.

"Thas' 'im," she said. "Ya know 'im?"

"'Tis a black mark on the face of all Irishmen, Matty O'Brien."

"Well, McKinnon O'Brien is a mirror image then," she said. "Mac O'Brien runs 'bout everything aroun' the Patch an' 'e doan like strangers."

"An' does 'e answer to anuther?" Newton asked. Both of them knew that a man like O'Brien had betters in a city this size.

"Mr. Malone, a much finer gentleman and the power among the Irish in the city."

"Well, I have no wish to be meetin' either of 'im," Newton replied. "Though I doan know nuthin' of Mr. Malone, the O'Briens either get their way or bury ya."

Mary smiled. "An' as you learned this morning they ain't the only ones." She leaned forward. "Newton Daines, ya 'ave a bit t' learn about St. Lou' an' where folks can go an' where they can't. So I'll be bendin' yer ear fer a bit."

"And I'll be grateful for the bendin'." Newton turned his chair to dry the back side of him.

"Where ya' was shot this mornin' is where the rich Americans, Germans, and even a few rich Irish live. They don' like vagrants an' bums, an' they would consider ya such, dressed as ya are. Tha's why they took aim at ya." She set her cup on the floor next to her chair. "They are surrounded by poverty that they do little abou' except keep it ou' o' their streets and away from their 'omes. If ya go there, they be havin' ya arrested or they send their own goons t' beat on ya goo' for bein' uppity. If ya persist, they either dump ya in jail fer a nice long stay or in the river, which won't be sending ya back."

Newton attempted to speak, but Mary raised a hand. "Let me finish givin' ya a tour o' our fair city. Freed blacks an' Irish doan get along. Stay away from the black sections o' town, or they'll beat on ya worse than the rich folks' goons. The Irish came an' took their jobs, and they 'ave not taken to it kindly. An' you'll be notin' that no blacks come into the Patch. They're either idiots or lookin' to die if they do."

She leaned forward. "The city is split between them wha' wants t' free blacks an' them tha' don't. Them tha' don't want t' free the blacks think slavery suits the blacks just fine an' they'll fight Northern abolitionists t' the death protectin' it. Didn't used to be tha' way, but since the labor wars most Irish 'round this place 'ave taken a 'ard view. Sure, they will visit coffee houses run by freed blacks an' steal their money at the gambling tables, even 'ire some of 'em to do work of a lesser kind they doan want to do for themselves. Some of 'em, especially the rich ones and the bosses, own slaves. So if'n you 'ave it in your 'ead to rant against slavery t' the Irish, you best plan on gettin' your 'ead busted. Most won't like it. We had an Irish printer, an' a fine one too, who refused t' keep 'is abolitionist views t' 'imself, and 'is press ended up in the street an' 'e was run out of town."

Newton felt a grim depression in the pit of his stomach. "An' th' views o' Mary McConnell on th' subject?"

"Mary McConnell 'as no views. Women git just as riled abou' this as men. I 'ave seen plenty a tangle between Irish women over blacks. They say the more ya free, the more the competition for jobs and the less food they 'ave for themselves and their young uns. Some o' our rich Irish gentlemen ev'n supported a law tha' denied blacks the right t' any kind o' book learnin' just so they could be kept at a disadvantage, and e'en the Catholic priests say slavery is nah contrary t' natural law an' 'tis nah wrong as long as ya feed 'em good and only beat 'em when they be deservin' it. Which is the same as sayin' that if ye be a good Catholic and go t' mass and confession once a year an' ya 'ave slaves, ya doan need t' worry 'bout God bouncing ya outta 'eaven."

Her distaste for the words she was saying was obvious, and Newton figured he knew where Mary McConnell stood on the matter whether she said so or not. She clearly did not like slavery, but she was a realist, and her livelihood depended on keeping her views to herself. He knew that she was warning him about the reality so that he wouldn't get his head beat in by someone who didn't take a fancy to blacks, freed or slave, in St. Louis.

"Now, I be tellin' ya one other thing," Mary added. "The Hudsons hate slavery. Word 'as it that Miss Elizabeth Hudson helps blacks get on the Underground Railroad and get outta this part of the country t' Canada where they can be free. Her brother is as fine a man as there is when it comes to 'ow 'e treats blacks and has freedmen workin' for 'im. Word 'as it that 'e 'as brought a few slaves out of the South aboard 'is steamers to get them t' freedom. So if ya hate slavery you'll find them agreeable. If ya doan they probably won't say much unless ya turn coat on 'em. If ya do, beware. They'll 'ave yer 'ide hangin' on the barn door fer it."

He stood. "I am grateful t' ya fer the warnin.' I'll do me best to kee' me mouth shut abou' such things." He glanced at the window. The sun shown through it, promising better weather. "I be leavin' ya now t' do a little explorin'—git me bearins an' all," Newton said.

"A good day to ya then, Mr. Daines."

Newton had a sudden thought. "I doan 'ave lots a muny, but it bein' me day off, would ya be willin' to find a coffee house an' 'ave a bit to eat wi' th' likes o' me? I be havin' further need a yer goo' counsel, Mary McConnell, and it would please me—"

"Ah, yer offer would please me as well, bu' Mrs. O'Grady is gone the rest o' the day, an' I will 'ave me duty 'ere." She smiled and seemed genuinely pleased at the offer. "'Ow 'bout another time?"

He bowed slightly. "'Twill be an honor. Ya be havin' a goo' day," he said, backing into the entry and then turning to the door, his face a bit flushed. The thought of a future dinner with Miss Mary McConnell made his heart pump furiously and his palms sweat like a flash flood. And what had gotten into him to ask her in the first place? He shook his head to clear his mind. A part of him wanted very much to be with Mary McConnell, while the other part was scared to death at the idea. He never was much with women but she seemed different, easy to talk to.

He was beginning to like St. Louis and America too. He did not like people telling him to stay out of their streets, and he wouldn't be pushed around in a free country, but there were possibilities here he never could have claimed in old Ireland, or even in England. He'd mind his p's and q's, but he'd stretch his wings as well and see where doing so would take him. If a woman like Mary McConnell could like him, even a little, it would be far. Far indeed.

Chapter 8

FELIX COULON HAD BEEN BORN the son of a rich slave owner and his black slave, who was also his household servant. When the pregnancy occurred, his mother and sister (the daughter of another slave who had previously been sold) were immediately put to auction so that the slave owner could avoid the unpleasant detection of his adultery. The new owners were good to Felix's mother and sister and to Felix when he was born. They were allowed to live in a small room attached to the owner's home, where Felix's mother became the personal servant to the mistress of the plantation and his sister was taught the duties of maid and cook. When he was of age, Felix was trained as a household steward. His family ate from the master's cupboard, though some items were forbidden, and were clothed better than most because of their positions in the home. As Felix grew up and looked around, he found that his life was good compared to the poverty and inhumanity endured by other slaves his white masters owned—but he also noticed the way white folk lived and knew there was more to life than his present condition allowed. He always wanted more.

Felix had stayed in the same household until his first master died and the mistress was left with debt; she needed to sell the plantation and its assets in order to survive. Unfortunately, his mother and sister had been sold separate from him and, though he had tried to keep track of them, he had not seen them since. As far as he knew, they still worked on a plantation near Boonville, Missouri, and continued to work as household servants. But he could not be sure, so he was determined to find the plantation and discover the answer. As a black man, he did not have free access to white courthouses, and thus the records of the sale of black folk, so it was the only way he knew how to find his mother and sister.

He heard wagons coming and pulled his floppy hat down, his eyes riveted on the ground. He found it best not to make eye contact with white folks and wanted no trouble. The wagons passed, and he glanced quickly at the sky. The sun was turning the edges of the horizon dark blue and would soon appear. It would be a clear day, but there was a chill in the air. He did not mind. Such weather was comfortable for travel and would allow him to walk longer, thus covering more ground in shorter time. He figured he would arrive near Boonville later in the day.

By the time of the sale that separated Felix from his mother and sister, he was a large, strapping young man whose new master felt could be put to better purposes than greeting visitors at the front door. Hired out as a laborer along the docks of the Mississippi River at St. Louis, Felix soon became a man known for his physical ability. At more than six feet tall and at least two hundred and fifty pounds, far above the average stature of the day, he found that the hard work toned his muscles even further and gave him strength that put most men to shame when it came to work along the docks. Because Felix was prized for his physical ability, it was his master who benefited, making a good wage from the grueling jobs accomplished by Felix. Yet Felix gained no advantage and in fact was housed in conditions no better than the animals on his previous master's plantation. It was then that he had begun to dream of and plan for his freedom.

But unbeknownst to most, Felix had been given an advantage foreign to nearly all slaves that both increased his longing for freedom and gave him the language, skills, and other abilities necessary to obtain it. When Felix was ten years old, his mother had convinced her mistress to teach Felix and his sister how to read so that they could be even more valuable to the household. This education in reading also led the two children to learn how to write and use basic mathematics and to think more clearly on a variety of subjects than other slaves. It also gave Felix the courage to sneak books from the master's library and read them.

He learned how to speak proper English and to express himself in words on paper, but most of the time he had to keep such talents hidden. Whites in general and slave owners in particular feared educated blacks. From such had come the rebellions of men like Nate Turner in Virginia, who had put fear into white slaveholders. Out of that fear had come laws that penalized those who taught blacks how to read and write. His mistress had broken those laws, and Felix had simply learned to "act the black man" so as not to cause her trouble for it. Such acting had been tiresome and even humiliating, but necessary, and had proven to have advantages while protecting his master's wife from serious trouble.

As conditions worsened under his new master at the docks, Felix began to put his secretly held education to work. While seeming to be just another slave, he carefully watched how things worked on the docks, subtly offering suggestions for changes that would improve the foreman's ability to be efficient and thus make him more money. This enhanced Felix's position in the eyes of the dock bosses, and over time the foreman saw Felix's value and improved his conditions. When the foreman was promoted to head foreman, Felix moved to the new offices with him and was allowed to sleep in a small but comfortable room in the back of the office, where foremen or overseers no longer watched his every move.

Finally feeling he had the trust of the head foreman, Felix revealed his ability to read and do numbers. The foreman, as illiterate a white man as Felix knew, was soon allowing Felix to keep his accounts and run important errands instead of breaking his back under bales of cotton. This gave Felix power to improve the condition of both the slaves and the few free Irish and German workers on the foreman's growing crew, and soon they were the most productive and profitable gang along the docks.

Making himself invaluable gave Felix the ability to negotiate with the foreman for extra work outside the master's contract, which allowed him to slowly hoard the money that would eventually buy his freedom. And freedom did not come cheap. The downside of becoming so valuable was that his slave price increased as well. Ten years passed before he had enough, and even then it was a delicate matter to buy one's own freedom. Even after he had the money, it had taken him another two years and careful planning to accomplish.

Felix knew that if his master discovered he had saved money to buy his freedom, his master would claim it as the master's property and that the courts, which considered anything earned by a slave to be the property of the master, would give the money to his master. He was very cautious in this instance, but when he felt he had finally saved enough, he learned that there were some whites who sympathized with the plight of black slaves and would aid their release. One of these was a man name Charles Hunter.

Back then Felix did not know Hunter personally, and Hunter lived across the river in Illinois, a place that might as well have been on the moon for a black slave. But Felix knew how to write, and as part of his duties, he delivered and received mail for the foreman. He wrote Charles Hunter a letter and waited.

It was nearly a year later when Hunter walked into the foreman's office and handed the boss papers signed and sealed by Felix's master stating that Felix Coulon was now the property of Charles Hunter. Felix thanked the foreman for his kindness and left with his few belongings and Mr. Charles Hunter. An hour later Hunter signed papers setting Felix free for the amount of twelve hundred dollars, which Felix paid. Hunter then gave him some advice: Do not stay in St. Louis. If the subterfuge were discovered by his old master, his master could go to the courts and attempt to get Felix back along with the money used to buy his freedom. Better to move on, go north. Felix agreed and eventually ended up in New York City.

He worked at odd jobs, saving every extra penny, but realized he needed to find work that paid better. Not long after that, he found just the job aboard a ship that sailed between the United States and Europe. Felix had sailed the high seas for nearly ten years and had finally saved the money he needed to free his mother and sister. Now he had the money to set them free, and he was looking for them.

Felix arrived near Boonville in early evening. He was smart enough to know that he could not approach whites for information about slaves, so he waited in the shade of a tall oak at a crossroads until black workers came by. Because families were often split up in the sale of slaves, the black community had learned to spread information among themselves in order to keep track of one another. A slave living on one plantation knew who lived and worked on every plantation for miles. Someone would know where his mother and sister were.

But Felix was disappointed. By dusk he had talked to a dozen black men and women, but none of them knew of his mother and sister. Dismayed and discouraged, with the cold of evening setting into his bones, Felix decided he must find a place to sleep for the night and went back to the road. He walked for nearly a mile before he came to a small farm that looked like it had several slave houses as part of the property. The candlelight in the windows looked inviting, and he could smell food cooking. His mouth watered as he rubbed his cold hands together. He had not had a good meal since leaving the ship and had slept under two thin blankets that did little more than keep him from shivering to death four nights in a row. It would be nice to sleep near a warm fire.

He approached the slave dwellings warily. If he were caught by the white owner, he would surely be flogged at the least and imprisoned at worst, but the cold in his bones drove him forward.

"You lookin' fer someone?"

The voice came out of the shadows near a small pen that obviously held pigs; Felix felt his heart stop. He took a deep breath and turned to face someone coming out of the darkness. He heard the snap of a match then saw the light flicker over the heavily creased face of an old black gentleman as he lit his smoking pipe.

"Yas, suh, I am. My motha and sista."

The old gentleman puffed twice, the smoke lifting off the bowl of his wooden pipe and drifting heavenward.

"You a slave?" the old man asked.

"Freedman," Felix answered.

The embers of the pipe threw a light on the old man's face as he eyed Felix up and down. There was glint in his eyes that showed years of a hard life and a good deal of wisdom learned in the process.

"Youse a big 'un, but them gray hairs says you been 'round awhile."

"Near forty years," Felix said. Most slaves didn't live so long, and both of them knew it. "You be even older dan me."

"Near sixty-five. I learned to git along, but won't be long fer me now, no sir." He blew smoke. "Name's Handsome." He chuckled. "As you kin see, it fits ma fine features. Come inside 'fore you freeze up and cain't move 't'all," he said, stepping past Felix. "An' fore you get us both in trouble with the Massa."

Felix followed and soon found himself inside a small shack that had been made as comfortable as could be expected. A young woman and three children were sitting at the table eating corn porridge out of wooden bowls. Several candles and a fireplace lighted the room, and the heat from the latter hit Felix in the face like a bucket of warm water.

The children stared at him with wide eyes, and the woman, who looked to be at least ten years younger than Felix, looked up from what she was doing and threw a questioning look at the old man.

"Freedman," said the old one, "come lookin' fer fam'ly." He looked at the woman. "Name's Abigail and she's ma daughter. The little 'un there with the pretty face is Flower, and them two boys is Abe and Tom. Tom is the one what's tallest and meanest." He smiled. "Baby in the cradle is named Rankin and ain't much older than a week."

The woman looked at Felix for a moment as if measuring him, then smiled. "We ain't got much, but you's welcome to a little."

Felix nodded his thanks and set his bedroll and knapsack down near the wall before removing his coat. A bowl filled with porridge and a wooden spoon were provided him as Handsome sat down at the head of the table, tore some bread from a loaf with his hands, and handed it to Felix.

"No grace 'bin said," Abigail intoned.

Handsome nodded and bowed his head. "Dear Lord, bless dis here gent'man in his search, an' bless dis here food. We knows it ain't easy fo' some folks to find, and we's glad we has it. Now, you bless them folks what's gone t' yo' kingdom. We hopes to see 'em again someday. Name of the Lord Jesus, amen."

Everyone ate but said little, including Felix. The little girl kept watching him with big eyes, but Abe and Tom attended to eat every bite they could.

"Youse a big 'un," the little girl finally said.

"Never you mind," Abigail told her daughter. "You jus' be eatin' fo' Abe steals it from under yer nose. Go on." Flower went back to eating and didn't look up again.

When he was finished with what he'd been given, Felix was handed another piece of bread slathered with some sweet honey; he relished every bite. The woman was a good cook. She had to be to make corn porridge taste that good.

Tom and Abe helped clean up while Flower, not more than five or six, sat on the old man's lap in an old rocker near the fire. "How long since youse seen yo' momma?" asked Handsome.

"Twelve years," Felix replied. "We was separated by sale."

"An' you think they's here, in Boonville?" Abigail asked.

"When they was sold, they come here. Don't seem like dey's here no more. Been askin' folks all day. No one sayin'."

"No surprise," Handsome said. "Been a lot of runaway slaves lately. The rest don't say nothin' to nobody anymore 'cause the white folk got smart and use some blacks to ask de questions and catch de run'ways. I be surprised they spoke to you at all. Who be your motha and sista?"

Felix told him.

Handsome's eyes saddened as he glanced at the woman, who was the one who actually spoke. "Yo' momma is dead. Not too long 'go, but she's gone."

"Yo' sista, she is alive," Handsome added. "She been sold to a new owner on a plantation near Fulton in Callaway County. Place called the Cedars. Mr. Freedman, you is headed in de wrong direction."

Felix only nodded, his head still reeling from the news of his mother's death. He supposed he should not be surprised, but he was, and he felt the need to cry. It was all he could do to hold the tears in. "Where is she buried?" he asked quietly.

"Plantation belongin' to Francis Dowd, 'bout two miles down de road going west. Cemetery's down by de river."

"Dowd is a fair man, but he has a hard overseer name of Perkins; a bad man, Mr. Felix. Even Dowd is scared of 'im," Abigail said, clasping her hands nervously in front of her. "You best not be goin' there, no sir."

Felix only nodded.

"You been gone from dis here country fo' long time, ain't you, Mr. Felix?" Handsome asked.

"Yas suh. I was on a big ship 'tween this country and Europe fo' more than ten years now."

"Has you heard 'bout Mr. Lincoln?"

"Some, in passin'. He be de new president, an' most blacks I talk to says he's a good man."

"Maybe. Some's says he is, somes says he isn't, but one thing is sure, Southern white folk *doan* like Mista Lincoln an' dey *do* like de slave laws, and deys afeard de president put an end to dem an' free de slaves. Why, one state, South Carolina, she already leavin' de Union 'cause of it, and Louisiana, she soon follow along wif others down South. De slaves, dey be hearin' about all dis, and dey talkin' 'bout risin up and runnin' away. De white folk 'round here, dey be afeard de slaves rise up. Dey clamp down hard on us black folk, and dey doan like strangers cumin' round no how. You best be real cautious, Mista Stranger. Real cautious."

Handsome rubbed his eyes tiredly and eased Flower off his lap with instructions to go to bed along with the others. The children climbed a ladder into the loft and disappeared.

Handsome sauntered to the door at the end of the small room. "You had best be leavin' 'fore sunup. Won't do us no good to have you found here." He turned and went through the door, shutting it behind him and leaving Felix and Abigail alone. She sat in the rocker and picked up some needlework.

"You can sleep over dere, 'gainst dat wall," she said, indicating with a nod of her head.

Felix nodded his reply and stood to pick up his bedroll. She was a handsome woman, thin with big eyes and pretty features. Her skin was not as dark as most, and he thought there might be some white blood in her. She removed her head wrap to reveal her hair was weaved tightly into strands that ended at the nape of her neck.

"Them yo' children?" he asked as he picked up his bedroll.

"Jus' two of 'em. The massa bought the oldest, put him here with us to feed and care for. Like one of our own now." She hesitated. "He run once. Has the marks to show it. Wants out, he does." She hesitated again, measuring Felix with her eyes. "I'd run myself if Pa could do it with me, but he can't."

"Runnin' is a fearful business," he said. "Was yer husband sold to another plantation?"

"I ain't got no husband," she said and looked away. "He's dead."

"You have a nice place here," Felix said, changing the subject.

"It's a comfortable place, but not a nice one," Abigail said coldly.

Felix nodded sadly at the answer but said nothing more. He lay down and decided he would sleep only a couple of hours and then be on his way. This master would not be one to wake up to.

Closing his eyes he listened to the creak of the rocker as the woman continued her darning. "Have you ever really tried runnin', Abigail?"

She did not answer immediately. "I ran once. I also have the marks— and the children—to show it, but the massa didn't mark dem. Too young and affect the sale price someday."

Felix felt his heart sink at the anguish in her words. He turned over, his backside to the wall, and tried to close his eyes, but sleep did not come. He listened to the chair and the crackle of the fire, his thoughts on Abigail and others like her. He had fled to earn money to buy the freedom of his mother and sister. Maybe he should have stayed and helped Charles Hunter.

After a few hours his eyes grew heavy, and he fell asleep. It was the best six hours he'd had in days.

Chapter 9

A SLAVE CEMETERY WAS USUALLY placed in a far corner of an owner's plantation—out of sight, out of mind. The sun was just rising when Felix found it. He searched the faded, incomplete, and destroyed headstones and wooden markers until he found his mother's name. He knelt beside her grave.

He felt to apologize for not coming sooner but didn't; he felt to tell her that he loved her but couldn't. He had spent the morning walk thinking about his regrets. He should have, could have, come sooner, but he had delayed. His excuse had been to save more money, even though he knew he had plenty for both his mother's and sister's freedom, but in reality he had learned to live without them. If he was honest with himself, he knew he had come to enjoy his own freedom more than he wanted to achieve theirs, and he had come too late. Now he felt sharing his excuses would only offend his mother.

The horse and rider were nearly upon him before he realized they were even there. He thought to flee but saw it was too late. The horseman brought his animal across the graves, stomping down the earth and knocking over dilapidated and rotting markers to get to him. Felix wanted to cower away but held his ground, stood, and faced the horseman.

The spotted gray horse pawed at the ground. "What do you think you're doing here?" its rider angrily challenged Felix. Felix knew this man was an overseer. He was an especially mean-looking one who fondled an imposing club while continuing to question Felix regarding who he was and what he was doing there. Felix answered each question as patiently as he could, his head to the ground, his eyes averted, and his tone that of a poor, uneducated black who feared the white man. It was a role, he was deciding, he had learned to play far too well.

"Let me see your papers!" demanded the overseer after several minutes' worth of badgering.

Even though the papers were in order, Felix felt unsafe as he watched the overseer's mind work over his options. Freedmen had been forced back into slavery by such men. Overseers would kidnap them, destroy their papers, and then create forged ones showing new names, birth dates, and sale dates in order to have the freedmen resold into slavery—at a tidy profit.

But this overseer was alone, and the size differential between him and Felix seemed to discourage any greedy idea of overpowering Felix. The man reluctantly handed back the papers.

"This is Dowd property. My name is Perkins, and I swear an oath that if I find you anywhere near this plantation again, you will regret it." He then whipped his horse's flanks and was about to ride off when he hesitated. Felix immediately saw why. Two other men were coming down the road in a wagon.

Perkins looked back at Felix, gave him an evil grin, then rode to meet the wagon. Realizing what all of it might mean, Felix turned and ran. Smart enough to realize that running toward the road would surely make things worse, he ran toward a river he had crossed on his way here. The open farmland quickly gave way to thick trees, and once in them, Felix took time to look behind him. His heart nearly stopped when he saw the overseer coming across the empty field in hot pursuit, the wagon and its two riders driving hard down the road as if to cut Felix off before he could get to the river.

Felix scrambled deeper into the woods, traveling a good distance even as he realized that the overseer was quickly closing the half mile between them. Limbs, branches, and underbrush tore at Felix's clothes as he forced himself through the thick undergrowth even more resolutely. He felt something hit the tree next to him even as he heard the loud sound of a weapon going off. The sound frightened him so badly that he lurched left, fell down a ravine, and came to a halt when he slammed against a log at its bottom.

Forcing himself to his feet despite the wind being nearly knocked out of him, he ran along the bottom of the ravine, where a stream had run in a different season of the year. It turned sharply downward, and he slid down a wet slope to find himself on the bank of the river. Stopping, he listened, heard nothing, and then listened more carefully, finally catching the sound of voices to his left. He felt the sharp pain in his shoulder just as he heard the weapon go off. The impact made him cry out but also launched him forward and over the edge of the bank into the dark, muddy waters of the river. He came to the surface only to see Perkins coming down the ravine, shouting for his friends while loading his rifle again.

"Don't kill 'im, just slow 'im down!"

Felix took a deep breath, thankful he had learned to swim while at sea, and forced himself under the fast-moving water of the river. He felt the cold chill of it as he sunk deeper and swam harder into its murky depths, wondering how he could possibly get away.

* * *

Felix pulled himself onto shore and lay there for a moment, exhausted but listening carefully to the sounds around him. He could still hear voices, but they were on the other side of the river. Knowing he had to get out of sight, he pulled himself to his feet and stumbled through the trees, traveling a good distance parallel to the river going east until he could no longer hear the voices.

Just after dark, Felix stumbled onto a half-destroyed, rotting cabin. After catching his breath he removed his nearly dry shirt and checked the wound in his shoulder. It was a graze across the top, near his neck, and would give him little problem. He counted it as luck, plain and simple.

He sat against the wall, thinking, listening, and wondering if the men had found his tracks, until he could no longer stay awake. He awoke with a start after sunrise, found no one looming over him, and was thankful. He listened for a time then slipped through the woods to an old dirt road and fled from the area.

It took another day of travel along the wider Missouri River before he arrived at a spot opposite Jefferson City. He turned north to where the old man had said his sister would be.

Felix found a number of small villages along the way and was able to buy enough food to survive, but he slept in the forest at night, grateful that it had turned a bit warm and wasn't raining.

It was late afternoon of the next day when Felix approached the plantation. Unsure of what he might find, he chose to wait, nervously building his courage to approach the slave compound and inquire regarding his sister. He located a spot in the nearby woods to rest and momentarily fell asleep, waking with a start at the sound of a wagon on the nearby road. After it passed he wrapped his money in a handkerchief and buried it under a nearby rotting log. Leaving his bag a short distance closer to the compound but still in the trees, he moved quietly out of the forest and across the open ground toward the rows of slave shacks.

He was standing in the shadows at the corner of the nearest building when he heard the sound of harmonica music. Peering around the corner, he saw a slave sitting on a porch by himself. Felix could see or hear no other presence except that of a few animals in a nearby pen, so he took a deep breath and approached the boy, who did not stop playing until he finished his tune.

"Youse a stranger to dis place," the boy said.

"Freedman, looking for my sister," Felix said quickly. "Her name is Susannah, and she came from the Dowd place down Boonville way a few years back. Usually does housework."

The boy looked about, slapping the harmonica against his ragged pant leg.

"Dey call her Miss Suzy. I knows her, but she done been sold," the boy said. "A slave trader, name of Ridges. He done bought her, took her to St. Lou. He bin goin' from plantation to plantation, payin' po' money fo' used-up slaves an troublemakers and takin' 'em to his auction house. Yo sista, she been sick some. Masta done sold her. Jes' missed her, two days," he finished.

Felix shuddered and realized that he had heard of the place she had likely been taken. Ridges Auction House in St. Louis. It was one of the worst ones around. Those who ran it were plain mean to black folks.

"If you goes afta her, best be careful. Dey look at you and try to sell you 'gain, dey will. If youse plannin' to buy her freedom, you best be usin' a white man to do it. Tha' way yo keep things right." Though he was young, slavery had given this boy wisdom and understanding about such things beyond his years.

They heard the sound of footsteps approaching, and the boy went back to playing his harmonica while Felix darted into the shadows and through the trees to gather his possessions and get back to the road.

Felix was scared by what he'd learned. Ridges would have no scruples about beating a worked-out slave he had bought cheap—beating her to death—just to show the others he'd do it if they didn't mind themselves and do his bidding. Word in St. Louis was that he and his white overseers had raped black women just to "create a good darky worth something." His sister was in awful danger.

It took Felix two more days to get back to St. Louis, all the time thinking of Newton Daines. His friend would surely help him buy his sister.

But first he thought he'd best check Ridges's pen and see if his sister was still there. Though it had been a weekend, Ridges might have already held an auction and sold Susannah to someone. The thought made his heart constrict in his chest. If that was the case, he didn't know how he would ever find her.

Ridges's slave pen was a warehouse about one hundred feet long, with two large, heavy wooden doors at the far end, held together by chains as big as a man's wrist and locks to match. This was where wagonloads of slaves were brought into the compound and housed until sold. The walls were made of logs at least a foot thick.

On the street side of the building, Felix stood out of view of the guardhouse and faced two rows of several small windows. Having been in a similar pen, Felix knew that the top row was on the upper floor, where the men were shackled; the bottom row was the women's quarters. The women were left unshackled in order to take care of the men, feeding them when food was provided, giving them water when it was passed into the cell, and providing buckets for their waste. If any of the men— or bucks, as they were typically called—were sick, the women were to minister them back to good health so they would bring the expected price. No one wanted to buy a sick slave.

In summer it was blazing hot on both floors, but the attic was the worst. And in winter one could nearly freeze to death, with no blankets and only old straw to keep him warm.

Felix discreetly kept his attention on the lower set of windows for more than an hour as several faces peered out to get fresh air. None was that of his sister. He was becoming discouraged, when suddenly a familiar face came to the window. He leaned closer. It could be her, though she looked older, different, heavier in the face. He checked the barred door to his left, where buyers entered the compound, saw no guard, and quickly crossed the street and drew closer.

"Susannah?" he inquired in a hushed tone.

She turned to his voice, showing no recognition. As she studied him, her eyes suddenly opened wide. Clasping her mouth with one hand and gripping the bar window with the other, she kept herself from falling in a faint.

"Felix! Oh, praise God, yo is alive," she said too loudly.

"Shhh, Susha! You will have them comin' if you don't keep quiet!"

The window was small and higher in the wall than he could reach; he knew she must be standing on a table or bench, something to raise her to the window's height.

"Wher' has y' bin, Felix? Mama, she ask fo' you ev'y day. She . . . she gone now and—"

"Not now, sister. I come to buy your freedom. When is the sale o' you folks?"

"He's bin preparin' us all dis mornin.' Say's it s'afternoon, but dis trader, he doan sale to colored folk," Susannah answered.

"Greedy folk like him, they sell to anyone if the price is right. How much you cost him?"

"Five hundred dolla.' Das cheap, but . . . well, I ain't bee' feelin' too good, and de masta, he need de money." She looked down. "Course, de chil', he be worth somethin' da's sure."

"You have a baby?" Felix asked.

"Still comin', but it be soon. Too soon, I kin feel it," she said with a worried look on her face.

"Then we have to get you free," he said with a worried smile.

Her face flashed fear. "Doan take no chances, Felix. Dis trader, he a bad man. He look at yo' size, an' him git real greedy. He find a way to make you a slave again, I knows he will."

"I'll be gittin' a white man to buy you, then tha' trader will have no cause to look on me as fresh meat for 'is pens." Felix forced a smile. "Now you settle in, take care o' yo'self. I'll be back real soon."

She began to speak again, but Felix was out of earshot, already bolting toward the docks as fast as his thick, muscled legs would carry him. As he disappeared she slipped down from the window, both hope and anxiety in her wide smile and wringing hands. "God in de heavens, hep him come quick!" She turned and headed for the ladder to tell her husband. Surely if Felix had brought enough money to free both her and their mother, he would have enough to free her husband. He had to, that's all. He just had to.

Chapter 10

November 20, 1860

"CARPENTER'S WORK HAS OPENED UP," Pitts said, drawing Newton out of his thoughts.

"Sir?"

Pitts's brow wrinkled, but he handed Newton a note to give to the foreman of the job. "One of Mr. Hudson's steamers had a fire and needs a lot of repair. Eads Boatyard, end of the docks to the south. Ask for Hendershott. German fellow. He'll put you to work at double the wage you're making now." Pitts grinned, and Newton thanked him with a wide smile of his own. "May the saints bless you, Mr. Pitts," he said.

"Just don't do ugly work. Remember who recommended ya. She needs no blemish on 'er goo' name."

Newton left the office and headed down the docks. Time had passed quickly. He'd worked every minute he could on the docks, going to Mrs. O'Grady's only for a few hours' sleep each night and staying out of the streets of the Patch, partly to avoid O'Shay and partly to avoid the drink.

And then there was Mary McConnell. They had spent some time talking in front of the fireplace of late. He found her both fascinating and beautiful and looked forward to each new opportunity to be with her.

As Newton neared the fire-ravaged steamer sitting at the end of Eads Boatyard, he found Hendershott near the gangplank and gave him the letter. Hendershott referred him to the head carpenter, and Newton was put to work tearing out burned wood for replacement. The fire had destroyed the back half of the main and upper levels, and the ship was charred from stem to stern. The work would take months—a fact that gave him comfort.

* * *

Since the election, the news had been filled with printed, caustic threats and denunciations between North and South. Riots by pro-Southern supporters in places like Maryland, Kentucky, and Washington, D.C., exploded across the headlines as the country began to rip apart. Mississippi would surely secede in the next few weeks when a vote was taken, while South Carolina had already voted and its citizens considered themselves the first of the Confederate States of America. Talk by other states in the South was rampant as well, and most were preparing to hold conventions of secession in the next few weeks. Some were already using militias to take control of federal forts and arsenals housed in their states, but President Buchanan remained idle, paralyzed by threats from every side.

St. Louis felt like a city with a heavy black cloud hanging over it, both sides walking on eggshells so as not to set the other off, while privately planning to protect their own interests. Atchison and Jackson were increasing their "visits" to prominent citizens, making threats and trying to force support. Some of those threatened were buckling, and Rand had put his plan into effect, docking some of his steamers at predesignated places along the Ohio where they could not be easily accessed by Atchison, his devils, or any other Southerner.

One of Rand's ships had caught fire from a faulty boiler and needed attention, so that afternoon he left his office and proceeded across the street to his personal livery. As he was about to go inside, he caught sight of his friend Frank Blair Jr. waving at him from outside a warehouse office a few doors down. Frank was visiting with someone else but hurried to catch up with Rand.

Rand was immediately struck by Frank's somber visage, his deep-set eyes displaying heavy concern. His dark beard hung to his chest, and his shoulders were slumped, making him look shorter than his usual five feet eight inches. "I thought you were in Springfield to see Lincoln," Rand said. It was rumored that Frank's brother, Montgomery Blair, was a candidate for Lincoln's new cabinet; consequently Frank had gone to the capital city of Illinois as Missouri's newest and only Republican congressman to positively influence his brother's fortuity.

"Lincoln's people assure me that Monty will get a position, probably postmaster general, so I came home." He put a hand behind Rand's back and moved him to a walk. "I hear Atchison approached you while I was away."

Rand put his hands in his coat pockets against the chill of the cold, humid day. "And has he come to you yet?"

Frank shook his head. "He would not approach me personally. He sent our new governor instead. These attempts of secessionists to force Missouri into the Confederate camp are infuriating." He paused. "And what he plans next has only worsened my feelings."

"And what would that be?" Rand asked.

"After his inauguration, Governor-elect Jackson will call for a convention to ask for support of the Confederacy. If he doesn't receive it, he will ask for authority to use the militia to keep the federal government out of Missouri—ostensibly to keep us neutral."

"Neutrality by force of arms. An interesting approach," Rand said.

Frank looked around. "I have learned since that his real intention is to use the militia to take the Arsenal here in St. Louis out of federal hands and turn those weapons over to Southern sympathizers, arming them to support the Confederate effort. He will use neutrality as an excuse."

"Can't have the North infesting Missouri land any more than he can the South. Shrewd," Rand replied.

"That Arsenal holds more than forty thousand rifles, a dozen smooth-bore cannons, and endless amounts of ammunition and powder, not to mention all the equipment to keep making arms in even greater abundance."

Rand's brow furrowed. "And he'll turn it all over to the Confederacy."

"Or use it to force Missouri into the Confederacy, whether the citizens of Missouri wish it or not."

"And what is the temperament of the legislature, Frank? Will they give him those powers? It seems they change their position as often as the wind changes direction," Rand said with some cynicism.

"At present one could flip a twenty-dollar gold piece and discover the answer as quickly as if he were relying on mood or language, but we must be ready in any event. We cannot let Missouri leave the Union."

Frank paused, glancing around them once again, before putting his arm around Rand's shoulder and lowering his voice. "Randolph, I need you to come to a meeting tomorrow night. It will be at my home but must be kept strictly quiet. I will explain more fully then. Can you be there?"

Rand knew better than to ask for details. Frank was clearly nervous, afraid they were being watched. It was most likely paranoia, but since Atchison's threat, Rand had found himself looking over his shoulder a good deal as well. "Yes, of course. What time?"

"Six in the evening. Be careful, Rand. I am being watched, even if you are not. We must move quickly but quietly."

Rand nodded and received a grateful smile and a pat on the arm. "To-morrow night then." Frank waved for his carriage, and it quickly pulled up beside them. Then he scrambled inside and was gone.

As Rand watched it roll away, he noticed one of his own carriages coming his direction, Elliot at the reins. It was Lizzy's carriage. Elliot pulled up in front of him, and Lizzy leaned out the window.

"Surprised?" she asked with a smile.

He smiled back. After hurting her ankle, Lizzy had taken ill and spent the better part of a week in the house mending. She was walking very well now, and he was glad of it. Lizzy was not one to be cooped up, and she was driving everyone mad, so he was glad to see her out. "Lydijah must be elated," he said.

She laughed. "Practically pushed me out the door." Then her expression sobered just a bit. "I did want to talk to you about something, though." Lizzy looked stunning in a simple silk hat that matched a silk dress of the same fabric. Her cloak was of maroon wool and gave her a bold look as well as warmth.

He climbed up beside her, closed the door behind him, and the carriage began moving. "What is worrying your pretty little head?" He asked the question while checking his pocket watch.

"This won't take long, I promise." She hesitated only a moment, now settling back and looking a bit apprehensive as she handed him a wire. He leaned toward the window so he had enough light to read it and found it was from Andrew. His invitation for Lizzy to visit Virginia was now official. Apparently Horatio Clay had agreed to his son's request. Rand bit his tongue to prevent verbalizing his immediate reaction. Once under control, he finally spoke.

"So you are going," he said.

"Unless you will be angry with me and think I have lost my mind."

"Have you?" He smiled.

She laughed. "I am not sure. You know I have feelings for Andrew, but I am also more curious now than ever. I have never been on a plantation of such size, never been to Virginia. I want to see both, Rand, with my own eyes. I want to know what his family is really like. How do *they* live with slavery? What are the people around him like, and how do they justify it all? I want to see *them*, Rand, before I allow myself to consider anything else with Andrew."

"When will you leave?"

"After Christmas," she said. "I will be gone for a month, maybe a little longer."

Rand nodded. He would miss her a great deal but still understood this was the only way. He leaned forward, took her gloved hand, and kissed it lightly. "Dear sister, promise me you will be careful. If things blow up politically, you must leave there immediately. War will trap you if you do not."

She looked lovingly at him. He had always protected her, made sure she was happy—a substitute for the father she had lost when so young. She could not help but love him deeply for it. But she knew that it was not war that Rand feared most when it came to his little sister; it was Andrew Clay. "I promise," she said. It was the easy way out, but she did not want to get into matters she could not fully explain. Was she in love with Andrew or just enamored with his charm and her curiosity? She didn't think it was the former, though falling in love with Andrew Clay would be easy . . . under proper circumstances.

"Thank you," she said to Rand. "Where can I have Elliot drop you?"

"At our steamer at Eads Boatyard. A boiler malfunctioned, and we had a fire. The steamer was towed in this morning, and we're going to work on her this afternoon."

"I hope no one was hurt," she said sincerely.

"Not many passengers aboard, and only one hurt along with two crew members, but they are all recovering well. Overall, we were lucky."

* * *

Shortly after he started working, Newton saw the fine carriage of Miss Elizabeth Hudson pull up. A gentleman in a dark suit and black wool coat climbed down to help Miss Hudson from the carriage. He recognized both. He'd seen Rand Hudson around the docks and was impressed with the fact that the man did not mind getting his hands and pretty suit dirty.

Newton forced himself to concentrate as the Hudsons came aboard and was working with the dirty timbers when he heard someone close behind him.

"Well, well, Mr. Daines, how are you?"

He turned to face Lizzy Hudson, her brother standing at her side. She looked stunning in her finery, and few men continued their work.

"So this is your knight in shining armor?" Rand Hudson asked.

"Umm," Lizzy said. "His armor does look a bit tarnished." She smiled at Newton, who was covered in soot.

"Miss Hoodsun, nice t' see ye again. Your foot seems ready fer ridin' once more. How's the mare?"

The other workers focused on listening to the conversation and had stopped working to be sure they were hearing correctly.

"She's healing well, but unfortunately, riding her again is probably out of the question. Come to the house sometime and I'll introduce you to her replacement." She turned to her brother while most of the workers picked their jaws up off the ground. "Randolph, I will see you at home. I have errands to run." She kissed him lightly on the cheek and went back the way she'd come. All eyes followed her until she was in the carriage and gone—with the exception of Newton, who went back to work with a wide and comfortable grin in place.

Hendershott ordered the others to do the same, and Rand visited with his project manager for a few minutes before returning to talk to Newton.

"Mr. Daines, I haven't had the chance to thank you properly for caring for Lizzy when she fell."

"No need," Newton said. "'Twas me fault in the first place."

"Just the same, thank you." He extended his hand for a shake. Newton looked at his own hand, wiped it off on his dirty pants, then shook Hudson's hand. When he withdrew, Newton found a twenty-dollar gold piece sitting in his palm. He watched in amazement as Hudson walked away. Most rich men were uppity and arrogant and had little concern for workers of the common class. Most would have had him fired for daring to touch any relative, let alone a sister.

He gratefully stuck the coin in his pocket and went back to work. One could not help but respect a man who did not judge another by the quality of his clothes or the land of his forefathers. Yes, he liked Mr. Randolph Hudson. He liked him a lot.

Chapter 11

FELIX HAD HAD NO LUCK locating Newton. He had searched the Irish section of St. Louis at the risk of taunts and even threats to his life and had knocked on the doors of a dozen boardinghouses before he found Mrs. O'Grady's.

A younger woman came to the door, a curious look on her face when she saw him.

"Sorry, miss, but I has t' find a Mista Newton Daines. Does you—"

"Newton lives here bu' is nah 'ere a' the moment," the woman said. She looked behind her, and Felix followed her glance to see the threatening visages of several men, and some were gathering close.

"This is nah a place fer talkin', Mr.—"

"Felix, Missy, Felix Coulon."

She nodded quickly. "My name's Mary. Newton has mentioned you, bu' 'e's at the docks workin', an—"

"I has to git 'is help, Miss Mary. I's desperate."

"I'll go an' find 'im, but ya 'ave to get off of O'Fallon Street, Mr. Coulon," she said.

"Hey, nigra, d' ya know where ya be?" asked one of the men with a brisk tone. Others sneered and catcalled at Felix.

"Ya be movin' along, Danny May," Mary said, "fo' I bust yer chops fer ya."

The crowd laughed as Felix realized he could be asking for trouble. "Dem pens, miss. Ridges's pens. Dat where I be, tryin' to buy ma sista." He shoved an envelope toward her and spoke in a low voice so that the others wouldn't hear. "Most of mah money is in dat, 'cept what I need to buy her. I knows I can trust youse with it." He quickly left the steps and hustled away down the street as the men continued to jeer at him. Mary watched him until she knew he wasn't being followed, then grabbed her wrap, shoved the envelope in her pocket, and headed for the docks to find Newton.

* * *

Felix circled the Irish section and hurried back to the pens to find that the sale had not yet begun.

Susannah, as thin and frail as a pregnant woman could look, stood in the middle of the line. Buyers stood about, poking the slaves, asking them questions, looking into mouths, ears, and eyes. They lifted the new, cheap shirts on the men's backs, checking for any lash scars. There was discussion and nods among others. Felix had been sold at such a sale. It had been humiliating, but he had learned to gauge when a group of sellers were pleased with the person being offered and when they weren't. This group did not seem pleased with his sister. He himself saw no visible reason for their dissatisfaction, but she had told him she hadn't been well, and she did look thin for an expectant mother, although this was not uncommon after being forced to work in the fields day after long day.

Felix knew the buyers' displeasure could help free his sister. If someone bought her for a low price, he would have that much more bargaining power. And if no one bought her, he might still have a chance. No slave trader wanted to hold slaves, especially sick ones. Surely the greedy Ridges was no different.

He positioned himself at the back of the group, where he could not be seen easily. He had kept fifteen hundred dollars from his envelope. He was sure it would be enough to secure Susannah.

Felix paced nervously, knowing he was on dangerous ground. Most of these men would not appreciate him trying to free another black. It made their system look bad when blacks wanted their freedom, since the slaveholders preached incessantly that blacks themselves depended on the slave system for a decent life—which, of course, the slave owner provided.

Worse still, Felix knew he could be in serious danger if the traders became aware that he had money. There were no more evil and conniving men than slave traders. If they were so inclined, they would figure a way to trap Felix and take his money. It all made him sweat.

He looked over his shoulder to see if Newton was coming. Felix was alone, scared, and wondering if he was playing the fool. He decided to stay quiet, pray his sister was purchased, and then follow the new owner to his wagon and offer him a price well above the amount he had just spent. If Felix didn't have enough, he could get the man's name and bring more. Surely the new owner would appreciate the profit, and it would keep Felix out of conflict with the trader.

The bidding began after the trader had praised Susannah's unusual abilities and skills—and the fact that she was pregnant by a strong buck who would be sold later. He pointed to a man at the far end of the line, and Felix felt the wind go out of his sails. A husband. He felt sobered as he realized that much more had happened in Susannah's life since he saw her last. He wasn't sure why he hadn't pondered this before. He should have realized she would have a man in her life and that children would have followed. Had there been other children besides the one Susannah carried now? And if there were, would they also be sold here, now? He looked at the children still waiting to be sold. Could any of these belong to her? His stomach tied in knots as he realized that his sister's life was far more complicated than he had allowed himself to imagine.

But he knew he must think only of Susannah now. He shook off his thoughts to discover that the bidding had stopped at only four hundred dollars and that the slave trader was trying to elicit more, his frustration palpable at not getting a better price. After all, he had paid five hundred for her—a price far below the value of one with her experience, but still a good deal of money. Felix realized that the trader might decide to pull her from the sale altogether, making it more complicated for him to free her. He began to sweat again.

Another bid was finally offered, then another, the bids going back and forth in small increments. But then it stopped. The final bid was five hundred dollars, and there were no more offers. The trader cajoled, used humor, and finally swore before ordering that Susannah be taken back inside. Felix felt a sudden fear as Susannah lowered her head in despondency and turned to go inside the compound.

Felix saw several men turn and look at him, and he realized that his hand was in the air. The trader noticed and smirked, then growled a response. "We don't sell to blacks here."

Felix knew that he must play the uneducated Negro again and spoke accordingly. "I's able t'give you a fair price."

"You?" The man laughed. Everyone had turned to look at him, and the whispers and derogatory mumbling began.

"I's a freedman. I has worked hard fo' money on de ship *Andrew Jackson*. I needs a wife and chil'. Dis un'll do jus' fine," he lied.

There were chuckles through the crowd.

"I's jus' lookin' for de fam'ly, massa, dat's all."

"Well, ya won't find yer wife here. I told ya, we don't sell t' blacks," the trader said with some irritation.

"Let 'im buy her. Nobody else will," said one white man, his small smile smothered by his plump face.

"Yes, let her go, and get on with it," said another impatiently.

"He's a freedman. If he's got money, let 'im have her. Let's get to them bucks," said a third.

"And them kids," said another. "We ain't got all day, Ridges."

"She ain't worth what you got in her, Sam, and you know it. She's been sick for months, and the child will never be born because of it. If it is, it won't be worth the money to bury it."

Felix's eyes widened. Sam Ridges was this man's name and he was the trader himself. Felix swallowed hard. He had never seen the man but he looked as mean and evil as his reputation implied. With his heavily unkempt beard and hair, thick shoulders, and pockmarked face with its large bulbous nose, the man looked like he could kill another human and enjoy it.

"That ain't true," Ridges said adamantly.

"Sure is. I live next door to the Cedars, where you bought her. Jackson Greene is gloating over getting the best of you 'cause you bought her from him," said the man with a laugh. "Says it was the only way he could keep you from cheatin' him on them bucks."

What could be seen of Sam Ridges's face went red as strawberries. He glared at Felix. "If you can give me a thousand dollars, you can take her, but you'll be buyin' her after I get done with these others, and not until." He said it through clenched teeth.

Felix felt the hair stand up on the back of his neck but knew he must respond. "Doan have no thousand dollars, got five hundred," he said. He glanced at Susannah, her eyes wide, frightened and elated at the same time.

"Get her inside," Ridges said to his men, before turning back to Felix. "Then you won't see her again, nigra, that's sure as day will come tomorra."

Felix looked down. "Then I'll pay."

Ridges scowled a smile. "After the auction, *nigra*."

Felix shivered, fearing the hate and thirst for vengeance he saw in the man's eyes. The trader had given in too easily for Felix to believe that all would go smoothly now. The idea of buying Susannah without witnesses present was a frightening prospect, but what other choice did he have? He looked around desperately for Newton. He still hadn't come. He dared not wait. If she was left in the pens, this man would punish his sister for his own humiliation. He must get her out.

He waited, sweating, staying back from the crowd until the last slaves were sold and the white folk had all hauled off their slaves or left in their carriages. Felix approached the trader sitting at his table counting his money, a guard with a club in hand and pistol in his belt standing next to him. Felix's anxiety increased, his heart near to exploding with its pounding as he sensed the danger of his decision.

"Massa," he said his eyes down, "I be pleased to buy dat woman now."

Ridges didn't look up until his money was counted and put in a steel box. He then stood and leaned across the table toward Felix. "You ain't got enough money, boy," he said, saliva landing on Felix's shirt sleeve.

"I got what youse said, massa," Felix said. He kept his eyes down but was also very aware of the movement of the guard by Ridges's side, his club lifted with the loaded end resting in his other palm. He tensed slightly.

"'Taint enough, nigra. Now, let's see your papers," he said, a hard set to his jaw.

"Ain't no reason—"

The attack came and Felix was ready, grabbing the club before it was in full swing. The guard went for his gun with his other hand, and Felix grabbed it as well. He twisted the man's arms, and the man cried out as Felix ripped both the club and the pistol from his hands, nearly breaking both wrists. He went to his knees in anguish as Felix tossed the gun and club on the desk. Ridges stepped back. "Ain't no reason fo' dat, massa. You git de woman now, and I pay."

The feel of hard steel in his back made Felix stiffen, and the smile on Ridges's face told Felix that there had been another guard and another plan all along. "Now, let's see those papers, nigra."

Felix removed the papers from his bag as the first assailant got to his feet and picked up his club, anger turning his face to stone. Felix handed the papers to the trader, but the man didn't even look at them.

"Look like forgeries to me. How 'bout you, Fulton?" Ridges asked.

"Yeah, sure enough," the injured man said harshly. Felix sensed that this man was aching to use his club.

Felix braced himself and tried to keep his wits about him, knowing that even a word would cause him great pain, but he was no coward and not willing to just let them take his freedom.

"They's real, an' you knows it," he stated boldly. The cold steel in his back pressed even harder against his flesh. The trader took out a match and struck it on the table.

"No!" Felix said. Felix grabbed Ridges' hand and flung it up and away from the papers with such force that Ridges was thrown back and off balance. Felix swept around and grabbed the man with the gun by the throat and squeezed hard, raising the man off the ground so that his hands convulsed and dropped the weapon. Then the club came crashing down on Felix's head and sent him reeling forward, blood gushing down his face. Another blow came to the back of his neck, and he fell to his knees. Ridges's voice seemed miles away, and though Felix wanted to focus, to force his muscles to work again, he could not move. As he tried to force his mind to stop the rush of darkness, he saw a flame pass in front of his unfocused eyes and knew his papers were gone, along with his freedom. As his mind collapsed into a dark hole, he wished he had heeded the old man's warning. But it was to late. He was a slave again.

Chapter 12

By the time Mary finally found Newton, it was after dark. She quickly told him about Felix, how he seemed desperate for help, and how they must hurry. Though confused by the rush of words through the exhaustion of her run to find him, Newton knew the matter must be very serious when she hailed a rentable carriage to take them where they needed to go.

"Ridges' Auction House," she urgently told the driver, then turned to Newton as she sat down. "Ridges is a' mean a' they come," she said. "Wha' yer roomies di' t' ya is nothin' to wha' Ridges will do t' yer friend if he can. I pray Felix had enuf sense nah t' try an' buy her on 'is own."

"If Ridges is tha' dangerous, you'll nah be comin,'" Newton said, "I'll nah be havin' time t' worry about ya."

"You'll have no need t' worry. Ridges will be less likely t'cause trouble if there's two of us an' one of 'em is an Irish woman he knows," Mary answered.

"All right then, but if danger comes you'll be runnin' in the direction I say an' you'll be doin' it withou' question."

"Ya can depend on it. I ha' no desire t' get me head busted," Mary said.

By the time they arrived at Ridges' pens, a few blocks south of Biddle Street and just about the same distance above the docks, the lamplighters had already lit the lanterns at each end of the street, giving Newton and Mary just enough light to read the sign above the business office at the end of the pens. The title *Ridges's Auction House* left Newton cold. To Ridges, slaves were apparently no different from old farm equipment.

"There be a light in the office," Mary said. "But any sale tha' too' place is over. Maybe yer friend succeeded in freein' 'is sister."

"Maybe," Newton said, worried.

"If he be inside them walls, you'll 'ave no chance fer savin' 'im," Mary said soberly.

A man stepped from the office and walked along the street to a barred door, which clearly led directly into the compound where slaves were held. Mary put her arm through Newton's and pulled him close, walking slowly down the street as if they were out for a lover's stroll. Newton's heart reacted as he felt her touch and warmth; it took a good deal of will to keep his mind focused on the man on the other side of the street and what he was about. He wasn't used to being close to women.

The jailer gave them a hard look before rattling the barred door and calling to someone inside. Another man appeared at the iron gate and opened it, letting the first inside. He took one last look at Mary and Newton; Mary grabbed Newton and turned him into her, kissing him hard and eliciting a chuckle from the jailer before he disappeared inside.

Mary, one eye open, saw him disappear but let her lips linger. When she backed away, Newton was speechless.

"Cat got yer tongue, laddy?" Mary smiled, her arms still around his neck.

"Uh…"

She turned and looked across the street. "He was gettin' nervous. Had to do something, so doan be takin' it too personal."

"No . . . uh . . ." He cleared his throat, grasping for his composure—something that seemed to be somewhere down the street.

"Now what?" Mary asked.

He cleared his throat again. "Ye be a waitin' righ' 'ere, Mary McConnell," Newton said. Before she could voice any concern to the contrary, Newton was across the street and against the wall near the barred entry of the compound. Mary held her breath, and even though the street was not brightly lit, she backed into the deeper darkness of an alley between two buildings. She had quite enjoyed the kiss, more so than she thought she might. Newton Daines was beginning to get a bit under her skin, and she found it to her liking. But the crack of a whip and the sound of a man crying out jolted her thoughts to the purpose of their visit. Next she heard laughter and vile curses. Though she could not discern every word, she heard enough to know a slave was getting a whipping either for the master's pleasure or from displeasing the guards. A moment later Newton hurried across the street from the compound and joined her.

"Did you hear it?" he asked hotly. "Tha's Felix they be beatin'. 'Tis a voice I know as well as me own."

"Did you hear anything o' use to us?" Mary asked as she put her hand on his arm to calm him.

Newton took a deep breath. "They say they be takin' 'im ou' by wagon t'nigh'."

"Tha's not surprisin'." Mary said. "They'll take no chances on anyone recognizin' 'im by sellin' 'im here." She cringed at the smack of the whip again, accompanied by a few more drunken laughs. "But sounds like they're havin' their pleasure first," Mary said with disgust.

It was torture for the two of them as the sound of the whip echoed in the street, and both racked their brains to find some answers. Suddenly a wagon approached from the area of the docks and parked outside the gate; thankfully the whipping stopped. Mary and Newton melted into deeper shadows as the teamster secured the reins around the wagon post, jumped down, and called to those inside. The gate opened, and the man slipped into the compound while the wagon and horses waited. A plan suddenly formed in Newton's mind. It would require guts and a good deal of luck, but he saw nothing else that would give his friend any chance at all.

"You nee' t' be leavin' 'ere, an' quick," he said to Mary.

"Wha' are ya plannin', Newton Daines? I can nah see anythin' tha' you kin do bu' git yourself killed," Mary said.

"Never ya mind. I ha' to try. Now you be goin'." He gently pushed her toward home and watched as she reluctantly obeyed his orders. He waited until she was out of sight, all the while becoming even more resolute. He darted across the street and slipped under the wagon near the tongue. Working with strong hands, he quickly loosed the crosspiece bolt and partially removed it. Grabbing hold of the undercarriage, he lifted himself into the shadows above the reaches that attached the front and back axles. He lay motionless in the darkness for a long time, his arms and back aching horribly by the time the gate opened. A woman and the shackled Felix were herded to the back of the wagon by three others. Felix stumbled, was smacked with a club for it, got up, and went on. It was all Newton could do not to show himself and beat the living tar out of his friend's cowardly attackers. He shook it off, concentrating on the woman who had to be Felix's sister. Sweat beaded on Newton's forehead as he realized that her presence might make freeing his friend even more difficult.

Peering through a crack in the floorboards, he watched Felix and his sister sit on the floor while the chain around Felix's wrists was fastened to an iron eyebolt in the bottom of the wagon. From his side Newton could stretch to reach the nut that would free the bolt, but its rusted condition made it impossible to turn with his bare fingers, strong as they might be.

The driver climbed into the wagon seat as his partner finished securing Felix and slipped from the back of the wagon onto the seat as well. Felix saw the glint of a rifle barrel in the driver's hands. The third man wished them well and walked back inside the gate as the wagon pulled away. Lowering his head so he could see the crosspiece bolt, Newton watched as it bobbled up and down in the hole. If a sudden jolt removed it too quickly, the guards from the prison would come to the rescue of their friends driving the wagon. If it took too long, Newton's strength to stay in place would be gone and his plan foiled. Newton clung to the reaches, praying for perfect timing.

They were nearly two blocks away when the front wheel struck a rut and the bolt exploded from the hole, the crosspiece simultaneously thwacking the ground behind the horses' heels. Both horses bolted, jerking the driver out of his seat and to the road with a crushing thud as the wagon suddenly spiked left, hit the wall, and sent both Newton and the guard reeling from the wagon. Newton felt the wind knocked out of him but forced himself to his feet to find the guard unconscious next to the wall, his head bleeding. The driver was still being dragged by the horses. Newton grabbed the guard's rifle, found the keys to the shackles, and quickly turned back to the wagon where a shocked Felix sat eyeing him through swollen eyes. His sister had been jolted against the wagon seat and lay stunned next to him. Newton quickly turned the keys to unshackle his friend.

"'Tis time to flee," he said to Felix. "Can ye be walkin'?"

Felix nodded as he stood, picked up his sister, and jumped from the back of the wagon. It was then they heard the shot of a rifle and the punch of lead-shot in the wagon near them. Newton pulled Felix back behind the wagon box then looked over it to see several guards standing under the light of a streetlamp two blocks away. They fired another shot, and Newton ducked again. Taking a deep breath, he ran through the darkness, Felix at his heels, lead balls chipping the stone pavement at their feet. He saw a side street and quickly turned and ran in the direction of the docks. Not sure of what to do next, he looked for anyplace to hide but found none. He could hear the footfalls and curses of at least a half dozen men far behind them and knew he didn't have much time. Then, to his amazement, he saw a carriage appear around a cross street and come to a halt in front of them. The door flew open, and Mary's pretty face appeared.

"Get in!" she called.

Newton stood paralyzed as Mary jumped from the carriage and thrust her arms around Felix's sister to help them inside. "Standin' there wi' tha' dumb look on yer face 'ill only git ya killed, and the rest o' us too. Now git yer carcass in 'fore I shoot y' meself."

Newton launched himself into the carriage, and Mary shouted for the driver to get moving. The horses felt the whip of the reins and bolted across the intersection as several balls breached the carriage walls but hit no human flesh. The escapees quickly expanded the distance between them and their pursuers until finally Newton dared to check through the window behind them. He then fell back into his seat.

"Yer a miracle, Mary McConnell," he said. "Where in the heavens di' ya fin' a carriage?"

Mary smiled. "Pure luck o' the Irish. Cabbie friend was deliverin' a customer t' 'is mistress. Ha' a few minutes fer rescuin' ya from sure death if'n I doan miss me guess."

Newton chuckled. "Tha's sure enough." He glanced at Felix, who seemed dumbfounded by what had just happened. "How is she?" Newton asked.

Felix looked down at his sister, who was moaning. "She needs a doctor, Massa Newton. Dis here chil'—"

"She's pregnant?" Mary gulped.

"Dat she is, Missy, and she bumped her head good, too."

"Got any idea on where to 'ide two runaway slaves?" Mary asked, concern in her voice.

Newton felt his mouth go dry as his mind worked it over. Then he remembered. Leaning out the window, he gave the order to the driver. He only hoped Lizzy Hudson meant what she had said.

* * *

Lizzy couldn't have been less prepared as the rumble of a hurried carriage sounded in the driveway. She was in her room, relaxing in her favorite chair, a cozy fire warming her as she read from her Book of Mormon. Rand was away for the evening, so she quickly crossed to the window, looking down on the torch-lit drive near the front door. The cab came to a halt, and she watched as the carriage door opened and a man lurched out and onto her front steps. She immediately recognized Newton Daines.

Thankful she still had on her work clothes from an earlier visit to check on her mare, she hobbled from her room, still feeling pain in her ankle. Reaching the wide stair, she found Lydijah having a hurried conversation with Newton.

"What is it, Mr. Daines?" she called from the top of the stairs. His anxiety prompted her to descend the stairs as quickly as she could, his story spilling out in a jumble of words as she hurried down. When the impact of them hit she quickly went to the door and ordered the cab driver to take the carriage around back. She and Newton followed, Lydijah a few steps behind.

Lizzy reached the carriage and opened the door to find a large black man and the two women, one in considerable pain, the other kneeling to help.

"She's deliverin'," the white woman said matter-of-factly.

Lizzy did not hesitate. "Then get her upstairs. My room. Lydijah, show them the way." She went to the front of the carriage and spoke to the cab driver. "There will be a twenty-dollar gold piece for you if you go to Doctor Samuel Richin's home and bring him here immediately."

The cabbie nodded as Felix exited the carriage. The cabbie then whipped the horses, made the circle, and headed for the gate with his team at a trot.

Lizzy quickly followed the others into the house and up the stairs while Newton unfolded the details of the night's events. Escaped slaves, and from Ridges's pens to boot. It was going to be an interesting evening.

* * *

Sam Ridges, red-faced and chewing hotly on his cigar, listened as his men related their misfortune. He'd lost two slaves, had three men knocked colder than tar, lost a team, and had nothing left of a wagon but busted-up boards. And it seemed it had all been done by one man and a woman in a carriage. He looked at his little brother. "You sure it was a woman?"

"Ain't sure. I didn't see it," Castle said. The younger of the two, Castle Ridges was even uglier than his brother—something most would consider quite impossible. His face was round, and he had a sunken cheek where a rifle butt had crushed it during a drunken fight. There was a wide scar on his forehead from a whiskey bottle used by Sam to teach him a lesson, and he was missing part of his right ear—chewed off by a dog while he lay in a near-drunken stupor outside the Black Swan. His beard was sparse in some places and a color somewhere between brown and dirty; two of his teeth on the right side were missing, having rotted out of his head for all the tobacco he chewed.

"But yer men thought it was a woman, didn't they?" Sam probed.

Castle spit in the general direction of the stove, and the wad splattered a foot short of his target. "They wasn't sure neither, Sam. I told you—"

Sam jumped to his feet in a rage, flipping his chair, as everyone cowered below him. "I know what you told me, you idiot!" He jammed his teeth around his cigar as he glared around the room.

Castle swallowed the rest of his chaw of tobacco and sat up straight.

"Twitchins, you said that when you went to the pens from the office you saw a man an' a woman loiterin' across the street. Seems like a strange coincidence, don't it, Castle? Especially since a *man* broke 'em out and a *woman* picked 'em up in a cab!" He spat his own tobacco in the direction of a spittoon and managed to hit its edge, causing most of it to stain the wall. "Don't suppose you recognized either of 'em, did you, Twitchins?" he asked mockingly.

Twitchins looked at the floor. "Couldn't see 'em clear, boss, but they wasn't doin' nothing but spoonin' anyway."

There were chuckles under the men's breath until Ridges glared it to a stop. Castle wasn't giggling and seemed deep in thought.

"Castle, don't think too long or you might hurt yerself. Did you see somethin' or didn't ya?"

Castle was feeling the pain in his gut from the tobacco but set it aside. "I think I seen that cab around. Special top fer holdin' luggage."

"Then I suggest you try to find it. If that freedman tells his story to the authorities—"

"He won't, Sam. He'd have to give up the black woman. She was legally ours," Castle said.

"A silver linin', right, Castle?" Ridges said angrily, spitting tobacco and mostly missing the spittoon. "An abolitionist judge won't give a tinker's toot about the woman. He'll fine us big for imprisoning a freedman and probably send us to jail to boot. I want 'em both back, ya hear? You find out where he took them nigras, and you find out soon."

Castle nodded while he nursed the goose egg on his forehead where he'd hit the wall after being launched from the wagon. "I remember somethin' else, Sam. When I got this lump, it knocked me near out, but I heard that varmint what helped the darkies. He was Irish, I swear."

Ridges picked up his chair and slammed the legs on the wood floor. "Then get down to the Kerry Patch and put out the word that we got an Irishman helping blacks escape."

"He's a freedman, Sam. Irish don't want no more blacks freed, that's for sure, but they don't hassle those that has been freed. Even come to their aid in tight spots."

Sam glared at his brother. "Then don't *tell* them he was a freedman," he said through clenched teeth.

Nobody moved. They'd seen this tension before. It usually erupted into a good thrashing for Castle, and anyone who got in the way was going to get it too.

"Get movin'!" Sam yelled.

The men scrambled for the door, leaving Sam sitting at the table. He stuck his feet up over the edge and pushed back so the chair rested on two legs. It creaked against the weight but held. He let his mind work on what had happened and who might be behind it. It had to be someone who knew his operation. No one got that lucky.

The door opened again, and one of his men stuck his head in. "Carriage is waitin', Sam."

Sam stood, threw the mutilated cigar in the fireplace, and left the room. He had a man inside Hudson Company who had informed him that there would be some sort of big meeting by abolitionist elements tonight. While his men were searching for the Irishman, Sam intended to follow Hudson and see what he could see.

Sam figured that Randolph Hudson was as dangerous as any man in the state to their effort to make Missouri part of the Confederacy. It was not just because he was politically connected to Frank Blair, but because he had enough steamers, when properly fitted for war, to tilt the scale in favor of the North when it came to holding the Mississippi. The Confederacy needed those steamers—and to get them, they had to either get something on Hudson or get rid of him so that his idiot of an uncle, Benjamin Siddell, could control the company long enough for Atchison to take every ship away from Hudson. Ridges wasn't particular about how they handled Hudson; he just wanted the privilege of making it happen—and, if lucky, pulling the trigger. For him it was a pleasant thought, one he entertained all the way to his carriage.

Chapter 13

THE EVENING WAS COOL, WITH a clear sky and a full moon draping the river in a peaceful, shimmering glow. Rand stood at his office window watching the *Elizabeth,* the premier hauler in his fleet, come into dock. He looked at his pocket watch: seven P.M. Right on time. She was one of six still docking in St. Louis, but he could not afford to make arrangements otherwise, and he was glad she was home safe.

Despite the late hour, the dock was busy. He counted seven ships and five barges still taking on goods brought by rail from Chicago and the industrial north, goods that would end up in ports all along the Mississippi drainage via tributaries like the Missouri, the Red and White Rivers, and the Illinois and Wisconsin. The movement west to Texas, Arizona, Utah, California, and Oregon was in full swing, and wagon trains carrying goods and supplies were becoming more common to the prairie than those taking people. It was a time of great expansion.

In fact, the boom of people and products traveling west was such that more efficient methods of transportation had been cultivated, in particular the railroad. Though river shipping was still integral to the smooth and efficient transport of goods north to south, railroads had hastened the pace east to west. Most immigrant traffic now came from New York by rail to St. Joseph, Missouri, where the travelers caught steamboats or land stages and wagons to Council Bluffs and were outfitted for the trek west. Another railroad line was being built directly west out of St. Louis, and Rand knew the day was not far off when train tracks would overwhelm the entire country and reduce to a pittance the wealth to be gained in river shipping. It was a worry for Rand, but he had already begun to adapt, moving his wealth to better use and protecting it against such changes, including the ravages of the impending war.

Last to leave the office, Rand doused the lamps before lifting his leather valise and descending the stairs to the street, locking the doors behind him.

He waited on the cobblestone pavement only a moment before his carriage pulled up; he quickly got inside after giving his driver instructions to go to Frank Blair's. As the carriage lurched forward, Rand looked through the small window at the rear to see a second carriage pull out of the shadows and fall in behind him.

He was certain that he had been followed ever since he and Frank Blair had visited on the street, and he had caught glimpses of Sam Ridges from time to time. It was gnawing on his nerves, and he intended to do something about it soon, but tonight was not the night.

The carriage headed up Poplar Street and soon passed the new train depot. Frank's place was another fifteen minutes away.

Rand forced himself to focus on other subjects and concerns until the carriage turned and stopped before heavy wooden gates. An armed guard came to the carriage and opened the door, looking inside, while two others stood at the ready. Frank was being cautious, and since someone was following him, Rand appreciated the effort. It was nice to know this was as far as Sam Ridges would get.

"Herr Hudson," the man said in a thick German accent. "Gut, gut, Herr Blair is vaitin' fer ya." He closed the door and signaled for the other guards to swing open the gate. Frank had a strong friendship with the large German community of St. Louis, especially its leaders. This was the community that had elected him. The Germans in St. Louis were, for the grand majority, staunch supporters of Northern views and had already expressed a forthright willingness to end slavery through peace or war; to them it did not matter.

The carriage traversed the long lane and passed by an open field covered in moonlight. At the front entrance, servants helped Rand step down, and he went quickly up the steps and into the house.

As he was helped with his coat, he looked around the entry and into the sitting room, eyeing the other guests. He had to smile; this was not Frank's usual political dinner party with the elite moneyholders of St. Louis in attendance. Though some of these men did indeed have money, they were far from high society.

"Guten Tag, Randolph."

Rand turned to see Niklas Hirsch, a wide smile on his square jaw, standing next to Max Rosenthal, who had his usual dour look pinned in place.

Niklas Hirsch and Max Rosenthal lived in the German section of St.

Louis. Hirsch owned a furniture manufacturing business, while Rosenthal had his own metal works. Gentlemen in their late forties, both had come to the United States twenty years earlier and immediately enlisted in the military, fighting in the war with Mexico. A sergeant, Hirsch had saved his company from total annihilation by charging a cannon emplacement, overcoming its gunner's crew, and turning it on the enemy. Rosenthal had gained a reputation as one of the toughest line sergeants in the army, and his troops had been in the forefront of most of the battles of the war. The fact that he had survived said something, but the fact that more of his men had survived than any other group told a more important tale. Like Frank, both men were rabid in their antisecessionist beliefs and were not shy about saying so. Rand knew of half a dozen brawls caused by these two, all sparked by the topics of slavery and secession. But most important for Frank Blair, these men had tremendous influence in their German community. They would need to use that influence if Frank were to succeed in what Rand assumed was his goal—the raising of a militia.

"Niklas, Max, how are you?" He shook their hands. Both sported beards and were dressed in fine suits saved for fancy affairs. Hirsch was balding and had let his hair grow on the sides, where it attached to a beard that ran around his chin and that was not accompanied by a moustache. He was stout, trim, and hard. Rosenthal was of similar build, though a little taller. His dark brown hair was tinged with gray, and his beard was short and neatly trimmed to match that of his head. The man looked like a barroom tough, and for good reason—he had a regular habit of finding trouble in such places and making it personal.

"Fine," Hirsch responded. Both men had lost their accents over the years, though each continued to use a little German around the English-speaking population.

"I don't suppose you have any idea what old Frank is up to," Rosenthal said with a raised eyebrow.

"Randolph." The voice came from behind Rand, and he turned to see Brendan Malone coming toward him.

"Maybe Malone knows," Rand said, smiling at the Irishman as they shook hands.

"Know wha'?" Malone asked.

"Nein, he don't know. The Irish are born ignorant, and from then on they're too drunk to do anything about it," Hirsch said with a wide grin.

"An' th' only men in thi' tow' who kin drink more German beer than any German that lives. Niklas, good to see ya," Malone said.

The men shook hands. They were all good friends. Malone had been in the city just as long as the others and had been one of the first Irish to volunteer for Mexico. Rosenthal had been his company commander until Malone had proven his equal and gotten a company of his own.

Brendan Malone was at least four inches taller than Rand, thick of shoulder and with arms and hands that could crush a man's skull quick as they could squeeze the juice from a lemon. His handlebar moustache was waxed at its ends and stuck out a good inch on each side of his hardened cheeks. With straight teeth as white as pearls and never stained by tobacco, he showed a wide and powerful grin. With well-kept hair as thick as straw, he struck a powerful picture in most people's minds when he entered a room—and that caused them to part like the Red Sea when he entered a saloon. Rumor was those thick hands had done more damage to hard-headed Irishmen than had the plagues of Ireland. He still belonged to the state militia, worked at training soldiers, and was a skilled marksman with rifles of any kind. He was also the controlling power in the Irish community. Though McKinnon O'Brien controlled the Kerry Patch, he still answered to Brendan Malone, a fact that irritated O'Brien a good deal.

Malone had married but lost his wife to cholera years earlier. He had two adult children, both boys who were living in New York City and who controlled a good deal of the Irish section there.

Frank's servants presented a tray of drinks to the four men. Rand declined as he always did, while his friends each grabbed a glass of preference.

"It seems we're headed for war," Rosenthal said. "My guess is that's what this little meeting is about."

All agreed, but the conversation ended as Frank approached.

"Gentlemen," he said, greeting each. "Good you could all come."

The front door opened, and a tall man with graying hair stepped through it.

"Well, I'll be. I thought he was still in California," Hirsch said.

"That can't be him," Rosenthal said. "He's all dandied up."

The man was nearly as tall as Malone and wore wool gentleman's trousers that were a bit too short, with a waistcoat and vest over a linen shirt; his boots were newly blacked, and he wore a stovepipe hat of beaver that he was just removing to reveal a head of hair that usually flowed onto his shoulders but was tied up in a tail at the back of his head. It actually looked washed. He wore a black leather patch over his right eye, had a dollar-sized scar that marred his cheek, and was missing a similar-sized patch of hair on the left side of his head, where an Indian had tried to lift his scalp. He glanced about the room now, an unlit cigar between brown teeth.

Isaac Hooker was the son of a prominent plantation owner in Mississippi but hated slavery because of what he had seen growing up; he had helped three slaves escape from his father's plantation and had been disowned for it. He had gone west to pursue fur trapping and hadn't spoken to any of his family since, spending nearly fifteen years in the Rocky Mountains before the fur-trading business declined. He had subsequently found work as a scout for the army. After being seriously wounded in defense of a wagon train against renegade Blackfeet Indians, he came back to St. Louis to recuperate from the loss of one eye and part of his scalp. Following his recovery, he continued to work as an occasional scout for the army then started his own outfitting company. That was ten years ago, and Hooker had become a wealthy man, owning outfitting posts in St. Louis, St. Joseph, and Council Bluffs, Iowa. He used Rand's steamers exclusively to haul his goods.

Rand broke away with a wide grin and greeted the man. "Isaac Hooker, is that you?"

The man flushed a bit as a servant took his topcoat. "Randolph, good to see you."

Rand looked Hooker over with a wry smile. "My, my, Isaac Hooker in a suit. The world will surely end by the morrow."

Hooker glared. "My wife gets her way more than I like these days. She tells me that Frank Blair's house is no place for leathers."

More than a year ago, Isaac had married a widow with two children who was poorer than a Irish tenant when they met but it hadn't taken her long to spend a considerable chunk of Isaac's money on a new mansion and all the trappings in an attempt to climb the social ladder of St. Louis's elite. Despite her spendthrift ways, Isaac adored her and the two children, and one had only to see him all gussied up like this to know just how much.

"Mighty fine of her to bring some culture to your miserable life," Hirsch said as he joined them. "Heaven only knows how much you can stink up a place in them grease-soaked leathers you usually wear."

The group laughed, but the merriment didn't last long as Isaac glared at them and shoved his cigar back between his teeth to chew on it—hard. "Never you mind about my duds, Nick. You ain't exactly at home in that tight collar a yourn."

Hirsch chuckled, putting a finger between collar and neck. "Ya, ya, that's the truth."

Hooker's brief smile turned serious again. "Randolph. I hear you been watchin' your docks pretty close."

"Everyone has been looking over their shoulder the last few weeks. Unless, of course, you think like Atchison does," Rand answered.

"You mean be willin' to join the Confederacy and betray yer country. The man hasn't got the sense God gave a buffalo," Hooker responded.

Frank cleared his throat. "I believe we're all here now. I have someone I want you to meet. He's in the dining room. Shall we join him?"

Still visiting with one another, the men followed Frank into the dining area, where a young man in a charcoal gray wool suit stood visiting with a young woman Rand knew immediately.

"Lovely this evening, isn't she," Frank said, leaning toward Rand so that only he could hear.

Rand smiled. Frank had been trying to match him and his niece for months, and so had Lizzy, but it was Ann's natural qualities that drew Rand to admire her—and tonight was no exception. She wore her long hair furled on the back of her head with several combs holding it in place. Her slender frame was draped in a linen dress that was buttoned just below the chin but accentuated all the right spots. As always, the natural sparkle in her eye gave the look of mischief and intrigue that could turn any man's head.

Turning to the others as Ann moved from the other end of the dining hall to greet them, Frank made the introductions.

"This lovely lady is my niece, Ann Alexander," he said to the group. The men all bowed slightly and greeted Ann as she stepped forward. She paused in front of Hooker.

"Handsome as ever, Mr. Hooker." She smiled and gave him a quick peck on the cheek. "How is your lovely family?"

Hooker blushed. "Fine, fine. Thanks for asking, Miss Ann."

"Mr. Hooker used to sell his pelts to my father years ago. Used to bounce me on his knee. Those dresses still have beaver grease firmly implanted in each thread," Ann said with a grin.

The group laughed, Hooker along with them.

Ann took Rand's hand next, squeezing it gently. "Mr. Hudson, nice to see you again," she said with a pleasant smile. Her hand was soft, and Rand held it a moment longer than he intended.

"Miss Alexander," he said. "You are lovely as ever."

She flushed slightly then turned to the group and smiled. "Gentlemen, you all look hungry enough to eat Frank out of house and home. Please find a seat, and we will see that you have a fair chance to do so."

"Ain't et since early this morning an' my stomach is gnawing at my backbone, so sounds like a right good challenge to me," Hooker said.

"Then I will leave for the kitchen immediately," Ann said. "We would not want Mr. Hooker to expire and leave us all mourning a horrible loss." She turned to the gentleman standing beside her, who was obviously feeling a bit left out, put her arm through his, and went on. "This is Mr. Elmer Ellsworth, a wonderful gentleman who lives in Springfield, Illinois, but will soon be housed in the White House as personal secretary to Mr. Lincoln. And gentlemen," Ann said with smile for Mr. Ellsworth, "he is also single and quite handsome, don't you think?"

Ellsworth's cheeks turned crimson, and the others either chuckled or cleared their throats. Rand felt more than a bit jealous but worked hard to keep his face from showing it.

As he gazed at her, she again glanced in his direction, and he gave her a quick smile before taking his seat. Though he often joked with Lizzy about Ann's headstrong nature and her powerful opinions, which she never failed to share, he appreciated her independence and self-reliance and very much enjoyed her company. Her family had been among the New Orleans elite until her father's death two years earlier. The debtors who had come calling would have taken her mother for everything if Ann had not stopped them. Her father had seen that Ann received a fine education and had put her to work in the family business as his bookkeeper. She was able to show some debtors' claims as fraudulent and worked with others to reduce their immediate demands so that her mother did not lose everything. Ann had eventually been able to sell her father's business assets for enough profit to keep their estate outside New Orleans, along with a monthly income that, if handled properly, would provide for her family for some time to come.

Ann's eldest brother had just finished his studies in law and was practicing with a prominent firm in the city while her youngest brother was finishing his last year at West Point. Ann had recently left her mother's affairs in the care of her eldest brother to come to live with Frank and his wife, Apolline, who had nearly lost her life during childbirth and needed constant care.

Ann was really quite a remarkable woman, but Rand had done little to really pursue her. For the first few months after she arrived in St. Louis, it

seemed she was at every event and every street corner where Rand was—
and though he felt drawn to her, he pushed the feelings aside because of
his mother's illness or business pursuits or a dozen other excuses. And at
this moment, he was beginning to regret every one of them.

The meal was served in grand fashion and progressed quickly. Conversation centered around Mr. Ellsworth and his thoughts on the progress of
Lincoln's establishment of a new government. He was guarded but pleasant, witty but frank, and particularly open with his own opinions. Among
other things, he acknowledged that Mr. Seward would be nominated as
secretary of state and that Gideon Welles would be the head of the Navy
Department. He also assured the group that Montgomery Blair would be
postmaster general. Rand noted Frank's approving expression following
Ellsworth's assessment.

As the conversation proceeded, Mr. Ellsworth pointed out the importance of Illinois and especially Missouri in keeping the Union together,
and he said that Mr. Lincoln would try to help where he could in that effort,
even though he had no real authority until after he was inaugurated. The
discussion quickly turned to Missouri politics and the increased tensions
between supporters of the North and South.

Rand smiled as he noticed that the kitchen door was blatantly ajar. He
could not picture any servant or the socially correct Apolline Blair breaking
such a basic rule of propriety. But Ann Alexander would not hesitate; her
curious nature simply would not allow her to resist.

His suspicion was verified when the door swung fully open and Ann
walked in with a tray to deliver dessert herself. The conversation, however,
was quite intense at the time, and the others hardly noticed as she carefully
sauntered around the table and placed a tasty-looking pastry in front of
each diner.

In spite of the weighty conversation surrounding him, Rand was more
than a bit distracted by Ann's presence, her dark hair tied up at the back
of her head and her olive skin beautifully flushed by her efforts to serve.
The high-necked dress of white linen was comfortable and fit her slender,
agile form perfectly.

Rand was drawn back to the conversation as Max Rosenthal
commented, "Mr. Ellsworth, we who support the Union in Missouri
are in constant turmoil. We supported Mr. Lincoln because we agreed
with his position on the unconstitutionality of secession, but more so
because of his position on slavery—surely we must prevent the South

from seceding, but we cannot do so while still allowing the continuation of this . . . this inhumane practice. There must be no equivocation in our effort to end the buying and selling of mankind." He leaned forward to emphasize his words. "And yet as these rebellious states secede, we hear rumor of compromise from Mr. Lincoln on the issue of slavery in order to keep them in the Union. Surely he will not make concessions on such a fundamental human right. We cannot stomach such weakness."

Ellsworth dabbed at his mustache-covered lip with a napkin, a slight smile on his face. "There is no equivocation in Mr. Lincoln on that subject, Mr. Rosenthal. He very much wants to end slavery as an institution. The quest at present, however, is whether he can accomplish it with the Southern states still in the Union. Surely all of you gentleman understand how devastating war would be to all Americans and that we must try to hold the Union together, even if it means an olive branch or two to accomplish it."

"Gentlemen," Frank said. "Mr. Ellsworth is right. Secession is surely our greatest concern. We must keep the states in the Union. Slavery can be dealt with legislatively."

Rand smiled inwardly. Frank Blair was a slaveholder. His servants— the ones serving their meal, taking their coats, cleaning their boots, and cooking their food—were all slaves, and yet Frank had called this meeting. He did not want it to be about slavery, yet he had invited the leaders with the most strongly held abolitionist views in the community. Why he thought he could do so and not make slavery the central subject of conversation was curious to Rand. He supposed the answer would be forthcoming and decided to hold his peace for the moment.

Hirsch looked at Frank with determined eyes. "Frank, secession will occur *because* of slavery. It is *not* a side issue—it is *the* issue. And the sooner you rid yourself of any hypocrisy on the subject, the better support you will have from those of us in this room."

Frank grew a bit red in the face. "I have freed nearly half my slaves— all of you know that. And you know that the rest will be freed if war breaks out. I have made that promise, and I will keep it." He leaned forward to emphasize his own point. "Nick, you know that a premature freeing of every slave I own would put me in the poorhouse and them in the street without any means of support. Like others who hold slaves, I cannot just walk away from them overnight. That is why this meeting must not focus solely on slavery. It must address the destruction of the economy through secession—the destruction of the Union, the destruction of our government, and a split that will be devastating to the future of all Americans."

Ellsworth came to Frank's rescue. "Slavery will end, gentlemen. President Lincoln will see to that, but you must understand that we cannot make it the central issue of our stand against secession if we have any hope of a peaceful settlement."

Hirsch's face became red. "I, for one, am tired of giving up the rights of our colored Americans so that we can compromise. It is time we stood against this horror and those who sustain it."

"And if we are not here to discuss war, why are we here?" Rosenthal asked, clearly a bit frustrated. He tossed his napkin on the table, his appetite apparently gone.

All was silent for a moment, the tension heavy.

"Gentlemen, gentlemen, you speak of the South as if they were your bitter enemies. Surely you cannot think so."

The room went quiet, and all eyes turned to Ann, from whom the words had come. She had a gentle smile on her face, her eyes on young Mr. Ellsworth. "Does Mr. Lincoln consider Southerners his enemy, Mr. Ellsworth?" she said, almost too sweetly.

Ellsworth forced a smile and seemed unsure how to respond. The source of the question had caught him quite off guard.

Ann went on, though a stern look from Frank tried to warn her to return to the kitchen. "As a girl of the South who saw slavery firsthand and learned to despise it with all her being, I am nevertheless appalled at this talk of war to bring it to an end. Mr. Hirsch, are you sure you want no further discussion, no compromise, when it might mean the death of thousands, even tens of thousands of our best men? Are we really at the end of that rope?"

Hirsch fumed in his chair. Frank, clearly embarrassed by his niece's boldness even though she was supporting his position, flushed an angry red that moved up his neck to his cheeks. Rand chuckled inwardly. A woman simply did not infuse her thoughts into a conversation to which she was not invited, and for Ann to do so was considered offensive by much of society—and by at least three of the men in the room. Though Rand liked them all, his beliefs about the place of women in society were quite different from those of Rosenthal, Hirsch, and Blair, and he was both amused and supportive of Ann's right to speak her mind. From the look Hooker and Malone had on their faces, they were also were amused and appreciative of Ann's audacity.

"Mr. Hudson, you seem thoughtful. Possibly you could answer my query?" Ann had picked up a steaming pitcher and poured coffee in Ellsworth's cup while glancing at Rand. "What course of action do you think Mr. Lincoln should take in handling what Mr. Hirsch and Mr. Rosenthal think requires war?"

Hirsch couldn't control himself another moment. "Miss Alexander, really, you have no right to voice any opinions in this setting, and to even ask questions is—"

"Niklas, let's not concern ourselves too much with propriety. Miss Alexander's future is just as much at risk as our own, and her question hits at the heart of the matter, don't you think?" Rand said.

Hirsch bit on his cigar, but the slump of his shoulders and the drop of his eyes to his plate indicated a reluctant willingness to keep his silence, at least for the moment. Rand saw that even Frank relaxed a little as all eyes focused on him, waiting for his answer.

Reaching for his cup, Rand held it out for Ann to fill. With a quizzical look at his action, she reached across the table, extended the coffee urn to his cup, and began to pour. He moved the cup slightly, and she spilled coffee on the basket of bread below. He held it still again until she tried to pour. Then he moved it again, and the coffee spilled once more, this time splattering on the white table linen. Her face flushed in embarrassment and a little anger as she pulled back. He continued to move the cup from side to side, up and down, slowly.

After a moment Rand smiled. "Answering your question is as easy as filling a moving cup, Miss Alexander." He held the cup steady. "Mr. Lincoln proposes to pay for slaves and their freedom in order to keep the peace, but the South requires exorbitant prices they know the government can never accept." He moved the cup. "Suppose Mr. Lincoln lets them keep slavery," he said, steadying the cup again, "but then they ask for more territory to carry it forward. They want Cuba, Arizona, or Utah." He moved the cup again then leaned forward. "On and on it goes. Unfortunately, every time anyone has tried to fill the South's cup, tried to compromise, they just keep moving their position, demanding more. How does one fill such a cup? At some point someone has to make them hold that cup steady."

"But wouldn't just letting them have their own country steady the cup?" she asked.

"If isolation were their only goal, yes; if they didn't want or need to expand in order to survive, yes. But it is clear that they would still want Cuba, or Arizona, or the entire West. And could we give it to them and stop our own expansion? If not, what then? Would they threaten war once more? Rattle sabers, intimidate, even as they do now, in order to get their way?" He placed his cup on its platter. "Everyone in this room, including you, Miss Alexander, knows that the institution of slavery must grow in order to survive. It not only requires more land, but it requires more slaves. The Confederacy has already said without question that they will begin purchasing new slaves from Africa once they have their own government. Can you imagine the outcry in the world, where we are nearly the last to end this horrid practice? Europe will demand that we take action, with the threat that if we do not they will do it themselves, but the result will be the same: war. And then we will find ourselves right where we are now, but with the South much more prepared to fight all nations who try to end slavery for them. How many thousands will die then? How many tens of thousands?" He looked directly at Ellsworth. "I agree that we must do everything we can to avoid war, except allow the South to continue slavery. If that is what peace requires, then war we must have, but all of us in this room intend to end slavery." He looked at Frank. "Have I misstated our position, Frank?"

Frank shook his head, a wrinkle of serious concern in his brow. "No, you have not. It was well stated."

"Thank you, Mr. Hudson. I appreciate your clarification," Ann said softly. Rand could tell her words were sincere, but she also smiled quickly, shoving it all aside. "Well, enough of my silly questions. Gentlemen, enjoy your dessert. Coffee, anyone?"

Rand lifted his cup. "Mine still seems to be empty."

Several laughed, including Ann, and the men busied themselves with dessert as the air cleared of its heaviness. Ann moved around the table, filling cups and making pleasant conversation until she stood between Rand and Frank, who was obviously still unhappy with his niece's temerity and projected a scowl in her direction to give her a clear understanding.

Ann poured coffee in Rand's cup, leaning down as she did. "I am staying this night with a friend who is nearing the time when she will bring her first child into the world. From the look on my uncle's face, I might not have use of one of his carriages. Mr. Hudson, could you possibly provide transport? I would hate to disappoint my friend." She whispered it just loud enough so Frank could hear.

Rand did not look up but nodded slightly. "If your uncle approves, I would be glad to see you safely there."

She glanced at her uncle. "Well, then?"

"You shall have a carriage if you need one, Ann, no matter the depth of my displeasure, and you know that. Therefore, I can only assume that your request of Mr. Hudson has a different motive." He looked at Rand, a hint of vengeance in his eyes. "Beware, Randolph, my niece is after—"

"Uncle, I would speak no further unless you want this coffee in your lap," she said with a determined and threatening smile.

Having gotten his revenge, Frank smiled. "Randolph, if you would be so kind as to see that my niece arrives at her destination, I would be most appreciative."

"It would be my pleasure," Rand said, a slight blush in his own cheeks.

Ann left the dining room, clearly pleased, and Frank leaned over. "She has been wondering how to catch your interest again. I see she has worked it out for herself."

Rand smiled. "She does not have to work very hard, Frank. I assure you."

Frank pushed his chair back and stood. "Gentlemen, let us retire to the study, where we can talk a bit more . . ." he cleared his throat ". . . privately."

There was light laughter as each man got to his feet and headed for the study, where a servant greeted them, pouring drinks and offering cigars. Rand took nothing and found a chair he knew would be away from the center of the conversation, while the others took what refreshments they wanted and found a seat. Frank stood near the fireplace, a cigar clasped between the fingers of one hand and a shot of liquor in the other. He placed the cigar to his lips, and a black servant lit it for him. The man was a servant Frank had recently freed but who had decided to stay at a fair wage.

Rand watched the others, who did not seem to notice or care that they were using the very system they declared themselves so adamantly against. But even he condoned it every day. Slaves poured his coffee at the hotel dining room, polished his shoes outside his office, and worked to load and unload goods his steamships hauled in and out of St. Louis. It was there, every day, and most people accepted it even though they abhorred it. War would change that dramatically, and Rand wondered just how many of the men in this room were going to be willing to pay the increased prices because slaves who worked for so little would be replaced by freedmen who would demand more.

Frank was a bit of a paradox for Rand. Ann had told him that Frank never mistreated or even raised his voice to his servants and that because of it, most of his slaves would stay and work if paid a fair wage, just as Mose and Lydijah had stayed with Baker and Mary Hudson when freed. But Frank continued to drag his feet. The system worked for him, saved him money, provided prestige among a large segment of society—especially in his role as a politician. Like Rand had told Lizzy, the system had corrupted even Frank Blair, and though he did not see himself in the same vile wagon as Atchison and Ridges, he continued to deny some men their freedom. Trouble was, he felt justified—considering himself a nobler sort than Atchison, whom he despised. Evil made even good men blind to their own faults. But as he did with Andrew, Rand had learned to put up with that side of Frank Blair. There was good in both men, and he had managed to find it in order to be friends and maintain their differences.

Frank cleared his throat. "Gentleman, I personally asked our president-elect to send a representative he could trust to this meeting tonight, and I assure you that Mr. Ellsworth has the full confidence of the president." He looked at Hirsch and Rosenthal. "I appreciate your questions at the table, but this meeting is not about Mr. Lincoln's present need to placate Southern and middle states as a part of holding the Union together. It is about the need to prevent Missouri from falling into Southern hands."

"Mr. Lincoln has no illusions about what most Southern states will do," Ellsworth said. "They will secede, no matter how much we try to placate them and leave them without excuse. The question is not whether some states will secede but how many and what they will take with them.

"Our state, gentlemen, is critical to the Union cause, both economically and politically. We must—*must*—prevent Missouri from joining the Confederacy."

Ellsworth spoke. "And you must move quickly. The southernmost states are already planning a Confederate government and have invited all middle states—such as Kentucky, Maryland, Virginia, and your state, gentlemen—to join with them. They will soon invite Jefferson Davis to be their president, and then they will begin printing their own currency. They will be sending ambassadors abroad to garner support in Britain, France, and Germany, and they are already declaring that President Buchanan must turn over all federal forts and arsenals housed in Southern states once they leave the Union. They are moving at a fast pace, and we must move just as quickly."

"Buchanan has the power to stop them. He should act," Hirsch said angrily.

"Buchanan will do nothing, and the South knows it. And they know that Lincoln will do something as soon as he is in office, even though he offers compromise now. That is why they will act before March, when our new president is inaugurated. And you and others like you in the middle states must move just as resolutely if we are to save the Union," Ellsworth said.

Frank threw his cigar in the fireplace with determination, leaning forward in his chair. "As you are aware, Governor-elect Jackson will try to take Missouri out of the Union. As soon as he is sworn into office the first of January, he will call for a statewide convention of the legislature and ask for a vote to secede. He will not succeed—I and others with strong political influence will see to that—leaving him only one option: military force."

"He will never go that route," Rosenthal said matter-of-factly. "He hasn't the guts for such an action."

"You underestimate him, Max, and you underestimate the influence men like David Atchison have on him. I do not know what will precipitate it, but eventually Jackson will be forced to use the militia. He will try to do it legally, but if he cannot, he will do it illegally. We must be ready for that eventuality," Frank said.

He paused, looking at Rand. "Randolph, please tell these gentlemen about your visit from Mr. Atchison and Mr. Shelby."

Rand gave them a summary. "They want transportation south. They are talking fifty, sixty thousand men."

"Atchison and Governor-elect Jackson and their supporters are preparing for what they think is inevitable." Frank looked directly at Isaac Hooker. "Mr. Hooker, please tell us about your conversation with Mr. Atchison."

"Because of my, uh, heritage as a former slaveholder, he thought he might have a friend in me. I let him think so, and after several meetings he laid out a plan to raise an army of the size Rand just mentioned and move it south into Mississippi. I asked him how he intended to arm such a large group. He said many would have their own weapons, and I told him they would not have nearly enough. He said there was a place he could get another forty thousand weapons. Said they were all but in his hands."

Rosenthal frowned. "The only place Atchison would be able to come by that number of weapons is in the St. Louis Arsenal."

"The federal government controls the Arsenal. They aren't about—" Hirsch started to say.

"The man responsible, a Major Bell, has already offered the weapons to Jackson the moment the state secedes," Hooker said. "I already checked on Bell. He's been braggin' about bein' a Southerner and doin' his part."

"Surely General Harney 'ill overrule Bell an' provide the necessary protection against any such action by Jackson an' Atchison," Malone said.

Brigadier General William S. Harney commanded the army of the west and was stationed at St. Louis. Rand had met him several times but did not know him well enough to make a judgment about his ability or his loyalties.

Frank cleared his throat. "General Harney is convinced there is no imminent danger to the Arsenal. He has reassurances from Jackson and a dear friend—Sterling Price, with whom he fought during the war with Mexico."

Rand's ears were pricked. Sterling Price was a moderate slaveholder who opposed secession but had Southern sympathies. As a former two-term governor of Missouri, he had made it known that he wanted to keep Missouri neutral. But he had also said that if war broke out, he would fight for the South and take every man he could with him.

"Price is as blind to Jackson's machinations as Harney is. They're both being duped," Malone said, "but when the fight comes, Price will not be sidin' with us, an' tha's as sure as hawthorn blossoms in springtime."

"And if Harney does nothing when Jackson acts, it will cost us the Arsenal," Rand said.

"If the general does not open his eyes, we will have him circumvented," Frank said.

Hirsch spoke. "Harney is a very powerful man in Washington. You won't circumvent him easily."

"I have approached Lieutenant General Scott. He is very aware of Harney's position and has given me his promise that Harney will be removed if it comes to that," Frank answered. "Confidentially, the man Lincoln will make his new secretary of war also agrees with us."

General Winfield Scott was over the entire federal military, and though he was from Virginia, he had made it clear that his loyalties lay with the Union. There was not a more influential military man in the country, including Harney.

"And what about Major Bell?" Hirsch asked. "Seems to me he's more of an immediate danger than Harney might be."

"We are very quietly working to have him replaced. A new man, one we can trust, should be in place in the next few weeks," Frank said.

There were nods of pleased agreement.

"Then all we need is more troops for its defense. Can't Scott order them here?"

Ellsworth shook his head to the contrary. "We have only sixteen thousand in the regular army. Most of them are stationed in the West, and at least half of them will resign or desert as secession proceeds. Washington will need to be protected by what remains, and there will be at least a dozen other hot spots between us and the South that will cry out for immediate attention even more than your good state. Do not plan on any help, gentlemen. I do not think it will come, at least not for several months."

"How many federal troops are at the Arsenal?" Hooker asked.

"Fewer than a hundred," Frank replied.

"Governor Jackson can raise double that without spittin', and if he gets authority to call out the militia, he can probably amass two or three thousand in a month. Three months, five to eight thousand," Hooker said grimly.

"And where do we ge' an army of such a size t' stop 'em?" Malone asked.

"We have that many in the Wide Awakes," Frank said.

Rand was a bit shocked, and from the look of the others, so were they. The Wide Awakes had developed out of organized marching clubs for young men called the Rocky Mountain Clubs and Freedom Clubs. Such groups had sprung up all over the North as a movement to get young people involved in politics. Marches, as well as speeches and rallies in which the group's preferred candidate was the speaker had become their favorite and most successful method of stirring up interest in politics among the young adults. Most were somewhat disciplined and even had uniforms patterned after old Prussian and German military uniforms. During 1860, opposition to Lincoln and other Republican candidates had become violent, and the Wide Awakes had begun to serve as a political police that escorted candidates and kept the peace at rallies—but Rand didn't think that qualified them for military service. Most of those who joined were more interested in some public display that made them look heroic and caused young women who followed such movements to swoon than in dying for their country.

"The Wide Awakes?" Ellsworth said, a little astonished. "They are a marching club for silly young men. Surely you do not believe they can be trained—"

"You'd have to be at least half crazy to use 'em," Hooker added.

"Mr. Blair has a disciplined group," insisted Rosenthal. "They have been drilled with military language and bearing and the importance of following command. In time they could be become army recruits. Other units of Wide Awakes in Missouri and in Illinois are just as organized."

"Even if you had a thousand of the best of them, they have a long way to go to be a fighting militia," Rand said.

"From what I've seen, Jackson's state boys could rout them in the first charge with less than half that. They aren't used to fightin', just marchin'," Hirsch added.

Frank's second cigar was thrown forcefully into the fire. "Then we will train them!" He took a deep breath and regained control. "Gentlemen, war is coming, and the moment it is declared young men will enlist, thinking it a glorious opportunity. They won't have much chance of training before being called to put their lives on the line. By starting them now, we will give them a better chance at surviving while also preparing a force that can keep this state out of the Confederacy."

Rand looked at Hooker, who shrugged. There really weren't any other options. "They will need weapons and a quality of training that gives them the mettle needed to kill another human being," he said.

"We have some weapons. They are older flintlocks, but they will do for training. I have arranged for them to be sent here secretly from New York. When we take control of the Arsenal, we will give them better rifles and will train them on cannon and mortar, both of which are housed there," Frank said.

Hooker's head came up. "Take control of the Arsenal? That would be an act of war, Frank."

"Not if the federal government asks for our help in protecting it. And they will—I will see to that. Our immediate attention must be directed to the training of a sufficient force to respond effectively to that invitation," Frank said.

Rand was beginning to see how much Frank had done in preparation for this meeting, and he was also beginning to see just how needful those preparations were. The Arsenal really was a critical point of control for the state, and if Missouri was lost, it would allow the South to effectively surround the North and cut them from any access to the western frontier. "How many of your Wide Awakes will respond immediately?" Rand asked.

"We already have a thousand at the ready. They continue to meet at a large warehouse I own, but by the end of January their number could double, even triple."

Rand nodded agreement as Malone spoke. "'Ow does one keep such an army secret?"

"One doesn't, but there is no need. They are a legal organization and have every right to meet," Frank said.

Rand's mind was already working on the structure and training of such a group. "You will need a commander for every hundred men—a *company* in military terms. To begin, that means at least ten qualified men. I assume you have others we can call on."

"That's where you come in, Mr. Hudson," Frank said with a sober look. "Because of your schooling in tactics and training at the military academy, I would ask that you accept responsibility for training our troops. Each of these men will work under your command. Is this agreeable to everyone?"

All nodded once more, which surprised Rand nearly as much as the request. "With all due respect, Frank, I am the least qualified and by far the least experienced."

"To the contrary, Rand," Rosenthal said. "All of us are used to taking orders, not giving them. Your abilities and experience in logistics and field operations are critical."

Rand swallowed hard, his mouth dry. He glanced at Hooker, who simply nodded his agreement.

Ellsworth was checking his watch. "Then we have a beginning. I will present the elements of this meeting to Mr. Lincoln. However, I doubt he will put anything in writing as far as presidential support is concerned. You will be on your own until your Wide Awakes are invited to aid the full army." His look changed to one of resolute surety. "I must warn you: Do not think that you can use such a group to break the laws of the state of Missouri or the United States. If the federal government asks for your help and you are ready, that is one thing. But if you begin something on your own, the president will denounce you as quickly as he will Southern secessionists set on treason. Never forget, the North cannot be seen as the aggressors—at least not now, not in the beginning."

He stood, putting his watch in his vest pocket. "Gentlemen, I must catch a train back to Springfield. Mr. Blair, I thank you and your family for your fine hospitality. Please give especial thanks to your lovely wife and the beautiful Miss Alexander for that wonderful meal. And gentlemen, thanks to all of you. I am sure Mr. Blair will keep Mr. Lincoln informed of developments. God be with you." He looked to Frank. "Mr. Blair, I assume you will accompany me to the train."

Frank nodded. "Give me but a moment, if you would."

Ellsworth nodded agreement and left the room. Rand heard Ann and Apolline both greet him in the hall before the door was closed again.

"Gentlemen, we must meet again. There is much to be done, don't you agree?" When it was clear that everyone did, Frank called the meeting to an end and thanked everyone for coming on such short notice. He reassured them that their contribution would not go unnoticed as future events played out. Rand smiled slightly. Frank Blair, ever the politician.

"Randolph, thank you for seeing that Ann gets to her destination," Frank said, frowning. Clearly he was not quite past his irritation over Ann's actions.

Rand nodded and smiled. "If it keeps her alive for one more day, it will be my pleasure."

Frank shook his head lightly. "I swear the girl is in need of a good willow." He sighed, then finally gave into a smile. "But I fear she may turn it on me as quickly as I raise it."

Chuckles from those who had been listening filled the room, and Hooker spoke. "One does not break the spirit of a good horse in order to control it, Mr. Blair. Miss Alexander will be a challenge for any man, but she will sure as day keep him entertained."

There was more laughter, and this time Frank joined in before bidding them all a good night and leaving the room.

The others soon rendered their good-byes as well, until only Hooker and Rand remained.

"Well, you will have your hands full this night, and I am glad for it," Hooker said with a smile.

"You're better qualified, Isaac, and we both—"

"I ain't talking about the army; I'm talking about Miss Alexander," Hooker said. "'Sides which, I ain't, and I already said so."

"Umm. More than any other woman, Ann Alexander is a mystery to me," Rand said in earnest.

Hooker grinned. "I have known you a long time, Randolph. There ain't another woman in this here world who would suit yer temperment more."

Rand looked over at his friend. "And I suppose such a thought has a sound foundation?"

"Sure does. Though ya both are headstrong and independent in yer thinkin', ya are also driven by a moral conscience that considers others' needs more than yer own." He paused. "But, more important, I believe she loves yer pretty hide. And that, dear boy, will give ya more joy than ya can possibly imagine." Hooker got to his feet and started to leave the room. Rand's mouth had turned to cotton, his voice box paralyzed.

"Let 'er reel ya in, Randolph. If'n ya don't, ya'll regret it the rest of yer life."

With that he was gone, and Rand was left alone to deal with thoughts that he had never seriously entertained.

And to his amazement, they felt very comfortable. Very comfortable indeed.

Chapter 14

RAND HELPED ANN INTO THE carriage, then climbed in and sat beside her. She wore a warm wool coat over her linen dress and a hat that most women would not be caught dead in, at least not in public. It too was made of wool and pulled down over her ears, fitting the form of her head and tying around her chin, covering her hair. A few unruly curls protruded from its edges and framed her face.

Amazingly, she made the whole ensemble look quite beautiful.

Their immediate topic of conversation dealt with her unexpected entrance into the dinner and Frank's irritation over it. She had shrugged it off as Rand had expected. Ann then tried to pull from Rand any details regarding the men's discussion, but he only smiled, replying with evasive comments.

As the carriage left through the gates, she spoke again. "You men are so incorrigible," she said with some frustration.

Rand laughed lightly. "You forget mighty quickly who broke with proper decorum during dinner."

"What do you expect? You never tell us anything for fear we don't have the intelligence to deal with the information properly. Some of you treat us no better than slaves. We are to pick up after you, press your clothes, cook your meals, do your laundry, and have your babies, but you don't think we have the ability to think for ourselves and discuss our feelings. Even worse, those of us who have servants to deal with the daily chores are treated like little dolls to be set on the shelf and looked at but not included."

"Well, you *are* nice to look at," Rand said with a smile.

She slugged him on the arm. "Oh, you know what I mean!"

"Ouch. Ann, I cannot tell you about what happened in the study because it was not for anyone's ears but those who were there. Surely you can understand the importance of my keeping confidences. If you and I had a personal conversation, you would expect it to be kept between the two of us, and I would do so. But I am not sure if you would or not, given your insistence on this issue."

She stopped in her tracks, thinking. Obviously she had not thought about the matter in this way.

She sighed. "Yes, I guess you're right." She sidled in closer to him as if chilled, then removed a hand from her muff and put it through his arm. As she snuggled closer, his heart picked up to double the pace.

"Do you think Frank discusses such matters with Apolline? Privately, of course."

Rand shrugged slightly. "The relationship between a husband and wife is different, I suppose. They must trust one another. Both need to be able to speak freely and know it will go no further. However, there may be some things they should not share."

"I cannot imagine it," she said emphatically.

"Let's suppose that your husband is privy to information concerning national security—information so sensitive and dangerous that it could bring harm to anyone who was in possession of it. Wouldn't it be insensitive for a husband to share that with his wife?"

She thought a moment. "I suppose in that case, maybe—yes, it would be best, but those situations are rare, aren't they?"

"Tonight was one of those situations, Ann."

She sat straight up and looked directly at him. "It was that important?"

"And if leaked prematurely could endanger others' lives, including yours."

Ann stared out the window for a long time before speaking again. "I worry about my mother and brothers," she said softly. "If there is really going to be war, I must be with them, especially Mother. She could never handle it alone. Never."

The thought sobered Rand as he sensed her genuine concern. It explained far more clearly her desire to learn as much as she could about what was about to happen.

"Will your family stay in the South?" Rand asked.

"Adam is already talking about seeking a commission in the Louisiana militia. Matthew, on the other hand, said in his last letter that he is torn. He says the talk of war is splitting the academy apart."

Rand knew Matthew was at West Point. "I can understand that. I have a dozen good friends from the academy who live in the South—my best friend lives in Virginia and serves at Fort Sumter."

"Lizzy told me." She paused again. "I suppose my brothers are old enough to take care of themselves, though it pains me a good deal to think of anything happening to them," she said sadly. "I fear that in their Southern pride they will fight for a cause that is both unjust and coming to an end anyway, and the thought of them dying because of such a thing brings me such anguish. I have spoken to them, and Matthew . . . well, he is noncommittal, even evasive. Adam, however, is angry to near violence. He seems to have forgotten how he used to abhor watching the treatment of the slaves at the selling pens in New Orleans. How it upset him! And how he told all who owned slaves that they were surely going to the devil. Since going to school and finding his job, he seems to have completely changed. But then most of the clients with which his firm deals are men who own slaves or buy and sell them. It has hardened his soul, I'm afraid."

"You say he is seeking a commission in the militia?"

She nodded. "The foremost partner in the law firm where he works is a major, and the man has Adam convinced that he can get him commissioned as a lieutenant."

"It's done all the time," Rand said.

"Will you go back to the army, Rand?" she asked with genuine concern.

"If there is a war, I won't have much of a choice. A man cannot take a position against secession and slavery as I have and then not defend that position with action. In my youth I read a book that talked of the necessity of fighting for our wives, and our children, and our freedoms. The book says we must stand up for others when they cannot fight for themselves. That principle definitely fits here, and I agree with it."

She shook her head lightly. "How can you stand the thought of fighting against men like Andrew . . . Andrew . . . ?"

"Clay."

Yes, Andrew Clay. He is your best friend, and Lizzy seems quite interested in him."

"I try not to think about it, but Andrew must also have his right to choose. If he chooses to defend Southern rights to slavery, then things have changed between us."

"But you will remain friends," Ann said.

"In some ways, I suppose." It was a hard question to answer, and he didn't have a complete answer. "Will you go back to New Orleans if your brother does fight?" he asked, trying to hide his apprehension.

"I too will have little choice. My mother will have no one else."

Rand only nodded, his stomach in knots. He had known that this would be her answer. He supposed it was one of the main reasons he had been reluctant to pursue her as his heart had impressed him, and now he wished he hadn't let such feelings stop him. Could it be too late? But he could not let it be so. He must not let the impending future and all it might hold paralyze him when it came to Ann. If he did, even his mother would never forgive him.

Mary Hudson had met Ann on several occasions and was one of her foremost admirers. Rand could not count the number of times his mother had told him of Ann's qualities and to get moving! She would be sorely disappointed if Rand let Ann slip away.

He had also wondered what his father might think. Baker Hudson was a good judge of women. After all, he had convinced Mary to be his wife. What would he think of Ann? It was a question with an immediate answer. Baker Hudson would have loved Ann Alexander—she was too much like Rand's mother to do otherwise.

"I have to do some Christmas shopping tomorrow. I am horrible at deciding what to buy, especially for the women in my life. Could you accompany me?" Rand asked.

She smiled, her round, dark eyes glistening in the light of the moon that came through the window. "It would be a pleasure."

Ann removed her glove and placed her hand over his but said nothing. He took her hand and pressed it gently in his.

They talked of gifts, of past Christmases, and of what each loved most about the season. Rand had never felt so comfortable and alive, and when they reached her address in St. Louis, he regretted it. She was about to get out of the carriage when she turned back, placed her hand behind his neck, and pulled him to her. Her lips were soft and exciting, and he wrapped his arms around her and pulled her into his lap, breathing in her passion and returning it in the strength of his arms and the gentleness of his kiss. As she melted into him, he felt love as he had never felt it before.

She pulled away and looked into his eyes, then took his face between her hands and drew him in to kiss him again—once, twice, gently and tenderly. "You have wasted time, Rand Hudson. Why? I must know."

"Fear, dear Ann, but I promise to make it up to you, starting tomorrow. Will you let me?"

"Let you? I will aid you. I have loved you since the first time I saw you, and I have waited patiently for you to feel the same. I am glad I will have to wait no longer."

"Then you think I am in love with you," he said with a slight smile.

"We both know it. It has always been in your heart. It is nice to see that your head has finally accepted it."

He chuckled, but the sound did not last long, as she kissed him again, then nestled her head on his shoulder. "Do you see what your silliness has cost you?" she said softly.

"Yes, my eyes are quite open to it now." He leaned in and kissed her this time, long and passionately, until they were interrupted by the sudden jolt of the carriage as the horses danced about in their impatience to be moving again.

"Come on, Miss Alexander. I'd best get you inside while I still have my wits about me."

He got out of the carriage and helped her down, and then they stood together for a moment in front of the modest, middle-class home. She again put her arm through his, and in their new reverie they walked together up the front steps.

After Rand kissed Ann one last time and went back to the carriage, he asked the driver to take him home.

He did not see Sam Ridges give his hack driver an order to follow. But he would not have cared, as his thoughts were on Ann Alexander.

* * *

It was nearly midnight when Rand's carriage entered the lane of his estate. The sight of all its lanterns and candles lit alarmed him greatly, and he was out of the carriage before it came to a full stop, taking two stairs at a time. He handed a concerned Lydijah his coat while she filled him in.

"And dat woman, she be upstairs in Miss Lizzy's room, tryin' to have dat baby. But it don't look too good, Massa Rand. Not good 'tall."

Rand saw movement in the parlor and turned to see two men—one white, one black—pacing the hardwood floors. He recognized Newton Daines.

"Mr. Daines," Rand said as he entered the parlor. "It seems you have had an eventful evening."

"Yes, sir," Newton said. He glanced over; noticing that the black man had come to a standstill, his eyes wide with apprehension, Newton quickly went to his side. "This man is Felix Coulon. He's a freedman an'—"

"Yes, I heard. Mr. Coulon, you are welcome in our home. Tell me what happened at Ridges' pens." Rand could see the worry on Felix's face and was asking him the question more to take his mind off his sister than any need to hash over Ridges' actions. He knew Ridges.

Rand motioned toward two chairs, and Felix began his story as they seated themselves. They were nearly finished when Lizzy and another woman came into the room, tears in their eyes and concern on their faces. Rand had never seen the second woman before. Lizzy looked at Rand, gave him a wan smile, and then turned to Felix, who stood. She forced a smile. "It's a boy, Mr. Coulon. A healthy, though small, baby boy."

Felix grinned but then saw that Lizzy hadn't told him everything. "An' Susannah, Miss Lizzy? How she be?"

Lizzy went to him as she took a deep breath. "I am sorry, Felix, but she was quite ill and very weak from everything that happened. She . . . she did not survive the child's birth."

Felix felt weak in the knees and began to crumple, forcing Lizzy to grab him by one arm while Mary McConnell grabbed the other. Newton and Rand came to their aid and helped Felix sit. Unsure if he had heard Lizzy right, his eyes searched hers, trying to make sure. It was all Lizzy could do to keep her own emotions in check. They had tried so hard!

"Mr. Coulon," Rand said. "We will see that your sister is cared for, and we will provide a place for you and the child as long as you need it."

Felix gave him a blank stare but finally nodded. "Thank you, Massa Hudson." He sat back. "I haven't seen her for a long time. Now . . . now she's gone . . . Just like my mamma. I waited too long, Mr. Hudson, I did, and now . . ." The tears and sobs started, and Lizzy knelt and took his hands in hers.

It was all any of them could do.

Chapter 15

NEWTON AND MARY ARRIVED AT the boardinghouse just before sunrise. As usual, the place was bustling, but they were able to slip in the back door to find Mrs. O'Grady cooking breakfast for her paying customers.

"Might' late to be comin' in," Mrs. G. said, giving the two a look.

"You tryin' t' be me mum now," Mary said.

"Not yer mum, dearie, just yer guardian. Word is that a man an' a woman picked Sam Ridges's pocket las' night, and he's lookin' fer 'em. Says the man is Irish fer sure. But you two wouldn' know nuthin' abou' tha', would ya," Mrs. O'Grady said cynically. "Word is they freed a big black buck abou' the same size as the one who showed up 'ere lookin' fer Mr. Daines."

Mary glanced at Newton, who was wondering how the word had gotten out so quickly. "E'en Dublin's underground doan ge' the word ou' tha' quick," he said, shaking his head.

"You'll both be wantin' t' stay clear of O'Shay and 'is boys. They be lookin' real hard at young couples matchin' abou' yer height and size."

"Thanks fer the warnin', Mrs. G.," Newton said. "We'll be owin' y' fer it."

"Doan be thankin' me jes yet, Mr. Daines," Mrs. O'Grady said, firmly folding her arms across her chest. "You be messin' with 'ard men, an' I doan wan' none o' it comin' back on me 'ouse an' livin.' So if ye be wishin' t' continue such foolishness y' best be findin' a different place t' live."

"It was a goo' thing he done, Mrs. G.," Mary said. "Doan be pushin' 'im out fer it."

Mrs. O'Grady smiled a little. "Tha's the way, is it?"

"An' doan be jumpin' to no conclusions neither," Mary said, firmly.

Newton felt the color rise in his cheeks and decided it was time to be moving upstairs to wash up before going out. "I'll nah be bringin' ya any truble, Mrs. G.," he said. "Felix was me only colored friend, an' I doan expect t' be havin' t' break 'im out again. An' with his sister dyin' . . ."

"The woman died?" Mrs. O'Grady asked.

"She was pregnant. She went into labor prematurely, bu' ha' other problems as well. Some kind of disease inside, the doc said. Jes too weak t' make it," Mary said.

"And the child?"

"In goo' hands," Newton said. He did not feel to say more about Lizzy and Rand Hudson or where Felix was. He and Mary had made a pact. No one would be told—not a soul.

"I 'ave' t' be goin'," Newton said. "Doan want t' lose me job, and I need a fresh look at a water basin afore I be goin'." He started from the kitchen, but Mrs. O'Grady caught him by the sleeve. "'Tis right wha' Mary said. 'Twas a goo' thing wha' ya done." She shook her head in the direction of the sink. "There's hot water on th' stove, and ya can wash up 'ere."

Newton knew this was a warm gesture of apology. No one used Mrs. O'Grady's kitchen for washing but her and Mary. While he washed, Mrs. O'Grady fried an egg, and by the time he was ready to go, she had put it on a slice of bread with butter and handed it to him. Mary gave him a cup of coffee as well. "You'll be bringin' the cup back this evenin'," she said. Even with gray circles under her eyes and her soft blond hair in disarray, she looked appealing to Newton.

"Ay, tha' I will," he replied. He looked into her eyes for just a moment. "Tonight then," he said finally, with a bit of a smile. He pushed through the back door and went quickly down the stairs and headed for the docks. Though he hadn't slept but a few moments all night, he felt alive and strong. The breakfast was gone and the coffee too by the time he reached Front Street. The place was packed with drays, wagons, carriages, and a mass of mankind as boundless as any he'd seen in Liverpool. Diving left and right to avoid any direct collisions, he was soon at the damaged steamer belonging to Rand Hudson. The work was progressing well, and they were already working on new walls for the lower hold and upper level. He boarded and approached Hendershott for his daily work assignment. Then he retrieved his tools from the hold and put his shoulder to his assigned task.

Newton did not see Mickey O'Shay standing across the street, watching, dressed in his usual wool pants, gambler-length waistcoat, and high derby hat, deciding just how to handle Mr. Newton Daines.

Mickey had heard Newton's name the first night Newton had come to St. Louis. He had been at Mrs. O'Grady's making sure a gambler knew his debt was due. Daines had gone inside quickly that night, but Mickey had been watching him off and on ever since.

Daines was heavier, and his short, neatly trimmed beard made him look older; besides that, both of them had added nearly eight years since Mickey had been Newton's watchdog in Dublin, but O'Shay knew it was Newton all right. Daines was one of the best boxers Mickey had ever seen but Daines had welched on a contract with Matty O'Brien—and when you welched on one O'Brien, you welched on the whole clan. That made Mickey O'Shay certain that if McKinnon O'Brien knew Daines was in town, he'd want to collect on that contract for his brother, one way or another.

But O'Shay hadn't told Mac O'Brien. Always one to play all the angles, Mickey figured there had to be an angle here—one from which he could profit. He just hadn't figured out what it was—at least not until last night, when Castle Ridges had come to the kitchen.

Of course, Ridges didn't know it was Daines who'd hornswoggled Castle and his brother, Sam. No one but Mickey O'Shay knew it, and even Mickey wasn't entirely sure. Not yet.

He removed his watch from his vest pocket. He had errands he needed to run for O'Brien. Daines would be headed back for the boarding house by sunset, and Mickey would make sure he paid Mary a visit before then. He took one last look at Daines. Ridges was willing to pay a pretty penny for any news about the man and woman who'd cost him a big buck slave as well as a woman with child, and Mickey intended to collect on that offer and maybe get a little out of Daines or Mary as well.

He put his watch back in his pocket and strolled away. He figured by evening he would make a tidy sum. A tidy sum indeed.

* * *

Lizzy sat with Felix in the living area of the small cabin on the back of her property, where Felix was living for the time being. Felix sat near the fire, the child wrapped in a wool blanket and sleeping in his arms. There was love in his eyes for this child, who at least partly assuaged some of his grief over the loss of Susannah. But the child was fussing, hungry; Felix dipped his thick finger in the goat's milk and let the child remove it with a powerful suck. For a few hours such a method would suffice, but what the child really needed was a nursemaid.

They had already buried Susannah. It had been done quietly, during the night. Rand had promised to visit with the Hudsons' attorney on the way to the office this morning so that Felix would not go long without papers, but the child had no such protection—and, legally, the baby belonged to Ridges. But after last night, after watching the baby be born and the mother die, Lizzy determined that if the Ridges boys ever did find this child here and tried to take him, she'd personally make sure that Ridges left with his boots pointing up at the heaven he would never see.

A knock came at the door, and Lizzy opened it cautiously to find Lydijah shivering in the cold, nothing but a shawl around her wide shoulders. She ushered Lydijah in quickly and pointed her to a spot near the fireplace. Lydijah looked at the fussing child as she warmed herself. "He'll be needin' a heavy breast real soon, Mr. Felix."

"Yes'm, I knows," Felix said. His eyes never left the baby's face.

"Dey is a woman who jus' los' a chil' a week ago. She's still holdin' milk an' could take de chil' an' feed him. Name is Jasmina Talking Rock."

"She ain't a slave, is she?" Felix asked, wiping away the tears from his cheeks.

"No, she's a half-breed—part colored, part Indian. A lady o' the evenin', you might say, but she'd feed the boy if'n you took care of her rent an' food. You could move her into dis place for a while. Course, you be havin' to sleep in the barn or somewheres."

Felix nodded while standing up to try to comfort the crying child, rocking him back and forth. "If y'all give me da address, I'll see dis woman you speak of. Miss Lizzy, I hate to inconvenience you, but I'd 'preciate a wagon an' yo' company. I doan know nuthin' about such things, an' this city scares me some without papers an' all."

Lizzy—still dressed in her riding clothes and her hair in a single wide braid down her neck and back—nodded, stood, and retrieved her heavy wool waistcoat while asking Lydijah to have their carriage brought to the house. Her ankle did not hurt much this morning. Just a light throb, and Lizzy was grateful. Lydijah pulled her shawl over her shoulders, told Lizzy the woman's address, and left immediately. Lizzy heard her yell to Mose to have the carriage brought up "this minute," and Mose hollered at Elliot to get moving. Since the carriages were harnessed up first thing each morning, she knew it would not take long.

Felix seemed a bit mystified about how exactly he should wrap the baby in the warm blanket, so Lizzy took the child and laid him on the small divan before wrapping him up. She handed the boy back to Felix, and the three of them went outside as the carriage pulled up, Elliot at the reins. Lizzy opened the door but Felix seemed a bit reluctant to step in, and she had to reassure him it was quite all right.

The carriage went quickly into St. Louis and through the streets before depositing them in front of a boardinghouse that was much worse for wear and tear than most of those Lizzy had seen in the city. She didn't hesitate but quickly led Felix inside, where she inquired after the woman they sought. They were told the room number and climbed the creaking stairs to the second floor, where Lizzy found the correct door and knocked. They heard movement inside then a woman's gruff voice telling them to go away.

Felix rocked the baby as the child grew more and more restless. Suddenly the baby's whimper escalated to a cry, and the woman spoke again, her voice nearer the door. "What you want?"

"I have a chil' that needs a mama's breast," Felix said. "If you is Jasmina Talking Rock, we hopes yo' will give us the help we be lookin' fo' befo' this young'un starves to death."

The lock turned in the door, and the woman's head appeared in the opening. She had large, round eyes and an equally round face, with a wide, flat nose and heavy lips. Her hair was long, parted down the middle, and spoke of her Cherokee background. Her skin was dark, though not black, and Lizzy thought her to be quite a handsome woman. Her longing eyes went to the blankets held by Felix, but she checked herself, then opened the door and let them in. The place was dark, a shambles, and smelled of smoke mingled with heavy body odor and even waste, probably from the chamber pot sitting in the corner.

A rocking chair sat in another corner with a baby blanket across its back. The woman told Felix to close the door as she went to the edge of the bed and picked up a cigarette.

"Boy or girl?" she asked. The baby continued to cry, his hands and feet jerking the blanket about. Felix pulled it back to reveal the face, and the woman stood to get a look. She had to rise on tiptoes to do so.

"Boy," Felix said. The baby cried louder.

Jasmina gave Lizzy the once-over. "What's she doin' with the likes a you?" she asked.

"She's a friend. Helped me an' dis baby's momma to hide from Sam Ridges's demons. She's a good woman, so you be careful what yo' say."

Jasmina looked ruffled but let it go, returning her gaze to the child. "How old?" she asked, inhaling more smoke.

"A few hours," Felix answered.

"Taking care of a chil' ain't no small thing. I won't be able to work."

"While the child needs your care, you can have a private house on our property," Lizzy said.

"I'll be providin' the food and such," Felix said.

"If you's an escaped slave, how is you gonna work?" Jasmina challenged.

"I is a freedman. Ridges locked me up cuz I tried to free my sister."

"Feedin' me an takin' care a' my needs tain't no small order. I eat good, and I like nice things," she said.

"Other than a room and goo' food, I got nothin' but the baby to give yo'," Felix said honestly.

Jasmina kept smoking, and the haze in the room thickened.

"That cigarette ain't good for the baby. If'n you feeds him, it'll sour your milk, an' how you can breathe with that infernal smog is beyond me."

She harrumphed. "Sour milk better than no milk."

"Not by much," Felix said firmly. "You feed dis baby, you quit smokin', simple as that."

"'Scuse me for saying so, but seein's how you is a man, it don't seem like you got the proper equipment to argue the point," she said indignantly.

"Dey is other women in this city, and I'll be lookin' for one who is willin' to care more about the baby than dat weed you be smokin'," Felix said firmly. He was wrapping the baby back up and rocking back and forth, trying to settle the child down at the same time. Lizzy could see the worry and sweat on his brow. He was bluffing, but rightly so, and though Lizzy wanted to say something, she decided to let Felix handle the situation.

Jasmina took one last drag on the cigarette and snuffed it out in a cup of cold coffee sitting on a table. "Give me the chil' then," she said stiffly, moving to the rocking chair. She planted her tall, ample frame in it and extended her arms for the baby.

"Soon as you give dat tobacco and them papers to Miss Lizzy. Tain't gonna be no more smoke roun' the child," Felix said. "I seen what it does on the plantation. Makes babies sick with the cough, and when they gets bad 'nuf some of 'em even dies."

Jasmina cursed him, removed the bag of tobacco and papers from her dress pocket, and slapped them into Lizzy's outstretched hand. "Is this darky always sech a know-it-all?"

"He's a fine man who reads and writes and was smart enough to free himself from the scourge of slavery," Lizzy said. "You would be smart to heed him, Miss Talking Rock." Lizzy had sat up most of the night with

Newton, Mary, and Felix and had been humbled by all their stories. The one Felix told was no exception. For him to have done what he did with his life when every white man he had known had tried to use him for his considerable size and strength was to be admired.

Jasmina eyed Felix and waved her hands impatiently for the child. Felix handed the baby to her, and she removed the outer blanket as he screamed for feeding.

"Now you folks can sit here and ogle m' breast while I be feedin' this chil', or you can go on out in the hall and be waitin' for me there. Make no mind to me, but I accept your offer, mister, and I'll be needin' you to stick around long enough fo' me to gather m' things so I can git out of this hole an' find a better." She was about to open her blouse when Lizzy turned to the door and Felix followed. "What be your name, darky?" she asked.

"Felix. Felix Coulon."

"Fine enough," she said. "I'm called lots a things 'round this part of town, but I expect you to call me Jasmina. Now you be waitin' in the hall."

Felix closed the door behind them, and they both lay their backs and their heads against the wall. Felix closed his eyes as he caught his breath. "Now dat is a nasty-tempered woman," he said.

Lizzy nodded and chuckled at the same time. "You bluffed her good, Felix," she said.

"Cain't bluff nobody who don't want to be bluffed. She's as lonely as that chil', and I 'spect they'll be gettin' 'long real well. It's me that'll have m' hands full."

Lizzy looked at him. "She isn't your wife, Felix. You needn't give more than what you promised."

"That don't mean she won't be constantly askin'," Felix said. "A woman like that tire out a man real quick-like with all her wantin' and talkin'."

They laughed lightly, then waited. Half an hour later, Jasmina came out with the baby cradled in one arm and a small bag under the other. It obviously contained everything she owned. Lizzy felt small in the presence of Jasmina and Felix, who were both taller than her by a good four inches—and she was not short by the standard of the day.

Jasmina scowled at them both as she walked past. "What are you waitin' for? An' you best know we need to be stoppin' at a market. I needs good food to produce good milk."

Lizzy glanced at Felix just in time to see him roll his eyes.

Chapter 16

NEWTON SAW THE CARRIAGE PULL up about an hour before noon. When Rand Hudson got out and came aboard, he visited with Hendershott for only a moment before he approached Newton.

"Good morning," Rand said with a friendly smile. He was dressed in his usual suit, with a warm black wool coat against the morning chill.

"Mr. Hoodsun," Newton responded. "I di' nah ge' t' thank ya for wha' ya done for Felix an'—"

Rand waved a hand in front of him dismissively then cleared his throat. "Newton, if you are willing, I have some work aboard another of my steamers that I would like you to consider. It will take a good deal of work and must begin as soon as the ship arrives. I'll pay you top wages."

Newton saw that Hudson did not care for the praise and admired him for it. At the same time, he felt to give it. He put down the half-burned beam he was carrying and faced Rand.

"I'll be takin' whatever work ye 'ave for me, but I be needin' t' thank ya, so if y' doan mind I be givin' it once more, an' you'll be listenin'," he said.

Rand smiled. "I do not care for words of thanks, Mr. Daines; they come a dozen for a penny. The work I have for you will tell me where your heart is. Are you willing?"

Newton noted that Hudson was about his same height and weight and had a piercing look to his dark eyes that would give a man pause about standing up to him. But Newton had seen such looks before and had no qualms about holding fast to his own position when he felt strongly about it. This time, however, he decided to leave things as they were. If he could show his thanks with actions, he was all for it.

"Then I be more than willin'," Newton said. "Where do I fin' yer other steamer?"

"She'll be in dock tomorrow around noon. She's called *The Constitution* and will be in the slip about halfway down the docks, just down from our offices," Rand said. He turned to walk away, then turned back. "I will tell Hendershott to let you go in time to meet me." He left the ship, and Newton went back to work, counting his good fortune.

* * *

Though exhausted as he neared the back door of Mrs. O'Grady's, the smell of fresh bread coming through a partially opened window revived Newton. Opening the door and entering the kitchen to the hope of a good dinner he now had hard coin to pay for, he was disappointed to find himself facing the barrel of a gun. Mary McConnell stood in a corner, both anger and fear in her eyes. A man held her by the neck, applying pressure upward and against her throat. Newton's first reaction was to launch himself through the gunman and at Mary's captor, but the barrel of the gun was pushed firmly into his solar plexis as a warning. Newton forced himself to stay still.

O'Shay stood to the left, drinking a cup of coffee. Mrs. O'Grady was at his side, fear in her wide eyes. O'Shay had a pistol in his free hand, which was pointed at Mrs. O'Grady's side.

"Well, well, look who we have here. How aire ye, Newton Daines?"

"O'Shay. I see ya bee' doin' wha' y' love most."

"Jes havin' a little talk with your accomplice, tha's all."

Newton suddenly realized that this visit involved more than his welching on the contract with Matty O'Brien of Dublin. He quickly looked at Mary and could see in her eyes that she had said nothing about freeing Felix. "Mary had nothin' to do with me runnin' from Matty O'Brien, and you know it," Newton said, calling O'Shay's bluff.

"Tha's the way of it, then. The two of you holdin' together real tight-like, hopin' I got no proof." He jammed the weapon into Mrs. O'Grady's ribs. "Maybe the sudden demise of Mrs. O.'s liver will convince ya both t' be more honest with me."

O'Shay did not expect the result of his threat. A stocky and powerful Mrs. O'Grady grabbed the gun and pushed it aside with such quickness and strength that O'Shay's jaw dropped. "I been puttin' up wi' yer beatin' up on uthers long enough, Mickey O'Shay, and it's gonna be stoppin' right here and now." She threw the gun across the room with such force it all but stuck in the plaster wall before it hit the floor. "I tol' y' before, Mary and Daines 'ere had nuthin' t' do with wha' ye say took place las' night.

They was 'ere, both of 'em. Now you go tell McKinnon O'Brien wha' I said, or I'll be tellin' 'im myself."

O'Shay's gun-wielding friend, unsure of how to react, kept his rifle on Newton, and the other man tightened his grip on Mary from behind. O'Shay's red face could have forced steam out of his ears. He was cornered, had lost his bluff, and was livid over it. A stocky man himself, he grabbed Mrs. O'Grady by the throat and pushed upward hard, as if to break her neck immediately. Then he let go and turned away, thinking better of it. Mrs. O'Grady had a lot of good friends, and they were tough ones as well. Changing tactics, he drew close to Newton and gave him a hard stare. O'Shay was an inch or two shorter than Newton but his whiskey breath nearly knocked Newton over. It was all he could do to stand firm and speak his mind. "Yer man there ought to be lettin' go o' Mary. As I tol' ya, she ain't got nuthin' t' do with me and wha' happened in Dublin."

"She's been a bit rude of late," O'Shay said. "Needs a lesson or two in manners." He nodded at the man holding Mary, who flashed an evil grin and turned Mary around in his arms to face him. It was his mistake, and Mary, though smaller, took advantage, raising a knee hard in his groin and forcing him to release her. He was bent over in anguish as she grabbed a butcher knife from the cabinet and extended it between them.

"I'll cut out yer gizzard if y' so much as move t' me," she said to the man.

"Now, Mary, tha' be a mite unfriendly," O'Shay said menacingly.

Mary threw back her mussed, long blond hair. "An' I'll be doin' worse to you, Mickey O'Shay, if'n y' ever come close to me again."

O'Shay glared at her with cold eyes. "I'll be comin' fer ya later, lass, mark me words." He looked at Newton. "Fer now, O'Brien will be wantin' to see Mr. Daines." He looked over at the man holding the gun and nodded toward the door. "Take 'im out."

The group made their way onto O'Fallon Street, where onlookers stopped their conversations to note that Newton was being guided up the street at the point of a gun. A curious majority chose to tag along, and five minutes later there was a good following.

To the disappointment of the crowd, Newton was shoved out of sight through the saloon's doors then guided to the back of the room, where O'Brien sat at a table with a few friends. Among them was a large, solid man Newton recognized as Mack Kernlin, a boxer purported to never have been beaten by anyone. Like O'Shay, Kernlin had done collections for O'Brien until he became too valuable as a boxer. O'Brien smiled when he saw them coming and sat back, a large mug of beer in his right hand.

"Mister O'Brien, this be Newton Daines from Ireland. He's a friend o' yer brother's." O'Shay smiled then looked at the man next to O'Brien. "Mr. Ridges, take a goo' look as well. I be thinkin' this be the man who stole yer darkies."

The group went silent as Castle Ridges stood and stepped closer before taking a hard look at Newton. Newton was not certain but thought that this might be the man who had been driving the wagon. His heart quickened its pace, and he struggled to keep his face neutral.

"Maybe. Same height, same weight . . ." Ridges walked around Newton, who figured he was about to be done in anyway so he might as well take the offensive.

"And you be . . . ?" Newton asked.

"Ridges. Castle Ridges."

"Well now, Mr. Ridges, wha' is it I is supposed t' 'ave done?"

"Hep'd slaves to escape."

Newton shrugged. "Being just off the boa' from Dublin an' come t' America t' ge' me freedom, it seems helpin' uthers do th' same woul' be an honorable thing t' be doin'."

"Well it ain't," Ridges growled, a thick wad of chaw bulging his right cheek. He looked for a place to spit but saw no official one and deposited his crud near Newton's feet. "Slaves is property, and they cost us good money."

Newton glanced at his splattered shoes but decided to ignore it. "How much?" Newton asked.

The question seemed to catch Ridges off guard, and he had to think about it a minute. "Two, maybe three thousand dollars."

Newton whistled. "Must a been a bunch of 'em. Tha's a lot o' muny."

"Just two, a man and a pregnant woman."

"So two fine folks worth a thousand each?"

"Ain't nothin' *fine* about 'em. Everybody knows darkies ain't *fine*, and the man was worth at least two thousand."

Newton's eyes went cold and hard. "An' if he was a freedman, how much was he worth?"

Ridges blinked again as the room went silent.

"How much, Mr. Ridges? How much for a freedman, 'ose papers ya burned so's ya cou' sell 'im again?"

"He weren't no freed—"

"'Is name is Felix Coulon. 'E *is* a freedman, and 'as me and a couple dozen uthers as 'is witnesses to prove it."

"You!"

"Tha's right, Mr. Ridges, it was me, and I'd be doin' it again. If we let the likes a ye imprison freedmen an' resell 'em, pretty soon ya be lookin' at us fer yer pens."

"You never said he was a freedman," O'Brien said, looking hard at Ridges.

Newton saw beads of sweat break out on Ridges's forehead as he turned to face O'Brien. "He's lyin,' Mac. 'Sides, he helped that woman, and she weren't free."

He turned back to Newton with a triumphant grin.

"No, she was sick, near dyin'. Did jus' that this mornin', thanks t' the beatin' y' gave 'er jus' before I 'elped 'er escape with 'er brother. Baby died too, thanks t' you." This last part was, of course, a lie, but Newton didn't figure the good Lord would mind if it protected the child.

Ridges's face hardened. "Then you owe us a thousand dollars."

"Then yer paid," Newton said.

Ridges fumed. "I ain't seen no—"

"Felix, the freedman, bought 'is sister at yer auction. Yer bruther took a thousand dollars from 'im as soon as the auction was dun. Plenty o' witnesses to prove it. But when the witnesses left with their own merchandise, y' beat 'im good, stole 'is papers and 'is muny, an' tried t' sell 'im again. Yer paid, Mr. Ridges, an' count yerself lucky I doan have y' arrested fer doin' what y' done."

"You can't prove none of this," Castle said, his dark eyes cold and threatening.

"I can an' I will if ya push it. An' I'll see it dun in a court o' law, an' you 'ill end up in jail fer it right along wi' yer bruther an' the rest o' them thugs."

Ridges looked around him, searching for a friendly face. He found none and turned back to Newton. "You ain't heard the last a' this."

Newton glared back. "If I hear o' it again, I'll be findin' the first bobbie on the block and havin' ya thrown behind bars t' let the coppers figure it out. I doan think you'll be likin' the results."

Fuming, Ridges turned and thrust himself through the crowd that had trickled inside and gathered between them and the door. He was soon in the street.

"You've made an enemy, Mr. Daines," O'Brien said.

"Jes one?" Newton replied.

O'Brien smiled. "Castle is a mean man, but he don't 'old a candle to 'is bruther, Sam. He'll be lookin' to 'ave 'is revenge." He sat back, looking at O'Shay. "Now maybe ya will be explainin' why ya hauled Mr. Daines inta me presence."

"He was a fighter under contract to yer bruther and welched on it. Matty be lookin' fer 'im," O'Shay said with a confident smile.

"Well then, tha's anuther matter, isn't it, Mr. Daines." O'Brien gave Newton the once-over. "Ya doan look like much t' me. Me bruther must be out o' 'is mind to be wastin' 'is time lookin' fer one as puny as you."

The group laughed as if on cue.

"I ain't nuthin' to yer brother," Newton said. "He made plenty off me, an' tha's sure enough. Now if'n ya doan mind, I'll be abou' gettin' back to Mrs. O'Grady's." He turned to go, but O'Shay put a stiff arm against his shoulder. Newton moved so quickly to twist it behind O'Shay's back that the man hardly knew what hit him. Newton shoved him away hard, and he hit the wall with a head-spinning blow. O'Shay turned back with a glare in his eye and a gun in his hand.

"Put it away, Mickey," O'Brien said with a cold tone. O'Shay reluctantly shoved the pistol in his belt again. "Sit down, Mr. Daines," O'Brien continued. "Ya won't be goin' nowhere 'til we talk abou' wha' ya owe me bruther an' how you'll be payin' 'im."

Newton turned back as Kernlin grabbed a chair and pulled it back for Newton to sit in. "I'd be pleased t' stan'. Mr. Ugly there is a wee bi' too close t' tha' chair fer me to be likin' it much."

O'Brien laughed as Kernlin's face flushed. Kernlin didn't move, but Newton knew that all it would take was for O'Brien to unhook the leash.

"If yer bruther thinks I owe 'im muny, he's welcome t' come t' America t' visit wi' me abou' it."

O'Brien stood so quickly that his chair flew backward, banging onto the floor. The entire saloon went as quiet as a church during prayer.

"You'll be talkin' t' *me*, an' you'll be doin' it now," O'Brien said with steel in his tone. "You an' I might agree abou' wha' Ridges done, bu' this is anuther matter an' it'll be settled 'ere an' now."

Newton could see he wasn't getting out of this easily, and only one last way occurred to him. He shuddered at its prospects but he figured it gave him a fighting chance—whereas he had no chance at all at the moment. Newton felt bile churning in his stomach, but he controlled it with a smile. "How much does Mister Kernlin there ge' fer a match between 'im an' a real boxer?"

"Enough to keep 'im in plenty of whiskey and women in the finest room in this place," O'Brien said with pride.

"My, a startlin' amount when ya consider the value o' a room in a dump like this un."

O'Brien bit hard on his cigar, nearly cutting through it.

"I'll take 'im in the ring. If I win, ya consider any debt owed yer bruther paid in full, an' ya call yer dogs off." He looked at O'Shay. "Him in particular. He doan come near me, and 'e stays clear o' Mary McConnell as well."

O'Brien smiled. "Yer concern fer Mary is touchin'."

"I doan like a beater like O'Shay threatenin' any woman with a thrashin', an' O'Shay jus di' as much t' Mary. But mostly I jus' be protectin' yer interests. Mary'll kill 'im if 'e comes round again, an' seeins 'ow he's yer bruther-in-law, I figured ye'd be wantin' t' protect yer sister's husband." Newton looked thoughtful. "Then again, maybe ya be wishin t' get rid o' 'im anyway. Looks like a wife beater t' me."

There were laughs in the audience, but O'Brien didn't smile and O'Shay turned purple with rage. "An' if Kernlin whips ya? Seems like whereas ya be askin' a lot, a lot should be given if ya be losin'."

"If 'e beats me by some bit o' the Irish luck, I'll stay an' keep fightin' fer ya 'til me debt to yer bruther is paid."

O'Brien grinned. "Kernlin will make mincemeat o' ya."

"Well then, ya 'ave nuthin' t' lose, do ya? But if I win an' ya welch on our deal, yer Irish honor will be forfeit as well as me services. Every man 'ere knows the deal an' will be holdin' ya to it."

"Me honor will be intact," O'Brien said. "Kernlin will see t' tha'."

"Then we 'ave a deal," Newton said.

"We do, an' the ring is this 'ere room. Ya 'ave but fi'e minutes before me man busts ya inta small pieces."

Newton stepped back. "Then I'll be needin' a towel an' a stiff drink t' warm up me muscles." He turned back to the bar, where the barkeeper poured him a whiskey and placed a greasy towel on the bar. Newton took note of Mary and Mrs. O'Grady near the door and signaled for them to come closer. They began shoving their way through as O'Brien spoke.

"Gentlemen," O'Brien said, "I'll be gi'en four t' one odds against Mr. Daines. If there be any takers . . ." The place erupted into bedlam as the two women drew close to speak to Newton.

"Mary, Mrs. O'Grady, you fine lasses should nah be 'ere."

"We heard yer argument with Ridges. Are ya as goo' with yer fists as ye are with yer mouth?" Mary asked.

"Better." He smiled.

"Then I'll be placin' a twenty-dollar gold piece on ya," Mrs. O'Grady said. She pushed through the crowd to make her bet.

"Are ya sure abou' this?" Mary asked softly "Kernlin hasn't lost in . . ."

"Kernlin's got 'is weakness, and I'll be after it." Newton smiled. "Then I'll be greetin' ya outside for a goo' pot o' yer stew," he added. "Now, I doan want ya standin' 'ere, so be off wi' ya." He bowed at the waist, and Mary turned and pushed through the jostling crowd as Newton wiped his face with the towel then began stretching and cracking his knuckles. He had left Dublin to get away from fights, from having his brains turned to mush, and now here he was again, fighting—this time to save his life. He only hoped his face could stand one more beating. Confident as he may have sounded to Mary, Kernlin was tough and had killed men with his fists. The end for Newton Daines might not be pretty.

Kernlin had removed his shirt and was downing a second whiskey when O'Brien told the crowd to back up and make a circle. Newton's whiskey went untouched. He knew he would need it later.

Chapter 17

NEWTON STEPPED TO THE TOE line, and the two boxers hit one another firmly on the fists to signal the start of the fight. Kernlin followed with a quick hard swing; Newton ducked under it, swept quickly behind the man, and punched him hard in the kidneys. Kernlin was knocked forward several feet and turned around, rubbing his back, grimacing in a forced smile. The crowd egged them on while O'Brien sneered at his boxer and nodded his head hard toward Newton, urging him to get on with it.

Kernlin came at him—he was quick for a man his size—and poked Newton in the face twice before Newton could dance away. He felt blood trickle from his nose and sour his mouth. Stepping back, Newton spat, even though he knew Kernlin would use the diversion as an opportunity to come at him again. As he did, Newton ducked and slammed a fist up into Kernlin's ribs just below the heart, stepped back, and struck his left fist into Kernlin's jaw, drawing blood with a cut to his chin.

Kernlin, already somewhat of a blur to Newton, swung from hard right and pasted a steely fist into the left side of Newton's face, stunning him. He stumbled back, and Kernlin took advantage of the moment. He hit Newton three times in the stomach, driving him into the bar and holding him there to pummel at his gut again and again. Newton felt the pain of each blow, the loss of air, but he somehow managed to free himself enough to get behind Kernlin, hit him once in each kidney, and then back away, shaking his head to diffuse the fog blurring his vision.

They danced in a circle, careful, slow, deliberate, each looking for an in. Kernlin finally thought he saw one and swung hard. Newton sensed it coming and dodged once more, cuffing Kernlin with a stunning blow to his lower ribs, feeling one snap as he did. Kernlin groaned with pain but grabbed Newton's head under his arm and held him tight. Knowing that he must get free before Kernlin beat up his kidneys, Newton slammed a knee into Kernlin's thigh and groin and pushed hard with his hands. Kernlin was rammed backward against the crowd; they immediately shoved him back toward Newton with a loud cry of "Get 'im!"

Newton stared ahead as Kernlin came at him, bent over for a powerful tackle. Stepping to one side, Newton drove a fist into the back of Kernlin's neck. He went down hard, and Newton danced away. He saw O'Brien's fury as his boxer struggled to get up, then felt the hush of the stunned crowd as they realized Kernlin was actually down and slow to recover.

"Stay put," Newton said as Kernlin continued to try to get to his feet.

Two men stepped from the crowd and helped the boxer up. He jerked his neck left and right and grinned hard at Newton before stepping onto the balls of his feet and coming at him again.

Newton saw the right-hand haymaker but was not ready for the left that caught him hard in the jaw and jerked his head backward. The blow hit him with such force that his feet left the floor, and he found himself looking up at the ceiling in a daze. He perceived the boot coming at his ribs with no time to roll away. Instead he grabbed the foot with both hands, turned it hard to the right, and thrust it upward. Kernlin flew off balance and fell into the crowd again, giving Newton enough time to get up and shake his head free of cobwebs. He grabbed the whiskey and dumped it on his wounds, the sting driving the cobwebs out and giving him new life.

"Y' 'ave more kick in yer fist than I 'ave felt fer a while," Newton said.

Kernlin grinned. "An' when did ye feel such a kick?"

"When a gent's 'orse knocked me 'cross 'is barn," Newton said.

Kernlin laughed lightly, charged hard, and tried the same tactic. This time Newton was ready. He planted himself firmly and hit Kernlin in the jaw and throat with all the strength of both his upper and lower body. Kernlin's head snapped back, and he landed on his back like a sack of flour dropped from the second floor balcony. He didn't move.

The crowd went quiet, waiting, tense with expectation. Finally someone knelt down and checked him for a pulse. "He's alive, but he ain't gettin' up real soon," came the verdict.

Newton turned toward O'Brien, who was chewing hard on his cigar, his eyes cold and gray.

"Yer a tough soul, an' a goo' fighter. I'll be offerin' ya a hundred dollars a munth t' stay an' fight all comers," O'Brien said.

Mumbled comments rippled throughout the room.

"I thank y' fer the offer, bu' I 'ave other plans," Newton said.

Newton noticed O'Shay a few feet away, his face red with frustration. He had a gun in his belt; his hand was on the butt, and his fingers nervously fondled it as if trying to make a decision.

"Mr. O'Shay seems to 'ave a nervous trigger finger attached to tha' there gun," Newton said.

O'Brien gave O'Shay a withering look; O'Shay busted through the crowd and left the saloon.

"You be costin' me a pretty penny this night," O'Brien said.

"Did ya think yer bruther wanted me back because I was a loser?" Newton asked.

O'Brien smiled. "I think not."

"Is the debt t' yer bruther paid, then?" Newton said.

Several of O'Brien's men moved out of the crowd and around Newton. "I think you'll be takin' me offer," O'Brien said.

Newton was about to say something when a fancy-clothed, tall, and tough-looking stranger stepped forward. "I be beggin' yer pardon, Mr. O'Brien, but Mr. Daines here, he won fair an' square, and we'd be a mite upset if'n y' welched on 'im, 'ay boys?"

O'Brien eyed the man with cold eyes. "Yer off your territory, Malone. Ya best be gittin' back t' it."

"Me territory, is it?" Five other gents stepped forward and stood behind Mr. Malone. "Doan test me mettle, Mr. O'Brien, or this fine place will be catchin' fire of a sudden, an' if yer forgetful of who says wha' around Irish town, my boys here will be gla' t' remind ya."

Newton was both confused and amazed to learn that McKinnon O'Brien was not the last tier of power in the Kerry Patch.

"No reminder needed, a' present, but the time 'ill come," said O'Brien.

"Yes, I am sure of tha', but it isn't yet is it?" Malone said with a hard smile.

O'Brien looked at Newton. "The debt is paid, but the offer will remain open."

"I'll not be takin' it, but I appreciate yer confidence." He looked at Malone. "Ya heard th' deal. Kin I count on Mr. O'Brien keepin' O'Shay in check?"

"Ya can," Malone said. "O'Brien will see t' it. We doan crowd our women-folk, do we, Mr. O'Brien."

"Mary kin take care o' 'erself, but O'Shay is warned," O'Brien grumbled.

Newton nodded. Malone raised a hand. "Thanks t' Mr. Daines here and a fine bet placed by meself, the drinks are on me, but O'Brien is payin'." He turned to the man he spoke of and put an arm around his shoulder. "Ya owe me two hundred dollars, Mac, but yer payin' fer the drinks will bring us even, and I'll not be expressin' no hard feelin's fer yer gettin' uppity."

O'Brien nodded, then spoke to the crowd. "One fer each—and boys, if yer a winner, get yer pay from the barkeep and the rest a ya start drinkin.' I lost a lot o' muny tonight."

The place erupted in relieved but raucous laughter, and the pianist began beating the keys again.

Newton started for the door with Mr. Malone and his other friends around him. Several men who had been lucky enough to bet on the underdog reached out and clapped Newton on the back. Another grabbed him by the shoulder and turned him around. It was a now-conscious Kernlin. "Good fight, but I'll do better in a rematch."

"Won't be a rematch, Kernlin. I got lucky an' doan intend to press it." He extended his hand, and Kernlin shook it. Newton followed Malone and the others into the street, where Mary and Mrs. O'Grady waited. Newton took his shirt from Mary, who seemed genuinely pleased and relieved to see him. Then he put on his jacket.

"Mary, Mrs. O., how ya been?" Malone said with a pleasant smile.

"Goo' as grass in springtime, Brendan," Mrs. O'Grady said.

"Brendan, glad ya were around t' save this 'un," Mary said.

"Nah t' worry, jus' in the neighborhood t' do recruitin'," Malone said.

"Recruitin'?" Newton asked.

"War is comin', lad, and if yer as interested in fightin' fer coloreds as I heard in there, you'd be welcome," Malone said.

"I'll gi' i' some thought," Newton said sincerely.

Malone nodded then eyed both Newton and Mary. "Ya both be watchin' yer backs. I can control O'Brien, at least most o' the time, bu' the Ridges boys is anuther matter." He tipped his hat. "Mary, beautiful as ever. You too, Mrs. O'Grady." With that, he and his men walked off up the street.

"And who woul' tha' be?" Newton asked.

"Ya 'eard 'is name. Good as the Irish come. Lives up on tha' bench a few miles south o' Mr. Hoodsun. They're friends, I 'ear," Mary said. "He doan come down 'ere often, 'cept to keep Mr. O'Brien from ruinin' the place. He's got power, Mr. Daines, but he uses it right."

Mrs. O'Grady tossed Newton a coin: a twenty-dollar gold piece. "Tripled me money. Ya deserve a part."

Newton felt the soreness in his face as he tried to smile. It would be swollen before morning.

"An' Brendan be right as rain," Mrs. O'Grady said. "'Twould be well t' be watchin' out fer Ridges, bu' doan be forgettin' O'Shay neither. O'Brien might say he'll keep 'im in chains, but O'Shay is a hateful man tha' lets perceived wrongs germinate inta full-flowered violence. He'll be thinkin' tha' even a thrashin' from O'Brien will be worth killin' ya."

"I'll be watchin' out fer 'em both," Newton said.

"I have fresh bread in the kitchen," Mrs. O'Grady said, "and ya need a little tendin' to after Kernlin. He's a hard-fisted man 'imself."

Newton gingerly touched his bruised face. "Tha' he is."

As they walked down the middle of the street, several men approached out of the crowd to congratulate Newton on his win. Most others sent either curious or admiring glances his way, and Newton was relieved that no one seemed filled with enough animosity to give him any trouble. When they arrived at the house, they found a large body of men waiting for them at the steps. Newton grew cautious, ready. One of the men stepped forward.

"Mr. Daines, we be thankin' ya fer settin' O'Brien back a step 'er two. If ya need sum backin' sum time, ya be lettin' us know."

Newton recognized the man as William Benton, an American-born citizen who worked at a gambling joint in a kitchen down the street. He was a stocky bruiser who had tossed more than one of his roommates out of his establishment without breathing heavy. As Newton looked around the crowd of maybe fifty men, he realized that all of them were taking his side, and it sobered him. He'd made a few friends tonight.

He extended his hand to Benton, who took it; they shook hands. Then he looked at the others. "Yer a fine lot a gentlemen, and I'll be thankin' ya fer yer confidence." He removed from his pocket the twenty-dollar gold piece Mrs. O'Grady had just given him and tossed it to Benton. "Mr. Benton, I'd appreciate it if you'd see tha' gold piece is spent givin' me new friends a drink o' yer finest sarsaparilla. As fer me, 'tis a bath an' bed tha' I'll be askin' for, if ya doan mind."

The men erupted in laughter at the kind of drink they'd be getting then gathered round to shake Newton's hand before walking down the street toward Benton's gambling hall.

"Sarsaparilla." Mary smiled. "Fine drink tha'," she said in a mocking tone. "Tryin' t' kill yer new friends, are ya?"

Newton chuckled. "Gave up the drink meself. Can't be encouragin' such a thing if'n I know wha' it does t' the heart and soul of goo' men, now can I?"

"No, I doan suppose, but sarsaparilla? One 'tis bad as the other from my view."

Mary and Newton went through the front door, where several men sat in the small parlor talking. One was rather animated, apparently demonstrating Newton's skills against Kernlin. Glad they were occupied, Newton followed Mary and Mrs. O'Grady to the kitchen, where he sat down and allowed Mary to attend to his wounds while Mrs. O'Grady fixed something to eat.

"You made some powerful enemies tonight, Mr. Daines," Mary said.

"Aye, but some friends as well, an' it seems t' me I 'ad little choice but ta do wha' I done. Felix was a free man, an' the likes of Mr. Ridges 'as no right to take tha' away from 'im."

Mary shook her head lightly, worry in her eyes. "I told you when you first come tha' e'en the Irish frowns on freein' more blacks."

"But they hate e'en worse men like Ridges takin' way freedoms bought an' paid for. Brings fear o' who migh' be next. I jes reminded 'em of it, tha's all."

"Still, you'll be watchin' yer back," Mary said with genuine concern.

"Aye, and you'll be a mite cautious yerself."

"I will."

"Then we'll both be livin' long and happy lives," Newton said. "An' how are things with the gambler, Mary McConnell?"

She glanced down at him. "Mrs. O'Grady booted him out today, an' I be glad of it. He was gettin' a might possessive."

"Glad to hear he's gone, an' if ya doan mind I'll be callin' on ya," Newton said.

Mary stopped working on his cuts, clearly a bit shocked, and Mrs. O'Grady simply grinned.

"'Bout time is wha' I'd say," Mrs. O'Grady mumbled pleasantly.

At last Mary seemed to find some words and stood back to speak them. "I don't mind yer callin', Mr. Daines, long as ya understand there'll be some ground rules for courtin' a fine lady like meself."

"I'll be behavin', if tha's wha' y' mean," Newton said. "Yer a fine an' pretty lass, an' I would be treatin' ya as such."

Mary bit her lip against a tear that was trying to force itself from the corner of her eye. She had admitted to herself that she had feelings for Newton days ago, but they had grown a good deal over the last twenty-four hours. He was an honest and good man, a better man than she had thought she could ever hope to have calling on her. The emotion caught hold of her heart, but she concentrated on cleaning his face to avoid embarrassing herself in the moment. It was not easy, and she was sure it showed in the quiver of her lip and her wet eyes as her gaze lingered on him.

Mrs. O'Grady came to the rescue of them both by putting food on the table. Mary gingerly took Newton's hand and carefully cleaned the blood and torn skin from his knuckles before rubbing salve into them. She found herself holding onto them longer than she felt she should and quickly turned to put away the salve, catching her breath and wresting control of her emotions.

"Thank y', Mary McConnell," Newton said genuinely, but his curiosity was piqued by the sudden change in her demeanor. Mrs. O'Grady gave him a look and dismissed herself. Newton slid his chair up to the table, took a spoon in his hand, and lifted it, then suddenly realized that Mary was wiping away tears. He stood, a bit unsure of what his next move should be. Finally he took her hand and turned her around. She peered at the floor, her lip quivering. Putting his finger under her soft and pretty chin, he lifted it as he spoke.

"Now wha' these tears be for, Miss McConnell? Will it pain y' tha' much to—"

She lifted herself on her toes and gave Newton a tender kiss that shot a welcome shiver to the very center of his heart. His arms reacted in an embrace that brought her even closer. He hoped she would not move away, hoped he would not offend her by his inept ability at such things, and hoped that this was real and not his sometimes unruly imagination. Mary placed her head on his chest, returning the embrace with her warmth and softness. It was a long moment before she could speak.

"Do ya mind if I fall in love wi' ya, Newton Daines," she said softly.

Newton responded by pulling her even tighter, her sweet intoxication holding him there for the longest of embraces. Surely his world could not get any better.

Chapter 18

SAM SPIT A GLOB AT the stove; it sizzled and filled the room with a hot stink. "He did *what?*" The words were hissed more than spoken, and Sam Ridges stiffened in his chair then stood, staring coldly across the table at his brother.

"He told 'em all, Sam. T'weren't nothin' I could do once O'Brien—"

The back of Sam's hand moved so fast that Castle had no ability to get out of its way; it hit with such fury that Castle staggered back, tasting blood in his mouth. He spat the taste at the floor, his eyes fixed on his feet, afraid to look up.

Sam's fists were doubled up tight, the anger turning his body to hard muscle. He had always had a sharp, beastly temper, and Castle had felt its fury too many times to count. Now he braced himself for it to strike again.

But Sam did not strike; instead he walked to the door and left the room, slamming the door so hard that the molding surrounding it partially broke. Castle spat blood again but did not follow. He knew someone was about to experience the pain of that uncontrolled temper, and he was glad it wouldn't be him. Instead he went to the window and looked down on the street, where Sam mounted his bay gelding and quickly spurred the animal in the direction of the Kerry Patch. Castle worked his jaw with his hand and tenderly touched his lip. He had gotten off easy; he figured Daines was about to meet his Maker, and the thought wasn't an unpleasant one.

Sam arrived in the Patch close to 8 P.M. and headed directly for the *Black Swan.* He noted O'Brien sitting at his table playing cards with several of his men but continued to scan the room. Catching the eye of a half-drunk Mickey O'Shay, he signaled for him to come outside. O'Shay gave a quick glance at O'Brien, saw that he was distracted, and nodded at

Ridges. Moments later, O'Shay sauntered into the dark alley at the side of the gambling house, only to be slammed into the side of the building by Ridges, whose large hand grasped his throat, thrusting upward. With Ridges's hot breath nearly burning his eyebrows, O'Shay sobered instantly. "You were supposed to find that nigra lover and bring him to me. You didn't," Ridges said through clenched teeth.

"I wasn't sure it was 'im! Then when Castle confronted 'im . . . well, it was too late. The guy is shrewd. I can tell ya where t' find 'im, but if ya try t' kill 'im around 'ere, you'll have t' deal with Brendan Malone."

"Malone? What's he got to do with this?" Ridges let go of O'Shay, and Mickey rubbed his throat, thankful his feet were back on solid ground.

"Doan 'ave a clue, but 'e made it clear to O'Brien tha' Daines and 'is girl Mary McConnell was t' be left alone."

While Ridges pulled his thoughts together, O'Shay figured he'd make amends. "Malone is raisin' volunteers. Callin' fer as many as want a part of keepin' the South in the Union."

Ridges had followed Rand Hudson to Blair's house the previous evening and had seen Malone enter the estate as well. If Malone was raising an army, Hudson was involved. He'd have to get word to Atchison.

"Find out where they're meetin', and let me know," Ridges said.

"Daines needs clippin', Ridges. Can't 'ave the man braggin' about makin' a fool of ya and yer bruther, now can we."

Ridges looked up. "And yer the man t' do it, ain't ya."

O'Shay shrugged. "I suppose I am. I can deal with O'Brien, make it right, but it'll cost ya two 'undred."

"You can do it but I can't—is that it?"

O'Shay shrugged again. "Yer dealing in the Patch, and Daines is Irish with Irish angels lookin' ou' fer 'im. The one who clips 'im 'as to get them angels t' look a different way."

"And Malone?" questioned Ridges.

"Made O'Brien mad enuf to spit nails. 'E'll cover fer me if I 'andle matters right."

Ridges gave an evil smile. "Wounded yer pride, did they—this Daines and the woman?"

"Le's just say they need a lesson in proper manners."

Ridges nodded, pleased with the way things had gone, then turned on his heel. "You have a deal, O'Shay. Get it done."

Chapter 19

December 22, 1860

RAND FINALLY FOUND LIZZY IN the barn, gingerly rubbing her mare's injured leg with ointment by the light of several lanterns hung about the saddling area.

"Do you have a minute?" Rand asked.

Lizzy rose from her position to greet him with a kiss on the cheek.

"How was your day?"

"Interesting and wonderful," he said.

"Really? Tell me more." She knew that he and Ann had spent a good deal of time together that day, and she had been on pins and needles wondering how it had gone. She went back to work on the horse's leg, anticipating an answer.

"I will not be seeing Ann anymore," he said.

Her sudden turn startled the horse, who kicked over her bucket of liniment. Seeing the grin on her brother's face, Lizzy threw the rag at him. Stooping down he picked it up, holding it by two fingers and letting it hang, dripping limply between them. She tried to take the rag, but he moved it. She tried again, but he was too quick. She tussled with him until she had hold of the rag and jerked it from his fingers, then tried to wipe his face with it. He grabbed her arm and held it and the rag away. "You are asking for a face cleaning," he said with good-humored threatening.

"As are you," she said with determination and a smile. The nervous mare pranced about until they stopped teasing one another. Too much movement on the leg would not be good for the mare, and they both knew it. Lizzy quickly placed her arms around Rose's neck in a calming gesture.

"I'm in love with her, Lizzy, and I intend to ask her to marry me," Rand said.

Lizzy's approval radiated through her smile. "You will never regret it, Rand. Other than you, I don't love anyone more than Ann."

"I do have one concern," Rand said.

She looked at him quizzically as she prepared bandages for the mare's leg.

"I understand now why you were reluctant to say anything about your religion to Andrew. I am not sure how she will react, and if I lose her . . ."

Lizzy didn't respond immediately. She had spent many sleepless hours wondering how to tell Andrew, when to tell him, whether to tell him at all. She fretted over all the possible arguments and rationalizations; she had not come to a final determination of her own. She could not judge Rand, nor did she feel clear about what to tell him.

But she did know Ann far better than she knew Andrew. Ann Alexander was deeply religious but had no religion to which she felt allegiance, even though she had been baptized a Baptist. She and Ann had talked of religion more than once, and Lizzy had taught doctrines she knew though she had never revealed their origins. Lizzy knew that Ann believed most of what she shared and was even quite excited about their discussions. Lizzy just hadn't admitted to being a Mormon.

Lizzy secured the final bandage on Rose and faced Rand. "I have talked to Ann about what we believe—at least the doctrines surrounding Christ— but I am ashamed to say that the conversation never went further than that." She took a deep breath. "Sometimes I wonder if I have a backbone."

Rand chuckled. "That makes two of us."

Lizzy gave him a look of teasing disbelief.

Rand laughed. "I mean, I wonder if either of us has a backbone."

Lizzy sobered. "The thing is, I know Ann would accept the gospel, and *still* I haven't told her. Maybe it is time I did."

"It is not your conversation to have, not now." He paused. "I've finished the book again. I had forgotten how it made me feel. If I can get her to read it . . . well, things will be as they should."

He turned to leave, and she watched him go. He was right, and she suddenly realized just how right. The book makes the difference, and she must get Andrew to read it as well. It would be her first duty once in Virginia. Surely he would see then. She went back to work putting away the bandages, her mind secure in this risky yet important decision. But in her heart there was still a small, empty feeling of fear. Andrew Clay was not like Ann Alexander, and that difference frightened her.

* * *

News had arrived by wire that South Carolina had seceded. St. Louis was alive with the report, and there was talk everywhere of which states would follow. Talk of Missouri's future was on everyone's lips as well, and discussions and arguments around the subject were lively. Rand walked from his livery to the office, where he found his clerks discussing the most recent news and rumors—and there were plenty of both. At his entry, the clerks quickly went back to their work, nodding to him as he passed through and into his office. He shut the door behind him.

A few minutes later, his office received a telegraph from the Overland Express offices in Jefferson City, Missouri's capital. Rand was friends with the manager there, and they kept each other updated on events happening in the two cities. The wire was no surprise: Secessionist talk was now at its height in the city.

Rand's clerk came into the office. "Sir, the *Sam Houston* is having trouble with her boiler, and they need you at the docks."

Rand picked up his coat and walked toward the pier where the *Houston* was docked. Once there, he and his mechanics worked to determine the cause and then sent messengers to Rand's machine shop to make the proper part to repair the boiler.

By midmorning he was back in his office, having a cup of coffee and watching the wharf out his window. It was a busy day, with at least fifty steamers docked along the five miles of waterfront. Others were treading water, waiting their turn to load and unload.

In spite of the frenetic morning, his thoughts turned to the last month with Ann. Could one fall in love that quickly? In the days since the meeting at Frank's house, Rand had come to know just how deeply he cared for Ann Alexander. Surely he had been falling for her since the first time they met, but now he knew through and through that the feelings were deep and had only one conclusion. He wanted to marry Ann, and he wanted to marry her soon.

Rand caught a sudden suspicious movement near the store across the street. Hidden from Rand's view, a figure had stepped into the shadows; from the way Rand's hair stood up at the back of his neck, he was sure it was Sam Ridges. The man was becoming blatantly annoying. Rand had a meeting planned with Hooker and the others at the warehouse later; clearly he would have to lose Sam Ridges and possibly give him something to think about as well. He was tired of being shadowed everywhere he went.

But first things first. He checked his pocket watch. He intended to visit a jeweler and pick out a ring before meeting Hooker.

Rand called for his clerk to send a messenger to the livery to have his carriage brought around as he glanced one more time at the darkened alley where Ridges had been. There was no sign of him now but Rand was sure he was there.

Rand pulled on his overcoat and picked up his bowler hat and umbrella before stepping to his desk drawer and removing his Colt five-shot pocket pistol. He positioned the weapon inside his right overcoat pocket. He didn't usually carry a pistol, but unusual times and having Ridges on his tail cried for caution as of late.

Leaving the building, he gave directions to the driver and then settled back to watch through the small rear window of the carriage. It did not surprise him much when Sam Ridges lurched out of the shadows and climbed into a waiting carriage. Yes, it was time to do something about Mr. Ridges. Past time.

Five minutes later they were on Mullanphy Street in the Kerry Patch. The jeweler was an immigrant from Belfast by the name of Conleth O'Reilly; he had learned the watchmaking and jewelry trade before immigrating to the United States. He had two sons, both of whom worked for Rand: Wayneth as a captain and Patrick as a first mate on two different steamers stationed along the Ohio. Hopefully Conleth O'Reilly would have a ring suitable for Ann that was already finished or well on its way.

The carriage passed the Emigrant House established by the street's namesake, Brian Mullanphy, a few years before his death in 1851. Irish emigrants were housed in its three stories and forty rooms until they could find work, move west, or locate other accommodations. Brian Mullanphy had been a friend of Rand's mother, and Rand knew him as a good man who had helped build the growing Irish community in St. Louis so that its citizens could stand up for themselves in the rough and tumble of Missouri politics. Unfortunately, many of the Irish still supported Breckinridge or Douglas and most were lukewarm to Lincoln, but all that was changing. Rand and Hooker had come here stumping for the railsplitter, and the reception had at last begun to warm, though there was still the fear in the Irish of freed blacks taking their jobs.

The carriage pulled up to a row of shops fronted with stone façades, and Rand entered the familiar door. Conleth sat at a workbench at the far end while his daughter Briana busied herself with dusting off beautiful clocks and shelves along one side of the narrow shop. Conleth looked up and over the top of his glasses, saw that it was Rand, and smiled.

"Well, Briana, me girl, look 'ere what ye dawg 'as drug up. Auld Randolph Hoodsun 'as come a callin'."

Briana smiled as her father came out from behind the worktable and greeted Rand with a handshake. "'Ow ye be doin', and 'ow is Miss Lizzy?"

"Fine, fine. And you, Conleth, and your wife and family?"

"We be fine as well. 'Eard from both me boys recent, an' they be movin' their wives and children to Cincinnati soon. They appreciate yer 'elp." He glanced at his daughter. "Briann is ta marry. After it be done, I'll 'ave only little Eric t' do with."

Briana blushed and bowed a thank you as Rand congratulated her before turning to business.

"I have come for a wedding ring myself, sir," he said.

Conleth's heavy eyebrows lifted as he looked over the top of his Hookerlin spectacles to be sure he had heard right.

"Ye be needin' a weddin' ring? 'Tis a day I'd ne'er though' t' see."

"Well, the young lady has yet to say yes, but I hope to know for certain tonight. I don't suppose you have anything finished that is worthy of one of this country's most beautiful women?"

Conleth laughed. "Ay, ay, I 'ave jes' wha' ye be needin', Mr. Hoodsun." He stepped behind a dark wooden counter, removed his keys, and turned them in the lock then gently lifted an ornate ring box from the encased cabinet. Opening the box, he showed Rand the ring. "'Tis a beauty, is it nah'?"

Inside the box was a Victorian masterpiece. Six antique gold flowerlets swirled to center a modest yet dazzling diamond. A tiny seed pearl nestled inside each flower.

Rand was impressed. "It is, and one any woman would be proud to wear." A deal was quickly struck. Rand paid the price, and as he moved to place the box in his right pocket, he felt it strike the pistol. Instinctively he pulled it out, moving it around to his left. He now had a wedding ring in one pocket and a pistol in the other. The irony was not lost on him. He left Conleth with a warm handshake and a hearty thank you as Rand returned to his waiting carriage.

Randolph immediately noticed Ridges's carriage waiting a block back from his own. He instructed his driver to go back to the office but said that he would not be riding with him. The driver responded with a questioning look but reined the horses away from the curb and pulled into the street.

Rand walked back toward the carriage that held Ridges but at the last moment turned into the Mullanphy's Emigrant House. Upon entering, he made his way to a room he had visited before and found a few young men working out and learning the art of boxing.

"Gentlemen," he said. The room quieted and most faced him, even gathered closer. "How would you like to make a little money?"

Smiles erupted all around.

* * *

Ridges instructed his driver to move the carriage forward so he could get a better view of the door of the Emigrant House. He waited for several minutes, all the while becoming more anxious. The man had sent his carriage away. Did he intend to stay here, or had he sneaked out a back door after catching on to the fact that he had a tail? Ridges's impatience finally got the best of him; he stepped from the carriage and tramped up the steps to enter the building. Confronting a woman at a counter to his right, he described Rand and asked for his whereabouts. She smiled and pointed to the door at the far end. "Jus' lef' through tha' back door. Ye might catch 'im if'n . . ."

Ridges was already halfway across the entryway before she could finish and did not notice the slight grin on her face. He opened the door and took the set of stairs two at a time. He threw open the door at the bottom and found himself in a small arena with a boxing ring in its center. As he stepped into the room, the door closed behind him. He turned to find a burly young man at least his height and somewhat heavier blocking the only exit.

He opened his mouth to order that the man move aside when several others gathered around.

"We 'ave been tol' tha yer good with the leathers," one man said, lifting a pair of fighting gloves and tossing them to Ridges. "Mr. Coorigan here is our champ, an' he be wantin' t' prove ya."

Ridges sneered at the boy standing next to the speaker. "If this boy wants a good thrashin' I'd be more than happy to give it to him." He tossed the gloves aside as he stared at the boy with cold eyes. "But I won't be needin' these."

"Oh, tha's not Mr. Corrigan . . . *Tha's* Mr. Corrigan." The man pointed over Ridges's shoulder.

Ridges turned around to see a giant of a man standing in front of him; he had a chest bigger than a wagon and arms the size of elephant legs. Ridges eyed the others as they circled around him. He knew he wasn't getting out of the room without a fight unless he used his pistol, but when he tried to remove it from his waist belt it was already gone. "Doan need tha' kind of distraction, now do we," said one of the men, who tossed the pistol to another man. Ridges didn't much care. He'd fought bigger men—harder ones as well—but still he slid off his coat while cursing Rand Hudson.

* * *

Rand walked to the warehouse where he was to meet Hooker. As he approached the enormous structure, he could hear the muffled sounds of marching inside. Hooker waved to him from near the large entryway door, and Rand quickly joined him.

"No wonder yer late," Hooker said with a smile. "Lose yer carriage?"

Rand smiled. "Had to lose Sam Ridges."

Hooker looked back up the street warily.

"He's busy getting a boxing lesson," Rand said and told him about his diversion.

"The Mulanphy boys," Hooker said. "Ridges will wanna tear ya apart."

Rand nodded. "How many men showed up today?"

"We have about twelve hundred and fifty now. Malone, Hirsch, and Rosenthal have 'em in companies of a hundred each, with the last group half that. Trouble is some of 'em are young fer joinin' the military. Time to weed 'em out."

"How many?"

"At least a hundred, but it's hard to tell from looks," Hooker said.

Hooker opened a small door, and both men went inside. The warehouse was so wide that it needed five rows of huge columns equally spaced from end to end to hold up its endless roof. It gave them more than enough space to drill and train.

Rand looked over and saw Malone, Hirsch, and Rosenthal working alongside the men, correcting a few, barking orders, and doing their best to bring order to their training in the basics of field maneuvers. They had already assigned company sergeants from among the ranks of the Wide Awakes, and Rand had been impressed with their willingness and ability. He watched and moved around among the different companies before he spoke again. "They're coming along," he said.

"Yeah, but we still got a long way to go with these boys, Rand. They're just kids playing soldier. They haven't got a clue about fightin'. And we need to be lettin' the young 'uns go. No sense to go to the next step draggin' 'em along if they can't stay."

"Then let's get it done." Rand took off his overcoat, jacket, and hat and laid them aside. "Get them over in front of those bales so I can talk to them."

Hooker gave a loud whistle and the order to gather; the men broke rank and swarmed together in front of the bales. When they were all bunched up, Rosenthal ordered quiet, and Rand looked them over before telling them that he was impressed with their progress and giving them a pep talk about working even harder. He then paused before telling them that no one under the age of eighteen would be able to continue. There was a good deal of mumbling, and Rand explained: If their training went well and war broke out, they would be given the chance to join the Union army and would be given full pay and privileges that required them to be eighteen—no exceptions. Those younger could hang around and watch, but they'd have to come of age before they could join. Most of the men seemed more agreeable after Rand finished.

"Those under eighteen, move off to the side," Rand said.

Only a dozen boys moved over at first, but after a few minutes the older boys nudged others in that direction. Finally a flood of nearly a hundred worked their way out of the crowd to stand against the wall, grumbling.

"Now I know there are still some in this group who are still too young. Mr. Rosenthal and Mr. Malone here will finish weeding you out with a stiff kick in the britches if you don't get out on your own."

Another twenty boys grumbled their way to the side. "'Taint fair," one said. "We're good as those boys."

"I don't doubt it, but rules are rules, and the first thing a good soldier must be is obedient—and honest as the day is long," Rand said. "Can't trust a man who isn't, and we won't have him around. But I'll promise you that when you're of age, if you're still wanting in, we'll take you and make a soldier out of you just like these boys."

The grumbling died down, and Rand nodded to Hooker, who cleared his throat and began his rant.

"You boys are a fine bunch of marchers, yes siree, but marching don't come close to making a soldier, and we're gonna make you soldiers. And I'm telling ya right now, we're going to beat you into the ground getting it done. If you think this is some kind of lark and good time and that girls will be on the sidelines for you to impress, you're in the wrong place. You will no longer be Wide Awakes. If you sign up with us, you will be members of the Missouri Home Guard, a militia organization that will teach you how to fight, both as an individual and as a regiment." He paused before going on. "You'll be preparin' for war, children, and you'll be needin' discipline and hard work to get it done or you'll get yourself and others killed the first time you walk into battle. If you aren't up to the rigors of such preparation, there is the door, and don't let it hit you in the backside on yer way out. We have neither the time nor the disposition to play games with children who need coddlin'. Understood?"

The mumble through the crowd was one of approval and agreement.

"Where do we sign up?" said one, then another, then more.

"What about weapons?" someone called out.

Hooker looked to Rand, who answered the question."When the time comes, you will be trained in weapons, and we'll have weapons for you. They won't be first-rate—those will come later—but stick with this regiment, gentlemen, and I promise you will be in the finest-fighting and best-equipped unit in the Union army."

"We're in," came the hollers, and a degree of pandemonium broke out.

Rand held up his hand. "My name is Hudson—Captain Hudson to you from this point forward." He pointed to Hooker. "That is Sergeant Isaac Hooker. He will be second in command. Don't cross him, gentlemen. He knows how to use that knife hanging from his belt, and he'd just as soon skin you as look at you."

Isaac was in his leathers; he looked mean and ugly, and nobody laughed. His reputation was well known.

"Sergeants Hirsch, Rosenthal, and Malone have all been in the army and know how to fight. They'll assist sergeant Hooker. Listen to them and they'll save your lives. Disobey them or get cocky, and they have my permission to give you a thrashing you won't soon forget. You will do this our way, or you won't do it at all. Is that understood?"

The answer came in nods and a hush of humility that fell over the group.

"Bring your friends. We need to raise an army of three thousand minimum in the next two months, but don't bring us boys still wanting to be boys—bring us men wanting to defend the Union against any rebel who gets in our way and is willing to die doing it."

The crowd erupted once more, and Rand had to settle them down again.

"We'll sign you up over the next hour, then Mr. Hooker will begin your training. Belly up to those tables over there, men. It's time to join the Missouri Home Guard."

The race for the tables was on, and Rosenthal, Hirsch, and Malone went to get the recruits signed up while Hooker stepped up to Rand as he jumped down from the bale of cotton.

"Well, ya done it now," Hooker said. "They're in. Now the work begins."

"Yeah, a bit frightening, isn't it?"

"What's that?"

"I just invited them to die for their country."

"We'll get 'em as ready as anyone can, Rand. That's all we can do other than pray that them knotheads in the South quit acting like fools."

Rand watched the boys' excitement and enthusiasm. It was still just a game to them, a chance at glory. That had to change, or they'd all get killed.

"Work them, Isaac. Beat them down and build them into soldiers. If you don't . . ." He paused then went on. "I want them in shape. Fifty-mile hikes with packs in mud, rain, every condition. I want them to be able to load and shoot faster than they can think, and I want them steeled against turning tail. The harder we train them, the more of them will survive."

Hooker only nodded. They had a long way to go.

* * *

They didn't leave the warehouse for four hours, and by the time Hooker was finished with the recruits' first training, most were dragging themselves away, some surely wondering what they had gotten themselves into. Rand stood back from the door and watched them leave until Hooker came out.

"It was a good day," Rand said.

"We're still scratching the surface, but they're a determined lot. I'll give 'em that."

Malone came out and joined them a few moments later, along with Hirsch and Rosenthal, who attached the heavy lock and chain to the warehouse door.

"Gentlemen, well done," Rand said.

"I think most o' these boys 'as the makin's o' good fightin' men," Malone said.

"Half a dozen slackers in my group," Hirsch said.

"More in mine, but overall, Malone is right. We can get them ready—there's just not enough of 'em," Rosenthal added.

"There'll be more comin'," Malone said. "They like wha' they 'eard from ya, captain, and 'ere ain't nuthin' tha' appeals t' a boy more than wha'll make 'em a man. They'll be braggin' abou' this over ale t'night, and others'll be comin' t' see abou' it."

"More Germans than Irish," Rosenthal noted, needling Malone.

"You'll be needin' five as many jus' t' make up fer one son of Erin," Malone responded. The others chuckled. "We'll be addin' t' our numbers. I've already spread the word in the Patch."

"We'll be needing more leaders," Rosenthal said. "Fighters, or West Pointers who know what they're doin'."

"Is U.S. Grant still around these parts?" Hooker asked.

"Moved to Illinois. Couldn't make a go of it on his father-in-law's place," Hirsch said.

"Too bad," Hooker said. "Met him when he served out west. Don't know of a more determined man than Grant. No better man at tactics, neither. Had trouble with the drink though. Rousted him out fer it."

"Randall Greenfield was a West Pointer," Rosenthal said.

"Washed out of the academy. Lazy from what I hear," Hirsch said.

There were no other names offered. It seemed that leadership would be a problem. "Look for company commanders among the boys themselves. We'll have to develop them, bring them along," Rand suggested.

"How soon must we be ready?" Hirsch asked.

"We have two months, maybe three," Rand replied.

"Then it's every day but Sunday," Rosenthal said.

"Some of these boys have jobs and can't lose them. They'll miss some training," Hooker said.

"Repetition," Rand said. "Teach a few things well, over and over. Discipline under fire and order of battle; how to load and shoot in record time. Get them in shape. Tell them to run here instead of ride, and get them in the habit of doing sit-ups and pull-ups, at least a hundred a day. They'll have to train at home as well as here."

"Tomorrow then," Rosenthal said. He smiled, tipped his hat, and headed for his mount, with Hirsch and Malone right behind him.

"You've got no carriage," Hooker said to Rand. "Good thing I brought my wagon today." Rand looked over and saw the wagon with a heavy set of Belgian horses in the traces and crates tacked up behind the seat. "I'll give ya a ride back t' yer office."

They walked a short distance and settled themselves into the oversized wagon, a good half again as massive as a standard. The Belgians' rumps were wide and broad, and Hooker slapped the reins against them to get them moving.

"And yer own life, Rand, what of that?" Hooker asked.

"Well, I'm just about to ask Ann to marry me," Rand said.

"Yer provin' to be a smart man, Captain," Hooker said with a grin. "Congratulations."

"I'd like you to be in our wedding party," Rand said.

"You just got dumb again," Hooker said. "I hate gettin' gussied up fer such affairs, ya know that."

"Wear your leathers. Ann said she liked the smell," Rand said with a smile.

"Yeah, she did, didn't she," Hooker said with a laugh. He slapped the horses' rumps with the reins again and gave out a shrill whistle to get them moving faster.

"So Ridges is followin' ya, is he?" Hooker asked after a moment.

"Yeah—I'm guessing it's by Atchison's order."

"Ridges and I go back a bit. He didn't like me movin' in on the dry goods trade up at St. Joe. Some friends of his thought they had a corner on it, and Ridges sorta acted as their protector. He came callin' one night. Left draggin' a leg I stuck with my knife. He still has a bit of a gimp. I'll have a talk with him if yer willin'."

Rand raised an eyebrow and looked at his friend. "I appreciate it, but we're not at that point yet."

They had arrived at Rand's office, and he climbed out of the wagon.

"Just the same, you mind yer back, Randolph. That's the way Ridges usually comes at a man."

Rand nodded, and Hooker whipped the Belgians and moved on. Rand hurried to the livery, where he found his carriage waiting. He checked his watch as he climbed in. He was late, and Ann would be waiting for him.

Chapter 20

RAND SPENT THE REST OF the afternoon enjoying what he would normally shudder at: hours of shopping. Ann somehow made it a pleasure. They moseyed from store to store, looking for special gifts for her mother and brothers and all of Frank's family, along with a dozen friends and associates.

As Ann made her first purchase, Rand slipped to the counter as well. "I'd like very much to pay for your gifts," he offered.

Ann turned with a look of disbelief. "I'll not take your charity, Randolph Hudson. In fact, I should pay you for escorting me all over town."

Rand smiled and held up his hands. "I've learned never to fight with a real lady," he responded.

She turned to the gentleman making the sale. "I am fond of this item; however, I feel that the price is somewhat high. I am willing to pay what it's worth."

Rand swallowed hard but felt a smile cross his face at this little scene. Ann's graciousness somehow made up for his discomfort, and she had made a new friend by the time they exited with the merchandise in hand.

Just down the street, on a table of handmade goods, Ann spied a charming set of wool gloves, which she determined to purchase for her mother. A tiny, stooped woman stood at the end of the table and observed Ann and Rand as they browsed. As Ann brought the gloves to the woman, asking their cost, she reacted immediately to the quoted price.

"Oh, I couldn't possibly pay such a small price for such quality as these. Did you knit these yourself?" The woman's affirmative answer prompted Ann to lay down double the requested amount. When the transaction had been finished, Ann turned to leave, obviously not noticing the look of admiration Rand gave as he reached for her hand.

Ann displayed an uncanny ability to treat everyone as if she had known them all her life. When she met someone she knew, and there were many for a woman who had lived only a year in St. Louis, she seemed to know the names of each of their children and even distant relatives. Rand knew there was no guile involved; Ann's concern was genuine. Everyone seemed to be her dear friend.

And then there was the help she gave him in buying gifts for others. He was clueless as to what Frank might need, or even want. He had thought of maybe just another shirt or links for cuffs, but then Ann spied a singular pocketknife—one of a kind, perfect for the likes of Frank. It changed Rand's absolute distaste for shopping to something akin to enjoyment.

As the hour grew later, Rand led them to the Lindell Hotel, where Ann spied a poster hanging on the brick wall just outside its entrance; she stopped to read it further. It announced an abolitionist rally that very night at 8 P.M. at the Palace Theater.

"Oh, we must go," she said.

Rand gave a tolerant smile. "You wouldn't like it."

"And why not?" she said taking his arm again and turning toward the hotel entrance.

"It will be long and loud, perhaps even violent."

"Violent?"

"Secessionists will heckle until they bring it to an end either by police intervention or an out-and-out brawl. Believe me, I attended such a meeting once. They can get nasty."

They entered the hotel's restaurant on Washington Street and went to the dining room, where Rand's clerk had made them a reservation. Their table was situated near a large fireplace with a window that looked out onto the street. Lamps inside and out lit up the dusky, cool evening.

Once seated, Rand looked across the table at an absolutely radiant Ann, who was checking her shopping list once more, her upturned brow showing careful thought. She finally stuck the list in her purse and smiled at him.

"Well?" he said.

She looked at him quizzically. "Well, what?"

"Did you find something for everyone?"

She lit up, clearly satisfied. "All but one."

He now returned the quizzical look.

She leaned forward, smiling. "Randolph Hudson, you have been looking over my shoulder all day, darling. I have not had a single moment to buy you what I know you need."

"Ah, and what would that be?"

She gave him a teasing smile. "A very nice try, Randolph, but you are not in love with a stupid person. You will see soon enough."

"Then you believe I am in love with you," he said.

"You are, and you have been for some time, but as I told you before, you refused to recognize it for the longest while, that's all." She gave him a playful smile.

"And you—how long have you been in love with me?" he asked, leaning forward and taking her hand in his.

"Since the day I saw you on board the steamboat that brought me here," she said with a shy but serious intensity.

Rand was surprised by the statement. "I was on the steamboat with you? I don't remember, and I would have remembered. I am sure of that."

"Ah, but you don't, do you?"

He leaned back, scrambling to remember. "We first met at Frank's home. I . . ."

"Came for dinner?"

"Yes. You and I, Frank, Apolline, my mother, Lizzy, your Uncle Montgomery, and his wife. I remember," Rand said.

"Uncle Frank was kind enough to arrange that meeting and introduction for me, but it all stemmed from that day on the steamboat. I wanted to meet you, and I asked for Frank's help."

Rand sat back, a wide grin on his face. "And Lizzy's pestering? And even what happened at the meeting at Frank's house? All of this you—"

Ann grinned, squeezing his hand. "Are you appalled? Is it unladylike for a woman to seek out a man she admires and then encourage his interest?"

Rand shook his head. "It just never occurred to me. Frank, Lizzy, even Hooker? No, surely not Hooker."

She pressed his hand. "I have known Isaac a long time. He was quite accommodating."

"Well, I'll be," Rand said.

"But it is for your own good. Hooker saw that immediately."

The waiter came, presented them with a menu and wine list, and gave his recommendations.

"I would like the beef stroganoff," Ann was saying. "Cover the rice with your lovely sauce as well."

Rand shook himself out of his stupor long enough to order a steak with steamed vegetables and brown gravy over rice.

"And shall I bring you a glass of our finest wine?" the waiter questioned. Both declined, asking for spring water.

Ann looked sheepish. "I have not been completely honest with you. You could not have seen me on the ship. It was nighttime."

Rand grinned. "You little devil. You made me think—"

She took his hand again. "You were with your mother and sister. I have a vivid memory of seeing you with them, talking, joking, and enjoying one another's company; I was very impressed. Few men have such wonderful relationships with a mother and sister, especially in public. Their egos simply won't allow it. But you were so genuine and caring, I knew I must get to know you. I asked the captain about you, then talked with Aunt Apolline. I was especially pleased that she knew you so well and agreed with my every feeling." She grinned, one eyebrow lifting. "Then you became my challenge."

Rand remembered that night on the ship now. He, Lizzy, and his mother had gone to a resort on the coast of Louisiana for a few days' vacation. It was something they rarely found the time for. It had been the last time his mother was really well enough, and he had thanked God more than once for that last trip.

"I remember now . . ." he began and reminisced of their trip, with Ann listening intently. Their food was served and proved to be delicious, but the best part of the meal was relishing this new excitement of little details they were learning about each other. Rand's love was even more deeply confirmed.

Ann broke the mood as she glanced at a small watch dangling from a pin attached to her dress. "Please take me to the rally, Rand. I so very much wish to see it!"

Rand held back a smile as he flashed her a "What shall I do with you" look, yet he couldn't ignore her excited request. He had been honest when he'd said that the rally might not be safe, and the atmosphere was not pleasant either. Most rallies had at least one speaker intent on working everyone into a feverish pitch that bordered on insanity. But he could see that for her it was just another challenge—an adventure to be experienced.

"Very well, but I warn you, it will not be what you expect," he said.

The waiter brought the bill. Rand quickly paid it with gold coins and stood, pulling back Ann's chair and allowing her to stand. She took his arm, and they left the dining hall, retrieved their checked coats, and stepped outside. Rand raised his arm to his driver, who was waiting at some distance down the street. As the carriage came to a halt in front of them, Rand helped Ann inside where she snuggled in close for the short trip; he was electrified by her warmth, and silently wished they were headed someplace quiet and romantic, or even staying right here inside the carriage. He would be content to travel in circles the rest of the evening as long as he had Ann with him. And he still needed to propose, but the time simply hadn't been right. And at a rally? Heaven forbid! It must be after, on their way to her home—though it would take a good deal of patience, he knew it would be the best time.

Rand's coachman stopped a short walk from the theater; it was impossible to pull up in front because of all the congestion surrounding the driveway of the building. Rand helped Ann step down and instructed his driver to wait in a side street just down the block and to keep a vigilant watch; if any trouble seemed imminent, he was to pull up as close to the building as possible. The driver nodded, flicked the whip over the haunches of the team, and moved quickly away.

Ann took Rand's arm once again. They walked to the entry and stepped inside, where they jostled their way to the ticket booth through a crushing crowd. Regular seats were sold out, but there were two box seats left, and they forced their way toward the stairs that would take them to the seats. The going got easier as a young man called for all to find their seats and the crowd pushed through the main doors. The program was about to begin.

Rand found the box and lifted the drape long enough for him and Ann to slip in. The kerosene lamps left a smoky haze around the ceiling, and the room seemed particularly warm. Rand removed their coats and seated Ann but stayed standing himself, watching the crowd while she searched her small purse until she found a fan, unfolded it, and pushed away the stale, smokey air around her.

Rand recognized several people in the audience. As the tumult settled and those participating walked out on stage, an uneasy feeling settled on him. Arguments were ensuing across the rows, building on the already tense environment. He caught a deep breath and finally sat down next to Ann, taking her offered hand in his while leaning toward her to speak.

"If at any time I think we should leave, will you trust my judgment and do as I ask?"

"Of course." Her eyes met his, and she smiled lightly, then kissed him lightly before leaning forward to catch the view of the stage below.

A gentleman arose and proceeded to a wooden podium. There was light applause, and then the incessant noise of conversation turned to a hush.

"Ladies and gentlemen," the man said. "Welcome to our Freedom of Life rally." Cheers and applause resounded throughout the room, but Rand also heard the first of the boos along with the distinct cries of a heckler, whose words he could not clearly discern. The speaker introduced himself as a Baptist preacher by the name of Rogers and then quickly thanked in advance all those who would participate.

"Now, brothers and sisters, we have for your pleasure a band with choir who will play and sing an opening song for us. It is not new to our rally cry, but listen carefully to the words and heed, one and all, their call to our duty!"

The applause and cheers were deafening as the band came on stage and began to play "The Liberty Ball." The choir quickly took up with the first verse to wild applause.

> *Come all ye true friends of the nation,*
> *Attend to humanity's call;*
> *Come aid the poor slave's liberation,*
> *And roll on the liberty ball—*
> *And roll on the liberty ball—*
> *Come aid the poor slave's liberation,*
> *And roll on the liberty ball.*

One of the choir members stepped forward. A buxom woman with a voice the size of all outdoors swung into verse two, and the house erupted once more.

> *The Liberty hosts are advancing—*
> *For freedom to all they declare;*
> *The down-trodden millions are sighing—*
> *Come, break up our gloom of despair.*
> *Come, break up our gloom of despair . . .*

She waved for all to join in, and suddenly the place erupted with the next three stanzas. Ann sat with mouth open, listening, watching, like a child trying to take in a carnival for the first time. She obviously did not know the words but clapped to the rhythm, caught up in the emotion of the roaring crowd as they finished the last words.

It was a good five minutes before the uproar and applause stopped. The band waved and bowed, then waved and bowed again. Ann applauded with all her strength, and even Rand found himself under the spell of the words and music. But everyone was not pleased; there were boos and catcalls, mostly from three large sections around the hall. The secessionists were obviously in good voice as well.

The preacher stood again and thanked the band and singers before introducing the first of three speakers. Rand was surprised—the announcement they had seen advertised eight speakers. He was somewhat familiar with the first speaker and the topic he would discuss; his view would represent Northerners who thought patience and conciliation with Southerners would ultimately lead to the end of slavery.

Just as Rand had surmised, the first speaker weaved the usual argument for ten minutes, receiving only occasional applause from an obvious section of secessionists on the left center in front of the stage. When they did react, they jumped up in applause, whooping and hollering for such inordinate amounts of time that they even embarrassed the speaker. Another group with the same apparent secessionist beliefs tried to stir things up as well by intermittently shouting out that the South would not accept conciliation and that peace would come only if Lincoln was never seated. A loud response of boos and catcalls from the rest of the audience nearly turned the place into a brawl, forcing the speaker to blurt out a finish and sit down.

Rand watched Ann carefully. She seemed to respond favorably to the idea of conciliation, just as she had at Frank's home the other evening. She seemed pleased when some of the crowd responded with similar approval and even gladdened when the secessionist corner applauded. But her expression fell when she realized who these supporters were, what they really wanted, and how unpopular their opinion was with the large majority of people in the hall. Concern and disappointment spread across her face. Rand took her arm and put it through his, holding her hand while rubbing it gently. She gave him a weak yet grateful smile.

The second speaker was introduced—a woman this time—and Ann once again sat forward in her seat. The talk was a brilliant discussion of the equal rights clause of the Constitution and how it must be applied to all men and women. The speaker bridged into the evils of slavery and the need for full freedom for women, including giving them the right to vote. The response was equally mixed with boos and "here, here." On two occasions women stood to applaud—including Ann. Several of these women were immediately pulled to their seats by their husbands, while Rand stood and joined Ann. She lit up with a smile of approval, and they applauded together.

When the second speaker sat down, the preacher arose, announcing only one more speaker. He apologized for any disappointment but said that he felt it would soon be replaced with elation when the crowd realized who the next speaker was. Further, he and the others on their committee felt compelled to allow sufficient time for the concluding speaker to make his remarks.

He then introduced the man as H. Ford Douglas. The majority were quickly abuzz, while the secessionists stood silent for a brief moment before beginning their show of opposition even as Ford approached the podium. Ann was wide-eyed as she watched the mixed reaction and confusion garnered by this man of slight build.

Rand offered an explanation. "He escaped from slavery and has been speaking on the subject ever since. Recently in Chicago he advocated violence and war to end the practice and called for slaves to rise up against their masters. He has told the president that if a war is fought, he will personally raise ten thousand colored men to fight against the South."

"Oh, my." Ann smiled. "His coming to Missouri surely indicates he is not a man of weak constitution," she said with admiration.

"No, but he won't be popular with abolitionists either, at least not those who are moderate in their views. And remember, Stephen A. Douglas was for compromise—and he, not Lincoln, won this state in the election. *This* Mr. Douglas has a purpose here. He wishes to stiffen our backs."

"What do you mean?"

"If war comes, hundreds and even thousands will die. There will be a cry for compromise that will be hard for Mr. Lincoln to ignore. Abolitionists and black representatives like Mr. Douglas there fear that we in the North won't have the stomach to see the war through and actually free the slaves. In any state like ours, where sympathy for slavery is very strong, even though we say we still support the national government, Douglas sees a real danger—support for compromise that will pressure the president to end the war without abolishing slavery. My guess is that Mr. Douglas has come to remind us that this war is not just about holding the Union together as some would like to think. It is about ending slavery once and for all."

"But here in St. Louis most people will be friendly to his cause, won't they?" Ann asked.

"Let's just say that they will be friendlier than if he were in Jefferson City or Springfield, and he would probably be hung if he were in Independence.

But his speech is meant for all Missourians, and my guess is that it will appear on the front page of every newspaper in the region over the next few days."

Douglas was clearing his throat to speak, and the place went still. Even the pro-slavery element seemed paralyzed by the man's audacity in coming here.

Douglas began. "John Quincy Adams said twenty years ago that the 'preservation, propagation, and perpetuation of slavery is the vital animating spirit of the national government,' and this truth is no less apparent today. Every department of our national life—the president's chair, the Senate of the United States, the Supreme Court, and the American pulpit—is occupied and controlled by the dark spirit of American slavery. We have four parties in this country that have marshaled themselves on the highway of American politics, asking for the votes of the American people to place them in possession of the government. We have what is called the Union party, led by Mr. Bell of Tennessee; we have what is called the Democratic party, led by Stephen A. Douglas of Illinois; we have what is called the Seceders, or the Slave-Code Democrats, led by John C. Breckinridge of Kentucky; and then we have the Republican party, led by Abraham Lincoln of Illinois."

There was a lot of applause for Douglas, and a fair amount for Breckinridge, but when Lincoln's name was mentioned an uproar of both applause and denunciations broke out, filling the air with palpable angst. Ford Douglas was quick to cry for quiet, and the majority finally succumbed, restoring a degree of calm tinged with an explosive undercurrent to the room. Rand smiled; Douglas was measuring the crowd. He was known for it—not because he was looking for friends but because he was looking for enemies. He wanted to rankle them, get in their face and challenge them. He was off to a good start, and Rand leaned forward with a mix of fear and excitement.

Douglas continued. "All of these parties ask for your support because they profess to represent some principle. But I tell you with all my soul that so far as the principles of freedom and the hopes of the black man are concerned, *all these parties are barren and unfruitful;* none of them seeks to lift the Negro out of his fetters and rescue this day from odium and disgrace."

A buzz bounced around the room, and a few shouts of "The Republicans will do it," or "Lincoln is your man! He will set you free!" resounded above the din, but Ford quickly pushed on. "No, the Republicans will not, nor will Lincoln. I know Lincoln's politics. I have seen them at work. He and Douglas are the same and have compromise at their heart! Already he says he will leave the states to solve their own troubles and run their governments. This is not a man friendly to the cause of the black man!"

"You're wrong!" and like remarks rang out along with loud discussion. Even the secessionists, taken by surprise at Douglas's message, were confused. Rand smiled. Douglas had all of them where he wanted them; now he would let them have it with both barrels.

"There is no politician who truly has the freedom of the Negro at the forefront of his mind—not yet. They talk of it and give us words that make us feel they hate slavery and its inhumanity. They understand that, like many of you, people do feel the pain of my people and that you do want our freedom—so they tell you what you want to hear. Douglas and Lincoln, they are the same. They speak of slavery's horrors on the one hand but then they say, 'But we must take time. We cannot end it in a day!' Well, my opinion is that if you do not *demand* it, Lincoln will never end it. It is you who makes the difference. You who will stiffen your backs and make our leaders free us! Not *sometime,* as they are wont to say, but *now*, as we are wont to have it!"

The place exploded with applause that drowned out the angry denunciations of the secessionists, who jumped to their feet in opposition. Abolitionists shouted them down; some demanded them to leave or they'd throw them out. Rand looked at Ann, who sat spellbound as she witnessed the anger spread like a thunderstorm over the plains. The preacher sponsoring the meeting finally came to the stand, pounding on it with his gavel, demanding that Mr. Douglas be allowed to finish his speech. Reluctantly all sat down, but an angry cloud hung over the crowd.

"We often hear, from almost every platform, even that of Congress and governors across this nation, praise for the Saxon race. Now, I want to put this question to those who deny the equal manhood of the Negro: What peculiar trait of character do the white men of this country possess, as a mark of superiority, either morally or mentally, that is not also manifested by the black man under similar circumstances? You may take down the white and black part of the social and political structure, stone by stone, and in all the relations of life, where the exercise of his moral and intellectual functions is not restricted by positive law, or by the arbitrary restraints of society, and you will find the Negro the equal of the white man in all the elements of head and heart."

The place exploded again, with opposing views voiced so vehemently that Douglas could no longer be heard. The secessionists let loose like angry, howling animals from all around the hall, while the abolitionists cried out bravos and applauded loudly to drown out the secessionist cackle. Ann grabbed Rand's arm as the bitter hatred cut through the air like a knife. The preacher arose immediately to the side of Douglas, his gavel banging the podium for order, while a few rifle-armed police slipped in front and separated the stage from the gallery. The preacher continued slamming the gavel until a semblance of calm returned again. He stayed put as Douglas, wiping his brow with a handkerchief, came to the front edge of the stage, defiant, challenging, walking left to right and then back again as he spoke.

"Even Mr. Lincoln and the Republicans will try to convince this great audience and all of America that if war comes it is not about slavery or freedom or the right of men like me to rise above the mud pit of slavery. They will say it is about holding the Union together, and to do that they will ask you to compromise. And as the death toll mounts, you will cry out for peace at any cost, and in your compromise my people will remain forever beaten and crushed under the whip of the taskmaster!" He stood directly in front of the heckling secessionist group nearest the stage. He pointed at them and boldly cried above the growing voices of the crowd, "And men like these will continue to rape our wives and rob them from us, steal our children, and deny us freedom and the rights of all men! Men like these will continue to call us animals and never let us go! Rise up, good brothers and sisters, and fight that we and all people of the African-American race can be free!"

The place went berserk. The secessionists came out of their seats, and clubs appeared out of nowhere. The preacher grabbed Mr. Douglas and exited as quickly as he could along with the other two speakers. Those police around the edges of the room braced themselves to intervene in the ensuing battle.

"This is it!" Rand said, pulling on Ann's arm while grabbing both of their coats. She hesitated, both mesmerized and paralyzed by this unbelievable scene. He had to pull harder. "Ann! We must leave. Now!"

Ann shook off the stupor and turned to the exit. They ran down the hall to the steps while putting on their coats, only to find that the fight had billowed out into the large gathering area. Ann was pale, frightened, and gripping his arm so tightly that her nails dug into him through his coat and shirt. He stayed near the wall, shoving men away and protecting Ann even as he pushed for the door. A club came out of nowhere and just missed his head. He turned to see the assailant setting himself to swing again, so Rand landed him a stomach punch and sent him reeling backward just as two others, beating on each other with closed fists, stepped between him and Ann. With great exertion he pushed them out of the way and grabbed Ann's arm, pulling her back from being crushed by a reeling body knocked back by a powerful blow.

Finally they reached the door and pushed their way out as more police forced their way into the foyer. Shrill whistles pierced the air, and clubs rained down from all sides to beat the rioters into submission. Rand took Ann's hand once more, and they dodged left and right, avoiding contact with anyone until they were in the street. Rand saw the carriage and raised his hand to signal when a sudden piercing pain struck him in the side. He caught his breath as he stumbled forward into Ann, who caught him as his knees folded. As he turned, he caught a glimpse of Sam Ridges, knife in hand, his face bruised and swollen.

"Didn't expect to see me so soon, did you Hudson," Ridges said, spitting on the ground.

He raised the knife again, and Ann screamed for help. Ridges glanced about, but when he didn't see any immediate rescue, he stepped toward Rand for the finishing blow. Rand had melted to the ground, nauseous with pain, his weakened senses searching for the plan he had made in the event that something like this would happen. Through a cloudy haze, he remembered the pistol in his pocket and quickly lifted his hand to find it. His fingers curled around the trigger just as Ridges brought his arm down with the knife. Rand fired the gun through his coat and Ridges stopped, a shocked look on his face. He looked down at the growing spot of red on his upper chest and touched it with his free hand, a questioning look in his eyes. Then boiling anger replaced any other emotion as he tried desperately to lift the knife and drive it home. But it was too late. His eyes simply rolled back as he toppled over to his right and onto the street.

Rand tried to breathe, tried to move, tried to find Ann, grasping for her as darkness seemed to gather around him.

Ann grasped his hand while screaming for help, and suddenly Rand felt strong hands under him, lifting him. His vision glazed over as he was lifted into the carriage, but then he saw Ann over him. Tears flowed as she pled with him, saying words he could not make out. He felt her warm hand on his, gripping it tightly. He wanted to squeeze back but couldn't.

He was too weak. Too tired. He felt her lips on his forehead as the carriage lurched forward and an inviting blackness enveloped him. Then he felt nothing at all.

Chapter 21

December 25, 1860

RAND AWOKE IN A HAZY fog, his eyes blinking in the bright sunlight streaming through the window. He raised his arm as a shield against the rays and grimaced, the pain a hot iron against his skin.

He saw the dark silhouette of someone against the sunlight and tried to decide who it was. As she leaned above him, looking into his face, he smiled.

"Hello," Ann said, relief in her smile. "Nice to have you finally awake." She took his hand and squeezed it gently, then leaned over and kissed him on the forehead. "How do you feel?"

"Hungry," he croaked. Clearing his throat, he tried to swallow the sour taste in his mouth. "How long have I been out?" he said, looking around him. He was in his own room at home.

"It's Christmas morning," she said while rubbing her finger across his face, pushing against the stubble. "Apparently, while you were sleeping, you decided to grow a beard."

"I hate being a nonconformist," he replied, trying to smile. Though beards were a most common feature for most men, Rand did not like them and had never had one. He rubbed his face. Until now.

They heard a knock on the door, and Lydijah came into the room. "Mercy, mercy, de' massa is finelee awake." She laughed her cheery laugh and called for Lizzy, who seemed to appear almost immediately through the door. She looked beautiful and relieved.

"He says he's hungry," Ann said with a happy smile.

"Den we has got jus' the s'lution. Ah bring da food real quick. Real quick." She disappeared to do just that.

Lizzy rested a hand on Rand's shoulder, a relieved grin on her face. "Merry Christmas," she said.

"And to you. I'd like to sit up, wash out my mouth, and kiss you both. Is that possible?"

"Very," Ann said with a sly grin and a wrinkled nose, "but in that order, please." They quickly drew back his covers enough to help him sit up so that they could prop pillows behind him. He felt the pain in his side sharpen, taking his breath away.

"How bad is the damage?" he asked weakly, lying back and taking a deep breath.

"No vital organs hit, but you lost a lot of blood," Lizzy answered. "That's why you slept so long."

"And the doctor is worried about infection. You must rest, Rand. The wound is deep and very wide. That monster broke two of your ribs," Ann said.

"And what of Mr. Ridges?"

The women glanced at each other. "We don't know."

"Don't know? I shot the man in the chest," Rand said.

"With a pocket pistol," Lizzy added. "Not the most deadly weapon one could use. But, if he was killed, his friends hauled him off to bury him before the police even noticed. They were a bit busy that evening."

Rand felt competing emotions. If his aim had been true, Sam Ridges was dead and the thought of having killed a man, even a man like Ridges, made him sick to his stomach. But he didn't like the idea of having to look over his shoulder for Ridges the rest of his life either, nor did he like the idea of Ridges being a threat to Ann, Lizzy, and other people he loved. If Ridges *was* dead, he died while trying to take a life, and Rand could see no reason for guilt. He took a deep breath and closed his eyes. Then why did he feel guilt?

Lizzy saw the dark look on her brother's face and took his hand, sitting on the edge of the bed. "It was self-defense, Rand. You had no choice."

Rand forced a smile and squeezed her hand in thanks. He forced himself to put aside the thoughts, at least for now. "Have I really been unconscious for three days?"

"In and out. Can't you remember?" Ann asked.

Rand tried to think. "Dreams—lots of dreams—and . . . yes, there were times . . . you . . . I remember you near me. Your warmth. The smell of your hair. . . ."

"Which needs a good wash, I'm afraid," Ann said nervously, a flush to her face.

Lizzy smiled knowingly at them both. "How does your wound feel now?"

"Like someone branded me, but the pain is tolerable."

"Good. The doctor says to keep you off the morphine from now on. He did leave some laudanum, but that can be just as bad, so—"

"I have no desire to be in a fog, and I need to talk to Frank as soon as I can. I am afraid I made a commitment I am already failing to keep," Rand said firmly.

"He told me to tell you not to worry—Hooker and the others are taking charge of things until you can return. But all of them are coming to see you this evening. So if you're up to it, you will be able to speak with them later today," Lizzy said.

Ann moved to the side table and poured a glass of water for Rand. He drank it without stopping. She poured another, this time adding toothpowder and handing him a toothbrush with a polished bone handle. He took it gratefully and quickly cleaned his teeth. She then handed him some mint leaves and flashed him a teasing smile.

"Not good enough yet?" He chuckled. He chewed on the leaves with a slight grimace, though they were better than the nasty taste that had been infesting his mouth.

Lizzy bent over and kissed him on the cheek. "I love you, Rand. Try to avoid men like Ridges from now on, will you?"

"My highest priority," he murmured.

Lizzy gave him a smile. "I think you did this just to keep me from going to Virginia."

He laughed but stifled it quickly because of the pain. After catching his breath he spoke. "I think tying you up and putting you in the attic would have been easier." He grew serious. "I'll be fine."

Lizzy nodded, "Yes, but if—"

"I am in very capable hands, Lizzy," Rand said, looking at Ann. "I insist that you stay with your plans."

Lizzy's relief was obvious. "Lydijah will have some food ready for you soon, and then you need to try to sleep some more," she said, starting from the room. "Thank your Father in Heaven for Ann, dear brother. She hasn't left your side for more than a few minutes since the moment Mr. Ridges tried to skin you." With that, she disappeared through the doorway with a wave. Rand nodded, still grasping Ann's hand.

"You scared me near to death, Rand Hudson. You really did," Ann said softly. "I thought sure my wicked desire to go to that horrible meeting had taken you away from me." Ann was biting her lip against tears that threatened to spill. She looked tired, even worn out. She was the one who needed sleep.

He lifted her hand and kissed her fingers. "Our going to the meeting had nothing to do with what happened afterward. Ridges was likely looking for vengeance for a good deal of pain I caused him earlier in the day. He just happened to find me there. If he had caught me alone—well, you saved my life, Ann. It is as plain as that."

Ann ran her fingers through his hair, leaned down, and kissed him gently. He attempted to lift an arm around her shoulders, but the pain shooting through his side reminded him to be content with holding her hand; he wrapped both hands around hers.

The sound of Lydijah clearing her throat resonated from the direction of the door, and Ann pulled away reluctantly. Lydijah came in with a tray and a relieved grin on her face. Ann grabbed a bed table and put its legs on each side of Rand's waist as Lydijah placed the tray on top.

"The girls ha' youse bath a ready, Miss Ann," Lydijah said. "Now youse get a goin'. Massa Ran' kin feed hisself. Shoo, now!"

Ann blushed and started for the door, pushing at her hair. "I won't be long," she said. Rand watched her until she disappeared.

Lydijah laughed lightly. "My, my, I ain' nevah seen a woman so in love with a man!" She uncovered the plates. "If'n you doan marry her real soon, Massa Ran', I whip you good, tha's wha' I do!"

Rand smiled. "In my coat pocket, Lydijah. The one I was wearing that night, there is a small box. Get it for me, will you?"

"Why, Massa Ran', thet coat is burned up. It sho is. Lot a' blood, Massa Ran'. Mo, he threw it right in the fire, he did. Lot a' blood."

Rand felt sick to his stomach. "The box . . ."

"No box, Massa Ran'. Ne'r saw one. No, sir." She started for the door.

"Lydijah," Rand said.

She turned back. "Yes, Massa Ran'?"

He sighed. "I've told you a hundred times—I am not your master and hate being called by that name. No more, Lydijah."

"Yes, Massa Ran'." She grinned and left the room.

Rand tried to put the loss of the ring out of his mind as he finished what he could of the food and laid his head back, closing his eyes. The pain was hard, and he felt weak and tired, but he could not waste away in this bed even another day. He would sleep a little, just a little, then he'd have Ann help him get up. Surely there would be holiday visitors, and he would try to see them. But he would not stay in this bed one minute longer than critically necessary.

As he began to drift off to sleep, thoughts of Ann filled his mind. She had been there, watching over him, praying for him when he was hurt. He recalled moments of the ride in the bumping, racing carriage—remembered her tears and cries for him to hang on. She had stayed at the house holding his head in her hands as the doctor worked over his wounds, trying hard to help him deal with the pain. She had stayed here, in this room, giving him water, rubbing his hand and arm, checking his bandages, and quietly talking to him when he was delirious, on the edge of sleep. He did remember the smell of her hair, her soft form against him when he was cold and shivering. Yes, he remembered now. She had held him tight to her, warming him, coaxing him to live. He was certain he could not love Ann Alexander more.

He drifted off and did not see Ann reenter the room and check him before sitting on the sofa and putting her head in her hands, quietly sobbing. She had not slept for more than a few hours for three days, and she was exhausted.

She had nearly lost him, and in the dark hours of the night she had realized that this was still possible. The anger and hate she had seen displayed at the rally had frightened her beyond anything she had expected, and for the first time she had realized that not only was war inevitable but it would be horrible and that she and Rand and everyone else she loved would be swept away in its raging, deadly current. It was a thought that overwhelmed her to near paralysis.

Taking deep breaths, she tried to control her sobs, afraid she would wake Rand. Searching for some distraction from her worry the first night watching over Rand, she had found the book next to his bed. She had recognized its title and wondered what Rand was doing with it. Then she had seen his name carefully written on the inside cover. As she spent the hours waiting for him to wake up she had read first the notes, then the marked scriptures, and then started at the first page. The words had given her comfort and peace, but she still wondered. Were Mary Hudson and her children Mormons? She did not know, but then she did not care. She had thought of asking Lizzy, who had caught her reading the book at least twice, but she had stopped herself. Rand would be the one to explain it, not Lizzy.

She put the book aside now, lay down on the sofa, and pulled the heavy blanket over her. She must not think about it. She must rest. Rand would need her in the coming days, and she must be strong enough to help him—to put on a good face and relish their time together no matter what might come.

She laid an arm across her forehead and closed her eyes. "A few minutes' sleep," she murmured. "Just a few minutes' sleep."

* * *

Rand awoke slowly to the dim light of a lamp on a table across the room. He sensed someone else present and lifted his head to see Ann sleeping soundly on the sofa. She was only partially covered by a blanket, and he saw that the fireplace on the outside wall was burning low and would need wood soon. The drapes on the windows were drawn closed. Rubbing the stubble on his face, he was relieved to find it no thicker than when he had first awoke. He could smell fresh-baked bread and ham, and he heard the sound of cheerful chatter coming from downstairs, probably in the kitchen. It must still be Christmas.

Guests would be coming. Lizzy would be left alone to entertain. He used his arms and hands to push himself up in the bed, his back against the wooden headboard. Though the pain was still fierce, he felt rested, stronger, and managed to throw aside the covers. He found that his midsection was covered with bandages and that he was wearing only ankle-length underwear from the waist down. He gritted his teeth and moved his feet over the side of the bed. He braced himself for the worst but found the pain bearable.

The room was cool, and the wooden floor was like ice against his warm feet. He stood up slowly and waited for his head to stop spinning, then shuffled to the closet and quietly inched open the door. Fingering the shelves for underwear, warm wool socks, a sweater, and pants, he retrieved them and turned back to the bed only to find Ann standing in front of him with tired, glaring eyes, her hands firmly on her hips.

"What in heaven's name are you doing?" she asked.

He smiled sheepishly, extending his arms filled with clothes. "I would think that would be obvious, love."

She lifted an eyebrow, but there was a slight smile in her eyes. She took the clothes from him and then supported him in his return to the edge of the bed. She put the clothes down, perused what he had retrieved, and picked up the undershirt. He tried to lift his hands over his head and felt his breath catch despite his best efforts. She reached over and supported his arm, and his hand finally slipped into the first sleeve. Then she knelt on the bed behind him and pulled the top over his shoulder, easing his arm in before she lifted the garment over his head and pulled it down his back into place.

They went through the same motions with the sweater, and she moved to help with his pants when he stopped her, pointing to the couch.

She stood back, a bit flushed, then turned away to grab the water pitcher and step out the doorway. "I . . . I will get some hot water."

"It is still Christmas, isn't it?" Rand asked.

"Yes. You probably slept eight hours or so," she called back. And then she was gone.

Rand used one arm to pull on his trousers and fasten the buttons. The pain was worse, mostly from the rawness of the wound—thankfully it was surface and not deep pain—and the broken ribs. As he forced himself to move more and stretch his muscles, he hoped his condition wouldn't worsen. At present he could deal with the discomfort for at least a few hours. It was then he noticed his Book of Mormon sitting on the couch where Ann had slept. His heart beat faster for a moment, but he did not allow his mind to jump to any conclusions.

Ann returned with the pitcher of steaming water. As Rand wrestled to get his socks on, she sat down on the bed and managed them onto his feet, then filled a bowl with hot water and used soap to mix up a lather for shaving.

"You've been reading," Rand said casually.

She glanced at the book and nodded. "Yes, I have. Sit back, darling," she said, pointing to the bed. He did, and she leaned over him, lathering his face and neck. She then took the straight razor and used the strap to hone its edge before carefully removing the lather and whiskers. Though Rand knew he could handle this job, he didn't complain or object.

"You have done this before," he said.

Ann washed away some of the remaining lather. "My father. When he was ill I learned to do his shaving for him."

He smiled at the tongue that poked through her lips as she worked.

"Your notes were quite interesting, as is the book," she said evenly.

"Then it doesn't disturb you that we are Mormons," he replied.

She pulled back a little, looking into his eyes. "If the Mormon religion has helped to make the man I love what he is, then I must learn more of it." She put the razor to his throat with a wry smile. "I do have one question though, darling, and be careful of the answer. The razor is sharp and it might slip. Do you want more than one wife?"

Rand couldn't help but smile as he pulled his neck back a bit. "One is quite enough, but thanks for asking."

Ann pulled the razor away and continued shaving his face. "I am sure there are other things about your faith that I must learn, but as long as we are clear about *that* particular thing, we should get along famously," she said.

He laughed lightly, ignoring the pain. "Until I found that book again a few weeks ago, I had forgotten a lot of it myself. Maybe we can learn together."

"I would like that. And is Lizzy . . . ?"

"Very much so. She has never stopped believing, and she—well, my guess is she knows that book like the back of her hand."

"Then she should help us learn," Ann said. She concentrated on finishing the job, nicking him only once. "But why hasn't she shared it with me before? And why don't others know you are Mormons?"

"A hard and very embarrassing question to answer, dear Ann. I am afraid we have been less than faithful to our religion in that way. We intend to change."

"Good. Christ denounced hypocrites and said they should repent."

"Ouch. You don't pull punches, do you?"

"Saving your soul will be my responsibility as much as saving your marvelous hide from men like Ridges. I am simply doing my duty."

Taking a towel, she moved to wash off the rest of the lather and a bit of blood when he slipped a hand behind her neck and kissed her softly.

"Will you marry me?" he asked as he pulled back a few inches.

The words didn't seem to register at first. She seemed to suspect that it was only a casual teasing, but as she looked into his eyes, she caught her breath as she saw his genuine expression of love. Yet she resisted throwing her arms around him.

"That depends," she said, using the cloth to wipe away a last bit of lather under one ear.

"That depends?" It was not the answer he had expected.

She set aside the cloth and opened the drawer in the table, removing a small black box. His heart leapt as he recognized it immediately.

"That depends on whether this was intended for me or for someone else," she said, smiling while opening the box.

He smiled in relief. "I thought it was gone."

"Burned up with your coat?"

"Yes."

"I heard Lydijah telling you that no box was found. It fell out of your pocket in the carriage. I kept it, just in case."

"Just in case?"

"Just in case it might be mine and you were just holding it for me," she said.

He removed the ring from the box, took her hand, and slipped it over her finger. It was a beautiful fit. "It's yours if you want it," he said.

"I want you, Rand Hudson." She put her arms around his neck and held him close but carefully. Then she pulled back and kissed him with all the love she felt before looking into his eyes. "You may take *that* as a yes."

She grinned and went on. "Now, I really must resist any further advances in this present environment; I have a reputation to uphold, you know." She kissed him tenderly on the forehead before turning away, tears in her eyes. She blinked them away as she picked up his boots, which were resting near the bed. She felt happier than she could stand and finally broke down, throwing herself into his arms and sobbing for joy.

Rand held her close, his hand gently stroking her hair as tears gathered in his eyes as well. It would be several long minutes before either of them would let go.

Chapter 22

LIZZY FINISHED CHRISTMAS PREPARATIONS JUST after dark. Guests would begin to arrive soon, and she needed to get herself ready. She dragged up the stairs; though she had slept a good deal more than Ann, apparently it had not been enough. At the moment she found herself wishing that the evening was past, that the guests would stay home, and that she could just go to her room and fall into bed.

As she passed the door to Rand's bedroom, she noticed it was closed but heard nothing from inside. Just as well. Though Rand and Ann had both been asleep for nearly eight hours, they could surely use more. She just hoped the expected Christmas guests would not wake them.

Closing the door to her own room, she leaned against it and stared at the mess scattered about. Suitcases and trunks lay open and half filled, and clothes lay scattered where they had been thrown across the sofa and chairs. They were strewn over everything but the small portion of the bed where she had tried to catch a few moments of sleep. She could not remember the last time she had lived in such a mess.

Sighing, she looked at the sacks in the corner. They contained presents still unwrapped for Rand and Ann and several others; she knew she must get them wrapped quickly. She pushed the trunk and suitcases aside to clear a space in which to sit on the floor, then retrieved some wrapping cloth and ribbon, scissors, and pins before removing her dress and plopping herself comfortably on the floor in her pantaloons. She quickly began cutting wrappings to fit each of the gifts and had them nearly done in half an hour. The last was a gift for Andrew. Though she would be unable to give it to him for at least another week, she decided she'd just as well wrap it now.

She had thought of buying Christmas presents for Andrew's family as well, but he had discouraged it. Though many in the United States, including Lizzy's mother, had begun celebrating Christmas some time ago, the holiday was not popular with all people, and Andrew's family was among that group. Strict in their religious faith of Presbyterianism, they were slow to—as Andrew had said, quoting his father in a humorous pantomime— "dishonor the memory of the Savior with such crass commercialism."

Lizzy respected this opinion but supposed that Christ had never lost the center of her worship *because* of buying gifts for family and friends at Christmastime. In fact, she felt that such giving would be applauded by a Savior who considered the needs of others more than He considered His own. She guessed the danger was in the wanting instead of in the giving, but most people she knew hadn't disintegrated to that point just yet.

She felt a familiar twinge in her heart. Oh, how she missed her mother at times like this. Christmas had always been such an important day for them as a family!

And her father! He enjoyed the holiday more than any man she knew, and she still missed his stories and the reading of Luke around a warm fire on Christmas Eve. She swiped at a wayward tear and told herself she must stop being so melancholy. If she had learned anything from her parents, it was that Christmas was a time for joy, not tears.

She busied herself with her work once more, the strength of her memories refreshing her. Finishing her wrapping she got to her feet, put Andrew's package in her trunk, then gathered the others and stacked them on the bed before going to her basin to freshen up.

She was glad Ann seemed to share her mother's feelings about Christmas, even though Ann was a Southern Baptist. They had talked about many things over the past few days, and Lizzy had come to see Ann in an even more wonderful light than before. Ann was bright, caring, and down-to-earth, and Lizzy had noticed that she had been reading Rand's Book of Mormon. To Lizzy's relief, it seemed that Ann's knowledge of Rand's beliefs hadn't bothered her in the least. If anything, it had seemed to soften her. Lizzy was not surprised. Coming to an understanding of the gospel had done the same for her.

Twice Lizzy had nearly broached the subject of her faith but had decided to leave it to Rand, though she felt some guilt for not having spoken of it sooner. There were many people she would never dare approach about her religion due to their judgmental and outspoken nature but Ann should not have been one of those. Lizzy determined to have more courage.

Rand was truly blessed to have Ann love him as she did. Lizzy could only hope for the same from Andrew.

She was excited about going to Virginia, but the impending trip was also causing her a good deal of apprehension. Once there, she would learn what the future held for her and Andrew; only then could she make a decision. There would be no prolonging or procrastinating. She would either be in or out.

She opened the closet and retrieved the dress she would wear for the evening. As she finished slipping into it, the bell in the entryway signaled the arrival of a guest, and Lizzy went quickly to the mirror, checking her face and hair. She looked tired and a bit disheveled, and another sudden ache for her mother swept over her. Christmas had always been the time that Mary Hudson was at her very best, the perfect hostess, renowned for her hospitality and ability to make all feel welcome. And Rand had always been at her side, acting the perfect host. Because of it, Lizzy had usually managed to stay in the background and mingle as she liked, showing little concern for making guests happy and seeing to their needs. How could she ever fulfill this role as her mother had?

"Oh, Mother," she said, mournfully and near tears. "I miss you dearly!"

She bit her lip, took a deep breath, and quickly swiped at her eyes. The bell rang again, and she knew she must hurry. Her mother would expect her to take her place, especially since Rand was still too weak to even think of getting out of bed. She powdered her nose carefully, put on her cameo necklace and earrings, then looked in the mirror at her appearance. Though she wore a day dress with long sleeves and high neck, it was made of silk in an ivory color that set off her olive skin and heightened the color of her blond hair, which was pulled back above her ears and held in place at the back of her head by her mother's comb. Deciding that she looked pale, she added a touch of rouge, finishing just as Lydijah appeared at the door, announcing that two couples had already arrived. Lizzy breathed deeply, lifted her dress slightly to accommodate her steps, and proceeded out the door and down the hall to the stairs, all the while ritually instructing Lydijah to ready the refreshments and see that the lamps were all lit and the fires kept burning.

Lydijah hurried down the far hall to the back steps that led directly to the kitchen while Lizzy gathered herself, put on a smile, and was about to descend when she heard someone behind her. Turning, she saw Ann helping Rand, fully dressed, into the hallway.

"What on earth? Surely you aren't going down there, Randolph," Lizzy said in amazement.

Rand smiled. "With the help of the two most beautiful women in St. Louis, I think I can make it. Besides, Mother would be appalled if I let such a small thing as a knife wound keep me from entertaining her friends on her most beloved holiday, don't you think?"

Lizzy laughed lightly then went to his side and took his arm so that he stood between her and Ann as they started down the stairs. She knew he would not last the whole evening, but she was very grateful that he was there at all. She glanced over at Ann, whose eyes, though still ringed with dark circles, were filled with joyful relief. So much like their mother, Lizzy thought. So very much like their mother.

* * *

Felix piled the woodbox high and stoked the fire before putting several additional log quarters on it.

"Wha's you doin'? Ain't it hot enough in here already?" Jasmina was at the table rolling dough for hot scones, the usual forced hardness to the set of her jaw.

"Man can't make you happy no how," Felix said. "First you tell me to go and get wood—dat it's cold in this place—then you tell me it's too hot. Make up your mind, woman."

"Don't yo' get uppity with me, Felix Coulon, or you won' be gettin' none a this here bread. I was cold then, now I'm hot, simple as dat. Where's them hog ribs you was given by Miss Lizzy?"

"In that cooler I built to keep such things," Felix said.

She glanced at him. "How's Mr. Rand?" Her voice softened.

"I just seen 'im 'fore I came down here. He was up walkin' and conversing with them folks who came fo' Christmas. He don't look real chipper though, and I 'spect he'll be goin' on back to his bed sooner than later."

"He's fine man, and Miss Lizzy a fine woman. Youse lucky to run into 'em the way you done."

Jasmina was grateful this Christmas. First time she had her own home and a child to go with it. It was mostly because of Randolph and Lizzy Hudson. Trouble was, she had a hard time saying *thank you* and *please*. Just wasn't in her nature. And now she was falling in love and didn't know what to do about that either. Though Felix slept in the barn because they weren't married, she silently hoped that would change someday, but how could she let him know?

She had never known a man like Felix. Most men she had known either used and discarded her or were just plain mean. It had taken a good deal of time and effort to realize that Felix was nothing like that. He was good, pure and simple. The only real quarrel she had with him was that he made her stop smoking. She still snuck one once in awhile when she went for a walk alone, but even that was nearly something of the past and she was proud of it, though she didn't tell Felix so. Not yet. Good as Felix was, he could still leave her at any time, and when the baby was no longer feeding off her breast, she feared that day might come.

She glanced at the child lying asleep in his bed. She had come to love him like he was her own. And he nearly was, at least as far as she was concerned. It pained her more than she could say to think she might lose him, but it was still possible and she hated the thought.

"We both gainin' from that luck, Jasmina." Baby Shaymish stirred a bit; Felix reached into the small bed and took the baby carefully into his arms. He winced some as he stood straight.

"You been sleepin' in dat barn too long, dat's why you have dem spasms. You need a bed, Felix, and we both knows it."

"Jasmina, we talked about this afore. I ain't getting' in your bed 'less we's married, and we ain't gettin' married 'cause you and I doan see eye to eye."

"Not many husbands see eye to eye with dey wives; dat ain't nuthin' new." She paused, getting the courage to say what she felt, then spoke softly. "I like you, Felix. Ain't dat good enough fo' marryin' me?"

"I swear you is a direct woman." He couldn't help his smile. "But no, it ain't enough. I want a wife who loves me, not just *likes* me."

Her frustration was instantaneous. "There ya go again, splittin' hairs. Like, love, it's all the same. I'll be takin' care of you, and you'll be takin' care of me. Seems like dat's love and like all rolled up in one fine package."

Felix didn't answer. He liked Jasmina as well, despite her hotheaded personality. She could be witty and kind when she put her mind to it, and she had taken to little Shaymish like he was her own. She was a fair-looking woman, and he had been tempted to let her reel him into bed once or twice, but that wasn't his way.

Right now he was content to let things be as they were. If their feelings grew as more time passed, so be it. But for the moment, the most important thing was staying safe and caring for Shaymish.

A knock came at the door, and Felix was glad of it. He got up and opened it to find Newton and Mary standing outside in a fresh snow. He brought them in quickly and closed the door against the chill. Mary and Newton greeted him and made a fuss over Shaymish as they took off their capes and coats and set them on the double bed against the far wall.

The two had come to visit before, mostly to check on the baby but also to meet Jasmina. Mary and Jasmina got along quite well, and after all that had happened, Felix and Newton felt more like brothers than friends.

The two women continued the preparation of Christmas dinner, and Newton pulled up a second rocker and sat with Felix in front of the fire. They talked of many things but mostly war, then finally the refitting of the *Constitution*.

"A slave keep for runnin' slaves out of Little Dixie. I'll be!" Felix said after Newton quietly told him what he'd been up to aboard Rand Hudson's steamer. "Massa Rand, he's freein' run'ways!"

Newton nodded slightly. "I nosed aroun' a bit among crew an' captains. He 'as at least three steamers workin' up and down the Mississippi, holds jus' like this one."

"Never met nobody quite like him," Felix said, shaking his head in admiration.

Newton glanced at the women to make sure they were distracted by their own work and conversation. "The *Constitution* is near ready, Felix. I 'ear he'll send 'er north, up the Missouri. That woman ya tol' me abou,' the one ya met when you was lookin' after y' mum. Ya said she wanted t' run, t' escape. . . . If Hoodsun is agreeable, we coul' go after 'er and 'er kids. Others too. I know 'e's lookin' fer men willin' to go and fin' runners."

Felix felt his heart thump harder in his chest. He had spoken with Newton about Abigail and her children several times. Her situation still pained him a great deal, and he was unable to shake the haunted look in her dark eyes. He knew that part of the reason was that her circumstances mirrored Susannah's a great deal. He didn't have to think long on Newton's proposition. "I'll go," he said firmly. "You make it right with Mr. Hudson. You show him I can be useful."

Newton only nodded as Mary brought the kettle to the fireplace and hung it to melt grease. They'd soon have hot scones and ribs.

"Year ago on Christmas I was in England sufferin' from a cold spell tha' killed folks," Newton said, changing the subject.

"I was at sea. Haven't had a real Christmas in ten years," Felix said.

"We go' it goo'," Newton said with a smile.

"We does fer sure." Felix paused. "Merry Christmas, Newton."

"An' t' you as well."

Both of them watched the fire, deep in their own thoughts as they wondered what the New Year would bring.

Chapter 23

RAND STOOD WITH HIS ARM around Ann watching the steamboat pull away from the shore; Lizzy waved from the balcony of the upper deck. She would go down the Mississippi to Columbus, Tennessee, then catch the train to Corinth, Mississippi. From there she would catch another train to Chattanooga, Tennessee, and a final train to Richmond, Virginia. Her journey would take at least five days. Andrew was to meet her in Richmond and take her by carriage to his family plantation.

Lizzy's journey had been delayed. Andrew had sent a wire asking for another three weeks because of commitments he could not get out of at Sumter. Lizzy had been very disappointed but busied herself with helping Ann with wedding plans. Rand had been grateful to have them both around, as his recovery had taken longer than he expected and Lizzy periodically got Ann out of the house. When he finally returned to work, he was so swamped with catching up and his duties with the Home Guard that he felt he would have neglected Ann if Lizzy hadn't been there.

Rand waved to Lizzy one last time, and he and Ann turned back to the carriage. Rand told Eilliot to take them to Frank Blair's house before helping Ann inside and then following.

Though Ann returned to her Uncle Frank's each night, she spent most of her time each day with Rand and Lizzy at their place. But this morning she would be packing for her own journey to New Orleans and would leave later this evening. The prospect was very depressing for Rand.

Ann had sent word to her mother about their engagement and upcoming wedding. Her mother, as Ann had expected, had insisted on coming as soon as possible to help with every arrangement. She set the middle of January as an appropriate time in which she could be ready, but Adam, Ann's oldest brother, decided for some reason he could not accompany their mother, so Ann had prepared as quickly as she could to go to New Orleans and bring her mother back to St. Louis.

Rand sensed Ann's disappointment that Adam could not make this trip. Not only did Ann dread leaving for at least two weeks, but she felt that Adam was acting like a child over her decision to marry Rand.

"Have you heard from Matthew?" Rand inquired, asking about Ann's younger brother at West Point. He could only imagine what was happening there as the country was decidedly splitting in two. Frank had received a report that many cadets from the South had already resigned to return to their states and accept commissions in their militia units in preparation for the organization of a larger Confederate army. Rand could think of no greater sign that the Southern states were serious about secession than the call to arms of their young men at the academy.

"Nothing yet," she said with a worried look in her eyes. "But I know Adam has arranged for a commission in the Louisiana militia for Matthew and has encouraged him to return home soon to accept it."

Ann had learned from her mother that Adam had received a commission as a lieutenant even though he had no military training whatsoever. He had managed this with the help of the lawyer he worked for, who had a good deal of influence and was a general in the state militia. Rand considered it a mistake to put such inexperienced men in positions of leadership in battle; after all, he even questioned his own ability and he had spent six years in the military. But such things were happening in every state in the Union as North and South prepared for war. It did not bode well if things really came to hard-fought battles.

Ann gave Rand a worried look. "I hate to leave you. You are still not well, and . . ."

"I wouldn't hear of such a thing, and I am fine. Now that Lizzy is gone, your mother must come to help you, and it is not a good idea for her to travel alone." He paused as if thinking.

She smiled. "What is it, darling?"

"I have a proposal you might consider. Your mother will not be safe in New Orleans if war breaks out. I want you to try to convince her to stay here with you, possibly for a very long time. We can protect her far better if she is here."

Ann smiled. "Thank for you caring that much. I had the same concern. I will send a wire this afternoon."

Rand felt some relief as Ann snuggled in close but grimaced a bit as she inadvertently pressed again his still-healing wounds. He had thought of going with her on this journey, but with all he needed do to help prepare the Home Guard and protect his business, he didn't think it prudent. Instead he had arranged for someone to look after her, though Ann would hardly be aware of it. The idea of a bodyguard had seemed a silly thing to him a few weeks ago, but Ridges's attack had made him reconsider.

Ridges had disappeared, his brother Castle now running the slave pens and the plantation in Little Dixie that the two of them owned. Rand figured the bullet had taken Ridges to another world and was relieved to know it, though he still had nightmares about being forced to kill a man. But his personal war with the the Ridges boys probably wasn't over. Rumor was that Castle Ridges was looking for vengeance.

As they crossed town, Ann chatted about a number of wedding preparations, and Rand was content to listen and offer an opinion when it was required while also mentally preparing for the day. He was in the midst of such double thinking when she nudged him, looking up into his eyes.

"Did you hear a thing I just said?" she asked, a playful smile on her face.

He returned the smile. "Of course."

"Then repeat it."

"You want to have the wedding at the Riverside Hotel with a reception to follow, and you hope the weather will be good enough so at least some time can be spent in the lovely gardens." He smiled.

She looked at him, clearly a bit amazed. "How you do that is beyond me. I know your mind was elsewhere, and yet . . ."

"A gift from my mother," he said.

She laid her head on his shoulder again. "I wish I had known her better."

"You would have been the best of friends. She would have loved you very much." He pulled her in tight and kissed the top of her head.

"And your father?"

"He would have adored you. In fact he probably would have taken me to the woodshed for having delayed so long."

"Then I would have loved him very much."

Rand chuckled. "Yes, I think you would."

The carriage pulled up the lane of Frank's home and stopped at the door. After kissing Ann warmly once more and bidding her farewell until they could meet for dinner, Rand watched her disappear inside the Blair mansion then instructed his driver to take him to his place of business. He checked his pocket watch—there was just enough time to get there before his invited guests would join him.

He settled back in his seat and tried to concentrate on the issues they would be discussing at this meeting. Their group of recruits had nearly doubled in size, and they desperately needed more leaders. At this morning's meeting, they would discuss names and possibilities. As usual, Rand would go to the warehouse to oversee training later in the day.

Secession was gathering steam, and Rand knew that time was short before he and others would be called to arms. At his inauguration on January 4, Governor-elect Jackson had requested the authorization of a state constitutional convention in order to consider the relationship between Missouri and the federal government. His wish had been granted by a special referendum, and delegates had been elected.

But Rand no longer concerned himself with how members of the convention would actually vote. He knew that no matter the outcome, those who supported the South would try to force Missouri into the Confederacy, and that would mean civil war for the state. It was no longer *if* but *when* this would happen, and the Home Guard would need to be prepared to protect the arsenal and keep the state in Northern hands.

The carriage pulled up to Rand's place of business. He went up the stairs, greeting his employees as he passed their desks and entered his private office.

His guests had already arrived and were waiting. After greeting each, Rand cleared his throat and asked Hooker for a quick update.

When Hooker finished, he leaned back against his chair. "In my opinion, things are goin' better than expected."

Malone and Hirsch agreed verbally; Rosenthal nodded his head.

"They don't lack for effort, that is sure, but we need more weapons training," Rosenthal said. "Not just target practice, but maneuver and fire."

They discussed how best to accomplish that objective and talked about several other items, then Rand leaned forward. "We still need more experienced leaders."

Hooker sat back. "It's our weak spot, that's for sure, but we've come up with some names." He handed Rand a piece of paper. "Look 'em over, see what you think."

"Word is everywhere 'bout wha' we're doin'," Malone said. "Tha's goo' and bad. More good men are wantin' in, bu' the opposition is startin' to stir."

"Bound to happen," said Rosenthal.

"If the slavers try to interfere with us, what then?" Hirsch asked.

"Nothing they can do legally, but if they come as a mob, our men are trained enough to defend themselves. Let's just not forget to remind them that we are not out to start a fight, not yet. We are training, and they are to avoid conflict for now if they can," Rand replied. "I am still concerned about disicipline," he said. "Weapons don't win wars, gentlemen; discipline does. These boys need you to teach them how to stay on the line when they're as scared as a rabbit in a trap."

Hooker leaned forward. "Live fire training will do it, but…" He leaned back. "Are sure you want to do it just yet?"

"Get 'em on their bellies, and hit 'em good with a club if they raise up even an inch. Tell 'em this is only an inkling of what will happen if they get hit by a bullet. You tell 'em to keep down, and they'd better learn to keep down. They have to get it through their heads that they are to do as they're told if they don't want to get killed."

They all nodded, and for some time they continued to talk of other particulars. After an hour of such discussion, the meeting wore down and the men parted. Rand asked Hooker to stay.

"Ann is going to New Orleans to accompany her mother back to St. Lou."

"You should go with her, Rand," Hooker said seriously.

"Too much to do here. But I do have someone looking after her."

"And who will be lookin' after you?" Hooker asked.

"I can take care of myself," Rand said.

"Ya, I kin see that," Hooker smirked. He leaned forward. "If ya don't mind, I'll be watchin' yer back fer a time; I have a couple of friends who would be more than happy to help."

"No need."

"Rumor has it that Castle has a half dozen men ready to kill you on sight. If he and Atchison want you as dead as it seems, you'll be needin' help to keep ya alive. I intend to see you get it, and I want no arguments."

Rand nodded, relieved. "Thanks, Isaac. I'll sleep better knowing you are around, but don't be too obvious." He smiled. "Needing a babysitter is embarrassing."

Hooker laughed. "I'll do my best. So yer meetin' the mother-in-law, are ya," he said. "I know about that part. Like trying to deal with Jefferson Davis."

The notion brought a smile, but Rand didn't comment on it. Instead he said, "You're better at this military stuff than I am, Isaac. I've told Frank that from the beginning."

"You're the leader, Rand. It comes natural. People just follow you. Frank's right about that and I still agree with him." He stepped toward the door. "And I'll be followin' you into the mouth of Hades if I have to, but for now I'll just be goin' to the warehouse to see that the children get their schoolin'." He looked back at Rand, shaking his head. "Rand Hudson gettin' married. Lands, the world really is comin' to an end." With that he was gone.

Rand smiled widely then called to his clerk, who came through the door almost instantaneously.

"Give me a status on the steamers?" Rand said.

The clerk took the next half hour to give Rand a complete update on the position, condition, and use of each steamer in his fleet. Rand trusted most of those who worked for him but especially his clerk, William Dickson. The man was as loyal as the day was long, and if Rand did have to go away to war, leaving Lizzy and Ann to run things, William would be invaluable. Most of the others were the same, though he had wondered about Pete Hicks, who seemed a bit too quick to argue for Southern rights. Knowing someone was feeding Ridges his whereabouts while Ridges was alive, Rand figured that someone would need to watch Pete, and Rand had asked William to see to it.

"The *Constitution* is ready for use and is scheduled to leave for Jefferson City tomorrow. The *Elizabeth* is ready to go to New Orleans. Miss Alexander will have the owner's suite, as you asked," the clerk said.

"You can call her Ann," Rand replied gently.

The clerk nodded. "I suppose Miss Elizabeth got away safely this morning."

"Yes. Is Mr. Arthur keeping an eye on her?"

"All the way to Richmond, sir." The clerk nodded and smiled. "She will not like being tailed, sir."

Rand gave a wry grin. "No, I don't suppose so, but it's for her own safety. Let's just hope she doesn't shoot the man."

The clerk chuckled. "Yes, sir, that would be unfortunate." He stood to leave. "Anything else, sir?"

"Pete?"

"He's gone, sir."

Rand looked up. "Then he—"

"Yes, sir. I finally found someone who verified his connection to the attack on you. He was seen talking to Ridges just the day before. I took the liberty of firing him this morning."

Rand nodded. "Did you give him a week's pay?"

"Yes, sir, as with all those who . . . uh . . . don't work out. I also told him that Mr. Hooker would be paying him a visit if his miserable carcass was seen anywhere near one of our ships. I hope Mr. Hooker won't mind."

Rand chuckled. It was hard to picture William telling anyone off. "No, he won't mind. Have my carriage brought 'round in about twenty minutes."

William handed Rand a stack of papers to sign, along with a few letters to read and respond to. "Possibly an hour would fit better, sir," he suggested good-naturedly.

Rand looked at the stack, took a breath, and nodded. "Yes, an hour would be good." He loathed paperwork.

After nearly two hours, the last paper was signed, and he was ready to leave when his door opened. Frank Blair poked in his head. "Do you have some time?"

"Always," Rand said, forcing a smile. He was tired and hoped this was important.

"You look pale, Randolph," Frank said as he removed his coat.

"So do you, but I have a reason," Rand said tiredly.

Frank laughed lightly. "I suppose hearing that there is a credible threat on Lincoln's life has given me a bit of a shock, and there is word that the secessionists may attempt to take Washington at his inauguration in March. These matters may have something to do with my poor countenance."

"Or you just need more sun." Rand smiled. "What is Buchanan saying?"

"He doesn't believe any of it. Won't take any action, so Simon Cameron, Seward, a few others, and I are circumventing him, with Lincoln's blessing. Plans are being made to bring loyal militias from adjoining states into Washington for the ceremonies, and the president will get special protection from the Pinkerton agency when he moves east."

Simon Cameron and William Seward had both run against Lincoln for the Republican nomination. Seward was supposed to win but had made too many enemies to accomplish the task, and Cameron had thrown his support behind Lincoln early. It was rumored that Cameron would become Secretary of War in exchange for his support, and once he finally got behind Lincoln, Seward had been promised the position of Secretary of State. Both were extremely powerful in Washington, and it was obvious Frank was choosing his allies well.

"The secessionists would be fools to try anything," Rand said.

"I'm sure Davis and the others aren't involved, but there are fanatics in every movement, and if they see killing Lincoln to be to their advantage, they will give it a go." He paused. "My bigger concern is Washington. Davis would try attacking the capital. If he can take Washington, then the secessionists are the Union and we are the rebels. It would also cause Maryland to secede, which would leave the North very weakened."

"And the latest from Jefferson City?" Rand asked.

"With each state that secedes, Governor-elect Jackson and his supporters become bolder—even belligerent. They are sure they have the votes to follow suit here in Missouri." Frank smiled. "They will be disappointed."

"Have you received word about a new commander of the arsenal?"

"Yes. General Nathaniel Lyon. Staunch Unionist. He should be here in the next couple of weeks."

"Major Bell may try to surrender the arsenal before he gets here." Rand remembered Frank's words. The present commander of the arsenal had told Governor-elect Jackson that the arsenal was his if he wanted it.

"Bell resigned his commission—under pressure, of course, but he is gone. A man we can trust has temporarily taken his place," Frank said.

"You have been busy."

Frank's beard was fairly thick but his smile was large enough that even a heavy beard could not hide it. "Yes, I have." He cleared his throat. "Let's just hope that nothing happens before Lyon arrives."

Rand finished his conversation with Frank a few minutes later, and both men left in carriages that took them in different directions. Rand's mind delved into a dozen matters until he reached the *Constitution,* where he got out and boarded the steamer. He found the hold empty but well lit. He could hear the sound of a hammer on the far side of what seemed to be the old wall that formed the front of the hold. As he walked toward it, the sudden sound of muffled cogs and wheels and the quick lifting of a section of the wall revealed an opening and brought him to a halt. Newton Daines appeared, intent on examining the revealed door.

"Impressive," Rand said.

Newton greeted him with a nod. "Mr. Hoodsun."

"Newton. May I?" Rand asked pointing to the opening.

Newton stood aside, and Rand entered through the opening to find a room that contained shelves and built-in benches along the walls. Food, goods, blankets, and even clothes were stacked for use. He saw a dozen small cushions rolled up that could be used for sleeping as well.

"All the comforts, but it could get stuffy in here," Rand said.

"There are vents—ya jus' can' see 'em."

Rand looked around the hold. "Did you cut in an outside exit?"

Newton walked to the port side, reached into a discreet hole, and pulled down on a lever. A panel disappeared downward to reveal an opening. "No seams t' be seen when she's closed. A rope ladder can be dropped an' entrance gained from th' river itself if need be." Newton pushed up on the lever, and the outside door closed and sealed in seconds. "All about cogs, wheels, and pulleys," he said with a smile. He cleared his throat. "I s'pose she'll be pu' to goo' use soon?"

"She leaves for Jefferson City tomorrow," Rand replied.

"I been thinkin', Mr. Hoodsun, tha' I'd like t' help in this bit o' business."

Rand looked at him, gauging his comment. "It is very dangerous, Mr. Daines."

"'Tis so, I'm sure, bu' I still be wantin' t' give a hand."

Rand thought only a moment. Daines was smart, resourceful, and determined; that much was obvious. Rand could use him. "Then you're welcome."

Newton cleared his throat. "Felix woul' like to come along as well. When 'e was up river, 'e met some folks, an' 'e wants t' try an' bring 'em out."

Rand nodded, but his brow was creased with concern. "It will be dangerous for both of you but especially for him. They hang coloreds who help with this business."

"He knows, and 'e's willin' t' take the chance. 'As some regre's abou' nah helpin' 'is mum and sis an' uthers sooner."

Rand once more deliberated but was just as aware of Felix Coulon's abilities as he was of those held by Newton Daines. Though a black man was in great danger, he was also trusted by other blacks—and as long as he had papers showing he was a freedman and kept close to Newton. . . .

"I assume he has his new papers?" Rand asked.

"Yes, sir. Yer lawyer friend saw to it. He got 'em this mornin'."

"Very well; Mr. Coulon can assist you if he is willing," Rand answered.

They shook hands. Rand left the compartment and went back into the hold. "How does this one open and close?"

Newton reached overhead, pushed aside a false panel, and pulled on a lever. The door closed, and Rand stepped nearer to see if he could find a seam. He could not. "Fine work. Apparently this is the old paneling that was on the outside wall—you just moved it."

Newton nodded as Rand removed his wallet and took out several bills. "This is your pay for your work here. You will receive the same amount after each run you make aboard the *Constitution*."

Newton's eyes widened. "The saints be praised. 'Tis a lot of muny, Mr. Hoodsun."

"You will remove at least half a dozen souls from slavery in the next few days, Mr. Daines, and you will do so at the risk of death. It is worth every penny. If you need time to think things over, take it. If not, I will see you when you return."

"No, sir, I'll be aboard in the mornin'. Is the captain and the crew aware of what we'll be doin?'"

"They are, but they'll be carrying on just as they normally would so as to avoid any suspicion falling on the real purpose of the *Constitution*." He removed a small ledger from his pocket and began writing, then tore out the page and handed it to Newton. "Here are the names and addresses of those in Jefferson City and other places who are helping with the effort. You can rely on all of them for anything you need. Memorize the list and then burn it." He extended his hand. "Welcome to the work of freedom, Mr. Daines."

Newton shook the offered hand and smiled, and Rand started for the stairs. "I assume you will send word to Felix before the day is over," he called.

"I will," Newton promised.

"Elizabeth will not be happy with you. Felix is doing wonders for our bookkeeping." Rand smiled as he went up the stairs and quickly left the ship. He admired Newton Daines's grit and lack of fear and had an affinity toward him that bordered on complete trust. He couldn't have asked for a better addition.

Rand ate a late lunch then decided to return home for a brief rest before going to the warehouse for the training of the Home Guard. When he arrived at the front door, Felix stood waiting with a telegram from Elizabeth. She had arrived at Cairo, and Mr. Arthur had been sent home. She did not need an escort. Rand could only smile. Lizzy was so much like their mother.

"How is the baby?" Rand asked Felix as they climbed the steps to the front door.

"Fine, suh, jus' fine," Felix replied with a pleasant smile. Rand removed his coat and hung it up as Felix returned to the small office at the back of the house. It was obvious that Newton had not yet sent word but Rand was certain that Felix would not hesitate to accept an invitation to be involved in the underground. The man had seen the pens from the inside.

Climbing the steps wearily, Rand went to his room, lay on the divan, and closed his eyes.

He had found it more difficult to sleep since the attempt on his life. Being confronted with one's own mortality did that, he supposed. It wasn't just that Castle Ridges was looking for vengeance; it was something deeper—a concern about whether or not Rand was really ready to face God. He had lived a good life by most standards, but life after death was an unsettling unknown to him, and he still wondered if the little he'd been taught about it was true.

There had also been the thought that killing a man—any man—would be frowned on by God. He had resolved that with a study of the Book of Mormon, which taught that killing the wicked to keep them from harming others was sometimes necessary.

But his biggest worry now was Ann. He did not want to lose her or leave her. That thought, more than any other, caused him to toss and turn rather than sleep. He knew about temple ordinances and had heard Joseph Smith and others teach about them often. He could remember sitting in the bowery in Nauvoo and listening to the Prophet explain how families could be united and how work could be done for those who had passed on so that the dead could be judged on equal terms with the living. But however much these teachings had resonated with him, he was a thousand miles away from anyone who could actually perform such an ordinance. And even if Brigham continued to hold the authority, wasn't a temple needed? He knew they were building one in Salt Lake but newspaper reports said it was a long way from being finished.

With a dozen questions for which he had no answers, Rand had finally decided to write a letter to Brigham Young in Salt Lake. He'd sent it the day after Christmas but did not expect a reply for at least another two weeks, probably longer, if he got an answer at all.

In the meantime, he and Ann had discussed the principle of eternal marriage, at least as much as he remembered of it. Though he did not have a copy of the revelation on marriage, it was indelibly imprinted in his mind, and Ann had enthusiastically embraced such a notion. She had commented that a lifetime was certainly not enough for the two of them.

But now, with war coming, would a temple marriage even be possible? The thought that it might not be possible was the biggest reason for his sleepless nights. If he went to war . . . if he didn't come back . . . and was he even worthy of such an ordinance?

Rand's letter to Brigham Young had included a dozen questions and had ended up nearly three pages long. But the effort itself had been a sort of cleansing—a reconnection to his old faith. A connection he desperately needed.

He read from the Book of Mormon for twenty minutes before a knock came on the door. Lydijah poked her head in and announced that it was time to leave for the warehouse. He thanked her and she disappeared.

Getting to his knees, Rand prayed for greater strength, greater healing, and for protection for Lizzy and for Ann. Then he prayed for understanding, both of how to best prepare for what lay ahead and for peace, which seemed much more important now.

He got to his feet. He always felt better after prayer and wondered why he had ever stopped. He still kicked himself for the years of spiritual apathy, for thinking he had outgrown God or was smart enough to get along on his own. What a fool he had been—but then, any man who thought he could get along without God was a fool. Either that or his ego was out of control. What arrogance! The Book of Mormon warned about that arrogance repeatedly, as did the New Testament. Unfortunately there were a lot of men who weren't listening, including him. He had determined to never let it happen again.

He looked at his watch; he was running late. He quickly changed clothes, stuck his revolver in his belt, and picked up his Sharps rifle before putting on his stiff-brimmed hat and leather coat. He must trust that God would take care of him and Ann, but there were others who trusted him to help prepare them as well. He could not let them down. He left the room and went downstairs, where Felix waited for him to sign a letter to a man who had overcharged them for feed for the horses.

Rand felt to mention Felix's request. "I understand you want to help us with the work in Little Dixie," Rand said as he signed the letter.

Felix nodded. "Yes, suh."

"Newton has your orders. You leave in the morning. Be careful, Felix. They'll hang you if you get caught."

"Yas, suh, I know. Suh . . ."

"Yes, Felix, what is it?" Rand said curiously.

"I been thinkin' . . . well, maybe I'd like to marry Miss Jasmina. I ain't 'cided fo' sure, but she a changed woman and—"

"Felix, if you want to marry, it is your decision. You do not need to ask my permission, but if you're asking for my blessing, you certainly have that and my permission to use that house for as long as you like. I ask only one thing in return."

Felix seemed relieved. "Yas, suh, anything."

"You let me be your first child's godfather," Rand said.

"It would be an honor, suh," Felix said, his eyes tearing.

"Good."

"But I ain't decided fo' sure yet, Mr. Rand," Felix emphasized.

"I won't mention it, Felix, but don't wait too long. My experience is that when you do, you miss a good deal of happiness." He went out the door and climbed in his carriage.

He already missed Ann. It would be a long two weeks.

Chapter 24

Benjamin Siddell slipped into the small pub on the outskirts of St. Louis and waited a moment to let his eyes adjust to the darkness. He scanned the room and noticed Atchison and Shelby in a far corner consorting with a man half hidden by a drooping, wide-brimmed hat. He felt mixed emotions as he realized who it was.

As he crossed the room, he felt his knees begin to weaken. When he heard that Sam Ridges had tried to kill Rand, he had become physically ill. Though he felt wronged by Rand and Lizzy, he had never wished them any harm. Thinking that Atchison's threats were mostly bluster and attempts at intimidation, he had gone along, even used the tactic himself to try to get Rand to see reason, but he had never believed that Atchison and Ridges would try to seriously harm—let alone try to kill—Rand. It had been a hard night for Benjamin that had grown into days of facing the reality of the part he'd played in it all. Atchison held debt that if called would ruin Benjamin, yet he no longer wanted anything to do with the former senator and had avoided—even ignored—his request for a meeting. Then he'd received a visit from the men who held his debt.

He felt his palms begin to sweat as he neared the table. He was in way over his head, trapped by his own desperation and foolishness. Even now he regretted coming here. He should have gone to Rand and talked it through, but he couldn't swallow that pill—not now, not after being such a fool.

As Benjamin reached the table, Atchison looked up and simply nodded toward a chair, a look of loathing and disgust in his eyes.

"Mr. Siddell, if you ever ignore my messages again, Mr. Ridges here will bring me your head, do you understand?" Atchison said with ice in his voice.

"What do you want, Senator?" Benjamin said the words as normally as he could, but inside he was falling apart with fear.

"Castle, maybe you should answer Mr. Siddell's question," Atchison said.

The shadow of his floppy-brimmed hat covered Castle's face but Benjamin could swear that fire burned in the sockets where his eyes should be.

"Your nephew killed my brother. I want him dead for it."

"Your brother's death is not my concern, Ridges. He was a fool to try to—"

Ridges was across the table with his hand around Benjamin's throat before he could even yelp, and Benjamin saw the blade of the knife edge toward his eye socket even as Atchison spoke.

"Not now, Castle, and certainly not here," he said.

Castle Ridges slowly backed off and sat down, laying his bowie knife on the table with a hard thump. Benjamin wanted to pass out. The blood was completely gone from his face, and he strained to fight down the rising panic.

"Your nephew is a hard man to bring around," Atchison said. "So we're going to teach him a lesson. I want you to get a man on board one of his steamers."

"For what purpose?" Benjamin said as evenly as he could muster.

"We're going to start robbing Hudson blind and sinking his ships, Siddell. Maybe then—"

"They aren't any good to you at the bottom of the river," Benjamin attempted.

"And they ain't no good to the Union neither," Castle chimed in.

"Shut up, Castle," Atchison said, his eyes on Benjamin. "Hudson needs to know I am a man of my word. After he loses a few steamers and a couple dozen lives, he'll begin to see things more clearly. But right now he has his fleet so well guarded that we can't get near 'em. You are going to fix that."

"I have no control over anything to do with the steamers, and you know that," Benjamin said, looking for a way out. He wanted nothing to do with killing innocent people.

"You will find a way, or I will see you ruined," Atchison said calmly. He pulled a paper from his pocket and slid it across the table.

"What's this?" Ben asked, unfolding the paper.

"Eviction notice," Atchison said. "If I don't have someone on board one of those steamers tonight and the steamer sunk by morning, your family will get tossed into the street." He leaned forward. "Find a way, or see your wife and kids out in the cold by morning." He stood. "Castle here will be at Webb's coffee shop on the waterfront at noon today. You'd better show up with papers our man can use to get aboard one of those steamers."

Benjamin tried to think fast, clear his head, but he was not normally quick of mind, and fear only made it worse. "I . . . I can't do it that quick. I have to arrange, pay someone to come up sick, then there are the papers . . . Rand has special forms for changes like these, and I . . . I'll have to arrange for a copy. With Pete Hicks being fired, I—I can't get it before six tonight."

Atchison glared at him as his mind turned over the information. "You come any later than six this afternoon, and I'll have these papers served. Now get out of my sight."

Benjamin got to his feet feeling faint but managed to make his way outside, where he fell against a wall. His world spun as he stumbled to his carriage and got inside. The carriage driver looked through the small opening and asked where to go. Benjamin told him it didn't matter—to just get moving. As the wheels began to roll, Benjamin looked out the small, round, back window to make sure he wasn't being followed. He tried to shake the fear and confusion out of his weak mind, tried to think. After five minutes of anguished inner struggle, he realized how trapped he really was. And though he thought as long and hard as his brain would allow, he could see only one way out.

* * *

Rand left the warehouse close to 6 P.M. and waved to Hooker, who was just mounting his gelding and giving orders to two of his men. One hurried off with Hooker, and one followed Rand, his guardian angel for the evening.

A few minutes later, Rand's carriage pulled up in front of the Barnum, and he went inside to find Ann waiting at a table he had reserved. He quickly checked his hat then walked across the dining room to join her. He garnered no attention.

"Sorry I'm late," he said sheepishly, hoping he did not look as tired as he felt.

Ann reached over and touched his hand, a genuinely worried look in her eyes. "You look worn out, darling, and very different. I don't see you in those clothes often." Rand was wearing a pair of leather breeches, a loose-fitting linen shirt, a handkerchief tied around his neck, and a thick leather belt around his waist; a pistol and a rather large knife hung from each side.

Sitting near her, he took her hand and squeezed it. "The maneuvers we practiced tonight required it. I hope they don't embarrass you." He looked at a large clock over the fireplace. They had two and a half hours before she would need to board the steamer.

"Hardly. You are very handsome in them." She leaned forward. "There isn't a woman in here who has not given you her attention. They are jealous, and I am elated."

He chuckled. "Then I will wear them more often. Have you ordered?"

She nodded with a wry smile. "Your usual. Raw meat served with a side of crisp vegetables."

He chuckled. "Thanks."

"And how are things with the Home Guard?" she asked.

"Better than expected. We have fifteen companies each at an effective one hundred men, and I find them more disciplined and serious about this business than I had first hoped. Hooker and the others have done a wonderful job." He leaned forward, warming to his subject. "Most of the evening we put the men through maneuvers that they will experience in a real battlefield environment. They worked very well together, very even transitions from one manuever to another. Another few weeks and I think we will hold our own against the state militia on any field."

"Fifteen hundred doesn't seem like very many soldiers," Ann said.

"That's just the ones in training. We have another two hundred in orientation—new recruits over the last week. Our challenge is developing leaders that won't get them all killed in battle, but we had a couple more promising prospects join tonight. One is an old-timer. Fought in the Mexican-American War and was stationed out west for twenty years. Indian fighter. Hooker met him once or twice when he was out there. He can do the job."

"The other?"

"A thirty-year-old lawyer who went to West Point and spent a couple of years at Fort Pickney. No battle experience, but he knows cannon. He was a captain of artillery when he left the army. Trouble is, he's from Illinois. Has to travel here every day. Says he doesn't mind but if he can't get here it could put us in a bind—but Hooker says he can manage." He paused. "I'm beginning to believe we can do this."

"Good," Ann said. "If you believe in them, Rand, they'll believe in themselves, and you are going to need them to be at their very best far too soon." A look of consternation crossed her countenance.

She reached down next to her chair and retrieved a paper. "On my way here, I noticed a good deal of commotion at the newsstand next to the hotel. I bought this as a result."

Rand took the paper and read the headline: "Louisiana Has Voted to Secede and Join the Confederacy." He put the paper down, a wrinkle in his brow.

"That is the sixth state, with Texas all but out as well. The secessionist fever is at a high pitch. In the process they are forcibly taking possession of federal forts, docks, and even ships across the deep South. South Carolina is no longer just requesting that Fort Sumter be turned over to them but has sent a commission to Washington to demand it."

Rand watched the red rise in her face as her anger grew. "And Buchanan is still sitting on his thumbs."

"The man is a disgrace to his office."

"At least a fool." She leaned across the table and spoke quietly. "They call the Mormon War Buchanan's blunder, did you know that? He was an idiot then, and he has lost his mind now. This is a catastrophe." She sat back.

"Surely a fool." He smiled. "Have I ever told you how beautiful you are when you're angry?"

She seemed a bit jolted then smiled and finally chuckled. "You beast. You're egging me on."

"Yes, well, a little." He sobered. "But you are right. I never thought I'd see the day when a U.S. president would stand idle while the country disintegrated before his very eyes."

"I heard something else today," she said, a worried look on her face. "What can you tell me about another marching group, one that supported Breckinridge in the election, something called—"

"The Minutemen," Rand filled in the blank.

"Yes. Frank seems genuinely disturbed by them."

"The secessionists around town have heard what we're doing. They've decided to counter by calling up their Minutemen," Rand said. "Another marching group like the Wide Awakes that supported Douglas."

"Frank says that Sterling Price is supporting them with training and weaponry and that Jackson has given a speech saying the Home Guard is an illegal organization."

A former governor, Sterling Price was a pro-Southern general in the state militia. He claimed he was for maintaining neutrality, but as far South as he leaned, Rand found it no surprise that Price was aiding the Minutemen.

"Price and Jackson cannot call out the militia without approval of the assembly, which they cannot get, at least not yet. So they have turned to the Minutemen," Rand explained.

"I can understand that, but what about this declaration that the Home Guard is illegal?" Ann asked.

"We are officially registered as a political marching club, and the papers are signed by all the right people. That makes our group just as legal as the Minutemen. They are desperate to stop our progress, that's all, and desperate that we snuck the paperwork by them. They know they haven't a decent challenge."

The waiter appeared with their food, and they stopped their conversation long enough for the man to set it in front of them. Once he had filled their water glasses and moved on, Ann spoke again.

"I see what you mean." She smiled. "Jackson must be having conniptions. He had a chance to get the arsenal, but now that Lyon has been assigned and Bell relieved of duty—"

"Lyon is coming?"

"On his way. Uncle Frank told me this evening—said to tell you."

"Wonderful news. Yes, they must be kicking themselves."

They ate without talking for a few minutes, both because they were hungry and they were mulling over the information they had just discussed.

Finally Ann spoke. "Frank says most of your recruits are German. Why is that?"

"Frank talks too much," Rand said with a smile.

She smiled. "Yes, well, I ask a lot of questions, and I suppose he trusts me more now that you and I are getting married."

"A wonderful turn of events, don't you think?"

She grinned. "Do not forget that I had to work very hard for your attentions, Rand Hudson."

"And rightly so. I am a fine catch," he said jokingly.

"And one to be refined and shaped into a man of even greater ability than he sees in himself," she answered.

He chuckled then leaned forward. "I was not even half a man without you, Ann Alexander. I thank God every day for prodding you to take me off the list of unfortunate bachelors."

"And I am glad to have done it." She made a clucking noise with her tongue. "Such a waste."

Rand chuckled even as her eyes seemed to move to something behind him. He turned to see Frank Blair coming across the room toward them, a sober look to his face.

"Ann, sorry to interrupt you," he said with a slight peck on her cheek. "Rand, may I join the two of you for a moment?"

"Of course," Rand said as Frank retrieved a chair from an empty table nearby. He sat down and then spoke.

"Jefferson Davis resigned as senator from Mississippi. He's been commissioned as a general in the Mississippi militia." Frank was visibly upset. "In a few days a Confederate States' Constitutional Convention—composed of Mississippi, South Carolina, Florida, Alabama, Georgia, and Louisiana—will meet in Montgomery, Alabama. They'll name Davis as provisional president of the Confederacy."

The three of them did not speak for a long moment.

"Surely they have all lost their senses," Ann said softly.

"Davis responded to reporters by saying that they are a new country with new laws, and if the Union tries to force them back by war, they will fight. He says they'll win."

Rand put his fork down, his appetite suddenly gone.

"As you know, South Carolina has taken Fort Moultrie. They are threatening Sumter and will not let federal troops return to the mainland for supplies unless they surrender the fort."

"They might just as well declare war," Rand said.

"They're not ready yet, but they obviously mean to do it," Frank said.

"I am confused; is Sumter an island or something?" Ann asked.

"Yes, it sits in Charleston harbor," Rand said. "It's the most important harbor in the South."

Frank nodded. "Three forts overlook the harbor—Castle Pickney, which is old and run-down and hardly any use unless rebuilt and fortified; Fort Moultrie, which is small and indefensible because of its position; and Fort Sumter, which is large and protective. It is the most important of all. Robert Anderson took his troops to Sumter earlier for their protection."

"Yes, I remember. The South was very upset about it. Called him a traitor. It won't be long before they fire upon it then, will it?" Ann asked.

"Southern members of the Union forces at Sumter have deserted for commissions in the South Carolina militia. They are preparing to lay siege," Frank added.

Rand had a sudden thought about Andrew and what he might have done, but he pushed it aside, at least for the moment. "They think they are backing Lincoln into a corner and that he will give up," he said.

"They're wrong. They've just given Lincoln a way to discredit their entire action. If they fire on a federal fort, he has every right to call for its protection. At that point, they become the aggressors, and foreign powers cannot support them. They are fools." He shook his head lightly. "But that is not why I have come. Buchanan is paralyzed. He's thinking of recalling the remaining forces at Sumter and surrendering it, the worst possible thing he could do. I've come to tell you I am leaving for Washington in the morning. We have to put some bone into his spine until we can get Lincoln inaugurated." He glanced at Ann then went on. "I will leave you in charge of preparations here. Are you well enough to—"

"He is fine," Ann said. "He will have the men ready."

Frank gave an amused smile. "The source of your strength is noted, Mr. Hudson." Frank stood. "I will leave you two alone. Ann, be careful in Louisiana. Things have become frenetic there. There is a rumor that its militia has been called to arms and that they intend to take control of the mint." He looked at Rand. "She really should have an escort sent with her, but I need you here, Randolph."

"Don't worry; everything has been arranged," Rand said.

Frank nodded to them both and then left Ann and Rand to their thoughts.

"Did you wire your mother and tell her she should be prepared for a long stay?"

Ann nodded. "Yes, and a good thing." Her brow wrinkled, and she placed her hand on his. "But it may mean a delay in my return. She has to get rid of some things, pack others . . ."

"You know I will hate it but I understand." Rand knew Sumter would not be attacked before the Confederacy had a president and a constitution. Nor would they act until after Lincoln was actually inaugurated. They had applied pressure, but they needed time for preparation. Until then the entire South would be in turmoil, with each militia acting on its own against what they considered Union targets. The South would be chaos and no place for Ann's mother; better a little delay now than no ability to get her out later.

He looked at his pocket watch. Two hours before Ann boarded the steamer. He put all thought aside and concentrated on her.

Chapter 25

BENJAMIN SIDDELL'S CARRIAGE PULLED UP in front of Webb's coffee shop, and he took a deep breath before stepping out and going inside. He saw Ridges on the far side of the room with two of his cronies. He recognized one of them as a man by the name of O'Shay, an Irish thug from the Kerry Patch and a man with the same hard heart and endless greed as Castle.

Weak in the knees at the prospect of what he had to do, Benjamin clumsily dodged a customer and wound his way through the congested tables before slinking in front of the table occupied by Ridges and O'Shay.

"You're late, Siddell. I was just about to send someone to tell Atchison to serve them papers." Castle's wry smile strangely gave Benjamin strength from sheer hate.

Benjamin had come late on purpose. It was a matter of timing now. Careful timing. "It couldn't be helped." He reached into his coat pocket, retrieved an envelope, and placed it on the table. Ridges picked it up and handed it to O'Shay. Benjamin had forgotten that Castle Ridges didn't read.

O'Shay opened the envelope and unfolded the paper. It seemed to take an eternity for O'Shay to read through it, but then O'Shay wasn't the sharpest tool in the shed.

"It says I am replacin' sum guy by the name of . . . Pushman," O'Shay said.

"Bushman," Benjamin said. "He works in the boiler room."

"Doan know nuthin' abou' boilers," O'Shay said.

"You can toss wood at a fire, can't you?" Benjamin said condescendingly.

"Doan be getting' uppity wi' me or I'll—"

"Leave it be O'Shay," Ridges said. "What time?"

"He can board her at 7:30 P.M. That won't give them time to ask any questions of Mr. Bushman." He looked at O'Shay. "And try to get rid of

that horrid accent. Bushman isn't Irish." Benjamin felt stronger speaking
to O'Shay like this, but now was the tricky part. "She's in the last position
on the south end of the docks. She'll look old, beat up, but she's the only
one going out tonight." He leaned forward, placing his hands on the table.

"You tell Atchison I expect a thousand dollars in payment. If he thinks
I am going to let you destroy Hudson Company and get nothing for it,
he is a fool."

Ridges stood quickly and leaned across the table until his face was
within a foot of Benjamin's. He turned his head just long enough to spit a
grim wad of tobacco on the floor before glaring meancingly at Benjamin.
"You ain't dictatin' nuthin', Siddell," he hissed.

It took every bit of his strength not to cower, but Benjamin had been
doing too much of that lately when it came to Atchison and the Ridges
boys; it was critical that he didn't do so now. He pushed back by standing
and leaning even closer. "You tell him, Ridges." With that he turned away
and left the coffee shop, his stomach churning. Again he felt faint as he
struggled to climb into the carriage, and he threw himself into his seat as
it pulled away. He took deep breaths to wrest control of his shaking hands
as the carriage moved down the street and away from Castle Ridges. He
had done all he could. Now he would wait.

* * *

Ridges gave O'Shay and another accomplice their final instructions then
climbed into the carriage that had belonged to his brother. He headed
south toward the designated point of rendezvous, where O'Shay would
blow up the steamer—the spot from which he would need a ride back to
the city. His carriage had just reached the outskirts of town and was in the
country when the carriage slowed, then stopped. Ridges leaned out the
window and looked up at the driver to find out the reason for the delay
when he felt a gun barrel at the back of his neck. Another man appeared
at the opposite carriage door and pushed a rifle in his direction then told
him to get out. Castle opened the door and got to the ground, his hands
in the air, when a third man appeared out of the darkness.

"You!" he growled.

He felt two sets of strong hands grab him from behind, and he was
quickly tied and blindfolded, then shoved back in the carriage; a cloth that
smelled of chloroform was placed over his face. His attempt to fight the
two men who restrained him was to no avail; he soon felt his mind drift
then dive into a heavy sleep.

* * *

O'Shay presented himself for boarding in the place of Mr. Bushman. Asked for his papers, he quickly presented the ones Siddell had given him, was questioned only briefly, then told to report to the boiler room to begin his work. He walked into the main hold, found himself alone, and quickly went through it and to the front of the steamer. He immediately went to the side closest to shore and peered over it.

"Swenson," he said as loud as he dared.

"Here," came the reply. Hands wrapped around a barrel appeared out of the darkness. O'Shay took the cylinder of black powder and hefted it on board then quickly shoved it out of sight behind a stale bale of cotton sitting near the hold. Two more followed before he saw Swenson rowing back toward shore as quickly but quietly as he could.

The plan was simple. Once the steamer was moving, O'Shay would retrieve the powder and place it in the hold below the boiler. Then, when the steamer reached the rendezvous point where Castle Ridges waited, he was to light the fuse and jump ship. Two minutes later the old steamer would go to the bottom and he would be safely ashore.

O'Shay sauntered into the boiler room and reported to the boss, who pointed at a stack of wood and told him to start feeding the furnace. Normally O'Shay avoided work, but this time he didn't mind. He was getting paid well for this piece of action, and a little grunt work didn't bother him.

It was Castle Ridges who had come looking for him. At first he'd thought it was because of the deal he and Sam Ridges had made for O'Shay to take care of Daines and Mary McConnell, but when he discovered it was not, he kept that information to himself. Castle was offering good money for this work, and O'Shay didn't want to complicate things by bringing up past promises, especially since Sam was dead and could no longer pay the two hundred for Daines's demise. No sense taking a chance getting hung if there wasn't money in it.

Half an hour after he threw his first piece of wood, the steamer left the docks and paddled into the middle of the Mississippi River, going south. O'Shay worked until midnight, and once he was replaced he went on deck and rolled himself a cigarette. The night was dark, with a thin fog already clinging to the water. But he could see the lights that marked Rafferty's Point, and he knew he was only about twenty minutes away from his point of rendezvous with Ridges.

Making sure he was alone, he retrieved the first powder barrel then quietly slipped into the hold below the main deck. Lighting a match, then a small lantern that hung on the wall, he went down the steps. He lifted the lantern and peered around the hold as his eyes adjusted. It was empty and even had some water on the floor at the lowest point. He stared for a moment then shrugged. Strange, but no matter. He pulled his pocket watch out and checked the time. He was running out of time.

O'Shay positioned the barrel where he figured it would be under the boiler, then quickly retrieved the others and put them beside it before removing a roll of fuse from his coat pocket. Quickly punching the wood cork out of the barrel top, he shoved the fuse into the powder and strung the remainder in the direction of the door. When he reached the steps, he pulled out his pocket watch and checked the time. He was a couple of minutes behind schedule, so he cut off a small section of the fuse before he lit it and quickly started up the steps.

As he came onto the main deck, he checked around him but saw no one. Walking to the back of the steamer, he looked up at the wheelhouse. No one there. Curious.

Hearing the sound of oars in the water, he squinted through the mist and finally caught a glimpse of two small rowboats heading in the direction of shore.

"What the—" He was cut off by a muffled voice coming from the shadows a few feet away. He looked at the water, knowing he had only a minute to get off the steamer, but he decided to check the source of the sound. After only a few steps, he looked down in amazement to see Castle Ridges—tied, gagged, and lying on his stomach on the deck.

"Castle?" he said as he rolled Ridges over. "What the—"

Ridges's eyes were wide with fear, and O'Shay quickly removed the rag from his mouth.

"The fuse, you idiot! Stop the—"

O'Shay gasped just as the fuse struck powder and the steamer's bottom was blown out from under her. The two men were launched upward then came down hard on the deck as the steamer slapped back on the water.

"Get me loose!" Ridges screamed.

O'Shay, who had been knocked off his feet and stunned to paralysis, didn't move. His eyes fixed on the gun shoved into the bridge of his nose.

"Up," Hooker said.

O'Shay scrambled to his feet as best he could as the ship listed left and round and wood tore away from wood as it was coming apart. He glanced at a stunned and wide-eyed Castle Ridges, who was still on the deck, water creeping up his legs as the front of the ship began to go under.

"Now git!" Hooker said, waving the pistol toward the edge of the ship. O'Shay glanced at Ridges once more then went for the side and was gone.

Ridges swore and screamed as he fought the ropes hard until Hooker pushed a strong hand into his chest and a bowie knife under his nose.

"Ridges. You seem to be in trouble," Hooker said almost casually. He was dressed in his frontier leathers.

"This is murder, Hooker."

Hooker only smiled as he stood and sheathed his knife. "This is your doin', Ridges. Let's see how you handle dyin' the death you intended for a hundred others." He turned as if to go over the side himself.

"No! You can't just leave me here!" Ridges said, his eyes darting wildly to the side of the steamer and the water that was lapping at his legs. "You're not a cold-blooded killer, Hooker!" He forced a smile, his eyes darting to the water climbing his legs. "Come on, cut me loose!" He was near begging now.

Hooker hesitated only a second more, then turned back, slipping slightly as the ship began to slide downward. The two ends of the steamer were separate now, and the river was forcing the forward end of the rear section where they were down at a fast rate. As Ridges started to slide into the rising water, Hooker grabbed him by the collar and held him.

"If I even hear you're within fifty miles of St. Louis or one of the Hudsons, including Benjamin Siddell, I'll be huntin' you down, and you won't like what I do to you then." He pressed the knife closer. "You hear me?"

Ridges nodded furiously, the water to his waist. Hooker lifted him enough to cut the ropes binding his feet and arms then unceremoniously threw him over the side before jumping into the river himself. He grabbed hold of the thrashing and sinking Ridges and dragged him toward shore. When he had him pulled up on land, he again pressed his knife against Ridges's throat.

"Get up and get movin' 'fore I change my mind."

Ridges scrambled to his feet, fear etched in every crease of his ugly face; he quickly stumbled into the trees and disappeared.

Hooker looked out at the river as the last of the old *National Belle* sank out of sight. Then he chuckled. Atchison had managed to purchase this old steamer just two days earlier. Somewhat serviceable, but in need of a license and some repair, it now sat at the bottom of the Mississippi and would not be aiding the secessionists in their efforts for the South. He wondered how Ridges was going to explain *that* to David Atchison.

Chapter 26

WHEN ATCHISON SAUNTERED INTO HIS usual coffee shop for breakfast, he found the place abuzz with the word of an explosion sinking a steamer a few miles down river. No one seemed to know the name of the steamer, and Atchison smiled to himself as he thought about one of Rand Hudson's flotilla sitting at the bottom of the Mississippi.

He was just sticking a large bite of egg in his mouth when a man stepped in with a stunning announcement.

"Name of the steamer that blew up was the *National Belle*."

Atchison nearly choked on the egg, then spat and sputtered to try to dislodge it from his throat.

"Ain't that your steamer?" someone said, facing Atchison from the adjoining table. All eyes were on him, and he heard whispering from around the room. More than a few people had the audacity to smile.

But Atchison didn't answer the question. Standing abruptly, he threw coins on the table then followed them with the thrust of his napkin before grabbing his coat and exiting the premises, his mind a blur of confusion and rage. Shouting for his driver to get to his office posthaste, he fell back into his seat and fumed. Ridges was stupid, but surely he couldn't be *that* stupid.

He was out of the carriage before it came to a stop. Rushing up the steps to the second floor, he opened the door to find his clerks in a sober, even fearful, mood.

"Then it's true," Atchison bellowed. The stark silence in the room screamed the obvious reply. He entered his office, slamming the door behind him, confused and angry as a nest of mad hornets, his stomach churning bile and his mind set on revenge. Benjamin Siddell had something to do with this, and he would pay for it!

There was a quiet knock at the door, and Atchison harshly called out for whoever it was to come in. His clerk stuck his head through a crack in the door, gulped, and then spoke. "Sir, Mr. Ridges—"

"What about him? Where is he?" Atchison hissed.

"He . . . he's gone, sir. He was here first thing and—"

"Gone? Gone where?"

"To Boonville, sir. He said to tell you . . . ," he swallowed hard again, ". . . tell you that it was Mr. Siddell, sir, and . . . and Isaac . . . Isaac Hooker."

Atchison stood, kicking his waste pail across the room and scattering its contents. "Uh, sir," the clerk said, even more pale than before and looking as if he might be sick.

"What is it?"

"Mr. . . . Mr. Hooker is *here* sir. He—"

"Here?"

The door suddenly pushed open. Hooker stepped past the clerk and into the office. "Excuse us, but Mr. Atchison and I have business." He shut the door solidly as the clerk scurried out of the way.

Atchison sat back in his chair trying to remain calm, though inside he was coming apart. Atchison saw the bowie knife in its sheaf, smelled the greasy leathers, and saw the cold look in Hooker's eyes. Some said that Jim Bowie had gotten the idea for his famous knife from a knife Hooker used to tame Bowie during a saloon brawl. Atchison didn't know whether the rumor was true, but one thing was sure: A knife like Hooker's could take a man's scalp in one quick, painful swipe. He swallowed as hard as his dry mouth would allow.

"Mr. Hooker, what do you want?"

"I understand you lost a steamer last night."

"So it seems."

"I have it on good authority that Castle Ridges and a man by the name of O'Shay were involved."

Atchison leaned forward and took a cigar from the box on his desk. "No small allegation. You must surely have evidence."

"They were seen smuggling several kegs of some kind onto your vessel just before your steamer launched. Seems O'Shay and Ridges purchased them from a local store about two hours earlier."

"Not much to go on."

Hooker shrugged as he stood. "Just thought you'd like to know." He started for the door.

"Tell Siddell he'll pay for this," Atchison said with clenched teeth.

Hooker turned back and had his knife drawn and its point sticking between Atchison's first and second fingers as they lay atop the desk so fast that Atchison didn't have time to even flinch. "If he does, I'll come back, Mr. Atchison, and this here knife will skin you alive as quick as if you was an apple."

Atchison didn't even move. His mouth went so dry his cigar stuck instantly to his lips.

"This little attempt at gettin' to Hudson Company cost you a steamer. If you go anywhere near the Hudsons, and that includes Siddell, it'll cost ya a lot more." Hooker pulled out the knife and let it hover. Atchison pulled back his hands and put them in his lap, barely able to keep them from shaking.

Hooker continued. "Mr. Atchison, as you can see, I ain't a patient man, and I promise you that the *National Belle* will be the least a yer losses if ya try somethin' like this again." He resheathed his knife. "Of course, that sounds like I'm sayin' I had something to do with it, but I didn't; it was O'Shay and Ridges who blew up yer steamer. You know it as well as the God of heaven." With that he left the office and closed the door behind him.

Once he was out of sight, Atchison started breathing again.

* * *

Rand couldn't believe his ears. "You did *what?*"

"He came to me, and I helped him. Simple as that," Hooker said.

Rand could not help the smile, but it changed quickly. If Hooker hadn't acted, the ship at the bottom of the river could have been the *Sam Houston*—and a hundred innocents, including Ann, would have gone with it.

"And Uncle Ben was the one who tipped you off?" Rand asked in disbelief.

"Ben ain't a bad man, Rand; he's just a bit on the lackin' side when it comes to money matters an' gettin' himself in a pinch. It's my feelin' he made up for it and you need ta give him another chance."

Rand sobered. "Right now I need to get him out of St. Louis. As frightening as you can be, Isaac, Ridges and Atchison will have their vengeance. Keeping Benjamin around would be a mistake."

"He may not want to go," Isaac said. "The foundry could turn a nice dime if war breaks out. The Union will be needin' foundries as much as them Southern boys. Something to consider, but I hope you'll close the gap between you and Benjamin. He needs to know that what he done is appreciated." Hooker stood. "I got work of my own to see to. Ridges has run for Little Dixie. He won't be a bother in the near term, but don't stop watchin' yer back."

Rand only nodded. "Thanks, Isaac, on all points. I'll talk to Ben."

Hooker left, and Rand sat motionless, then closed his eyes and thanked God for Isaac Hooker.

* * *

Rand didn't have to wait long to talk to his uncle Ben. Ben showed up on Rand's doorstep at two in the morning. Rand welcomed him in, and they sat down in the den in chairs facing one another, the fireplace to the left warming them against the chilly night.

Benjamin told Rand what he had done—how he had been involved with Atchison and finally how he had asked Hooker for help. Rand just listened, knowing that none of this confession was easy for his uncle. Though the bad side of Rand Hudson wanted to lecture, Hooker's plea kept him from doing it.

Finally Benjamin finished and sat back, pale and drawn.

"Thanks for telling me, Uncle Ben," Rand said softly. "It took a lot of guts." He sat back, sobered. "Atchison will want his revenge. You should consider leaving St. Louis."

"I won't be runnin' anymore, Rand. I've done enough of that in my life."

"A fine sentiment, but you have a wife and two daughters to take care of. You'd best work them into your thinking," Rand replied.

"I've already told my wife." Ben took a deep breath. "I'll lose the foundry, even if Atchison's friends do wait until the loan is due, which I doubt."

"Maybe, but the Union will need foundries when war breaks out, so hang on as long as you can."

Ben shook his head. "No sense. I went there today, took a good look at it for the first time. It's a mess, Rand, just like you said. I let Atchison convince me; refused to see that the place was too small and too old and too beat up to ever be productive, because I was flattered by smooth talk and promises. I was desperate, and now I'm ruined, pure and simple."

"How about coming back to Hudson?" Rand asked.

Benjamin looked up. "You . . . you would let me after all—"

"You saved lives, Ben, including Ann's, and if war comes I am going to need you to help Lizzy while I'm away. But you have to promise to listen to both her and me. If you can do that, we have a spot for you."

Benjamin was overcome with emotion and couldn't speak for a moment, but it was a good silence and Rand let it remain.

"I can do that," Benjamin said softly.

Rand leaned forward and offered a hand. "It's a deal then. Be at the office tomorrow, and don't give up on the foundry just yet. We'll take a look at it and see what we can do when the time comes."

Benjamin only nodded, then got to his feet. Rand joined him, and for the first time Rand could remember, Benjamin Siddell gave him a hug. His mother would have been pleased.

Chapter 27

February 8, 1861

ELIZABETH HUDSON ARRIVED IN RICHMOND, Virginia, as the afternoon turned to evening. Her luggage had been removed from the train and placed on the boardwalk; she stood next to her bags and looked about her but saw no sign of Andrew. She began to pace, puzzled at her circumstances. It was a bleak, gray, snowy day, and Lizzy felt chilled to the bone. Finally, she decided to wait inside the depot.

The trip had been long, the train's wheels seemingly square instead of round; the smoke from the small stove in her compartment had been stifling. When she had opened the window for fresh air, the engine's fumes lay in wait to make her life just as miserable. Though she had a bed in her compartment, it had been nearly impossible to sleep, and she felt bone weary from a lack of sleep.

But the train ride had had one positive—it had given her time to think. She had determined that if she were to even consider marrying Andrew, he would want her to live here—and she had come to wonder if that were at all possible. How did one get along with those who practiced slavery without implying at least partial agreement or acquiescence of it? How could she love Andrew or his family if he and they were not willing to give up the practice? She could not. Living where slavery was practiced would be impossible for her. How could she live where she could not think and speak as she felt?

But if one loved someone enough. . . .

And so it had gone the entire trip, arguing herself into circles that had no end, making her question even the wisdom of this trip to meet Andrew and his family.

And then, as if she did not have enough on her mind, there was the problem of her faith. Though in her mind it was a much smaller barrier to their relationship than slavery, she had never been sure how Andrew would feel about her beliefs, and she had found a hundred excuses to put off telling him. During the trip she had determined a dozen times she would no longer do so, only to lie awake wondering. Even now she wasn't sure how to tell him or when to broach the subject, afraid of what it might cost her.

Out of it all came a genuine realization of just how much she liked Andrew. In fact, she knew now it was beyond "like" and was into at least the first stages of love. And that only confused her more. Even as late as last night, she had pled with the Lord to show her the way and had gotten what she thought was the resolve to do it, only to have it flee as she disembarked from the train.

"Elizabeth! There you are." Lizzy turned to see a woman of slight build and proud carriage coming across the depot from the main door. Lizzy met her halfway across the depot, and the young woman spoke again.

"Hello, Elizabeth. I am Andrew's sister, Emily," she said with a stiff smile. "I am afraid I must inform you that Andrew is stuck with duty at Fort Sumter and will not be coming to meet us, at least not today. Father sent me to bring you home."

Lizzy felt sick inside, her apprehension at Emily's news nearly overwhelming her.

"I can see you are very tired," Emily went on. "I will have our servants get your luggage loaded. I suppose it is the large stack on the boardwalk just outside? You really shouldn't leave such expensive things unguarded, Elizabeth. Though Richmond is a wonderful city, we do have our riffraff and . . ." She went on but Lizzy hardly heard, her mind reeling with this sudden change of events. Before she knew it, they were in Emily's carriage and leaving the depot.

Lizzy finally managed to shake off her angst enough to concentrate on what Emily was saying. She went on about the beauty of Richmond, the awfulness of politics—especially those of Abe Lincoln and the Northern abolitionists—and finally the wonderful qualities of Southern institutions. Lizzy forced herself to simply listen. It was difficult, and she realized that any thoughts she had entertained about holding her tongue and looking for the positive might prove more of a challenge than she had supposed.

"That is the church we attend," Emily said with a turned-up nose. She was pointing to a large building. "It is Southern Baptist." She looked at Lizzy. "So much better than the Northern Baptists, don't you think? I mean, their views about scripture and what it says about, well, everything, are so . . . so . . . odd."

Lizzy continued to bite her tongue. She saw in Emily what she had seen in her uncle and aunt; religion was something to be worn as a sort of medal, and the larger and more prominent the church, the bigger the medal.

Lizzy took a close look at Emily for the first time. Her face and neck were pale; she was tall and far too thin. She had dark brown hair with too many hairpins, small eyes, and an expensive hat that did not flatter her. Sitting atop her long face, the hat actually made her look quite comical. Lizzy had the impression that any beauty Emily had was overshadowed by her eagerness to display her place in society, but Lizzy tried to shove the thought aside. She was already being unfair.

"Will Andrew be coming soon?" Lizzy asked, trying to steer the subject back to safer waters.

"He really has no idea. Surely with the North being so intransigent about the obvious turnover of Sumter to our new country, well, he simply cannot leave. As a part of the force that is laying siege—"

"What?" Lizzy said.

"Laying siege," Emily said impatiently. "You know, trying to force them to surrender. Surely—"

"But that makes no sense," Lizzy said. "As part of the federal force protecting—"

"Oh, no, no. Andrew is no longer with the Union," she said in a mocking tone, as if Lizzy were being silly. "He resigned and was given a commission in the militia of South Carolina. The refusal of abolitionist Northerners to accept our new country—well, they are forcing us to take action, aren't they? And Andrew knows his duty. Very much so."

Lizzy felt white-hot anger burn into her chest. "And when did Andrew accept this new commission?" she asked as evenly as she could.

"Two days ago. It is the reason he could not come to meet you," Emily said as if repeating herself for a young child.

Knowing that Andrew could not have made her aware of this information himself, Lizzy tried not to feel deceived, but it concerned her more than a little that Andrew had joined a militia that belonged to the South's most obstinate state. He had never seemed at all predisposed to such an action. Had he been deceiving her after all?

"My father made the arrangements," Emily was saying. "He is a very powerful man, you know. Why, Andrew went from a lieutenant to a captain nearly overnight!"

Lizzy did not answer, but her doubts were growing by the minute. *Why had she come?* It now seemed like the worst possible timing, and without Andrew even here, the thought occurred that she should tell the driver to turn around and deliver her to the depot for a return trip—the sooner the better.

She shook off the thought. "And your father wants his only son to go to war?" Lizzy asked after a moment.

Emily chuckled. "Heavens, no. The North will never go to war. They are fools, but they know they cannot stop us now. Why, that old railsplitter Lincoln—he hasn't got enough backbone for such a thing, and Northerners, they are cow . . ." She stopped herself, suddenly realizing she might be walking onto thin ice.

"Cowards? Is that what you meant to say, Emily?"

Emily's pale skin turned a splotchy red. "I only meant—"

"Is this view of those of us who live in the North a personal view, or is it just what a good Southern girl is supposed to believe?"

Emily seemed shocked. "Why, it is what every good Southerner knows—and believes—and therefore it is my personal view as well. Father says—"

"So it is your father's view," Lizzy said. "And does Andrew hold the same view?"

Emily seemed trapped now and did not speak for a moment. "Andrew agrees with father, of course."

"Are you sure?"

Emily glanced out the window. "Of course."

Lizzy found herself feeling more deceived than ever. How could Andrew have possibly felt she would be comfortable if this were the view she would be pummeled with every day she was here? He *knew* how she felt. She had not decieved him in the least.

They left the city behind and rode in silence between rows of tree-lined fields. Houses became progressively less frequent as the carriage wound its way along hardened roads. She saw several large mansions set back off the main road with large barns and rolling fields, surrounded by forests covered in a growing layer of snow. Ordinarily Lizzy might have considered the scene idyllic, but today it looked horribly dark to her, and she wondered how she could maintain any degree of civility when she felt both deceived and stupid.

The carriage slowed then turned down a long lane. Lizzy could see the house at the far end. Large by any standard, six tall pillars three stories high held up an overhanging roof. A large cobblestone drive surrounded a marble statue of Hermes, the Greek god of hospitality and animal husbandry. She supposed Horatio Clay intended to convey the purpose of his plantation with such a statue, but Lizzy couldn't help but consider the irony. She saw nothing hospitable about a plantation that used slaves.

A half dozen black servants seemed to appear from nowhere as the carriage drew up to the front steps and wide porch, each dressed in a long dark coat and white shirt with scarf and top hat. As the carriage stopped, the servants moved into action. One placed a step, another opened the carriage door, and a third offered Emily a hand then did the same for Lizzy.

Lizzy looked about her as she started up the steps. Andrew said it was called the Meadowlands and had described with a proud look in his eye the endless hills and streams that gave it the name. It *was* a beautiful place, even in winter, and though she was still very upset about Andrew's absence, at least she knew she would have a house around her for a few days instead of a cramped, smoke-filled railroad car compartment.

She waited as the luggage was unloaded and Emily gave a few instructions, then she followed Emily up the steps onto the porch, where several more servants waited to open the door, remove their boots, and take their coats and bonnets. Lizzy was beginning to wonder if anyone did anything for themselves in this place as she looked about her at the large entry with a heavy chandelier in its center. There was a wide staircase that went up one floor, with an expensive-looking Oriental rug acting as runner up its center. Emily, whose expression was still drawn in tight-lipped disapproval, motioned Lizzy into the sitting room to their left, and a servant opened heavy oak doors to allow them entrance.

Horatio Clay stood next to his wife, his tall frame rising a good foot above hers. He was thin of face and build, and Lizzy saw instantly from whom Emily had received her least appealing physical traits. With mostly gray hair and a somewhat ashen face that was made even starker by a natural tightness in his lips, Horatio seemed much older than his wife. He stood stiffly, looking down his aquiline nose at Lizzy and forcing a smile. Andrew had prepared her for this type of reception, explaining that his father's demeanor was more often considered that of a fire-breathing, no-nonsense Baptist preacher than it was of a parent or even a politician, and she saw that he had been quite right.

Horatio's smile grew a little as he extended his hand for Lizzy's. When she gave it, he bent over and kissed it lightly. "Welcome to our home, Miss Hudson," he said without emotion. "Andrew has told us how lovely you are. He was quite correct." Lizzy sensed immediately that his words stemmed from habit or form and were not intended as a genuine compliment, but she returned a pleasant smile and a thank you as she curtsied.

Horatio Clay turned to his wife and introduced her as Mrs. Clay. Lizzy knew from Andrew that her first name was Naomi. She had a kind eye and cherubic countenance and was rather thick head to foot, but Lizzy recognized immediately that she was surely the warm-hearted center of the family. Naomi stepped forward and greeted Lizzy with a kind hug and smile.

"Welcome, Elizabeth. We are so happy you would come and spend a few days with us. I am so sorry that Andrew is not here to greet you. I am sure he will join us tomorrow, won't he, dear?" The last part was said with a sideways glance at her husband, who simply cleared his throat. Obviously Naomi was not happy with their son's absence at this critical time.

Naomi went on. "We were so sorry to hear about your mother. Andrew admired her so." Her tone was sincere and kind, calming Elizabeth's fears a little.

Naomi turned to Andrew's sisters and introduced the first as Patricia, or Patty for short. Patty, who was the prettier of the two girls, was a striking thinner and younger version of her mother. Lizzy guessed she was no more than seven or eight and that there were at least ten years between her and Emily. Patty curtsied, then welcomed Lizzy with a smile very much like Andrew's, though she avoided any direct eye contact with Lizzy and spoke with a slight stutter in a low, timid voice. Lizzy stepped forward and gave her a warm hug, which made Patty blush and lower her head even farther as she stepped away, though her smile broadened as she peered at her own feet. It was then that Elizabeth realized that as pretty as Patty was, she was also a bit slow of mind. Lizzy knew that Patty's condition was probably an embarrassing concern for her parents, especially her father—who, by Southern tradition, likely put much weight on family bloodlines. She pondered why Andrew had not mentioned this about Patty before, but she pushed the thought aside when Horatio Clay spoke.

"Patricia is very shy, as you can see. Now, if you will excuse me, I must get back to matters of business." He bowed abruptly then left the room. Lizzy noted that Naomi seemed less than pleased with this sudden and somewhat discourteous exit. But Naomi simply smiled and put an arm around Lizzy's waist then moved her toward the entryway and subsequent stairs. "You must be very tired after such a long trip. Let's get you to your room. Matty," she called, looking at one of the younger servants waiting in the entry. The woman, who wore her hair in a scarf, was thin of form but had a pleasant face and large dark eyes that seemed to awaken when she was addressed.

"Yes, missus," Matty said in a high-pitched voice.

"Bring Elizabeth's personal belongings to her room, and help her get settled." She turned back to Lizzy. "Dinner will not be until seven, so take your time, relax, and rest. If you need anything, anything at all, Matty will see that you get it. I am sure the servants have put your luggage in the room already, and Matty can help you unpack. I have already had the room warmed and a bathtub placed therein. The servants are probably filling it with hot water as we speak." She took both of Lizzy's hands. "We are so happy for our Andrew. He has obviously chosen well. Now, off with you, and we will see you at dinner." Lizzy felt a bit shocked at the remark, an indication that Andrew might have presumed more than he should. She felt wary of such presumptions at this point, but she let it go simply because it had caught her so off guard that she could not think clearly what to say. Giving a courteous smile instead of a reply, she hastened up the steps with Matty behind her, carrying her coat, hat, and bag.

Matty directed her to a room at the far end of the left wing, where the servants were carrying buckets to fill the tub. As she entered, she found the room warm and comfortable. The half-full tub, which had been placed near the fireplace, looked especially inviting. At the opposite end of the room was a massive poster bed, canopied by damask curtains. Her luggage stood near a towering armoire and an imposing standing mirror. A giant picture window overlooked the back of the property, where buildings dotted the landscape and fields seemed to run on forever. As Matty closed the door behind them, Lizzy went to the window and noted that there were a good many slaves moving about working at various chores even on a cold, snowy day.

When she asked Matty about the houses and buildings she saw, Matty replied, "Dem long houses is fo' de field workers and der fam'lies. Lots of de slaves work all dem fields what you sees."

"What about those large houses? Do slaves live there too?"

Matty hesitated only a moment then responded in her high but pleasant voice. "Dem biggest homes is whar de ov'seers lives, and dat," she pointed to a building nearest to them situated in the midst of leafless trees and shrubs, "is de massa's place o' bis'ness." She glanced at Lizzy and added quietly, "De black folks doan like goin' to dat house, no sirree."

Matty moved to Lizzy's largest trunk, which stood on end, and opened it from top to bottom. She began removing the dresses and hanging them in the armoire. Lizzy checked the water for temperature then sat on the bed while the tub was filled the rest of the way by servants who hustled in and out of the room. She asked Matty several more questions about the house, the grounds, and the daily routine of family and business. Matty seemed to be friendly and even talkative, willing to answer her questions. Lizzy decided to venture into a little more dangerous water.

"Matty, are all the servants on the Clay plantation slaves?"

Matty shrugged, looking at the closed door. "Yes'm, dey is," she said softly.

"And if I wished to pay you for your services to me, would Mr. Clay object?"

Matty gave her an incredulous look. "Oh yes, missy! We doan git no money 'round here."

Once more Lizzy's curiosity got the best of her, and she decided to ask another question. "Are you well taken care of, Matty?"

Matty had to think about her answer for a moment. She looked once more at the door, hesitated a moment longer, then answered. "I's happy, missy. I eats ev'y day and has a husbin and chil', and we lives in a nice room over de summer kitchen. We's happy, missus."

Matty's tone left Lizzy less than convinced.

"And how many slaves does Mr. Clay have?"

"Dey's too many to keep track of, an' I nevah goes where dem workers live. Massa Clay, he doan allow that kin' a foolin' 'round. Dem workers, dey come and go, so's I jes doan know, missy."

Seeing that Matty was becoming uncomfortable, Lizzy changed the subject. "Is your family here with you? Your mother and father?"

Matty looked down. "No ma'am, dey was sold to dif'ren' folks." She smiled. "But like I said, I's married now, an' we has our own room. It's nice. Jim be my husbin's name, an' he drives de massa's carriage—de big'un what youse come in." She obviously loved and was proud of her husband, but Lizzy knew that their marriage might last only as long as it took to hold next week's slave sale, though Matty's chances were better than most. She and her husband were producing offspring, which enhanced their value. The situation was also bettered because Matty and Jim were both clearly trusted by their master, or they wouldn't have the jobs they did. Breaking them up for sale was unlikely.

"Did you live somewhere else before coming here?"

"Yes'm. It was a bad place in de deep South. Very bad. I's happy here, I is."

"Have you ever thought of being free?" Lizzy asked quietly.

Matty stopped what she was doing and looked at Lizzy quizzically. "Ev'y slave thinks on it, Miss Lizzy. Ev'y one. But God, He makes i' so. Nothing us po' nigras kin do 'bout freedom. We'n's waits on de good Lord fo' such miracles."

"Has Mr. Clay ever set anybody free?"

Matty stopped her work to think. "Dey was ol' Billy Blue." She thought a minute more. "But dat was Massa Andrew's doin', I believe." She glanced at the door as if she might have said too much. "Doan know nuthin' 'bout it though, Miss 'Liz'beth. Nuthin' t'all."

Elizabeth felt some relief at the report and found herself even more curious about the matter, but it was obvious that Matty wasn't going to say anything else, so she let it go as the woman closed the trunk.

"Please, finish that later. Right now I would like some privacy to bathe." Lizzy reached to pull the curtains shut when Matty ran to her aid and promptly did the chore.

It was dark in the room, so Matty hurriedly lit several lamps then waited, her hands fidgeting with one another. "I's s'posed to hep you, missy. I always hep Miss Emily," she said.

"Well, I am used to doing such things for myself and wish to be alone, Matty. Possibly Emily needs something."

Matty nodded lightly, still unsure of what to do. Lizzy put her arm around Matty's back and moved her toward the door. "I really appreciate all you've done. Now, come back in about an hour and you can help me with the rest of the luggage." She opened the door, and Matty went out then turned to face her with concern in her eyes. Lizzy gently closed the door and then locked it. She knew that when she opened it again, Matty would most likely still be standing in the same place, waiting to follow orders, but Lizzy wasn't about to mold her life to a Southern norm just because she was in the South. She would accept some help from Matty just as she would any other servant, but she did not need someone to help her dress or undress, or do every other little thing for her. She had seen what such dependence and use of others did to slaveholders, especially women who simply became spoiled and pampered and the worst kind of snobs. She feared that she saw that in Emily.

From Lizzy's perspective, slavery created a false but very deeply ingrained pride because of the power one felt to command another human being, to use them or abuse them at will. In doing so, the slaveholder's view of himself and others changed dramatically. A false sense of power gave rise to a false sense of right and wrong and a nearly godlike sense of self that caused people to believe they had the right to treat others however they wanted; and anyone who tried to stop them was certainly less sophisticated, if not unworthy of their society.

She undressed quickly and lowered herself into the still-hot water of the tub. As she let the water wash away her feelings, she closed her eyes and drove all thought from her mind. She drifted into what she thought was a light sleep but awakened fully when she heard a loud knock at the door.

"Matty, I am fine. I will call you when I need you," she said, sitting up in the now-cool water of the tub and looking at the door across the room.

"It's me, Elizabeth. It's Emily."

"I am in the bath, Emily. Can you give me a few minutes?"

"It is nearly dinnertime, Elizabeth; you must have fallen asleep. Matty is very concerned."

Lizzy shivered slightly, glanced at the clock on the mantel, and knew instantly that Emily was right. "Yes, yes, I am sorry. You are right. Tell Matty to wait just a moment and then she can help." Lizzy felt horrible. She grabbed the soap from the dish on the table next to the tub and quickly washed her hair and then scrubbed the rest of her. Grabbing the towel from the same table, she got out and dried herself before slipping into clean undergarments and pantaloons. She rubbed her hair more thoroughly as she went to the door, unlocked it, and opened it. She found Emily and Matty both waiting.

"Matty is your personal servant, Elizabeth," Emily said with irritation. "She is instructed to help you in *everything*. Surely you understand that it disturbs her a great deal when she is not allowed to do her duty."

Lizzy smiled, even though she was a bit ruffled by the attack. "Emily, does Matty usually serve you?"

"Yes, she does, and she knows her duty better than any other. That is why she was given to you. She is obedient and knows her place. She—"

Lizzy's feelings wrinkled with the word *given,* but she let it go. "And she is with you every minute? She does your hair, helps you bathe and dress, everything?"

"Yes . . . well, not everything, but those things, yes. A lady needs someone to make sure that she is properly clean and that her appearance—"

"I am quite capable of determining how clean I am, and a good mirror can do the rest. If Matty needs more to do, then she may return to your quarters and continue her duties there. I am quite capable of doing things for myself. However, if she is willing to do only what I need, she is quite welcome to stay and assist me just as my servant at home would do."

"But my father sets the rules in this house, and if they are not followed he becomes most unhappy. Matty and I are quite concerned that he will . . ." She stopped, as if someone had suddenly gagged her.

"He will what?" Lizzy asked in a low voice. "Punish her?"

Emily looked up sharply. "I did not say that. I only meant to warn you that Father assigns each servant specific duties, and the servant's happiness comes from accomplishing those duties as he asks," she said.

Lizzy had to bite her tongue and take a deep breath to keep from saying what she really thought. "Emily, a servant helps me manage my time so that I can do the things I want to do for myself, especially personal things. Bathing and dressing and taking pains about how I look are activities I enjoy by myself. Now, you have had a good look at my appearance, and if you think it needs someone else's touch to make it more acceptable, please say so. If not, please forgive me, but I do wish to dress privately, and then I will join you for dinner." She smiled and slowly closed the door as the two girls stood side by side but said nothing. Emily was visibly angry, while Matty seemed mostly shocked. But Lizzy had noticed a slight smile on Matty's face even though her head hung in its normal state of obeisance. It was obvious she had never seen anyone speak to her mistress like this and that she was frankly deciding whether to risk enjoying it.

With the door fully closed, Lizzy slipped to the mirror to manage her hair. Muffled tones from Emily's grumbling and Matty's "Yes'ms" quickly diminished as they moved down the hall. Lizzy considered the matter to be a victory.

Unfortunately, she had not heard the last of it.

Chapter 28

It was only half an hour later when Lizzy opened the door to find Matty sitting in a chair in the hall. Her expression fell when she realized that Lizzy was nearly ready for the evening, but she quickly stood as Lizzy smiled and asked her to come in. "Matty, please help me with those bags. Put everything from the brown one in the armoire and everything from the tan one in those drawers. All my personal items need to be organized on the dressing table, and I need you to prepare my nightgown for when I return. Also, the tub needs to be emptied and removed, and please thank each of the servants for their help. Please thank them, Matty. Do you understand?"

"Yes, missy," Matty said with an attitude of both relief and continued curiosity.

"Good. Now, how do I look? Is there anything I have missed? Is anything out of place?"

Matty circled Lizzy, carefully looking her over. Then she smiled. "You is so beaut'ful, ain't gonna matter much what you missed. Nobody gonna notice."

"Thank you," Lizzy said, touched. "And thank you for being patient with me. I will need your help, but you will have time for other things as well. Do you read?"

Matty seemed to hold her breath. "No, missy. Massa Clay, he doan—"

"You said you have a child."

"Yes'm, a baby boy." She grinned. "He be takin' goo' care of by one of de other slaves."

"Then this arrangement will give you more time with him," Lizzy said.

"But Miss Emily, she *nevah* let me do such a thing. An' Massa Clay, he . . . I doan think . . ." She looked at Lizzy, clearly a bit mystified. "Why you doin' this fo' me? It ain't how things be 'round here," she said in frustrated confusion.

"No, I don't suppose it is, but I own no slaves and do not like the institution as a whole. It is immoral, and you deserve better." She smiled.

"Massa Clay, he . . . he said yo' was . . . dif'rent," Matty said.

"Oh? And what did he mean by that?" Lizzy asked, patting her hair.

"Well, Massa Clay, he . . . he say you has no sense when it come to Southern ways. Why, he told Massa Andrew he was makin' a big mistake, 'cause you . . . you don't think like Massa Andrew." Her voice dropped a little lower with each word.

"Does Andrew think like his father about everything?" Lizzy asked, Rand's words to her coming back. He had told her that Horatio Clay controlled everything about Andrew, and she had thought it ridiculous at that time. Now she wasn't sure.

Matty looked at the floor. "Can't say, missy. Massa Andrew, he doan say much to his pappy. Not since that other woman . . ." She suddenly put her hand to her mouth as if she had said too much.

"There was someone else before me, is that it?" Lizzy pressed.

Matty looked down at her feet. "Yes, missy, dey was. She a Southern girl, but she pappy died and didn't leave no money. Dey was po' as chu'ch mice after the debtors come. But worse dan dat, dey was part Injun or some such. Pretty woman, but not like you, no ma'am, not dat pretty. But Massa Clay, he put his foot down, he did. He tell Massa Andrew if'n he married dis woman, he disown 'im fo' good."

Lizzy felt her throat tighten. "And did your mistress, Mrs. Clay, feel the same?"

"No ma'am, she was mad as I evah see her. She made Massa Clay's life miserable, she did." She leaned toward Lizzy and spoke softly, a smile on her face. "The missus, she doan say much out fron', but she makes the massa know her feelings. Even wif de slaves, if'n she doan like what he do, she tell 'im and he best listen." She paused, lowering her voice even further. "He be a hard man if'n she doan git his 'tention some times, but she has t' pick her battles too."

"That's good to know, Matty. Thank you. I think I'm ready now. Will you lead the way?"

"Yes, Miss Lizzy, and I take care of dem tings you ask me."

They left the room, and it occurred to Lizzy that for two years in a row, Andrew had come to their house for Christmas and for about every other holiday allowed by the academy. The first year he had seemed distant and sad, but the more he visited with the Hudsons, the more he seemed to get past whatever had been bothering him. "Was all this about two years ago?"

"Ma'am?"

"When Andrew had to break things off with the other woman, was that about two years ago?"

Matty thought a moment, then whispered, "Yes'm. Dat girl come here wif her mama, and Massa Clay, he treat dem no good. De missus, she be mad fo' weeks, but he doan care dat time. He say his son ain't marrying no half-breed." She smiled. "Dat when de missus make his life miserable."

"What did she do?" Lizzy asked.

"His clothes jus' come up missin' sometimes, and she quit runnin' de house and buyin' de food. And she say she sick, but when he gone she up and lookin' healthy as evah I seen." Matty rolled her eyes. "She was too sick to have guests and too sick to 'tend to parties and sich, but when he go she feelin' fine. Den one night I hear dem have a good talkin', and she tol' 'im if'n he evah done such a ting again, she kick 'im out and he kin sleep in de office. Tings go back de way dey was afta dat." She paused. "De only time I see 'im win dem battles was when it come to nigras. She doan push dat button now. No sirree, she doan." Matty lowered her voice. "Not since Billy Blue, dat is."

There was that name again. Lizzy found it quite irritating to be left in the dark, but they were nearing the dining room and she did not think it wise to pursue the conversation further right now. She would simply have to do it later.

Naomi Clay smiled warmly and greeted her with a hug, then invited everyone to be seated. "Mr. Clay will eat later," she said with a concerned look while forcing a smile. "He is attending to an emergency."

"Di-di-did Ja-Ja-Jackson run?" Patricia began to ask innocently.

"Shush, sister," Emily said firmly, while glancing at Lizzy furtively. "It is a matter for Daddy to take care and is none of our affair."

Naomi smiled at her youngest daughter, who seemed very worried, even a bit frightened. She reached over and clasped Patty's hand, stroking it softly. "Everything will be fine, Patty. I promise."

Lizzy tried to help calm the girl as well. "Is Jackson a friend of yours, Patty?" she asked.

"Of course not," Emily said. "He is a servant. A nigra, and—"

"He, he sa-saved my life," Patty said softly, her head down.

"Not exactly, dear," Naomi said, "Your father was there too. He pulled you from the water."

"Fa-fa-father was sc-sc-scared," Patty said.

"You know that isn't true, dear," Naomi said with a nervous glance at Lizzy. "Jackson was just closer, that's all." She smiled and quickly changed the subject. "Would you say grace for us, Elizabeth?"

"Of course, but may I ask a question first?" Lizzy ventured boldly. "Was Patty's speech different before she nearly drowned?"

Naomi seemed a bit taken aback by the question but looked tenderly at her young daughter and answered genuinely. "Yes, quite different."

Lizzy had heard of such damage to the brain from near-drowning and wondered what had happened that day. She bowed her head and began her prayer.

"Father in Heaven, we thank You for our bounteous blessings, and especially for Your Son and His great love and sacrifice for us. May we always be worthy of such a gift. And please, bless those who are looking for Jackson with compassion so that he can come home safe and sound. Comfort Patty and give her peace. We pray in the name of our Lord, even Jesus Christ, Amen."

Lizzy opened her eyes to see Patty looking at her with a fixed gaze, a slight smile on her face. She got out of her chair and stood next to Lizzy, looking even closer into her eyes. Then she touched Lizzy's forehead with her finger and spoke. "Is . . . is Je-Jesus in there?"

Lizzy smiled and adjusted her chair a bit as Patty leaned over to give her a hug. As she lay her head against Lizzy's breast, Lizzy kissed the crown of her head then glanced at Naomi, who was using a napkin to dry a tear. Lizzy could only imagine the anguish she must feel for this young girl.

"Mother, can we please eat now?" Emily said, making no attempt to hide her selfcentered impatience. Lizzy could see that anything involving such tender feelings bothered Emily. She had seen the same tendency in some of her friends when growing up, especially at Emily's age. They were so conceited and full of themselves that they seldom thought of others as anything more than a nuisance. Her friends had grown up miserable and unhappy. There were never enough things, never enough parties, never enough attention. She felt sorry for Emily because she saw that same canker of soul growing in her.

"I have a friend like Jackson, Patty," Lizzy said. "His name is Elliot, and he works for my brother and me. He has a wife and a baby son and has always been very protective of me."

"Is he c-colored?" Patty asked innocently.

"Yes, and a very hard worker. He does many things to make life easier and less costly for us, and—"

"Hmph," Emily grumbled, "then he is the exception. Our nigras are a great deal of expense, and you practically have to beat them to get any work out of them." She was looking haughtily at one of the servants, who was doing his best to quickly ladle gravy onto her potatoes. It gave Lizzy heartburn.

"Well, there is a difference between your servants and ours, Emily," Lizzy said as she gave Patty one last squeeze and helped her to her own chair.

"Oh, and what is that?" Emily asked.

"Elliot is free; your slaves are not," Lizzy said evenly. She realized the statement bordered on rude but Emily left her little choice.

Naomi, who had so far kept silent, suddenly came alive with instructions to the servants and began telling Lizzy about the food and about shopping in Richmond and its wonderful people and culture. Lizzy was quite impressed by how effectively she kept the discussion from even broaching slavery or politics for the rest of the meal. Such avoidance of the most important subjects of the day was no small feat.

In her attempt to honor her hostess's apparent quest, Lizzy did her best to keep the conversation on neutral ground and asked the girls about their interests. Emily's response was a simple shrug and words to the effect that she had little time for such things. Lizzy thought this an interesting answer, since a girl of Emily's age had little to do in the way of anything else, especially in a home with endless servants, where she hardly lifted a finger to feed and dress herself. She wondered if Horatio Clay was even aware of what was happening to his daughter because of his pampering and indulgence.

"Do you play the piano?" Lizzy asked.

"A little, but it is very boring. Chopin and Mozart make little sense to me."

"Have you tried some of the newer writers, like Stephen Foster? He produces lovely music, and his songs are not hard to play."

"Father does not allow any such music," Emily said with her typical haughty air.

"Emily, you know that is not entirely true. Why don't we have Elizabeth play something for us after dinner?" said Naomi.

Emily looked a bit stunned by her mother's suggestion but determined to poke firmly at her food instead of responding. Lizzy could see now why Emily was so thin: she had the appetite of a door mouse. But this seemed fitting, since her hardened soul probably took in very little nourishment of any kind either.

The meal was lovely, and when they were finished, the four women moved into the sitting room, where the piano stood in one corner. It was a Broadwood Grand in wonderful condition, and Naomi sat down and quickly played Beethoven's "Moonlight Sonata." The piece was well done, and Lizzy thought she would surely embarrass herself when it was her turn.

"Now, let's hear something from Mr. Foster," Naomi said, getting up and waving for Lizzy to sit. Lizzy thought she would lighten the mood a bit and played "Some Folks," singing the lyrics as she did.

> *Some folks like to sigh,*
> *Some folks do, some folks do;*
> *Some folks long to die,*
> *But that's not me nor you.*
> *Long live the merry merry heart,*
> *That laughs by night and day,*
> *Like the Queen of Mirth,*
> *No matter what some folks say.*

She played a short interlude between the chorus and the next verse then sang again.

> *Some folks fear to smile,*
> *Some folks do, some folks do;*
> *Others laugh through guile,*
> *But that's not me nor you.*
> *Long live the merry merry heart,*
> *That laughs by night and day,*
> *Like the Queen of Mirth,*
> *No matter what some folks say.*

Patty started clapping to the tune, and Naomi joined in as well, while Emily did her best to remain aloof and disinterested. Lizzy wondered briefly if she was bothered by the words. They certainly fit Emily's arrogance, but Lizzy knew that the arrogant were the last to recognize this negative in themselves. Humility usually had to be brought about by some difficult trial that made one look more carefully in the mirror, and Lizzy wondered if the possibility of war—of losing everything—would do that to Emily. In fact, she wondered if it would take anything *less* to change her. Lizzy kept singing.

Some folks fret and scold
Some folks do, some folks do;
They'll soon be dead and cold,
But that's not me nor you.

She sang the chorus again, and this time Naomi, who had a lovely voice, chimed in; Patty tried hard as well. Emily flushed but still refused to participate. A moment later Lizzy ended the music with a flourish, and Patty and Naomi applauded enthusiastically. Emily clapped softly, a slight smile on her face, looking like a queen giving her royal nod to a barely acceptable performance at some distinguished concert.

"Let's try this one," Lizzy said after a moment as another song popped into her mind. She played "Amazing Grace" and watched the three women. She did not sing the words but simply played a rendition that used the quality of the piano at its best. As she finished, both Naomi and Patty brushed away a few tears. Emily just seemed agitated and impatient. Lizzy sighed inwardly.

"Thank you, Elizabeth," Naomi said. "You do play wonderfully, and I was especially touched by that last piece. How magnificent. I can tell you feel strongly about our Lord. For that I am grateful."

Lizzy only nodded. She couldn't help wondering how Mrs. Horatio Clay would feel if she knew why Lizzy felt as she did about the Lord—a feeling for which she had the Book of Mormon to thank. However, she shoved the thought aside for now. She was very confused about what Andrew's absence meant for their relationship; if he did not come back, her religion was a moot point.

At the rumble of voices, wagons, and horses outside, the three members of the Clay family immediately tensed. "Come girls," Naomi said, forcing a smile and waving impatiently. "Lizzy, would you join us in the library for scripture, meditation, and prayer?"

"Of course," Lizzy said, following them from the room. As they crossed the entry area, she spoke to Naomi. "I will get my Bible and be with you in a moment." She smiled and started up the stairs.

"But—" Naomi started.

"I will just be a minute," Lizzy insisted and hurried up the stairs.

She hastened down the hall, entered her room, and immediately crossed to the window. Standing in the shadows, she watched as torchmen rode up to the office building and surrounded a wagon carrying at least two men and a young boy. In the light of the torches, Lizzy could see that they were black and shackled. Orders from Horatio Clay to take them from the wagon and to the post came clear and distinct to Lizzy's ears. Two men jumped in the wagon and jerked the first man to his feet, threw him from the back of the wagon, and then jumped down, prodding him with clubs until he got up, stumbled past the office, and moved out of sight. Two more men did the same with the second black man, and then another man grabbed the boy by the arm. He was dragged from the wagon and shoved in the same direction as the others. Lizzy's gut wrenched as she saw Horatio Clay dismount with a coiled whip in hand.

Lizzy thought quickly, grabbed her cape, and went down the back steps that led directly into the kitchen. Her sudden appearance seemed to shock the servants, who were talking among themselves near the back window. It was clear to Lizzy that they too were distressed at what was happening. Gathering her courage, she sprinted across the courtyard, alarming the hitched horses, and rounded the outbuilding to find an unknown man about to uncoil a whip. She slowed her pace. Horatio Clay stood near the man, a look of disinterest on his hardened face. He no longer held the whip; apparently he expected others to do his dirty work.

"There you are, Mr. Clay," Lizzy said, slightly out of breath. Horatio stiffened as he turned to see her approaching. "Oh my, I seem to have come at an inopportune time, but your wife said—well, never mind. I need a carriage to go into the city. Could you provide one immediately?"

Horatio glared at her. "It is too late to make a trip into the city, and *this* is no place for you, Miss Hudson. Go in the house. Now." He said it with a cold edge to his voice that allowed for nothing but obedience.

Lizzy watched the man with the whip. His eyes were filled with a thirst for blood that sent chills up her spine.

Lizzy ignored him. "What did these men do?" she asked. "And this child, surely you do not intend to whip a child."

The man with the whip scowled, and Lizzy could see that if Horatio were not present, he might just as well use it on her as anyone else.

"This is none of your affair, Miss Hudson," Clay said again, his impatience obvious.

"Inhumane conduct," Lizzy said, her smile gone, "should be the affair of each one of us, and I will not be leaving here until I am assured that these men will not be beaten." She looked at the man with the whip. "You, what is your name?" she demanded.

He sneered at her. "Slade, and you will be leaving as Mr. Clay has asked, or I will—"

"Whip me as well? Yes, you look like a man who would whip the innocent and enjoy doing so."

"Slade, shut up," Horatio said. "Miss Hudson, these are runaways. Two of them have tried to escape twice, one a third time. I have no choice—"

"What are their names?" Lizzy asked.

Horatio stiffened even more, and Lizzy pictured him in a corset with every tie and button busting. "Their names are of no consequences to you, Miss Hudson," he said flatly.

"Do you even know their names? Is it because you have so many slaves, or is it just that you don't care to know who Mr. Slade is going to torment with that vile whip?" she asked hotly. She could not believe she had completely lost her composure. Surely this would do no good, but she could not help it. This was wrong—vile—and she must do something or she would never be able to face herself in the mirror again.

Lizzy moved close enough to both Slade and Horatio that she could nearly touch them, but her stomach was churning violently from the fear she felt. It was not Horatio she feared but Slade. In those eyes she could see a threat to her life. But she refused to back away—she could not do it. The fear of what would happen to the men and boy was more horrible than her fear for her own life.

"I have no intention of beating the boy. I—"

"Good, then the whip will not be needed." She reached out and grabbed the whip handle, jerking it out of Slade's hand so quickly that he could not prevent it. She threw it some distance away as Slade reacted by grabbing her free arm and squeezing so hard Lizzy felt he would break it in two.

"Slade!" Horatio barked. "That's enough!"

Slade pushed Lizzy away, fire in his eyes. Lizzy wanted to flee, but her stubbornness kept her solidly in place. "Mr. Slade, if you ever touch me again, I will have you thrown in jail for assault or kill you myself."

Slade sneered defiantly, but Lizzy turned her attention to Horatio.

"Why did they run away, Mr. Clay?" She pushed back a curl of hair that had fallen into her eyes, her voice as calm as she could make it.

Horatio stood cemented in shock, absolutely speechless.

"Did they run away because of the food you feed them? The kind of work you make them do? The whipping of other slaves? Surely fear over a similar fate would cause me to flee as well. What, Mr. Clay, is their reason? Have you even tried to understand it?" Lizzy asked, stepping closer. "From what I have heard tonight, I believe that boy saved your daughter's life; how can you even consider beating him?"

"Miss Hudson, that is enough! You know nothing about any of this. Go! And do not come back out here." Horatio had gathered himself. He had been challenged, something absolutely foreign to him. Never had he been denounced by any man, let alone a woman. "I have put up with enough from you, and even though you are our guest, at my son's insistence, I will not hear another word from you. Not one! If I do, I will have you manhandled back to the house."

Lizzy felt the hair on her neck stand up. This time she knew that the threat carried weight, but if she left now, empty-handed. . . .

Biting her tongue, she walked resolutely to where the boy named Jackson where he sat scared and confused on the ground, his eyes wide and his shoulders shaking. She stooped down and took his hand, then lifted him up as she stood. "Come with me, Jackson."

Jackson got to his feet, wiping away tears beneath his wide-open eyes, and Lizzy started back toward the house. She stopped in front of Clay as she was about to pass him. "That man you have shackled over there may be nothing but property to you, but to this boy he is a father. How would Andrew feel if you were the one tied to that post, Mr. Clay?"

She saw an almost imperceptible change in his cold stare, but it disappeared just as quickly. "Go, Miss Hudson."

Lizzy walked a few steps and picked up the whip, then coiled it before extending it to Clay. "If you want the man whipped, at least have the courage to do it yourself."

Clay said nothing, and Lizzy walked away holding the hand of young Jackson. She prayed she would not hear the crack of the whip and the screams that must surely follow. She prayed harder than she had ever prayed in her life.

Chapter 29

ABIGAIL HAD WORRIED ABOUT THE baby most of the day. He seemed to have developed a cough during the night that had turned harsh and was accompanied by a fever. She was assigned to prune the trees of her master's orchard, but she left her chores regularly to check on him, to feed him, and to make sure he wasn't getting worse.

It was late in the day and the sun was nearly set when she finally retrieved the child and started home with the other slaves. She was tired, near exhausted, after getting hardly any sleep and spending the day doing hard manual labor. Between faltering steps and stopping to comfort the fretting baby, she soon fell behind the others.

She watched them as they walked away, singing, seemingly happy, and she supposed many of them were. Most were very good at being slaves. They did exactly as they were told, never talked back, and never, ever even let the thought of freedom enter their pretty little slave heads. She saw things differently—mostly because of Rankin, her husband. He had been free, at least for a short time, and he had known what it was like. He had run so far and so fast that he had managed to get clear to New York, where he found a job and had his own room and friends and could go where he wanted. He had been poor, but at least he had been free to do something about it—and free to try to save the money to come back and get them to freedom as well.

Rankin had tried to sneak back and free them, but Sam and Castle Ridges had caught them and beat them all—but beat Rankin half to death—before delivering them back to Massa Harrison. But even this hadn't broken Rankin. Instead, he'd told Abigail about every stop, every place to go, where to hide, and how to get across the river. "There are white folk," he'd told her, "that will help you if you find them."

She would find them someday. She would.

But she would have to do so without Rankin. He was dead as dead could be. He'd walked in on Massa Harrison raping her, and Rankin had nearly killed him. Rankin had been hung for it, and they'd made her watch. The Ridges boys and her master were all bad men, and she prayed every day the good Lord would do something about it.

"Miss Abigail."

The sound came from the brush and trees that grew along a small stream at her left. She stopped.

"You keep on movin', Miss Abigail."

She recognized the voice immediately and felt her stomach knot. "Mr. Felix, what is you doin'—"

"I come to take you and dem kids outta dis mess. If you still be wantin' it anyway."

She looked at the other slaves some distance in front of her. They were still chattering away and had not heard. "I does, and I mean it, but how—" She heard a wagon coming up the road from behind and turned to look. She nearly froze when she saw who it was.

"Massa Harrison is comin'," she said urgently. "An' Perkins, that overseer what works fo' dem Ridges, he be with 'im. You hassa run, Mr. Felix."

"I's all right. Now you bring them children an' yer pa ta that washout down by the river. There be a small cave—"

Abigail took a breath and gathered her courage. "Yes, yes, I knows de place. All right, I be comin' tonight, but it be late."

"We'll be waitin'," Felix said.

Abigail heard a rustle in the bushes and caught a glimpse of movement across the stream as Felix disappeared. She stopped in the road and rocked the fussing baby, her eyes on the men and wagon approaching. They didn't seem to be paying much attention to her, and she started walking again, quickening her pace to catch the rest of her group. About the time she fell in behind the others, a horseman caught up, the wagon just behind him, and the slaves all stepped off the road to let them pass. Castle Ridges pulled up directly in front of her.

"Well, well, Miss Abigail, how is that new half-breed yer carryin'?"

She glanced up quickly before forcing her eyes back to the road. "Massa Ridges, he's fine, suh." She said it in a quiet voice, but her heart raced and her hands began to shake. She held the baby more tightly.

Ridges leaned forward enough so he could reach out and pull back the ragged quilt from the baby's face. "Sick-lookin' little nit. Must be the darky in him."

"Yes, massa. S'pose, massa," she said. Though she was afraid, Abigail fervently wished she were holding a weapon, any weapon. If God granted it to her, she would crush this man where he stood.

"Looks like his pa some though, don't you think?" he said low enough that only she could hear. He leaned back and grinned, and Abigail felt the hate surge in her heart, but she kept her head down and her body controlled, the loathing roiling through her in waves without reaching the visible surface. But the anger mingled with self-disgust because she had let this man take her without a fight. She should have died then, killed him, but she had thought only of her children, what would happen to them; Ridges's threats to them had ripped at her desire to beat him off and had made her give in.

In an attempt to keep from complete rage, she forced her mind to other things. It was then she noticed the pine box coffin in the back of the wagon. With her eyes still on the ground and knowing she could get whipped good for it, she spoke. "Beggin' yer pardon, Massa, but who dat coffin fo'?"

"Sam." Castle said. She felt the white-hot hate in him, and it elated her. Sam Ridges, dead! "Thank you Lord, fo' dis little miracle." She did not realize she had spoken out loud until Castle cursed and raised the whip to punish her. She turned to protect the baby against the blow, but Ridges's horse suddenly reared up, nearly throwing him. She backed away as he brought the animal under control and pushed him in her direction. She cringed at the raised whip, but it never came down. Instead he used the horse, pushing her to the edge of the road, where she toppled over and fell down, rolling into the ravine. She tried to protect Rankin Jr. but felt the baby beneath her, then heard his screams. She scrambled to her feet as quickly as she could and unwrapped the wet, muddy blanket. She daubed the blood coming from his nose and tried to mollify his terror. She looked up at Ridges, his eyes filled with satisfaction. "There'll be more comin' nigra, you can count on it." With that he rode away after the wagon.

Abigail finally got Rankin quieted but was concerned about the growing lump on the side of his head. Muddy and wet, she scrambled up the side of the bank as best she could. Several of the other slaves gathered around and tried to help clean off the worst mud as she examined Rankin. She had seen worse bumps—had had them herself—but she did not like the color of this one.

She looked after Castle Ridges. He would come—she knew it. She thanked the others and fell in step as they headed on home. Felix Coulon had come at the right time. She would leave tonight. There was no longer any other choice.

* * *

Felix awakened with a start and strained his ears to identify the stirring outside. The dim moonlight revealed a black shadow stooped at the cave entrance; Felix froze.

"Mista Felix," came the whisper. He recognized the voice as Abigail's and relaxed a bit.

"I's here," Felix whispered back.

The opening of the cave suddenly darkened as Abigail shimmied through it, and Felix quickly lit the candle he had brought with him. He had waited so long he'd fallen asleep. He kept still until everyone seemed to be inside; he quickly noticed that Handsome wasn't with them.

"Where is yo' pa?"

"Pa told us t' be leavin' 'im. He was beat on today and can't walk good. He say he old and near dyin' an' he only slow us down, get us caught 'gain. He says if we has a chance at freedom we should take it. 'Sides, he says he can cover for us. Tell Massa we's sick, give us extra time."

Felix only nodded. No master would accept such excuses and they both knew it. The old man simply knew he couldn't make the journey.

"We have to get movin'," he said. "They be a wagon we have to catch if we is goin' to git to the ship on time."

"Ship? What ship?" Abigail asked, looking concerned.

"A steamer. It's sittin' at Jefferson City waitin' fo' us, but we has some walkin' t' do t' meet that wagon."

"You is talkin' in riddles. What wagon is we to meet?"

He explained. "My friend Newton will be meetin' us back at the last village. Come on, now."

She didn't question any further. They crept from the cave.

"Abe an' Tom, you be worryin' about Flower. If she needs carryin', you put her on yer back," Abigail ordered.

"Don't be worryin' 'bout us. We's strong and able enough," Tom said confidently.

"You'll be doin' what I say, when I say it," Abigail said firmly and looked at Felix.

Felix nodded gravely. "All of you listen to Abigail. This is a dangerous thing we're doin', and we has t' move fast, an' I has t' know you'd do what we says when we says it."

They all nodded in the darkness of a half moon.

Felix led out, Abigail at his side with the baby in her arms. Abe, Tom, and Flower followed close behind. Abigail reached over and touched Felix's arm. "I nevah thought I'd be so happy t' see a man as I am t' see you, Felix Coulon. Nevah."

Abigail's touch strengthened Felix's resolve, but it also gave him the sudden realization that her life was in his hands now, and the thought sobered him. When he and Newton had started off with the wagon, anything had seemed possible, but now that it was just him and these poor runaways all depending on him, the stakes seemed incredibly high. And though he had been in this part of Missoiuri once before to fetch his mother and sister, this was still unfamiliar country to him—especially at night. He knew he could lose his direction easily, and then they'd be in real trouble.

"I doan mind sayin' I am a bit worried, Miss Abigail. This be dangerous fo' you an' yo' children."

"Ever' day of my life I wake up wondering if I kin please de massa, if my chil'luns will make 'im mad and git a whippin'." She paused, her eyes turning sad and dark. "Ever' night I wait fo' de massa to come . . ." She glanced in the direction of the children. "If I doan do what he says, he say he kill dese chil'luns and me. He beat me when he's drunk, he . . ." She bit her lip. "I's leavin', Mr. Felix, with or without yo' help. If I dies, so be it. I's tired a livin' like some animal to be used as de massa pleases. No mo', Mr. Felix. No mo'."

Felix only nodded. He could only do his best, and he resolved to do just that. He just hoped it would be good enough, but if not he'd die protecting this woman and her kids. They had seen enough of misery.

* * *

Newton heard them before he actually saw them. He lit a match as a signal, and Felix quickly appeared through the darkness and the trees. Newton quickly put out the match.

"'Twas a might worrisome tha' ya be so late in comin'," Newton said with relief. He counted the people with Felix. "You're missin' one."

"He stayed behind. This is Miss Abigail and her children, Flower, Abe, and baby Rankin. And this here is Tom. He ain't Abigail's blood but same as." Felix pointed to each before turning back to Abigail. "Abigail, dis here is Newton."

"We 'ave only a few hours of darkness still, then we'll 'ave t' stop an' 'ide," Newton said. "Ge' 'em in th' wagon wi' the uthers." He pointed at the two dark shadows already in the back. "Tha's Bella and her 'usband Amnon. This is their second attempt. If they ge' caugh' again, the owner 'ill beat on 'em goo', so let's get movin'."

"Same as us," Tom said. "An I doan cotton to it." He jumped into the back of the wagon and helped Abigail and Felix get the children in before Felix helped Abigail into the front seat to sit between him and Newton, the baby still held close in her arms.

Newton flicked the horses' rumps with the reins, and they leaned into their traces. Then he whipped them into a trot and they began to move quickly along the road, half blinded by darkness.

Neither Newton nor any of the others saw the horseman come around the bend behind them. Slavers were watchful of places they suspected of harboring runaways, and this slaver had been watching the house where Newton picked up Amnon and Bella. It would be a mistake he would regret.

* * *

The rider had stopped his horse, afraid the runaway slaves would get onto him. The distance and the darkness did not allow him to see that Newton had picked up Felix and the others. He thought a moment about his options and, thinking he was still up against only three people—only one of whom might have a weapon—he decided to take them himself rather than go for help and face having to share any reward.

He rode another four miles and drank half a pint of whiskey before he worked up enough bottle-driven courage to remove his revolver from his belt and kick his horse in the flanks enough to attempt to catch up with the wagon. The buzz brought on by the whiskey blurred his vision and his good sense, and he rode too fast around a small bend in the road, where a large and dark object suddenly stood in the middle of the road. The gelding set his hooves to avoid it, bolted right, and the half-soused rider lost his stirrup and flew into the top railing of Newton's wagon. He felt his ribs give and heard an audible crack as a piercing pain shot up the side of his chest. He careened from the wagon onto his back, suddenly sober and fighting for breath. A warm, sticky liquid ran down his side as he blinked at the stars and tried to stay conscious. Forcing a hand to touch the spot, he fingered a large wooden chunk lodged in the side of his chest. He had been skewered, and he wondered if he was about to leave this world for another.

He heard voices behind him, reached for his pistol, and realized he'd lost it in the fall. A feeling of panic and helplessness overcame him as a large figure darkened what little light loomed in the sky above them both.

A match was struck and used to scan his body, coming to a stop at the jagged piece of wood lodged in his side. He felt it move with the touch of a hand then screamed as it was jerked from his flesh. He went out like the lights had been turned off.

* * *

"He'll bleed to death if we don't get 'im help," Felix said as he looked at the grave scene in front of him.

Newton was already looking for clean rags and quickly used them to fill the hole in the man's side and stanch the flow of blood while Felix unpocketed his candle and lit it. Tom came running out of the bushes after relieving himself, coming upon the unfortunate fellow and exclaiming, "Lord, save us. Who is dat?"

Newton had pushed aside the man's coat, and the light from Felix's candle glinted off a badge.

"I seen him b'fore," Abigail said. "He's de sheriff's deputy of Boonville an' works for slave hunters in his spare time." Her hand went to her mouth, and she swallowed hard.

"He's a bad man, he is. He good friends with Massa Ridges," Abe said, his eyes wide.

Castle Ridges?" Newton asked.

"Dat right," Abigail replied. "How you know 'bout him?"

"Let's jus' say he an' 'is bruther hold no place of affection in the 'earts of me and me friends," Newton said. "Includin' Felix, who was 'is prisoner once."

"Prisoner, what dat mean? When—"

"Never mind, and quit askin' so many questions. Lands, you is bad as Jasmina," Felix said, feeling a little nauseated by the sight of so much blood.

"An' who is Jasmina?" Abigail asked.

"Nevah mine dat, Miss Abigail," Tom said with some frustration. "Dis man got wha' he deserves. Let's git on our way." He flipped his makeshift suspenders over his shoulders.

"He'll die if we leave 'im," Abigail said and shook her head. "An' den dey be comin' aft' us fo' sure. Not even dem good whites'll have anythin' to do fo' us den. Day not only whip us good, dey hang us." She told Tom to kneel by her and hold the rag while she wrapped another around the deputy's waist.

"I ain't hep'n 'im," Tom said angrily.

Abigail glared at him. "'Tain't gonna do no good to hate dis depity, Tom. He ain't done nuthin' to you. Not yet anyways. Save it fo' dem what has. Now get down here 'fore I gives you a lickin'. An' doan you be thinkin' you's too big fer it, 'cause you ain't."

Tom knelt down reluctantly, and Newton got up to check the horses tied to a nearby tree. He was somewhat surprised they hadn't bolted with the jolt of the horse and rider. Though the deputy's horse stood with his head down, he seemed to be sound in spite of the hit he had taken.

"We has to take 'im with us, Mr. Felix," Abigail said. "Dey has to be another town soon, and we can leave 'im."

Felix and Newton both knew she was right, but just how to accomplish this task without revealing themselves was another matter.

"We'll sneak 'im in somehow an' get movin' on before dey knows what way we gone," Abigail said.

Felix knelt down by the deputy, who was moaning as he returned to consciousness. As Felix examined the bloody bandage, the man opened his eyes.

"What . . . what . . . ?"

"You run into the wagon. Hurt yerself pretty bad. Don't be worryin' none; we'll git you to a doctor," Felix said.

"Ain't wantin' no darky handling me no how," the deputy said, his language a bit slurred.

"Then you can be doin' it yerself," Newton said, stooping down.

The deputy grimaced as he looked at the other faces looming above him. "I knows this bunch. They belong to Burt Harrison, neighbor to the Ridges place. They hunts runaways for pleasure down there," he said through clenched teeth, "and Harrison will be after you by now."

"Then the question is, does we leave you here t'die or does we take a chance tryin' t' save yo' miserable hide," Felix said.

The deputy lifted his head enough to try to see his wound. The bandage Abigail had applied was thick with blood. His head lolled back heavily from weakness. "Jes' get me back on my horse and—"

"You couldn't sit on a 'orse even if I tied you on," Newton said. "Felix, bring 'is 'orse over 'ere, an' let's load 'im over the saddle. Then I'll take 'im into the next village. The rest o' ya 'as to keep goin'."

"Won't be leavin' you behind," Felix said firmly. "Put 'im in the wagon fer now. When we gets close, we'll load 'im on the horse and send 'im in so's one of us don't have to explain it."

Newton shrugged. It was a good idea. A moment later they had the deputy, who continued to drift in and out of consciousness, in the back of the wagon. Newton mounted the horse, and Felix motioned for everyone to get back in the wagon as he took his seat at the reins. Moments later they were moving again, Abigail sitting in the back with the baby cradled in her arms, the children around her, Bella and Amnon huddling close to each other. Felix noted with concern that the sun was just beginning to show on the horizon, and they were still a long way from Jefferson City. They'd have to spend the night at the safe house Newton had told him about. That meant they would be cutting things close getting back to the *Constitution* before her scheduled return to St. Louis. Any further delays and they might not make it all.

Tom sat in the corner of the wagon, his hands half behind him. He'd found the deputy's pistol, practically stepped on it, while mounting the horse. Before they entered the next town, he intended to use it.

Chapter 30

AFTER A SLEEPLESS NIGHT OF wrestling with the decision of whether to stay or leave, Lizzy decided to put off any decision at all. She had heard no whipping or screams last night, and when she went down for an early cup of coffee before breakfast, Jackson was working in the kitchen, and Patty, who was sitting on a chair near the fireplace, was all smiles. She glanced at Lizzy, grinned, and then ran to give her a hug. "Ja-Ja-Jackson sa-says you sa-saved him."

Jackson gave a shy smile as Lizzy looked his direction, then he quickly retreated through the back door as the voice of Horatio Clay echoed down the hall from the front entrance.

Patty rushed back to her chair while servants bustled about to put food on the table for their master. Lizzy, not sure she wanted to see Horatio just yet, exited the kitchen by the back stairs and returned to her room, coffee cup and breakfast roll in hand. She ate and drank while watching the plantation come to life along the rows of slave houses, barns, and sheds. The bustle of it all suddenly gave her an idea, and she quickly changed into warm underclothes, riding pants, and wool coat and hat before leaving the house by the front door and working her way around back. Near the tool shed, she saw Emily visiting with Slade—or, more accurately, flirting with him. Slade was obviously returning the flirtation. She wondered if Horatio knew of his overseer's advances toward his oldest daughter. Glaring at Lizzy, Emily defiantly sidled even closer to Slade, who gave Lizzy a look that would burn the hair off a horse's back.

"Good morning," Lizzy said, smiling pleasantly just to needle them. She then looked away as she approached the barn. Her arrival garnered immediate attention, and workers paused in their labor to whisper comments to one another. There was not a white man among them.

"Good mornin', missy," said a tall, thin black man with a wide smile. "Kin we hep youse?" His voice was kind and his demeanor stately in spite of his condition. So far this man had not been broken by the fact that he was a slave. He wore worn wool pants, a threadbare linen shirt that was loose at the neck, and a beat-up slouch hat that shadowed his eyes.

"I would like to go riding. Could you show me your horses?"

"Yes'm," he said with a wide grin; Lizzy noted that several teeth were missing. "Dis way." He pointed down the center of the large barn. "You all git back t' work," he said in a kind but commanding voice to the other servants. "You has gained some note'riety, missy." He smiled again and glanced at her. "De account o' what you done las' night to save po' Jackson and his pappy and an' another of our people is being spoke of by all us folks."

"And how is Jackson's father this morning?" Lizzy asked. "And what do I call you, Mr.—"

"M' name is Asher, missy. Asher Bentum, and Jackson's pappy be doin' time in de pit fo' runnin', but he be out soon. Dey's plannin' t' send 'im to Richmond fo' de sale." He smiled. "But he warn't whipped, and that's goo' news 'round here as of late." He looked over his shoulder as he spoke.

Lizzy felt a sharp sting of disappointment. "What is Jackson's father's name, Asher?"

"Henry, ma'am."

"Is Mr. Clay sending only Henry to Richmond?"

"Yes'm, his wife and Jackson will be stayin'."

Lizzy bit her lip hard. So Horatio Clay would punish the man by splitting up the family.

"Now you doan be worryin' 'bout dat. He'd a been sold anyway, whippin' or no. Mr. Clay, he doan like trouble. No indeed, and when a slave runs, well, he doan keep him around if it happen twice, no matter how much he worth." Asher visibly stiffened as Slade entered the barn at that moment and came toward them. Every worker seemed to cringe at his presence, and Asher stepped back, his eyes on the floor.

"You don't belong here," Slade said coldly to Lizzy. He carried a short whip in his hand. "Go back to the house. If you want to ride, send us word and we'll bring a horse to you."

"Mr. Slade, you might be able to order the servants around with the threat of that whip, but you forget your place when you try such a tack with me," Lizzy said with a forced smile. "Asher, you were going to show me a horse."

Asher still didn't look up, and Lizzy could see he was afraid.

"I am overseer here, and these nigras do what I tell 'em." Slade glanced toward the barn door, and Lizzy saw Emily standing near it, a pleased smiled on her face.

"Mr. Clay says to get you back to the house," he hissed.

"Mr. Clay or Emily?"

"It's all the same to me."

"Well it isn't to me. Now if you'll excuse me, I have a horse to select." She turned and started to walk away but immediately felt a firm grip on her arm. She jerked free. "You have a short memory, Mr. Slade. I told you last night—"

"Mr. Slade, leave her be." The voice came from a door at the side of the barn, and Lizzy turned to see Naomi Clay facing them both. Dressed in a plain linen dress with a shawl and a man's slouch hat, she looked ready for work.

Slade scowled while biting his tongue, and Lizzy saw Emily turn on her heel and angrily tramp from the barn.

"I am sure my husband has other things for you to do at this moment, Mr. Slade," Naomi said firmly.

Slade hesitated then turned and grudgingly left the two of them alone. The air of tension in the barn seemed to leave in the darkness that followed him, and the sound of work and low talk began again.

"The man is a beast," Naomi muttered, coming to Lizzy's side. "Unfortunately he is right; you should not be out here, Elizabeth."

"But you are here," Lizzy said with a smile.

Naomi returned it. "Yes, well, I received word that there are several of our people down at the quarters who are ill, and I need to attend to them. I was just passing by on my way there."

Lizzy nodded, aware that "the quarters" referred to houses set aside for slave laborers. "May I accompany you?" she asked.

Naomi smiled and sighed. "No, you may not, Elizabeth," she said in a frustrated tone. "I am sure you have strong opinions about our way of life, but can't you just try to leave things be?"

"I am sorry if I have caused you some discomfort, Naomi, but I would like to help. Let me come along and—"

"No, not there. It would only make things worse for you, and besides, I would not want you to catch something and be ill when Andrew arrives." She looked at Asher. "See that Miss Hudson is given a horse for her ride. You will also accompany her and be her guide; is that understood, Asher?"

"Yes'm, Mistress Clay," Asher said.

With that, Naomi Clay turned and left the barn.

"I do not seem very popular with the Clays and Mr. Slade, Asher," Lizzy said, shaking her head, a wry smile on her lips.

Asher chuckled. "No, ma'am, but den Jesus warn't too popular wif dem Sadducees neither." He chuckled again as he approached one of the stalls. "Dis here is Bandera, ma'am. Finest horse in dese here parts. Belongs t' Massa Andrew. I think he'd like it if you was to ride 'im, missy."

Coal black and lively, Bandera nickered softly as Lizzy took a step closer. She stood back as the gelding was led out of his stall and given oats; she was instantly agreeable to the proposition of riding such a fine animal as she stroked his neck and felt an immediate connection. "Bring me a brush then saddle and bridle, Asher. No better way to get to know a horse than to take care of him."

She brushed Bandera well and had him saddled and bridled and ready to mount as Asher led out another bay mare ready to ride. He helped Lizzy into the saddle, and they walked the horses past the barn and into a small valley, then up a grassy hillside on the far side. As Lizzy looked back from the top of the hill, she could see the buildings surrounding the great house. A half mile to the left were a number of houses she assumed were the quarters. She had seen endless numbers of such houses when traveling through Little Dixie and had even been inside one of several owned by a girlfriend's father in St. Louis. Normally they were built of rough logs and daubed with the red clay or mud of the region to fill cracks but these seemed to be of wood and plank construction and larger than most, possibly having at least two rooms instead of the more common one. Usually there were two medium-sized windows, a door, and a large fireplace, with a floor of hardened dirt, but these had more windows—and from appearances, they might even have real floors.

"How many slaves do you have at the Meadowlands, Asher?"

"I nevah tried to count 'em all, missy, but I guess it be 'bout hundred fifty, maybe more."

Lizzy knew that would make Meadowlands one of the largest plantations of its kind. She counted the slave houses, knowing that as many as ten slaves lived in such a place normally. If that were the case here, Horatio Clay had at least as many as Asher said living in the quarters, with more living in houses near his mansion.

Spurring Bandera, they continued their ride until they came to a large building near a river. A large waterwheel stood on one side, and Lizzy reined up in front of it. A sign on the front indicated it was a textile mill. She was about to dismount and go inside when two other horsemen appeared at the top of the small rise she and Asher had just descended. Lizzy put up a hand against the bright sun and saw that it was Slade and Horatio Clay. They rode quickly down the hill toward Lizzy and Asher.

Clay reined in his horse between Lizzy and the building. "Miss Hudson," Horatio said stiffly.

"Good morning, Mr. Clay." She glanced at Slade. From the look of the arrogant smile on his face, Lizzy figured this interruption was his doing.

"A fine mill," Lizzy said, looking at the building behind them. "What do you manufacture here?"

"Miss Hudson, what we do on this plantation is none of your affair. Asher, keep Miss Hudson on the main road and return her to the house."

Asher nodded and was about to spur his horse when Lizzy raised a hand to stop him.

"It is a shame that you must hide your affairs from view, Mr. Clay. It makes one wonder if they are less than honorable."

Horatio frowned. "I know you, Miss Hudson, and I know your abolitionist ideals. You have come here to ram them down my throat, and I will have none of it."

"Then why did you allow Andrew to invite me at all?" Lizzy asked.

"Because Andrew seemed to think you could change, but after last night I see that is quite impossible, and your belligerence with Mr. Slade in the barn—"

"Mr. Slade is a brute but you are right—it is quite impossible for me to sit idle while a man whips another, and that will never change."

The muscles in Clay's set jaw seemed to relax. "What you saw last night was the exception. I would never have had the boy whipped, but his father. . . . As I told you, it was his third attempt at escape. He left me no choice."

"Them darkies ain't got the brains God gave a turnip," Slade said defiantly. "They have to be taught what ain't right and what is."

Slade was struggling to hold his temper, and Lizzy knew it. She also knew that such treatment of the slaves by *him* was probably not an exception. This was a man with both a temper and a hatred for the African race. Putting him in charge of slaves was like allowing a fox in the henhouse. And Horatio probably did not know half of what Slade did. As the overseer, Slade would have the ability to hide his horrors.

"And do you reward them, Mr. Slade, when the rows are straight, when the work is done well, when the crops are planted on time, when the harvest is plentiful because of their hard labor?" Lizzy asked as evenly as she could muster.

"Yeah, we *don't* whip 'em," Slade said.

"Enough, Slade," Horatio said firmly. "Go on about your duties."

Slade glared hatefully at Horatio, then at Lizzy, his hand gripping the short whip firmly, making Lizzy wonder which one of them would get the first lash across the back. Then she noticed that Horatio Clay had his hand on the butt of a revolver tucked behind his belt. She wondered if even he feared Slade.

Slade seemed to gain control, yanked on his horse's reins, and spurred the animal to movement. He rode quickly up to the mill, dismounted, then angrily stomped through the door to disappear inside.

Lizzy watched Horatio carefully and saw the relief in his eyes. "You fear him as much as Asher and the others do, don't you," she said.

Clay stiffened again. "Mr. Slade serves my purposes, Miss Hudson. I trust him completely."

He was lying—she could see it and feel it, but she let it go as she dismounted to tighten her cinch. "Is that really the only reward your workers get for doing good work—they don't get a whipping?"

"They get better food and better clothing. We take very good care of our workers."

"Compared to what?" Lizzy asked, looking up at him. "The care other slaveholders give?"

"Our servants are better off than your factory workers in the North," he replied hotly. "I have been there, and I have seen the conditions in which your freedmen live. I have seen how they starve because of poor wages. Do not chastise me, Miss Hudson, when what you offer these people is even worse."

Lizzy saw the argument for what it was—an attempt at deflection—and she was not about to allow it. "You are rationalizing, Mr. Clay. I have been to factories in the North as well, and for every one that treats its paid workers poorly, there are five that do not. If you feel you treat your workers as well as anyone in the South, then compare that treatment with the very best factories in the North. What do you see then? How do you compare?"

Clay's jaw hardened but he said nothing. Lizzy decided to press him.

"And please, do not give me those old arguments about poor Southern plantation owners who just don't have the money to make things better. It's balderdash, and both of us know it." She looked at the building. "My guess is that you are trying to compete with a Northern factory in this building. It is a textile mill, so you are probably trying to make cloth rather than send your cotton to England to have it done. Cutting out the middleman could give you much greater profits, am I right?"

Horatio gave her a hard look. "Yes, for the most part. We can add a good twenty percent to our profit margin by manufacturing the cloth here, and we save retailers nearly the same amount if they don't have to import it from England."

"But your production is down. It is slow, cumbersome, probably less than one-fifth what an English or even a Northern factory can accomplish in the same amount of time with the same equipment."

He seemed a bit startled at her grasp of the situation. "About one-fourth, but how—"

"Not all women stay at home and darn their husband's socks these days, Horatio." She smiled. "I have a college degree in manufacturing and have helped my mother and brother establish a very profitable business in shipping. But that is not the point of this conversation. A slave economy will never produce what a free economy can. Workers have no reason to give their best when you stand over them with a whip and threaten to take away their food or their families if they don't. They find ways to hinder your work, to get their revenge. But Mr. Slade says they need to learn their lesson, and so he gives the orders for the other overseers to make them suffer, and all the time things get even worse. Buy more slaves, Mr. Slade says—that's the way. Build a bigger factory and put more people in it. So you pour in more money, and still production doesn't seem to improve much. It is like a dog chasing its tail."

Horatio listened but then shook his head adamantly in the negative. "Our slaves work hard. You are wrong. That is not what is happening here."

"How many good, strong workers—*bucks*, I think you slaveholders call them—has Mr. Slade recommended you sell downriver because they are impertinent or unmanageable? How many of your women and children have become less productive, even seeming ill all the time, since their husbands were sold? Count the costs, Mr. Clay. The answer to your lack of success in this venture lies in cruelty."

Bandera was already nervous from standing about too long, and at Lizzy's slightest nudge, he bolted up the road toward home and a bucket of oats. Asher followed.

Upon arriving, breathless and upset from both the ride and her conversation with Horatio Clay, she put Bandera in his stall and began to unsaddle him. Asher joined her as quickly as he arrived and had his own horse tied.

"Dat's my job," he said, gently pulling her to one side. She stood back, folding her arms and watching him finish and then retrieve a comb and brush.

"Tell me about Billy Blue," Lizzy said softly.

Asher looked at her, then stepped to the stall entrance and looked out before going back to Bandera and using the comb on him. "Mr. Clay, he say nobody talks 'bout Billy." Wiping his mouth on his sleeve anxiously, he fell quiet. She waited while he decided.

"Billy was Massa Andrew's friend, missy. Massa Andrew love 'im like a brother, but Massa Clay, he doan like it none and put de fear o' the good Lord into 'im 'bout it." He smiled. "But dat doan stop Massa Andrew and Billy from runnin' off sometimes to go swim in de river or take de raft dey built down to Richmond. Dey love bein' on de water an all. But Massa Clay, he find out an' he say he sell Billy if Massa Andrew doan leave 'im be."

He looked about, making sure they were still alone. "Massa Andrew have t' be real careful, but he sneaks off at night an' he and Billy hide in a cave nea' by, an' Massa Andrew teach Billy Blue how t' read an' write so's he can run 'way. They does that for several years, 'til Massa Andrew ready t' go t' dat military school up north. Nigh' 'fore he leaves, Billy done take off fo' freedom."

"But Matty said that Andrew set Billy free," Lizzy said.

"Yes'm," Asher said patiently, "but dat was de second time. Billy go t' de Noth on his own first time, but Mr. Slade, he hunt him down an' bring him back. He beat Billy bad, real bad. Even Mr. Clay was upset 'bout dat when he find out." He looked about again, nervous. "Dey sticks 'im in dat mill and hides him from Massa Andrew evah time he come home. Mr. Andrew don' know Billy even here 'til when he come back from yo' mama's funeral. Massa Clay, he ain't home when Massa Andrew come and neither is Massa Slade. Massa Andrew decide he go down to de quarters and he see Billy Blue den. When his daddy come dat night 'fore he go to Fort Sumter, he find out and has a big fight wid his papa an' Mr. Slade. Next thing evah body knows, he go off t' Richmond and draw up papers dat say Billy a freedman an' he comes home and sends 'im off again. Massa Clay, he don' do nuthin' 'bout it, but Massa Slade, he so mad he spit nails." He smiled. "But nothin' dey can do. Billy got dem papers, an' he walked right up dat der road t' freedom." Asher's face saddened. "Massa Andrew, he just go away an' doan say nuthin' mo'. I s'pose he figure he won, an' so does ever'body else 'round here." He shook his head. "Everyone 'cept ol' Massa Slade. He swear he find Billy Blue an' make 'im pay. But he never did, least not dat we knows."

Lizzy frowned. "And yet Andrew still wanted me to come here to meet his family. If he hates them so much—"

"Oh, he doan hate dem, missy. He just doan like dem much. They didn't used t' be so mean 'bout things, not even his pappy. Maybe he just think dey need an outsider t' wake 'em up." He chuckled as he lit an old, hand-carved pipe. "So far, missy, you doin' right fine."

"Why, thank you, Mr. Asher. You flatter me." Lizzy felt relief at Asher's revelation. Andrew had committed to her that he would free his slaves someday. She thought he'd been sincere, and this relieved some of the doubt she had felt since arriving. But she wondered if even Andrew could ever change Horatio Clay, ever bring freedom to Asher and the rest of the slaves working the Meadowlands. Surely it could be an even more beautiful place if freedom permeated its forests and fields, but getting Horatio Clay to commit to such a thing would be monumental—a miracle, as Rand had put it. And what if Andrew couldn't do it? What then? How could she live here? She could not. If things did not change, this would be the last time she would see the Meadowlands. Lizzy was a bit surprised at how much the thought disappointed her.

Asher chuckled then grew sober. "Massa Slade be a danger, missy. Massa Andrew kin handle 'im, but I fear fo' you if'n you pushes 'im anymo'." He paused. "Mr. Andrew be comin' home in a day or two. You best wait fo' 'im."

"I'll try," she said. She patted Bandera on the neck. Changing the subject, she said, "If I remember correctly, Bandera is from the same sire as my brother's horse, Samson."

"Yes, missy. Massa Andrew and Massa Rand buy dem at de same time." He paused. "Ain't no man since Billy Blue dat been better for Massa Andrew dan yo' brother."

"Unfortunately, things have changed some, Asher," Lizzy said with a sad tone.

"'Cause Massa Andrew take sides wid de South. Massa Andrew tell me 'bout dat. Thing Massa Rand need to remka, Massa Andrew is Virginian to his bones. Fo' him it ain't 'bout us black folks bein' free. He say he do dat eventually anyway; it ain't even 'bout a man's right to decide fo' hisself what he do. It about de folks what live in Virginy. He nevah desert dem."

He shook his head. "He feel it dishonor 'im and 'is whole fam'ly, an' he won't do it."

"And you believe him," Lizzy said.

"Yes'm, missy. I wish he wasn't so stubborn 'bout such things but he always been dat way."

"And you believe he wants to set you free as well?" Lizzy asked.

"Yes'm, I does, and he already tell his papy 'bout his feelin's too." Asher shook his head, a sad look in his eyes. "His pappy doan like it much, an' dey been fightin' 'bout it most Massa Andrew's life. His pappy say he never git the chance. Dey doan see eye to eye on it, not t'all. An' ain't no one who kin change de massa on dat issue. No one."

Lizzy felt sick—and if Rand knew just how Andrew really did feel . . . "Thank you, Asher," she said softly.

"Missy, I . . . if'n Massa Clay hear I tell you dis, he—"

"Everything you have told me will be our secret, Asher. I promise."

Asher looked relieved. "I thank yo', Missy."

She patted Bandera one last time and then left the barn and went to the house, proceedng upstairs to her room without seeing anyone. She found Matty waiting just outside her door. Matty stood as Lizzy approached.

"Good morning, Matty," Lizzy said.

"Missy." Matty extended a hand with what looked to be a telegram in it. "Dat come from Massa Andrew, jus' now."

Lizzy quickly opened the envelope and read the telegram. Disappointment followed. "Thank you, Matty. Please tell Mr. and Mrs. Clay that Andrew has been delayed."

"Fo' how long Missy?"

"He doesn't say," she replied. Matty walked toward the stairs as Lizzy opened the door and went inside, throwing herself on the already-made bed. Could she stand even another day? She looked at the telegram again, then wadded it up and tossed it at the fireplace before rolling over to look up at the ceiling. She must stay. She had to talk to Andrew!

But if she did. . . . Slade was a dangerous man, and she felt to protect herself.

A knock came at the door; it opened slightly, and Matty poked her head around it. "Does ya need anythin'?"

"Matty, how would you like to go shopping?"

"Oh yes, missy, I love t' see all dem things." She grinned.

"Very well then. Have Asher prepare a carriage, and then come and help me get ready."

"And breakfast?"

"Bring it up with you. Just biscuits with butter and jelly, and juice if they have any."

Matty seemed to skip toward the back steps while humming a song Lizzy recognized. She had played it on the piano last night, and it once more brought a smile to her lips. She began humming it as she changed her clothes, her thoughts on what she would say to Andrew when he finally arrived and how she could help him open his father's eyes. By the time she was dressed, she had determined that she would find a way. For the sake of her and Andrew, she must.

* * *

Lizzy knew that Matty would not be allowed to enter any public restaurants, so she had a lunch prepared by the cooks before they left for Richmond. Matty gave instructions to the driver to take them to the shopping district, and they spent an hour in and out of several stores. Lizzy bought several items of men's and women's clothing, a fine set of shoes, and a high top hat.

"Mr. Andrew will be pleased wid dem purchases, missy. Fine clothes dey is. An' you be lookin' real good in dat pretty new dress," Matty said approvingly.

Lizzy only smiled, her mind elsewhere. An hour ago, when she and Matty had stopped for a rest, she had picked up a newspaper after hearing the hum of anti-Union discussion in the stores. Her apprehension over what she had read had been growing ever since. The front page had declared Lincoln an enemy to peace and demanded that Virginia leaders meet immediately to support "our Southern friends in the defense of their rights to property." Another article talked about Sumter and demanded that Virginia be "taken in peace if you can, but by force if necessary." Every other article was filled with endless rhetoric and hot support of Southern views, a less-than-subtle warning to Lincoln that he would lose Virginia to the Confederacy if he made any effort to force Southern states back into the Union. Lizzy had found herself wondering if Andrew would come home at all and how long she could wait before she was trapped here.

After a few moments of thought, Lizzy looked at Matty. "I need to go to a dry goods store."

"My goodness, Miss Lizzy, what for? Why, we has at de big house evathing dey has in dem places."

"Never mind, Matty. Once I make my purchases there, I want you to take me to the freedmen's section of Richmond."

Matty was scratching her head. "My, you is a mystery, isn't you!"

"I will need to see the pastor of a church among the freedmen. It's called the Holy Church of Our Lord." She fixed Matty with a serious gaze. "And Matty, you cannot speak about any of this to anyone."

Matty swallowed hard then nodded. "No ma'am, you kin count on me. I keep it quiet, but dis is dang'rous business, dis is. I know dat church. Some of my folk say dey helps run'ways." She smiled mischievously. "Excitin' though. Sho' nuf."

"Matty, if you ever need help . . . if war does come and you need to get away, remember that these folks will help you."

Matty's eyes opened wide, but she only nodded, unsure of Lizzy's intent in telling her this information.

"Never mind such talk right now though. I just need to visit with the pastor," Lizzy said. She pointed to the picnic basket. "Our driver is your husband, isn't he?"

"Yes'm."

"Well then, while I am inside, you and he will enjoy a picnic. I will eat when we get home." The carriage stopped and Lizzy got out, a bit apprehensive. She wasn't sure why she felt so strongly about coming here. But she did, and she had learned to trust such feelings. It was possible that she would have to use this stop on the Underground at some later time, or maybe she just needed to better understand a few things about its operation. Regardless, this might be the only chance she had to be in Richmond, and she decided to take the opportunity.

Chapter 31

CASTLE RIDGES SLOWED HIS HORSE and dismounted, handing the reins to one of his men. An old black man he knew only as Handsome hung limply from his wrists where he was tied over the limb of a strong, old oak. Even in the half-light of dawn, Ridges could see deep whip marks marred his back. Handsome's owner, Burt Harrison, sat shirtless on a nearby stump, sweating from exertion while downing a large swig of home-brewed corn liquor. Harrison had sent for Castle.

Sam had said he didn't want a permanent hole in St. Louis, and his widow wanted him buried in the family plot as well, so Castle had gone to the trouble of digging up his brother and bringing his rank body home for burying. Then he got as drunk as a man could and still be kicking the next morning, just so he could rid himself of the stink. He woke up in a bad mood and was trying to figure how to get his vengeance on Hudson and Siddell without running into Hooker when Harrison's slave showed up with a message that slaves had run. Thinking it might include Abigail, he had come without even eating breakfast. He had a mean itch that needed scratching, and if Hooker prevented it, he'd find another way.

"Did he tell you anything?" Ridges asked, looking at Handsome.

"Nothin'," Burt said angrily, taking another chug on the bottle.

Castle went to Handsome and lifted his chin, then dropped it. "Won't be gettin' nothin' neither. Ya killed 'im."

Harrison was putting on his shirt and only shrugged. "He wasn't worth nothin' anyway."

"How many did you lose?" Ridges asked.

"Five, including that kid Tom. Yer old girlfriend and her three kids are the others," Harrison said.

Ridges didn't react to the mention of Abigail as his old girlfriend. Now wasn't the time. She was property—nothing more—and though he didn't like Harrison alluding to anything else, he'd wait for the right moment to let the man know. "How long they been gone?"

"Eight, maybe ten hours. I came t' git Tom this morning, and old Handsome tried to tell me they was all sick. I knocked him out of the way and found 'em all gone."

"We'll find the others, but it'll cost you that young'un, Tom," Ridges said.

Harrison had to think a minute. Tom was worth at least a thousand dollars, maybe two, but he was a troublemaker as well and didn't pull his share without constant watching. Abigail and the other two surely hated him, but he could put the fear of God into them. Tom was getting big enough to fight back.

"You sell him, give me half the money, and it's a deal," Harrison said.

"We'll give you a third, no more," Castle said.

Harrison eyed Castle. Castle was expensive, but he seldom came back empty-handed. If Castle chased the runaways himself, it would be worth Harrison's while.

"If you bring the other three back, it's a deal," Harrison said.

Castle pulled some papers from his saddlebag and had Harrison put the deal on paper and sign it. Harrison was one of the few men Castle knew who could write. Castle looked the paper over then shoved it in his saddlebag. "You wrote down four runaways. I thought you said there was five."

"The baby is a sicklin'. I don't care much if it don't come back," Harrison said.

He handed Castle a piece of cloth. "This was the woman's. It'll give yer dogs the scent." He looked at the tree-lined ravine north of his closest fields. "I figure they snuck off along that way."

Castle nodded and was about to mount when he remembered Harrison's earlier remark about Abigail. Turning back, he put a fist to Harrison's jaw that knocked Harrison back into the tree, where he melted to the ground. Castle knelt beside him and got real close, grabbing the collar of his shirt. "Watch yer mouth, Harrison, or next time I'll kill ya. That woman ain't nothin' but property t' me."

He got up and mounted his horse, his cold eyes watching Harrison, who was trying to get up, blood dripping from his lips and down his chin. He said nothing more, and Ridges spurred his horse down the lane from Harrison's house to the road. The woman couldn't get far on her own, not with two kids and a sick baby. Tom would be some help, of course, but the others would slow everything down considerably.

When he reached a ravine near the slaves' cabins, he whistled to his dogs, dropped the piece of clothing to the ground, and let them sniff it for several minutes. One by one the four animals peeled off and began sniffing along the ravine. After a short time, one seemed to catch a scent, and they were off. Castle spurred his horse and rejoined his men, who had been waiting some distance away. This was going to be easier than he thought.

They went nearly half a mile before the four hounds gathered around a small stand of thick bushes. Ridges dismounted just as one dog disappeared. He pulled back the brush and found a hole. He called the dog, and it immediately rushed back out as two of Castle's men collared them all so Ridges could climb inside.

After a few moments, Castle resurfaced with a scowl. Nothing! Then he saw it. A large footprint in the dirt stopped him cold.

"Man's boot," he said to the others. "Look's like they got help." This changed things considerably.

"From the looks a that thar print, 'e's a big un," commented one of his men.

Castle called for his men to set the dogs loose, and they were off again. To his liking, they found the wagon tracks an hour later.

"The dogs've lost the scent, but them wagon tracks ought to be easy enough to follow," said one of the men. "Must be someone gathering up runaways. And from the look of how deep them tracks are, they's got a few."

They spurred their horses and headed off at a fast clip. The runaways' transportation would even the odds, but they all knew that when they caught a wagonload of slaves, they'd get a good price from the owners.

* * *

It was after sunup, and Felix knew they were nearing a town, as the houses grew less scarce. He figured they'd start seeing wagons and riders soon, so he guided the wagon down a narrow trail through a stand of trees until it could not be seen from the main road. Newton came behind on the horse. Securing the reins on the wagon's brake handle, Felix jumped into the back of the wagon. He lifted the wounded deputy into his arms as Newton dismounted and pulled the horse next to the wagon. Felix slung the man over the saddle. He was now barely conscious but mumbling.

"His bleedin' ain't as bad," Abigail said, relieved.

Felix and Newton saw that the blood on the bandages had dried some; they exchanged a relieved glance, though they both knew the man had lost a lot of blood. "I'll ge' 'im t' town an' catch up," Newton said. "Ya keep goin', Felix. We'll meet a' the hidin' place I tol' ya abou' unless I catch ya sooner."

Felix knew this plan was their best option and nodded agreement, but when he turned to go back to his seat, he found himself staring down the barrel of a gun.

"Ain't no reason t' take a risk," Tom said coldly. "We leave 'im an' jes keep goin'." Though his voice trembled slightly with fear, it was also edged with cold anger.

For a big man, Felix moved very quickly. He grabbed the gun and ripped it from Tom's hands before Tom could blink. Shoving it in his belt, Felix stared hard at Tom. "We kill 'im an' we got no friends between here an' St. Louis. Now, you sit down where you was an' stay put."

Tom was stunned but wasn't through getting his scolding. Abigail, who was now finished nursing the baby, closed up her dress and wrapped the baby more tightly in the blanket while she gave Tom her mind. "Youse go on now, do as you was told 'fo' I gets a stick and puts it to yo backside. Felix only tryin' to save yo skin and what's you do? Turn a gun on 'im, dat's what. I has learned t' love you, Tom, but sometimes yo does play de fool. Now git in dat wagon."

Tom did as he was told even though he was still angry. Abigail turned to eye the deputy and spoke to Felix.

"If'n he tells others, they'll be comin', won't they?" She asked it with worry in her voice and soft enough only Felix could hear.

"We be doin' right, Abigail, so don't be botherin' yerself about it. How's baby Rankin?" Felix asked as he pulled back the blanket so he could see the child's face. He was shocked to see the size of the lump on the boy's head. He hadn't ever seen one on a baby before.

"He be gettin' weaker," she said softly. "Ain't eatin' hardly nothin' t'all, and that bump on his head—it doan look right."

Felix nodded. "You should a told us about that bump, Abigail."

"Didn't make no matter," Abigail said. "Massa Harrison don' like Rankin Jr. Says he has the sickness and won't last. He wouldna paid a cent for him to get a docta."

He signaled to Newton, who came over and looked at the child.

"He be needin'a doctor," Felix said. "Maybe he should go to town with the deputy."

"No!" Abigail said and pulled Rankin back. "We git caught, and you knows it!" she said with wide, fearful eyes.

Felix and Newton looked at each other, unsure of what to do.

"He be all right," she said. "If'n you git us a docta when we git's to Illinois, he be fine."

Both Newton and Felix were uneasy but saw little choice. "Let's ge' on wi' it then," Newton said. He called for everyone to get moving and then started for the village himself.

* * *

When Newton reached the village, he checked the deputy, who was now completely unconscious. As he passed the first store, a man came out and stood on the porch, staring at him with a hard look; then he reopened the door and called to someone inside the store. A moment later three men appeared and walked toward Newton. Two of them wore badges.

"If this is one o' your boys, he be needin' a doctor," Newton said, matter-of-factly. He extended the reins for one of them to take. They ignored the effort and one of them lifted the head of the unconscious deputy then indicated a shop across the street. "Not one of ours. Deputy from Boonville."

Two men grabbed the wounded deputy and gingerly removed him from the horse before taking him to the building indicated. Newton stayed put but watched as the door was opened by a tall, thin man with a two-day beard who saw their need and immediately ushered them inside. Newton turned around and started walking back the way he'd come.

"Hey you! Where ya think yer goin'?"

Newton turned around to see the two officers coming after him.

"Jefferson City," Newton said easily.

"Not until we know what happened." The man who spoke had his hand on his revolver, and Newton began to regret his decision to bring the wounded deputy into town.

"I 'aven't any idea wha' 'appened. Maybe ya should ask 'im," Newton said, turning and beginning to walk again.

"Hold on."

Newton heard the revolver hammer pulled back. He turned slowly around. "He was back there on the road," Newton insisted, clinging to the hope that he might still be able to talk his way out of this mess, "From the looks o' it, 'e was drunk an' run into a tree. Poked 'imself good. 'is horse was still standin' there, so I brough' 'im in." He looked directly at the man with the gun. "Coulda left 'im t' die, I s'pose, an' would ha' I known I'd be starin' at tha' pistol for doin' me goo' deed."

The man with the gun seemed embarrassed and let the hammer down, then holstered his pistol. "Just the same, you'll be stayin' until the man wakes up."

"An' if he doan wake up, wha' then?"

The officer apparently hadn't considered this and seemed to ponder as he looked at the others for some kind of support. All he got was a shrug.

"Unless ya 'ave some reason t' be arrestin' me, I'll be goin' on me way."

The two men looked at one another as Newton turned about and started walking again. As he reached the main road, he glanced back over his shoulder and saw the two officers still standing in the middle of the street jawing with one another. Newton picked up the pace.

* * *

Felix and Abigail did not reach the rendezvous spot appointed by Newton.

They had been delayed by the death of Abigail's baby, Rankin.

They hadn't gone far before the baby began to cough horribly. Then, all of a sudden, he had stopped. Abigail had worked to force him to breathe again but to no avail. Felix stood by in shock, horrified by how quickly it had happened. When it was clear that the baby had taken his last breath, Abigail fell apart, wailing that she should have listened and taken him to the doctor. This set off guilt in Felix for not having forced her to do it. Tears of sadness were accompanied by wailing in Abe and Flower—and panic in everyone else for fear that the uproar would attract attention and get them caught.

Feeling a good deal of panic himself, Felix pulled the team and wagon into the first opening in the trees. He drove deep into the forest in the direction of the river while also trying to somehow comfort Abigail, who continued to wail so loudly he thought slavers would surely be able to hear them back at Boonville.

Finally Felix pulled the team to a halt and attempted to settle everyone, wrapping his arms around Abigail to soothe her. Bella came to his rescue as she slipped into the seat on the other side of Abigail, whispering words of comfort.

After a few minutes, Abigail managed to quiet herself somewhat, and Felix turned his attention to the others, whose eyes had been drawn to a different kind of emergency. Amnon pointed below the wagon. "We's sinkin', Massa Felix," he cried and looked at the others in a panic.

Felix leapt to the side of the wagon and realized that he had driven it into a bog; he swallowed hard as he saw that they were at least a foot deep in mire, and though the horses were struggling to get free, the wagon was stuck.

"Get out!" Felix warned everyone. "Tom! Help with the horses!" Tom leapt from the wagon, and Amnon jumped from the back to work with Felix in helping the women and children trudge their way to higher ground. All the while Abigail held tightly to her lifeless child.

Tom was ankle-deep in the bog within minutes, but he somehow managed to unhitch the horses. Felix grabbed the reins and coaxed the animals forward, a nearly impossible task since they stood in the worst area of the bog, the ooze above their hocks holding them like cement. Felix slapped the reins against the horses' backsides again and again while Tom and Amnon pulled them with a lead rope, and at last the animals were able to break free. Felix exhaled in relief as they chugged their way to higher ground.

When he was finally able to get the horses settled down, he tied them to a tree but stayed close as he surveyed the wagon's predicament and continued trying to catch his breath.

The wagon was at least a foot deep in mire now, and putting the horses back in the bog to pull it out seemed unwise at best, downright stupid at worst.

"Tom, go back to the main road. Watch fo' Mr. Daines, an' bring 'im here when you sees 'im, but doan get seen by no one else, ya hear me?"

"Yes, suh," Tom said as he headed toward the road.

The others had found places to sit while they waited, except for Abigail, who remained on her knees, rocking back and forth, sobbing quietly now, her eyes on her baby. Felix knelt beside her, reached around her shoulders, and sat in silence as she wept. His tenderness seemed to calm her crying, and he wished he could do more to alleviate her pain. "My baby," she whispered. "If . . . if I had just listened to youse . . ." She sobbed more fiercely again, her head in his shoulder.

Felix felt grief of his own but figured if the baby was that close to dying, there probably wasn't much even the best doctor could have done about it. "Ain't no blame to give but on Mr. Castle Ridges," Felix said. He paused, looking around him, his anxiety increasing over their predicament. They had to keep moving. "We has to bury him, Abigail. We has to keep goin' or Abe and Flower and you and all of us gonna git caught, and it all be fo' nuthin'."

Abigail seemed to stiffen at these words, her eyes wide as if she were suddenly coming out of a dream. She took a deep breath and fussed with Rankin's blanket, pulling it tight around his cold body. "You be diggin' then, Mr. Felix, an' I'll be sayin' m' g'byes."

Felix got to his feet and went to the wagon. He and Newton had thought to bring some tools with them, and to Felix's relief there was a shovel among the lot. He sloshed through the ooze to retrieve it and several other items they would need then found a place that seemed high and dry enough to dig a small grave. Amnon joined him, and they quickly had the small hole dug and ready.

They were just finishing placing the body when Newton and Tom appeared on the path they'd forged through the woods. Felix looked up and nodded at Newton, then removed his floppy-brimmed hat to say a quick prayer. Abigail stood a short distance away, tears coursing silently down her face, Flower and Abe hanging tightly to her fragile frame.

Felix took a deep breath. "Lord, he's innocent as dey come and free o' any sin, so we be hopin' you'll accept him unto yo' bosom and give 'im comfort because he's away from 'is mama. And Lord, please bless her and these other chil'uns with yo' peace to know that he's free o' this torment and in yo' lovin' arms. Amen."

He put on his hat and motioned for Amnon to fill in the grave. Abigail knelt down, overcome with emotion, grasping her two remaining children. Felix let Bella comfort them while he went to Newton and Tom, who were surveying the wagon.

He spoke quietly to Newton, explaining what he'd told Abigail. Newton agreed with what he had done.

"I was a fool to come down dis way. I—"

"Ya 'ad no choice, so doan be beatin' yerself up over it." Newton looked back the way they'd come. "Tom an' I put sum deadfall o'er the spot where ya left th' road."

"If they're after us, they be catchin' up soon," Felix said.

"'Tis likely." Newton thought a moment. "We be abou' ten miles from Jefferson City but if we stay on the road they be catchin' us f'sure."

As the two of them looked out over the Missouri and considered their best course of action, Newton remembered that he'd seen places along the river where steamers had put into shore, cut down timbers for their boilers, then put out to water again. There were none here—it was too swampy—but down farther. . . .

He turned to the others as an idea formed. "Ya keep goin' downriver an' find a spot as far down as ya can go where a steamer 'as put in fer wood. I'll take one o' the horses an' ride 'im back t' the city then bring Mr. Hoodsun's steamer up t' meet ya. It'll ha' t' be daylight t' find ya, so we 'ill both have t' make goo' time."

Felix nodded. "Just as well take both horses. The second would jus' slow us down in these here thick woods."

"I'll be leaving the rifle with ya. Keep the powder dry," Newton said.

Felix nodded in agreement, and the two men went to the horses, then removed the unneeded parts of the harness. Felix gave Newton a leg up to climb aboard the wide back of the workhorse and handed him the reins of the other. Both knew the trouble they were in without saying another word about it, and Newton rode off while Felix gathered the others and gave each something from the wagon to carry.

Abigail still stood near the baby's grave, her eyes on the small mound of earth that had been piled over her child by Amnon.

Flower went to her and pulled on her hand. "Mama, we has to go. The Lord, he'll take good care o' Rankin now, I knows it."

"She's right, Mama," Abe said. "We has to go now."

"I know, darlin's," Abigail said, forcing herself to her feet. "I know." She put an arm around her daughter's shoulder before joining Felix and the others.

With the flintlock over one shoulder, Felix led off, and the others followed, a softly falling rain adding to the somber mood.

Chapter 32

ABIGAIL FELT DISCONNECTED FROM THE events that were happening around her as though she was in a dream, the ache and fear in her heart nearly crushing her. The rain had soaked them all clean through, and all of them shivered in the cold, increasing their exhaustion. Abigail, dog-weary and unable to pick up her feet, stumbled and fell into the mud. Bella came to her side, then called out to Felix, who came back quickly and knelt beside her, Flower and Abe next to him.

"Tom, go back and see if we is bein' followed," Felix said. Tom left as Abigail spoke.

"I has to rest," she said. "I *has* to."

"How far we got, Mr. Felix?" Flower asked. Felix hesitated in his reply. He knew they needed to stop, but they couldn't start a fire, not yet, and without a fire and no movement, they'd all freeze up worse as they sat on the soaked ground. But he didn't know how much farther either. Though he'd been watching for a place a steamer could come to shore, he still hadn't found any.

There was a rustling in the brush as Tom came up through the woods in a hurry. "Massa Felix, listen."

Everyone went very quiet, and there was a collective gasp as they heard the sound of baying dogs.

"They got our scent, they do!" Abe said with wild eyes. "We gotta keep goin', Massa Felix! We gotta."

"I told you, doan be callin' me massa,'" Felix admonished, then handed Abe the rifle and quickly slid his arms under Abigail and picked her up. "We has to git goin'! We has to move!" Tom picked up Flower, Amnon grabbed Abe's hand, and with Bella at his side, they all ran through the forest toward the river.

Though the trees and brush were thick and limbs ripped at their clothes, Felix pushed them to run faster, the dogs sounding closer with every passing second.

Within moments, they came to a jolting stop as the river's edge suddenly appeared and the rush of the muddy torrent cut them off. Tom and Felix set Flower and Abigail on their own feet and quickly looked around for some solution. It was a sheer drop of ten feet to the water here, and the furious torrent had carved out the bank below them. Felix glanced over his shoulder, heard the dogs nearer than ever, then cried for everyone to run along the shoreline, where there seemed to be a path in the grass. Tom went first and, in an attempt to look back, stumbled and plummeted over the edge and into the river. He came gasping to the top and found himself in water up to his waist. Thankfully, a small outcrop of trees protected him from the full fury of the current, but it was still no small struggle to get back to shore. Amnon scrambled partway down the bank and hung onto the roots of several trees as he reached to grab Tom's hand and then pulled him out and up the side of the muddy slope. When they reached sure footing, they fell to their knees, shivering hard as the cool breeze sliced through them.

"You all right?" Felix asked them. Tom nodded his head in the positive, but his teeth were already beginning to chatter.

"Hey, dis is a boat," Bella shouted from behind them, her voice tinged with wonder.

From the baying of the hounds in the night air, it sounded as though they would burst through the brush at any moment.

Felix hurried to Bella, and everyone helped shove tree limbs aside to uncover an old dugout canoe with no paddles and no oars. Though it was partially rotted on the outside, Felix could see no place where it was rotted completely through.

He stood and, with Amnon and Tom's help, picked up the canoe and hurried downstream, looking for a spot to launch it into the water. Just past the outcrop of trees, he found a small ravine leading to a muddy shore. He hurried back for the others and gave Tom and Amnon the order to get the canoe down to the edge of the river.

When Felix returned with the others, they slipped and slid down to where Amnon and Tom had the canoe half in the river. When Felix looked inside and saw no water, he flashed a smile. "It'll hold."

But their troubles were not at an end. There was room for two, maybe three—certainly not all of them.

"Flower and the women get in, the rest of us will be swimmin' and hangin' on," Felix ordered. He looked over his shoulder, knowing the dogs weren't far off, then looked back at the frightened faces looking up at him.

"We got no paddles," Tom said.

"Doan need 'em. Now git them women in."

Still they hesitated. In frustration and fear, Felix cried, "It's the river or the hounds and a good whippin', maybe worse. Which a them does you prefer?"

No one said another word as Amnon quickly helped Bella and Flower into the canoe. Felix lifted Abigail easily over the side and scooted her to one end. The vessel nearly tipped over, but he caught it with a firm hand as he waded into deeper water. Tom held to its side in front of him, and Amnon stayed on the other side of the canoe. It was then that Felix noticed Abe still on the shore, rifle in hand. Felix called for everyone to stop, then trudged back and took the rifle, handing it to Abigail.

"Keep it dry," he cautioned, then went back for Abe and put him on his back. Taking a breath, he pushed out into the frigid water.

They were at the mercy of the river.

* * *

The dogs had caught the runaways' scent where deadfall had been put in place to cover the wagon tracks. Castle had set the hounds loose then, and they had found the abandoned wagon and tracks leading toward Jefferson City. The dogs began to dig up a small grave and had to be pulled off when Castle figured he no longer had to worry about the child Harrison didn't want.

They had followed the tracks through bog and thick forest for nearly five miles, finally having to abandon their own horses in order to keep on the tracks. It was another mile before the dogs seemed to work up to a full frenzy as they reached the edge of the river, barking and sniffing at the muddy bank.

One of Castle's men, Cole Dunn, checked the tracks. "Some kinda boat was launched here. From the looks of the underbrush, it was an old one. These nigras got lucky."

"Old dugout," said Castle. "Probably rotten and won't last long."

"They'll be downriver," Dunn said. "We got 'em now."

Castle instructed the men to leash the dogs and tie them up; they would return for the dogs later. Then they hurried as fast as they could along the shore. All of them could smell a catch.

* * *

It took all their strength to keep the canoe straight in the flow of the strong current and still stay somewhat close to shore, but it carried them a good distance, and Felix couldn't hear the hounds anymore. Finally Felix knew that he, Tom, and Amnon could go no farther; the frigid water was turning their blood to ice. When at last he saw a place they could stop, he gave the order for everyone to head for shore, and they quickly beached at an embankment that sloped up to a stand of deadfall. A small stream of water poured out of it, creating a muddy bank where they were able to pull up the canoe. The women and Flower got out and helped the shivering men get to shore. With no blankets, all they could do was huddle close together and try to share their warmth.

Felix looked at the sky. It would be dark soon. He feared that Newton had been delayed or had found a place and was waiting for them farther downriver. One thing was sure: This spot wouldn't do, and they had passed none other. They had to keep going.

Abigail handed Felix the rifle and then wrapped her arms around him against his shivering. He felt her warmth immediately and was grateful for it, but he forced himself to check the gun and make sure the powder was not wet.

"Listen!" Tom said.

The boy had good ears, that was certain. The sound of someone coming through the woods could be heard, as well as dogs much farther away.

"They's still comin,' but they's left the dogs behind," said Amnon with resigned fear.

Felix tried to control his shivering as he stood up to take a look into the woods. He could see movement through the trees a short distance away. Looking to his right, he felt a cold spike of fear as he saw even more movement.

"They must have seen us comin' ashore. We're surrounded." Felix's mind struggled to come up with a plan for escape. "Pile up that wood. We got no place to go," he said.

The men and Tom scrambled to accomplish the task and quickly had a barricade in place.

"What we goan do now, Massa Felix?" Tom asked.

"Pray, Tom, or we can go swimmin' again. Them seems the only choices left, unless you want to give up and go back to what you was doin' for that white man."

"No, suh, I ain't goin' back, lest I's dead as dis here old wood. And dat water, we go in now and we jus' be sittin' ducks. I'll pray fo' sure, but it be for my soul, 'cause I ain't leavin' here with dem men no how." His expression was determined, and Felix knew he would do it.

Felix pulled the revolver out of his belt and handed it to Tom. "Do you know how to use it?"

"No, suh, but I's a quick learner." Felix quickly showed him what to do. When Felix was aboard a ship as a freedman, the captain had showed him how to use weapons in case of pirates, and he was glad of it now. "It has only one shot, and we got no reloads, so you save it, hear? You save it 'til they gets real close."

Tom nodded, his eyes wide.

"They won't stan' to let you git 'way, Massa Felix. You is a free black man, and they'll come fo' you 'cause what you done fo' us," said Amnon with obvious concern. "Maybe you should run, Massa Felix."

"I told all of you to quit callin' me 'massa.' I hate that name, an' you knows it. An' I ain't runnin' neither. If they comes after me, at least one of 'em is goin' with me to meet St. Peter." Felix was speaking with more bravery than he felt. He was downright scared, and he did not relish the idea of either dying or getting a good whipping and being sold downriver. He had grown fond of Jasmina and the baby, and he wanted to see them again, but unless the good Lord did something quickly, he didn't think that would be the way of things.

"Hey, nigras!" came the voice through the woods. It was close, almost upon them. Felix cocked the old rifle, checked the percussion cap, and prepared himself.

"What you want?" Felix asked in as calm a voice as he could.

"We want you all," came the reply. Then there was some mumbling and several laughs. "You the one who helped that pretty little Abigail escape? We's comin' for you, mister. Black or white, you gonna be a dead man when this is over." Felix did not miss the sneer and hate in the man's voice, but it only made him more determined.

"I figure there's maybe five or six a you. I can load this here Enfield twice before you get to me, so's not all a youse will be seein' any hangin'. Now you come on, mister. You be first. I'm sure them other boys will dig you a fine grave for bein' such a hero."

Felix had no Enfield, just this old flintlock, but if he nailed one of the men with his first shot, it would give the others pause and maybe give him enough time to load again. He removed the powder and shot bag from his shoulder, getting the gun ready.

The swearing stopped and rifles boomed, but the lead balls all struck a nearby thick grove of trees. Obviously the woods were too heavy for slavers to tell precisely where Felix and the others were, and though Felix wanted to fire, he knew that when he did, he'd give away their position. Then the bullets would be flying much closer and much more deadly.

He looked at the folks behind him. These folks would not die, though most of them would get a good whipping, and the bucks would be put in shackles and punished in some horrific way. Only *he* was in any real danger of dying, and it was all he could do to keep from jumping back in the river and taking a chance in its frigid waters.

"If you give up, go out with yo' hands up, you might get outta this," Felix advised the others.

Abigail harrumphed. "That's Castle Ridges. I ain't givin' up to him no how, and if'n he come down here, he gonna have to shoot me, 'cause if he doan, I break his head good." She had found a large, heavy stick and gripped it firmly. "But you kill one or two first, 'cause I kin't handle 'em all."

Felix saw that the woman had pluck, and it stiffened his own back.

The others picked up similar sticks and prepared them for use. Amnon spoke boldly. "She be right. If'n we want t' be free, we has t' fight fo' it. If youse doan mind, Massa Felix, we be fixin' to break a few heads ourselves if'n dey come."

"An' I'll be shootin' at least one of 'em, Massa Felix," Tom said. "Ain't goin' back no more. No, sir."

"Quit callin' me 'massa,' Tom!" Felix hissed. He heard the crack of a dead tree branch only a few feet away and raised his eyes over the top of the log only to find that he was looking into the barrel of a gun. Paralyzed, he thought for sure the end had come.

He heard the explosion but felt nothing and opened his eyes to see the man lying on the ground on the other side of the log jam, moaning. The other slavers had come out of the trees and seemed to be looking to their left, a shocked look on each of their faces. Felix turned to see several men coming out of the woods, armed, their rifles pointed at the slavers.

"You boys best be putting down your weapons if you want to stay alive."

Felix knew that voice. He got to his feet and aimed his rifle at the nearest slaver, just to make sure the slaver knew Felix was armed as well.

"That ain't no Enfield," the slaver said.

"No it ain't, but it will make you just as dead. Now you put yo' weapon down and git over there wid yo' friends."

The sound of a gun made Felix jump; he watched the slaver he was talking to go down like a felled tree. He turned to see Abigail holding the pistol he'd given to Tom, smoke coming from its shaking barrel. Her eyes were wild with anger. He took two steps and eased the pistol out of her hands.

Outnumbered three to one, the other four slavers set aside their weapons and eased together at a spot about fifty yards away. The person who had shot the man who was about to kill Felix came forward, her men's clothing, soot-covered face, and slouch hat hiding her real identity.

"Miss Mary," Felix said quietly. He had an arm around Abigail, holding her arm as she suddenly grew weak in the knees. Moving her to a nearby log, he helped her sit while Bella took over.

"We were a bi' late in arrivin', but when we 'eard those gunshots, we figured we'd better come at a quicker pace."

"Jus' in time, Missy," Felix said as he noticed Newton and several others come up behind the slavers.

"Youse sure is a sight fo' sore eyes," Amnon said.

The rest of the runaways gathered as the man Mary shot rolled over and moaned then sat up holding one arm with the other. Two of the steamer's crew knelt to look him over and then help him get up and put him with the others.

"He'll not be using that arm any time soon," Mary said. She went to the man shot by Abigail and knelt down.

"Da ya know 'im, Missy?" Felix asked.

"Castle Ridges," Mary said.

"No wonder Abigail shot him," Felix said, his eyes on Abigail.

Mary was curious but let it go. She knew Castle Ridges, and that was enough.

Newton stepped up and looked down. "Seems th' Ridges jus' can't win."

"He's still unconscious, but the wound isn't tha' bad. Maybe a concussion," Mary said. "He'll travel well enough, an' 'is friends can take him t' a doctor."

Felix protested. "You gonna let 'im go? We should take 'im to jail, or—"

"We're the ones breaking the law, remember," Newton said with a wry smile. "Believe me, I'd like t' see 'im in jail. I' woul' 'elp 'im understand wha' these folks 'ave been goin' through 'cause o' people like 'im." He looked at the slaves huddled together a short distance away. "But this is best, Felix."

"Yes, suh."

"You mus' be freezin'. Mary, take these folks an' get t' the steamer. I'll send these boys on their way." Felix could see that Newton was not happy with Mary but didn't ask. Instead he went to Abigail and helped her to her feet. She was weak, pale, and needed help.

"Did I kill 'im?"

"No, but he'll be feelin' it for a while," Felix said.

"I . . . I . . . I don' know what come over me. I. . . ." She lay her head against his shoulder as they walked. "Da goo' Lord don' allow no killin' do he, Mr. Felix? I coulda lost my soul."

"I doubt that, Abigail, but never you mind. The good Lord understan's."

They followed Mary through the woods, with Abe, Tom, Amnon, and Bella just behind them.

Mary had heard the conversation. She had few qualms about killing a man like Ridges and wished the bullet hadn't been so lenient. Castle Ridges saw black men and women as the equivalent of insects. Killing Felix and the woman with him would have been as easy for Castle as stepping on a bug. The woman would have done the world a favor sending Castle Ridges to the devil.

As she stepped onboard the steamer and helped distribute blankets and hot food to the slaves, she was grateful Newton had allowed her to come along. She hadn't expected it to be like this and had no intention of shooting someone, but she figured each time one went to free slaves, the chances were good it might happen again, and that worried her—not because she had fired her weapon and nearly killed a man, but because it might cost her Newton.

She watched him appear from the trees a moment later and hop aboard with several other crew members. The captain blew the whistle as a sign for the crew to get the steamer underway; the runaways were taken downstairs, where they would be made comfortable in the new hideaway Newton had built. The crew pulled in the gangplank as Newton stepped to Mary's side.

"Fine work, Miss Mary, but I believe I tol' ya t' stay onboard," Newton said without a smile.

"Since when do I do wha' ya tol' me?" she said, putting her arm through his.

"'Tis a good point, bu' ya know tha' when we be tyin' the knot, things 'ill be havin' to be changin'." He smiled.

"Tha's fer sure. I expect you'll be *changin'* diapers and doin' as yer told, or I'll be standin' ya in the corner with no breakfast."

Newton chuckled. "Ya 'ave the better o' me, love." Then he sobered. "But findin' ya there, it frightened me, Mary; I won't be havin' it again."

Mary put her arms around his neck and gave him a warm kiss. "Possibly that 'ill be helpin' ya to forgive me, and doan forget Felix is alive because I happened along."

"'Tis a start, and yer right, but still . . ." Newton smiled.

As the paddles drove the vessel quickly into the middle of the river, Mary and Newton watched the final rays of the sun settle on the western horizon. One thing both of them knew for sure as they headed for the Missisippi, then Illinois to send the slaves on their way—there was not a more satisfying work than that of freedom.

Chapter 33

LIZZY RETURNED TO THE CLAY home late in the evening with her purchases in hand. As the carriage pulled up to the door, she noted that no one came to greet her and Matty—an immediate sign that something was amiss. Climbing down, she and Matty went into the house to find Emily, who sat stiff-backed on the divan in the sitting room; she was pale, her eyes blank with confusion.

"What is it, Emily?" Lizzy asked with real concern.

Emily stared into oblivion. Lizzy went quickly to the divan, sat down, and placed her hand on the girl's shoulder to shake her lightly. "Emily?"

Emily attempted to focus on Lizzy. "Sick. They are all sick." Her voice was quiet, even despondent.

"What? What are you talking about, Emily? Who is sick?"

Agitated voices resounded from the back of the house, and Matty ran to see what the ruckus was about.

"Emily, who is sick?" Lizzy asked.

"All of them." She seemed distant, unable to really focus. "Mother went. She . . . she found the sickness . . ."

Lizzy felt her stomach lurch. "What kind of sickness, Emily?"

Emily swallowed. "The doctor says it is cholera, Elizabeth."

Lizzy felt weak, and her heart began racing. Cholera here! How could it be?

"Emily, where are your father and mother?" she asked, sounding calmer than she felt.

Emily looked at her with a blank stare. "They must stop it, you know. It would ruin us if we lost all our nigras. Why, Mr. Slade says we have to get rid of the ones who are sick. That's the only way to save the others. We have to burn everything. Everything."

"Slade is a fool, but we must go and help." Lizzy rose to her feet.

Terror filled Emily's eyes. "No, no, we cannot. Surely we will be infected. I will not do it. I cannot do it." Her lip began to quiver, and Lizzy felt her fear. She understood. She was afraid herself. Cholera was considered a contagious disease transmitted by proximity to a carrier. Doctors believed that if you breathed the air an infected person expelled, you might catch the same illness. Most would not even enter the same room as the ill, leaving them to suffer and eventually die alone.

But Lizzy knew better. Recent studies had proved that the spread of cholera was caused by contamination of the water supply by human or animal waste. In 1854, a Dr. Snow had proven that an outbreak in the suburb of London could be traced back to one particular well on Broadstreet. Lizzy had read the newspaper report of his detailed findings and found them impressive, even conclusive. But even with such evidence, the scientific world remained reluctant to break away from its fears of contagion—after all, even if a person *was* made sick by bad drinking water, that did not eliminate the possibility that the same person could then spread the disease. Such concerns and doubts in the medical field left a good deal of fear in everyone, including Emily.

Despite her knowledge on the matter, Lizzy was fearful as well. Yet she knew she could not let such fear stop her from acting. She would take precautions against contact but she knew she must not become paralyzed. She must do what she could.

Getting to her feet, Lizzy immediately started for her room and was up three stairs before Matty came running down the hall from the kitchen. "De cook, she say dat lots of dem folks is real sick, missy. De doctor is out dere, and Massa Clay and de missus, an—"

"Thank you, Matty. I will change clothing and be there as quickly as I can." Lizzy ran to her room and quickly changed into warmer clothes while trying to recall information from the studies she had read. Then she got to her knees and prayed for strength, for courage, and for mercy on them all. She grabbed her coat and headed downstairs, where Matty and the other house servants were anxiously chattering in the kitchen.

"Matty, we will need all the hot water we can get, and if Mr. Clay has not sent word to do so, I tell you now to start removing every blanket, every sheet, and every linen in this house for use out there. How many of you live in the slaves' quarters?"

"None, ma'am," Matty said. "We all live in dem houses by de barn, remember? We's separate. Mr. Clay made it so."

"Yes, I had forgotten. Do you drink from separate wells?" Lizzy asked.

"Yes'm," Matty said. "Dey use de old well, we use dis new one jes outside."

"Are you or any of the other servants feeling ill?"

"No ma'am," said Matty, shaking her head.

"If any of you or your families become ill, come and find me or Mr. Clay immediately. Until then you are not to drink from either well. Do you understand?"

Matty nodded her understanding, and Lizzy opened several cupboards until she found one filled with whiskey and other liquors. She removed two and signaled for Matty and the other servants in the kitchen to join her at the sink. "I am going to pour this over your hands. It will disinfect them." She used the entire bottle to thoroughly cover each set of hands. She surmised there might be some value in giving them confidence that they were clean. The next step would be to give them something to do. "Now, clean this place with hot water and any soap you can find. We must also make certain that food we prepare does not become a carrier of this disease. Nothing is to be served that is not thoroughly heated and cooked. And please, keep your hands washed."

Each of the servants nodded, but everyone still looked worried, and Lizzy understood why. Plantation life lent itself to repeated contact with everyone. If you believed in contagion, you believed that the cholera could hunt you down one way or another.

Lizzy took the other bottle of liquor and went outside, running along the path toward the slaves' quarters until she found herself in a mix of people standing about, their eyes on one of the slave houses where two men carried someone on a makeshift stretcher through the door. The men had rags tied tightly around their lower faces so that only their eyes were visible, wide and frightened. She saw an unfamiliar gentleman trailing behind and assumed he must be the doctor Emily had mentioned. Whispers through the crowd gave her the shakes; someone had already died. She hurried to the doctor.

"How many are ill?" Lizzy asked him.

At first he looked hesitant to respond to her question—after all, she was both a stranger and a woman, but after only a moment he shook his head and answered. "Half a dozen. The first has died. We are trying to isolate them in this place so that the illness does not spread."

"Then you are sure it is cholera," Lizzy said.

"Yes, quite sure. The fecal matter is extensive and gray, and the afflicted have fever and—"

"Have you told them not to drink from the well?"

"Yes. Mr. Clay has put a guard around it." There was stiffness in the man's voice, and he finally said, "I am sorry, but I do not recognize you."

"Elizabeth Hudson. I am a friend of Andrew Clay."

"Well, Miss Hudson, you should go back to the house. There is nothing you can do here." He glanced at the whiskey bottles. "Disinfectant?"

She nodded and handed them to him. "You will need all the help you can get, Doctor, and we both know it. Where are the Clays?"

"I do not need interference from someone who is sure to question me at every turn. Now—"

"I have studied the journals, Doctor. I know that contagion is still a possibility through fecal matter even though it has been determined with a good deal of certainty that the water supply is the place from which the illness springs. If that knowledge is somehow offensive to you, then you are right, I am of no use here. On the other hand, perhaps my understanding and willingness can be put to good use."

The doctor paused and considered her statement. His expression softened a bit, and he said, "Yes, I apologize; you are right. Mrs. Clay is inside, and Mr. Clay is burning the house where I believe all of this started. At least most of the cases have come from people living there. There is a good deal of fecal matter about, and if Mr. Snow of London is not entirely right, there is still the possibility of contagion." He paused. "We have one cauldron heating, but three or four more may be needed. Away from here would be best." He looked at the growing crowd of workers. "They will need places to stay until we can clean or burn the remaining houses. As a precaution, I think it best that they all be washed and cleaned and receive new clothes. The old clothing must be boiled and hung out in the sun to dry, or it must be burned."

"Does Mr. Clay agree with you? There will be a considerable expense involved in all this, and Mr. Clay may not want to pay it."

As the doctor pushed open the door of the house where the sick were being kept, Lizzy was stung by the sudden odor that came from within.

"Mr. Clay has torched one house and will torch others as needed." He gave Lizzy a stern look. "Do not underestimate his concern for these people, Miss Hudson. Though you and I may not agree with his position, they are property to him, and Mr. Clay will do everything he can to protect himself from losing them. It would ruin him. But I have not talked to him about the need for clothing. I will leave that to you."

"You are too kind," she said facetiously. He was about to close the door. "Doctor, you are a brave man if you believe this illness is contagious."

He smiled. "We have both read the studies about what causes cholera, but these people have not. What we are going to do is give them peace of mind that we are doing everything to put a stop to it and that we do not fear it. That has to be worth something even if it means the loss of some buildings and my looking like a fool." He closed the door behind him.

Lizzy looked up to see Asher and signaled to him; he quickly joined her.

"He a brave man, goin' in dat place," Asher said, shaking his head.

Lizzy smiled. "Come with me."

They went around the first row of houses and found Horatio watching one of the slave houses burning. She walked up to him but he didn't turn to see who was behind him. "Your servants will need a place to stay until all this passes," Lizzy said quietly.

Horatio didn't answer for a moment but simply stood watching the flames rapidly climbing up the dry wood and igniting the roof. Lizzy noted the dozens of slaves standing about confused, unsure of what the future might hold.

"Miss Hudson, you are not needed out here," Horatio finally said.

She took a deep breath, tired of the chauvinism. "Mr. Clay, I do not see anyone else rushing out to give you a hand. Or am I missing something?"

He looked at her. "Andrew would not want you in danger. Now please, go back to the house."

"Andrew has no say about what I do or don't do. You need help. *Now where do you want these people to be housed?*"

His eyes reflected a mixture of emotions, but Lizzy thought she noted just the slightest hint of relief.

"The textile mill you saw yesterday. It is the only place large enough."

"The doctor has asked that I see that they are all bathed and given clean clothes and blankets. I think we should take care of those matters away from here but before you move them to the mill so that any sickness borne in their clothing does not go with them. All the water must be boiled, and we will need more cauldrons, plenty of wood for fires, and lots of water, but not from this well. It will have to come from one we can absolutely trust."

Horatio thought a moment. "The one at the mill." He turned then and called out to several male slaves who stood about in uncertainty, ordering them to fill barrels from the mill well and take them to the pasture west of the barn in the wagons, along with the five cauldrons they would find at the mill. He then gave directions about where to build each fire and instructed the men to have others start hauling wood to the same location.

"Get going then," Clay said. He looked at Lizzy as Asher ran in the direction of the barn, all the other slaves with him. "The mill was not in use today. One of the waterwheels is broken, so most of the slaves have been here. That's both good and bad—good because there is a chance the mill is not infected, and bad because there are more here who may be."

"I may have overreached, Mr. Clay, but I have already asked that the cooks wash down the winter kitchen. They are also to gather every blanket and linen they can and bring them here."

"You did not overreach, Miss Hudson. Both are good decisions."

"Doesn't Richmond have a hospital?" she asked.

"It does—but as many will die there as will die if we keep these people isolated and cared for here, and I do not think the city will be fond of receiving cholera-infected servants into their midst, do you? Of course, I have sent my personal driver to notify the authorities, and when they come, we will decide if anything else should be done."

"Where is the well these people use?" Lizzy asked, knowing that time was of the essence.

"There." He pointed in the direction of a stone formation beyond and to the right of the burning house. Lizzy skirted the hot flames of the fire as she headed over to inspect the well's location. It lay only a few dozen feet from a small gulch with a creek at the bottom. She walked upstream along the tree-lined ravine until she came to a steep slope down which a waterfall cascaded.

Horatio followed and quickly caught up to her.

"What's up there?" she asked.

"A small pond. The creek feeds it on the far side," he said.

Lizzy nodded and started climbing, Horatio at her heels. They wound up the side of the steep hill on a path that quickly led them to the crest. It was another short walk along the tree-lined creek bed before she found the pond. It was a beautiful spot. Calm and apparently clean, it wasn't more than a hundred feet across at any point. Then she noticed the small cabin at the far end.

"Is that occupied?"

Horatio smiled. "No, not anymore. It was my parents' first home. I was born there. As is obvious, it has seen better years."

He was certainly right; the roof timbers had broken loose in at least one spot, leaving a gaping hole, and the door was hanging from a single bottom hinge. There was no glass in the windows, and part of a wall had caved in. Lizzy quickly walked around the pond to the cabin and examined it more closely, pushing aside the dilapidated door as she stepped in; Horatio followed. As her eyes adjusted, her breath caught as she realized she was not alone. A set of frightened eyes stared in her direction from a rancid straw mattress shoved against one wall.

"What on earth . . . ?" Horatio said as his eyes adjusted to the dark and he saw the black man sitting on the reeking mattress. He was shackled and obviously quite ill, near skin and bones. He cringed as Lizzy found a candle and lit it. By even its dim light, she could see that this man had been beaten recently, had been given little to eat, and had a horrible crook to one leg, as if it was broken and unset.

Horatio stepped closer, a stunned look on his face. "Billy? Billy Blue, is that you?"

The man began to cry, and Horatio knelt down in front of his emaciated frame. The man then fell against Horatio's shoulder and began to sob even harder.

Lizzy was stunned by the scene and was unable to speak as Clay held his old slave to his chest and tried to comfort him.

Then Lizzy heard the sound of horses' hooves outside and quickly went to the window to see Slade and two others riding up a trail from the back of the small cabin.

"Mr. Clay," she whispered. He pulled himself from a frightened Billy Blue and both simply stood and waited until Slade stepped through the door. The shock in Slade's eyes told them that he hadn't expected to find them here.

"What have you done, Slade?" Horatio asked angrily.

Slade gave a wry smile. "This ain't none of yer business, Clay."

"That man is a freedman. You went after him, didn't you? You just couldn't stand having him walk away."

"But why keep him here like this?" Lizzy asked softly as pieces of the puzzle started to come together. "Why not sell him, Slade?"

"He's healin' from a broken leg. No good broken," Slade said angrily. Lizzy saw Slade's hand go to a gun in his belt, and she reacted by pulling her own revolver from her pocket and pointing it at him. "That would not be a good idea," she said, glad that she had purchased the gun. Her hands felt cold and clammy, and she had to control her breathing. She had considered the revolver for just such a situation, but considering and actually accomplishing it were two very different things. Her mouth was dry, and she couldn't swallow.

Slade glared at her but his eyes also betrayed his surprise. "Boys," he said to the two men behind him, "Miss Hudson has a pea shooter in her hand. Now you be goin' 'round behind her and give her something bigger to look at." He smiled.

"If they so much as move, I'll see that you get a new navel." Her voice did not betray her anxiety. She *would* shoot them, she decided, as she glanced at the emaciated body of Billy Blue. Her anger returned, and she gripped the gun harder.

Slade quit smiling. The two men did not move.

Horatio quickly stepped forward and removed Slade's pistol from his belt, then swung it in a high arc and pummeled it unceremoniously across Slade's head. The man went down like he had no legs. Lizzy couldn't help but smile at the sudden and decisive action.

"You two, pick him up and get him aboard his horse," Horatio ordered Slade's accomplices. "Then you gather your things from the overseer's house and get on your way. If I see you or Slade anywhere near this place or even in Richmond, I'll have you hung for what you've done to this man, and I swear it before God and this woman!"

The two men seemed to sense the depth of Horatio Clay's wrath and moved quickly to drag Slade by his heels over the threshold and to his horse. Moments later Lizzy heard the thunder of hooves as they rode frantically away.

"Miss Hudson," Clay said, extending the revolver toward her. "I . . . I thank you for being prepared." His lip quivered slightly. "If you will take care of Slade's weapon, I . . . I will carry Billy."

Lizzy, shocked by this sudden change in Horatio Clay, only nodded and took the gun as Horatio went back to the terrified Billy, who was hunkered against the rotting cabin wall. Horatio tried to quiet his fears as he slipped his arms under his former slave and lifted him up. Lizzy felt a sudden softening in her heart as she saw how tightly Billy clung to his old master and how much tenderness there was in the eyes of Horatio Clay. It was a side of Horatio she had never dreamt existed.

And one that she hoped she would see again.

Chapter 34

ANN AND HER MOTHER ARRIVED back in St. Louis tired and apprehensive. At each stop the steamer made to load wood for the boilers, fervent talk of war was rampant, especially now that Lincoln had taken the oath of office. Though Lincoln had been conciliatory, the Southern states saw it as a sign of weakness and were becoming even more belligerent, demanding he not only release them from the Union but that the federal government turn the federal properties in seceding states over to those states intact—including navy yards, forts, and arsenals. To Ann this seemed the same as asking a man to arm the enemy who wanted to shoot him.

At Vicksburg, Ann had seen dozens of armed men deboarding Texan steamers that had come down the Red River. It was obvious that the South no longer intended to keep secret the intention to secede—peacefully if possible but by the waging of war if necessary.

Rand waited eagerly at the dock and gathered Ann into his arms, relieved and happy. He intended to kiss her lightly as was proper in public, but she would have none of it and kissed him good and long.

"Apparently I have missed you more than you have missed me," she teased, looking up into his eyes.

"I doubt that," he said with a wide grin. "But it is my duty to protect your public honor, remember." She and her mother had been delayed for nearly a month wrapping up her mother's affairs. It had seemed like an eternity to Rand.

She kissed him again. "I love you deeply, and because of it I have no shame, and it has been so very long!"

"That is my fault. I do apologize, Randolph," Amanda Alexander said with a worried frown. Amanda was about the same height as Ann and had held her form well for a woman of nearly fifty-five. Her hair was still dark, with a slight graying at the temples, and her face was of such beauty that it needed no enhancement. She wore a plain linen dress with a small flower print, and she wore no hat—unusual for a woman of her age. There was a glint in her eye that bore witness of her own mischievous nature, and Rand knew this was a woman who, like her daughter, would speak her mind.

Rand pulled back and smiled at his future mother-in-law, then released Ann long enough to kiss her extended hand. "Mrs. Alexander, now I see where my lovely Ann gets her breathtaking beauty."

Amanda's eyebrow lifted. "Yes, he is a gallant one, isn't he," she teased.

"Come, both of you, I know you are tired," Rand said.

A young black girl waited close by, and Rand turned toward her. "And who is this pretty young lady?"

"Adelia, my friend and servant," Amanda said with a smile.

Ann had given no indication that her mother owned slaves or even had a freedwoman servant, but Rand decided that now was not the time to question either woman on the subject. "Well then, ladies all, let's get you home." He took Ann's arm and walked to the carriage. They were all soon seated, and Ann was the first to speak, telling Rand of their trip and their harrowing experiences.

"Yes, things are getting worse," Rand said with a frown. "There is great concern that the Confederates are moving men to the east to either attack Washington or to secure a border and keep us out of the South."

Ann's brow wrinkled. "There are armed men everywhere—hundreds of them at Vicksburg."

"I overheard talk from a passenger who boarded there that the Southerners have a camp outside the city with hundreds more," Amanda added. "I'm glad to be out of the South. Such fools. I wish to thank you for allowing Adelia and I to come here, Randolph. I cannot express—"

"There is no need. You are both quite welcome, but I am afraid you are not entirely out of the South."

"Yes, Ann has told me, but she is confident that Missouri will be safe enough." She paused. "I wish to see that Adelia is set free. Can that be arranged here?"

Rand glanced at Ann, unsure of what to say.

Ann flushed as if she had been blindsided but quickly regained her composure and said, "Adelia is a runaway, Rand. Adam brought her home to make himself appear a good Southern gentlemen. Mother was very upset by it and decided the best way to send a strong message to Adam was to bring Adelia here."

Rand could not help his laugh.

"It is not a laughing matter, dear boy," Amanda said sternly. "Surely they will send someone looking for her. She did not really belong to Adam; he was only paying another man for her services on a monthly basis. A man who traffics in such business ought to be shot, but there you have it. What can be done?"

Rand cleared his throat. "Yes, you are quite right—this is serious business. I was not laughing at the situation but rather at how much you are like your daughter. How on earth did you get Adelia away without Adam knowing?"

"Well, of course he does know now, but he was gone to that silly military training camp the day we left, and I just told Adelia to pack her things and come along. Because she is with us, no one has asked a single question. It was quite simple really."

Rand choked down a chuckle. After all the money he had spent helping slaves escape, these two had walked away with one in broad daylight. The humor was in the irony.

"Yes, we can help Adelia," Rand said.

"Good. That gives me great comfort," Amanda said. "She is all by herself now—sold away from her parents last year. I know that horrid owner was planning to force her to be with someone she did not even love, and now she can choose her path for herself."

Rand noted the grateful look on Adelia's face.

"Adam must be livid," Rand said with a smile.

"I would not be surprised if he showed up looking for her himself, but I left him a note and told him it would do no good."

"Well, he does have some liability. The owner will want payment," Rand said.

"My son has always been a man who has had to learn life's lessons the hard way, and I have found over the years that when something hurts him monetarily, he learns more quickly."

There was a brief silence, and Ann took the opportunity to change the subject. "And the inauguration, did it go well? Being on the steamer the last two days with no news—"

"As well as can be expected, I suppose." He pulled a newspaper out of his pocket and handed it to her. "The story is there, on the front page."

Ann quickly began reading.

"Dear girl, what does it say?" her mother asked. "You are not the only one starved for news."

"Sorry, Mother. It says that Lincoln does not approve of slavery but that he has no intention of interfering where it now exists. He insists that the Union is perpetual and that no state by an internal vote can simply leave it behind. Secession is unconstitutional."

"In that he is right, but Southerners surely must be excoriating him for it today. They will not like it—not at all." She frowned. "I will not miss Adam's incessant preaching on this subject. He has become unbearably opinionated and would not even allow me to speak of Lincoln in his presence. Needless to say, he was not at home very much." She smiled.

Rand laughed again. He very much liked Amanda Alexander. She reminded him of his own mother, and he now saw where Ann got her fire.

"What else does the paper say, dear?" Amanda asked.

"Lincoln considers the Union still unbroken, despite a few misguided souls trying to organize a Confederacy, and he intends to enforce the law." Ann paused, reading further. "Oh my. He says he intends to retake any property that has been inhabited by rebellious states." She looked up. "That alone is a declaration of war."

"Not quite," Rand said. "The next paragraph is a direct quote. You will want to read it aloud."

Ann read directly. "'In your hands, my dissatisfied fellow countrymen, and not in mine, is the momentous issue of civil war. The government will not assail you. You can have no conflict without being yourselves the aggressors. You have no oath registered in heaven to destroy the government, while I shall have the most solemn one to preserve, protect, and defend it.'"

"Coupled with his tacit support of letting slavery alone where it now exists, Mr. Lincoln is doing his best not to start a war," Rand said.

"And rightly so, don't you think, Mr. Hudson?" Amanda said.

"No one wants war, but note that I said he is doing his best not to *start* it. He knows it will come, but he will not fire the first shot, and once made he will do everything it takes to win it."

"Well if Adam has things his way," Amanda said, "he will be the one to pull the trigger. The boy has simply lost all reason."

"Lincoln is very shrewd, isn't he, Rand," Ann said. "He acts as if nothing has changed; he will expect payment of taxes and tariffs, involvement in Congress, and business as usual."

"Yes, and the Confederacy will hate him for it. If you do not believe me, look at the second page."

Ann opened the paper. "'Declaration of War.' Is that the one you mean?"

"Yes, and to make a long story short, the so-called president of the Confederacy, Jefferson Davis, said that Lincoln has raised the gauntlet and that war cannot be avoided. Lincoln's speech has ignited the Confederate spirit, and even here there is a great feeling of support for the new Confederacy."

"Here, in Missouri?" Amanda said in shock.

"Governor Jackson has given a passionate speech on the matter, reiterating that we must 'stand by our sister slave-holding states.'"

They slowed for an intersection, and Rand heard the cry of a newspaper boy. "Davis orders siege of Sumter! Read all about it! South prepares for war!"

Rand leaned out the side of the carriage, flipped a coin to the newshawk, and received a copy of the afternoon daily in return. He sat back in his seat and unfolded the paper while Ann looked over it with him.

Rand read several headlines out loud for Amanda's benefit but there really wasn't anything new to report except that additional cannons now seemed aimed at Fort Sumter in an attempt to intimidate those holding the fort into submission.

"It seems we are on the very brink of war," Ann said.

Rand nodded, thinking. "This will embolden Governor Jackson."

"Then the arsenal is in immediate danger," Ann said.

"Until war is declared, he won't move, but he will be prepared to act the moment it is. We will have to move first."

The thought was sobering for all of them except Adelia, who seemed thoroughly confused.

"'Scuse me, Massa," Adelia said.

"Adelia, you have no master here. You are free to speak what you think, do you understand?"

"Yes, Massa, but I is confused a bit. Is you plannin' on fightin' them Southern folks to free us slaves?"

Rand thought of trying to explain about the Southern smokescreen of states' rights, constitutional mandates for unity, and economic considerations, among others, but he thought better of it. "Yes, Adelia, in the end the war will be fought to get rid of slavery."

Adelia seemed to be thinking. "But that mean you be killin' other white folks, don't it?"

"Let's hope it doesn't come to that, but yes it could."

Adelia looked even more thoughtful. She spoke softly. "Ain't nevah had no one care 'nuf 'bout me to even let me marry who I want, let 'lone kill 'nuther white man." She shook her head lightly. "Doan seem possible t' me, Massa, not t'all."

They rode in silence for some time after that, each lost in thought. Rand knew that as far as any official declarations went, the war would not be fought over slavery—not at first. In fact, most in the North said that if the war was to be over slavery, they would not fight. To them the central issues were union and rebellion. They would fight to hold the Union together, not to free blacks from slavery. But in the end, Rand was sure men would see that they could not separate one matter from the other. Disunion *was* about slavery. It was the central issue, and it would become the crux of the war one way or another.

"Darling, I want to have the wedding as soon as possible," Ann said, breaking into Rand's thoughts. "Do you think Lizzy could get back by the middle of April?"

Rand squeezed her hand, a worried look in his eyes. He had received only a brief note from Lizzy since she had arrived, and it did not carry a pleasant message.

"Lizzy has her hands full at present, so I am not sure—"

"Her hands full? What do you mean?" Ann asked.

Rand told her only what he knew. "She says it is a minor breakout and is contained but she—"

Oh, my!" Ann said. "She is in great danger."

"What have you done to get her out of there, Randolph?" Amanda asked, shocked.

Rand explained about cholera as patiently and quickly as he could, and both of them seemed to relax a little. "We will stop by the telegraph office and send a wire. I am sure she is fine and will be well free of the—uh . . . the inconvenience by now." He said it with as comforting a feeling as he could, but he had sent other wires and had not received an answer. But she had told them that she might not be able to respond. She and the others would be quarantined. But he did not think it wise to share all that with Ann and her mother now.

"I am sure she can arrange to return by the middle of April, Ann." He hoped that it was true, not only because of the wedding but because when war broke out Lizzy would have to run the family business. Though Benjamin was doing very well at the tasks Rand asked of him, it was always clear to Rand that Ben would not be able to handle the whole business. Fortunately it had also become clear to Benjamin, who was already expressing his support for Lizzy taking the reins.

"Good! Then April twentieth will be the date," Ann said.

Amanda seemed to suddenly wake up. "Oh no, no, the twentieth is much too soon, dear. I cannot send word to all our friends by then. I need at least a month, and what about Matthew and Adam?" Amanda said.

"Mother, the wedding will be small, family and very close friends only," Ann said. "We will send wires to those few, including Adam and Matthew, in the next few days. That will give them plenty of time to make arrangements, but I can wait no longer. And no matter what the day is, it will be the luckiest of my life."

"I'll need to check my calendar at the office," Rand said mischievously. "As I recall there is a meeting that day, and—"

Ann slugged him on the arm. "Dear boy, do not rile me or I may cancel the whole affair."

"She has a cold heart, does she not, Mrs. Alexander?" Rand grinned.

Amanda gave a sad smile. "I think not, Mr. Hudson. I think she fears she will not have you here much longer."

Ann lay her head on Rand's shoulder, and he pulled her in close and gave her a squeeze before turning halfway around to speak to the driver through the small window.

"Take us to the telegraph office," he said. He had decided. The wire to Lizzy could not wait until morning.

Chapter 35

LIZZY HELPED THE DOCTOR CLEAR OUT the last of the blankets used by previous patients so that they could be burned. She was near exhaustion and glad the worst was over as she gazed around the room of the quarantined shelter.

It had been nearly a month since they had found Billy Blue. Horatio had located the root of the contamination as waste matter that Slade and his men had been dumping into the creek behind their cabin. Horatio had it cleaned up, then shut down the well immediately. The number of patients dropped, and by the sixth day there were no new cases. Of the thirty people who had gotten ill, only three had died. The last of the patients, all past the critical point, had been taken to disinfected quarters to complete their recovery.

The door opened. Horatio Clay entered and greeted them before looking over the few remaining patients now tucked safely under clean linen sheets and blankets.

"The last of them?" he asked in a pleased tone.

"Yes," the doctor replied. "I don't expect any other cases, but we will monitor things carefully just to be sure."

"Then the houses they were living in can be burned," Horatio confirmed.

The doctor only nodded, and Horatio brought out his pocket ledger and made a few notes. "And Hyrum was the last one to be brought in here?"

"Yes," said the doctor, glancing at Lizzy with a slight smile. They had grown used to Horatio Clay's incessant note-taking.

Lizzy had watched as Horatio had made small but significant strides in the past few weeks—making an effort to learn the names of his slaves and what they did on the plantation and noting it all in his little book. He had remarked that it was all a matter of business now with Slade gone. But he couldn't hide the fact that a change had taken place in him. He smiled a good deal more as he oversaw his servants' work and even gave individual attention to some of them now and then. It was a bit mystifying, and some of the slaves were skeptical, waiting for the old Horatio Clay to return.

Horatio cleared his throat and announced, "I have hired a new overseer."

Lizzy stiffened, and the doctor came to attention as well.

"He is a man Andrew recommended some time ago. Unfortunately I hired Mr. Slade instead. His name is Boltright, Heber Boltright. You may know of him, Doctor. He worked for a time as overseer on the Lee place."

The doctor seemed relieved. "Yes, a good man." He glanced at Lizzy. "Never uses a whip, kindly, the workers love him." He looked again at Horatio. "He must have cost you a pretty penny."

"Yes, well, some things are worth the expense, aren't they?" Horatio seemed a bit uncomfortable with the attention on his benevolence and rushed quickly on. "And it's just too much to do for one man. I intend to stay more involved, but I find that my other affairs are often left neglected. Naomi and I may even travel, and Emily needs . . . well, a stronger hand."

"How is Billy?" Lizzy asked.

Horatio's countenance darkened. "Unfortunately, his leg will never be the same, but he is getting stronger and wishes to do some kind of work. I have asked Asher to give him some duties around the barn for now. But we will make him comfortable until he is ready to leave us."

Lizzy had not pursued further understanding of Billy and why Horatio had been so affected by his discovery. She intended to, and would, but the time just didn't seem right. Maybe she would have an opportunity to do so before she left.

Horatio gave her a searching look, a furrow of worry in his brow. "Miss Hudson, when was the last time you had a hot bath and a full night's sleep?"

Lizzy smiled, looking down at her plain linen dress. She did not know how many changes of clothing she had been in and out of during the last two weeks, and though she had washed many times, there had never been time for a full bath. Nor had she slept in her bed. The hayloft over the barn had become her new residence when she had time to sleep. It was closer to the patients and did not endanger the house servants by her coming and going. "It's been much too long, Mr. Clay."

"Doctor, are we finished here?"

The doctor smiled. "Yes, thank the Lord of heaven, I think we are."

"Can my servants see to the care of these few patients now that they are on the mend?"

"Yes, we're past any serious danger," the doctor confirmed.

"Then you should go home to your family, Doctor. You can return tomorrow to check on us." Horatio smiled. "And Miss Hudson, it is time for you to go to the house and take care of your own needs."

"A hot bath sounds wonderful."

"And is being prepared as we speak."

"I will give some instruction to your servants and then be on my way," the doctor said. He looked at Lizzy. "Miss Hudson, your effort here . . . these people and I owe you a debt of gratitude."

"I did very little. It is your genuine concern and skill that kept this situation from being much worse," Lizzy said sincerely.

Horatio cleared his throat as he removed his wallet and pulled out a generous handful of bills and handed them to the doctor. "If that does not cover your services here, please send me a bill for the difference. Your quick action saved many lives. You have my deepest gratitude."

The doctor looked at the wad of bills in his hand, then back at Horatio. "This is more than generous, Mr. Clay; thank you."

"No more needs to be said then. Off with the two of you." He motioned toward the door just as it opened and one of the servants peered inside, a look of apprehension on his face. Lizzy and the doctor stepped outside; Horatio followed as he hurriedly closed the door.

"What is it, Henry?"

It was then that Lizzy recognized the slave. It was Jackson's father, the one who tried to run away the first night she was here. He smiled at her briefly then answered Clay's query. Apparently he had not been sent to Richmond after all.

"A message from the city, Massa. De man who brung it say de governor, he needs t' see youse right 'way, suh." He handed Horatio a sealed envelope.

"Thank you, Henry. Have Mrs. Clay and the girls left for the city yet?"

"Yes, Massa, 'bout an hour 'go, suh." The quarantine had been lifted from the Meadowlands only the previous day, and Naomi and the girls had rushed off to make purchases of new linen and fill the larders again.

Clay was already reading the letter, concern in his eyes. "Have Asher prepare my carriage and the good doctor's as well."

"Yes, Massa." Henry rushed toward the barn.

"It seems that Lincoln has decided to send supplies to Fort Sumter. There is talk of Virginia seceding now, and the governor has summoned a few trusted associates to counsel with him."

"But if Lincoln is only going to send supplies—" the doctor began.

"Davis cannot let him resupply the fort. If he does, it is an admission that the North still has rights to property in the South. It disparages the whole concept of two separate governments." He paused, his face dark with concern. "If the South fires on the American flag and her troops, Lincoln will have all the excuse he needs to take the fort back. When that happens, Virginia will be pulled into the war, whether we continue to declare our neutrality or not." He shoved the note in his pocket. "I must leave immediately. Miss Hudson, I would be pleased to accompany you to the house." Horatio shook the doctor's hand. "I will let you know if we have even the slightest hint of any further illness, and my thanks once more. You saved me."

The doctor nodded and smiled in thanks at Lizzy, who gave him a quick hug before she and Horatio took the path toward the house.

"Mr. Clay, I have been meaning to tell you, I must leave for St. Louis as soon as I can. My brother's wedding—"

"The twentieth of April; yes, I know."

She was a bit surprised that he did know. She was sure she had not told him, but she decided to let it go.

"I would stay if I thought Andrew would return soon, but now it seems quite impossible."

"Well, if you left this afternoon could you make it home in time to give a hand to Randolph's future bride?" Horatio asked. He put his pince-nez glasses in his jacket pocket. It seemed to Lizzy that his thin, sallow face had filled out and even tanned and that a new glint had come to his dark eyes. She could see Andrew in him now, and that surprised her as much his statement.

Lizzy nodded. "With a few days to spare, I would think."

Horatio pulled an envelope from his pocket and handed it to her.

"What is this?"

"A ticket on the three o'clock train."

"Why, Mr. Clay. If I didn't know better, I would think you were trying to get rid of me."

He chuckled. "I assure you that is no longer the case." He took Lizzy's hand and kissed it. "Miss Hudson, I wish . . . I wish I had the time to express to you how grateful I am for your coming here. I allowed my son to invite you even though I was not pleased with his desire to do so, and I intended to make every effort to run you off. But I did not expect to make the acquaintance of someone quite so—"

"Stubborn?"

He laughed lightly. Lizzy thought it a pleasant laugh. "Forceful and direct would be more accurate. You completely caught me off guard." He grinned. "Please, come back when you are able. Not just for Andrew, but for all of us." He kissed her hand again and then walked quickly up the steps and into the house.

Lizzy watched him go, her thoughts a jumble. So much had happened; so much had changed; and yet so much was still the same. Discouragingly, she felt more confused than ever. Horatio had surely changed and clearly saw his servants in a new light but they were still slaves and would remain so for some time to come. And where did Andrew really stand in all this? He had not come, and she had so many questions for him.

"Missy?"

Lizzy did not register the soft-spoken word at first, then realized someone was behind her. She turned to find Henry standing there. She gave him a broad smile and grasped his hand. "I am so glad to see you are still here!" she said.

He looked furtively over his shoulder. "I . . . I had t' thank ya, missy. If'n I'd been sold down rivah wid out mah fam'ly. . . . Anyways, I had t' say it. I be workin' in de barn now wid Asher, and I doan run' way no mo'." He glanced at the house. "Massa, he promise he doan whip us no more and dis time I believes him, so I be stayin' and I . . . we . . . we all thanks yo' fo' it." Without another word, he turned and hurried away.

Lizzy felt to say something but could not get it out, her overfilled heart choking her vocal chords. Dumbfounded, she simply stood and watched him disappear.

"Miss Lizzy, come on now, it time fo' dat hot bath." Lizzy turned toward the house to find Matty waiting a few feet away. She had a blanket in her hands and stepped forward as if to place it around Lizzy's shoulders.

Lizzy blinked twice, trying to get her brain to change tracks. She cleared her throat as she reached up to take the blanket onto her shoulders. "Matty, I have to pack immediately."

"Yes 'm, I's already done started it. Massa, he tell me dis mornin' you'd be leavin'. He knows youse has to be dere for Mr. Rand and his new bride. Now we has ta get yo' outta dat messed-up dress an' dem shoes an' into dat hot tub."

Lizzy smiled. The thought that Horatio was concerned about what she wanted meant a good deal more than the thank you or the ticket.

Lizzy and Matty went into the summer kitchen, and Lizzy pulled off her dress and shoes and dumped them in a garbage bin. "These need to be burned," she said.

"Yes'm, we been burnin' ev'thing that comes outta de quarters. Miss Naomi, she make sure."

Lizzy suddenly realized that she hadn't seen Naomi or her daughters, not once since the first week of the cholera outbreak. "How are they?" she asked with sudden concern, remembering that Emily had said Naomi was ill.

"Oh dey's fine. Miss Naomi wanted t' go out an' he'p when she got t' feelin' better, but Massa an' Miss Emily, dey say no. No sense of it, says Miss Emily." She finished wrapping the blanket around Lizzy's shoulders. "Miss Emily, she scared, but not for Miss Naomi. She doan come close to her for near three days 'til she know fo' sure her mama don't have dat sickness no mo'. She nevah had it, just exhausted, dat all, but make no nevah mind to Miss Patty. She hold her mama tight all de time. Miss Emily, she just stomp around all day on account of Mr. Slade goin' outta dis place like a raccoon got him by de backside—praise de Lord for dat. Miss Emily be mad as a hornet's nest. She rail against her daddy like dere ain't no tomorra'." Matty chuckled. "It beyond me why, but I think she has de goosebumps fo' Mr. Slade." She leaned forward and added in a whisper, "An' I think it be a fine match o' personalities. Both mean as weasels." She gently pushed a smiling Lizzy toward the door. "Come on now. Nice hot bath waitin' fo' you in yo' room."

Lizzy danced across the cold ground to the stairs then up and into the kitchen, where she was greeted with a steaming cup of coffee and some hot bread and honey. Her blanket slipped away, and she stood in her pantaloons to devour the bread before Matty had the blanket back on her shoulders and was shooing her up the back steps.

Moments later she was completely immersed in a tub of clean, steaming water, Matty carrying her soiled clothes at arm's length from the room, her nose turned up and holding her breath. When the door was shut, Lizzy closed her eyes and let the tension and fear of the past few weeks slip away from her like honey from a spoon. A few minutes later, Matty returned but Lizzy didn't open her eyes, the exhaustion rolling over her in one very large wave.

"Which things you want in which suitcase, Miss 'Liz'beth?" Matty asked. There was no answer, and Matty asked part of the question again until she noticed that Lizzy was sound asleep, both arms hanging limp over the edges of the tub.

Matty only smiled. She would take care of everything.

Chapter 36

SEVERAL HOURS LATER, LIZZY STEPPED out the back door and found the carriage ready. She wished she'd had more time to say good-bye, but after her nap in the bath, there had been little left. Asher held the door open to the carriage, and Lizzy hugged him as she thanked him for his friendship.

Asher smiled. "It has been a joy, missy. You come back now."

Lizzy only nodded then climbed into the carriage. As she signaled for the driver to leave, her gaze drifted to the head of the driveway that led to the quarters, where all the slaves stood in a bunch and waved good-bye—Jackson and his parents on the very front row. She returned the wave and kept waving as they turned and passed along the side of the house where Matty and the other house servants were also waving to her and saying their good-byes. She kept waving until the carriage moved through the gate and onto the main road. Then, without warning, she burst into tears at the thought of leaving. She had come to love them, and she so hoped that Horatio really had changed and would make their lives better. Finally, cried out and still exhausted, she dried her tears and settled back for the ride to the city. Pulling the coverlet over her, Lizzy lay her head against the side of the carriage and fell asleep, awakening only when she felt the wheels of the carriage go from dirt to cobblestone. Knowing she would be at the depot momentarily, she sat up straight and stretched, then straightened her hat and folded the coverlet. She lay it aside as the carriage came to a halt in the bustle of the circle in front of the depot.

When the driver opened the carriage door, Lizzy was about to step out when someone stepped up to the carriage and offered his hand to her. She looked up to find Andrew smiling at her. Overwhelmed with joy, she threw herself off the step and into his arms, wrapping her own around his neck and hugging him close.

"My goodness, I wish I could have come sooner," he said, laughing.

"And you should have. Where on earth have you been?" she exclaimed.

"Trapped," he said grimly, shaking his head and still holding her close.

"But how—"

"My father carries a good deal of influence, Liz, and once you impressed him enough to bring him to use it—well, here I am." He smiled.

"Horatio? He arranged this?"

"He did. Unfortunately, even his influence is limited, so I am here only to see you off. My train returns even before yours departs." Andrew looked over her shoulder, and Lizzy turned around to see Naomi and Patty Clay standing a few steps behind them, wide grins on their faces. Emily stood to one side, her usual frown firmly in place.

"They wanted to say good-bye as well," Andrew said.

Lizzy hugged Naomi and then Patty, who tried to help Lizzy put her hat back in place, since her leap into Andrew's arms had skewed it. Lizzy then stood before Emily and took her hands. "Good-bye, Emily."

Emily forced a smile, her eyes on Andrew, who gave her a stern look.

"Andrew, you and Lizzy have a lot to talk about and very little time," Naomi said, smiling at her son. "But I must talk with Elizabeth for just a moment. Do you mind?"

Andrew smiled. "For just a moment, and I will not mind."

Naomi was pulling Lizzy away and talking in a low voice at the same time. "I must tell you something, not because you need to hear it, but because I need to speak of it," Naomi said. "I know Andrew—"

"It is quite all right, Naomi." Lizzy tried to look vested in the conversation, but her mind was really behind them and on Andrew Clay. But what Naomi said next riveted Lizzy's complete attention.

"Years ago, two days after Andrew was born, another little boy came into this world above Horatio's father's summer kitchen. His name was Billy. His mother was a house slave, and his father was her master— the man who owned the Meadowlands before he died and left it to my husband."

Elizabeth felt her heart nearly stop. "So Billy Blue is your husband's half-brother?"

"No one knew, but everyone suspected. To Horatio's father's credit, he did not do what some owners do when they take a slave as a mistress and it becomes known. He did not split the family up through sale. He kept them, and life seemed to go on as usual until almost a year later, when he joined Horatio's mother in the world beyond after dying of consumption. Of course, we then became the owners of the Meadowlands."

"And of Billy," Lizzy said softly.

"Horatio had known his father's mistress all his life. He was only six when his mother died, and Sarah—Billy's mother—had cared for Horatio as if he were her own son. But later, when Horatio found out what his father had done, he hated him for it and swore to me that he would get rid of Sarah the moment he had the power. I tried to reason with him, but he would not listen. After all, his father told him every day that we were a superior race, and to mingle his blood with that of the coloreds was a betrayal of that race. Elizabeth, every day that man's words and actions took root deeper in Horatio's soul."

Naomi stopped to swipe at her eyes and then continued. "When his father tried to justify his hypocrisy, Horatio would not listen. He was angry—very angry—and did not speak to his father until the day he died. Though he would not say so until a week or so ago, he regretted selling Sarah but at the time selling her was Horatio's way of avenging what he saw as his father's betrayal."

"But he kept Billy. Why?"

"At the time, he said it was because Billy was a future asset—that he would grow up into a fine, strong buck with value. But I knew better. Horatio hung on to Billy because he was a part of his father and was his only brother. A part of him loved Billy, but another part hated him. It was a horrible time for Horatio and, unfortunately, his pride hardened him. He kept Billy on the plantation but he treated him like every other slave. He worked him hard and even beat him once for insubordination. I was horrified and said so, but he lashed out at me, telling me that if I ever interfered he would send me away. I knew then, and I know better now, that he felt horrible guilt for what he was doing—guilt that made him meaner every day."

She shook her head back and forth. "Over the last twenty years, he became a monster, Elizabeth—a hard, cruel tyrant. That's when he hired Slade." She guided Elizabeth around several people getting out of a carriage.

"I nearly left him, especially when Slade began flirting with Emily. I told Horatio to keep that man away from her and from the house, or he would be the one in the street looking for food and home. He tried, but Emily . . . well, never mind, that is a different story. I am telling you all this because you need to know that my husband has not always been the way he was when you first came to our house, and I am so grateful to you for giving him back to me."

"It was Billy who changed your husband, Naomi, not I."

"Yes, but if you had not come . . . oh, I hate to think of what might have happened to poor Billy and to Horatio. What you did that first night—the way you went after him and Slade both. I have never seen such a thing by any woman." She grinned. "I have wanted to stand up to them myself, but my heart would surely have failed me." She grasped at her chest and rolled her eyes toward heaven. Then she chuckled. "Horatio was furious when he came in the house that night. It took him nearly an hour to calm down enough to even undress, let alone sleep. He tossed and turned all night, but it was just what he needed! You opened his eyes, Elizabeth. Thank you."

Lizzy felt some relief. Horatio really was changing, and it could only mean better things for all those who worked for him. Naomi turned and headed back in the direction of Andrew and the girls, but Lizzy still had questions and so little time.

"Did Andrew know about Billy?"

"Not at first. Horatio gave Billy to another slave to raise, a field worker who had lost her child while giving birth. She took him to the quarters and raised him by her side. For the most part, he was out of our sight, but Andrew and Billy seemed to have an affinity for one another and played together from the time Andrew first started wandering the property on his own. I did not learn of it because Andrew hid it from both his father and me. Horatio had made it clear that he was to have nothing to do socially with the colored people, and he told me explicitly to keep Andrew away from Billy. He made sure to tell Andrew incessantly that Billy was a troublemaker and should be avoided. Andrew saw right through it. Billy was as kind a boy as I have ever known. Nothing seemed to bother him, and Andrew loved to be around him." She smiled. "As with most young boys, I suppose, disobedience to Horatio's rule became a game for Andrew and probably even enhanced his friendship with Billy. Needless to say, they grew very close."

"Then Horatio found out and threatened to sell Billy if Andrew didn't stop the secretive relationship?" Lizzy guessed.

Naomi nodded. "Of course Andrew was very angry, and we found out later they met secretly through Andrew's youth and even into young adulthood. That was when they began making plans for Billy's escape."

"And Andrew taught Billy how to read and write."

Naomi chuckled. "I see Asher has filled you in on some of this story."

"Yes, but he never said anything about Billy being your husband's half-brother."

"He wouldn't. Horatio sold all of those who might know—his need to rid himself of the taint of his father's sin, I suppose."

"How did Andrew find out?" Lizzy asked.

"Other plantation owners suspected that Billy was Horatio's father's child. Some of them were jealous of our family's position in the community and in our local church. One of them made sure his son knew about the indiscretion of Horatio's father and ensured that word would be spread. When Andrew heard the rumor, he came to me and asked if it was true. I lied to him, and he knew it—I am a horrible liar. Then he went to his father, who told him it was none of his business—that Billy was no different from any other slave and that he should leave the whole matter alone. Andrew said nothing in response, but suddenly Billy disappeared." She smiled. "I will never forget the day Horatio confronted Andrew about it. Andrew simply shrugged, but his demeanor said it all. He had bested his father, and they both knew it. Of course this did not set well with Horatio for a multitude of reasons, the foremost of which was his refusal to accept Billy as anything but property—property to be controlled and disposed of at his pleasure. That was the point at which Horatio sent Slade after Billy."

"He really had become a monster, hadn't he," Lizzy murmured. She wanted to ask how on earth she had ever remained so loyal to Horatio but let it go. That was not the story Naomi was trying to tell.

Naomi nodded sadly. "When I saw Slade coming down the lane with Billy in shackles, I felt shattered. I sent word to Andrew immediately, and when he came he confronted Horatio. Receiving nothing but lies and a lot of angry denunciations, he went directly to the city to have papers drawn up to free Billy. He presented them to Horatio the next day, but Horatio showed him he could not do it—Billy was not his to set free, and Horatio would not let him do it."

Naomi and Lizzy were nearly back to Andrew, who was pacing impatiently. Naomi stopped. "And this is what I must tell you, Elizabeth. Andrew made a deal with Horatio for Billy's freedom. Andrew agreed to leave the federal army and join the militia of South Carolina. Horatio arranged everything."

"Andrew is trapped," Lizzy said, understanding dawning on her.

"Yes, but I pray you will not hold it against Andrew. If he lost you because of this—"

"I understand, Naomi. I assure you, he will not."

"Andrew has always hated slavery. Not just for the usual reasons but because of what he saw it do to his father. Though Horatio has finally awakened to a sense of the man he has become, he will not end slavery at the Meadowlands." She sighed. "He just cannot see how, but Andrew does, I promise you."

They did not speak for a moment as Naomi tried to get her emotions under control again. "When you found Billy, Horatio came home and cried all night, then stayed in his study without allowing even me to enter for two more days. I finally refused to let things continue that way and told the servants to break open the door." Her lip quivered. "He was a mess, but for the first time in our married life we talked, and then we prayed. Though I do not think he is fully at peace about what he has done, he is a better man and will never whip another servant again. Never. He will make changes, will make life easier, and will keep families together, but it is all he can see doing for now. For me it is a good start."

"And for me," Lizzy said softly. She put her arm around Naomi and hugged her tight. "Thank you for telling me. I cannot tell you how much it means."

Naomi drew her handkerchief and wiped at her tears. "We are not saints, Elizabeth, but we will try to be better Christians."

They walked to where Andrew waited. "Andrew, I have said my piece, the whole ugly story regarding Billy and your father. She is yours now. Do not lose her, or I will take a switch to you." Naomi stepped forward, hugged Lizzy again, and whispered in her ear, "Thank you for everything, Elizabeth."

It was obvious to Lizzy that Andrew knew about Billy and the firing of Slade, and she wondered just how long the letter must have been in which Horatio told him.

Lizzy's lip quivered slightly at Naomi's words. Patty had wrapped her arms around Lizzy's legs, and Lizzy stooped down and kissed her on both cheeks. "I love you, Patty. You take care of Emily, all right?"

Patty only nodded, her thumb in her mouth and her head lowered a bit in shyness. Emily, who stood nearby, rolled her eyes slightly.

"Good-bye, Elizabeth. Please come back soon," Naomi said. And with that, Naomi and her daughters hugged Andrew and said good-bye to him before walking off toward their own carriage.

"You seem to have won them over. Well . . . most of them," Andrew said as he watched Emily get into the carriage, obviously upset and letting her mother know it. "Come, we do not have much time," he said taking her by the arm.

They returned to Lizzy's carriage, where Andrew instructed the porters regarding her luggage and tipped them handsomely. Grabbing his own carpetbag, he opened the carriage for her to step in, instructing the driver to simply take them on a ten-minute ride.

Once seated next to her, he pulled her to him and gently kissed her. "I have missed you," he said.

She gave him a mischievous grin and then slapped at his face lightly. "That, my dear fellow, is for leaving me alone for these few weeks to deal with your father."

He laughed lightly while rubbing his face. "Yes, it was horrible of me, wasn't it?"

She settled in next to him, her arm through his. "Why didn't you tell me about Billy?"

"There were lots of things you needed to discover for yourself, Liz. And my family needed to learn about you as well. From what I just saw, everything has worked out pretty well." He paused while looking at his watch, his brow wrinkled. "I really am sorry I could not come sooner, but things are critical at Sumter. I was only able to spare these few hours." He rolled his eyes. "You would think Father had asked for Beauregard's right arm. If I am not back on time, I will be court-martialed."

"Will the South Carolina militia really attack those poor, starving fellows at the fort?" Lizzy asked in concern. Andrew belonged to that militia now, and if they attacked, surely he would be involved; that both bothered and concerned her.

"Foot soldiers, not cavalry," he said, reading her concern. "But I served with Anderson, and though he will put up a good defense of the fort, he will make sure that things do not go so far as to cause loss of life." Andrew sighed. "It will only be after the dust settles around Sumter that we will gain an inkling of our future."

"You mean whether there will be peace or war."

He nodded. "I am sure it will be peace. It must be." At the time of his father's blackmail, Andrew had asked to be commissioned as a captain in the cavalry, but the position had come with an unbreakable two-year commitment. At the time he still hadn't believed that war would actually come, but now he was beginning to fear he would be trapped in it and unable to be with Lizzy. His father was trying to reverse his bargain, but now. . . .

"Your father told you about finding Billy," Lizzy said.

"In a letter. A very long letter. You have changed him, Lizzy—you and Billy—and I do not know how to thank you."

"Holding me tight would be a good start," Lizzy said, snuggling in.

"An easy and quite profitable payment," Andrew said, holding her closer. "How are Father's servants? Are they recovering well?"

"The worst is past," Lizzy answered, "but the doctor will watch them carefully."

"Good. And Slade has not come back since Father gave him the boot?"

"No, he has not—something Emily is not happy about it, but he is gone."

"Emily flirted with Slade because Father told her to stay away from him. With him gone, she will only find some other way to rebel." He paused. "Father has changed, Lizzy, and I know he will treat them better, but I don't know that he will ever free them." He paused a moment, gathering his words. "I can only promise you . . ." he paused again. "I used to think I could never live any other place than the Meadowlands, but now I see only that I cannot live without you. And if you will have me, I promise that we will never own slaves, even if it means starting all over, poor as church mice. I want to marry you, Lizzy, more than anything else in this world."

Lizzy felt the love and sincerity of it clear to her toes and quickly reached up, put a hand to his neck, and kissed him lovingly once, then again. She remained in his arms, her heart full.

"Can I take that as a yes?" he asked softly.

"Yes, I think you can."

They kissed again before he smiled and spoke. "Then I have something for you." He reached into his pocket and pulled out a small box and handed it to her as she sat straight again. To her disappointment it was not a ring box but much larger. She opened it to find a beautiful cameo necklace.

"It was my grandmother's, and my mother's, and it has been passed to me as the oldest child. It is to be given to the one I will marry."

She looked up at him, her eyes brimming with tears as he removed the necklace and reached out to fasten it around her neck. When he had completed the task, Lizzy put her arms around his neck and pulled him close as the fears of the past melted away.

"Tell me when," Andrew said.

"Tonight if you like. I can always catch another train," she said softly.

He looked torn. "Unfortunately, I cannot. I have to return to my unit."

The possibility of war suddenly loomed large again. "Can you leave the military, Andrew? Surely. . . ."

A dark cloud seemed to wash over his countenance. "I have taken an oath, Liz. To break it now would force us both to live in shame for the rest of our lives. Cowards are not thought highly of in this world." He forced a smile, trying his best to lift the cloud from his feelings. "Besides, it will all be over soon. Sanity will rule in the end, and a compromise of some kind will be managed."

She wanted to believe it but saw that even he was unsure, his words not nearly as confident as they had been in St. Louis. Unable to find something to say—something that would give them both comfort—she decided to leave it alone altogether. His father had put him in this position, and to dwell on it would only force that hurt to the surface, and what good could that do?

"Then you must try to come to Rand's wedding. It is on the twentieth of April now, and—"

"Yes, I know. He needs a best man and wrote to ask."

"Then that is how your father knew that I must leave," she said. "Surely they will let you leave long enough for that. And you and I have plans to make, and we could begin them at least. Please try."

He smiled. "I will try."

She could see that he had little hope of success, but she let it go. There was nothing else to do but her heart began to sink as she realized this might be the last time she would see him for some time to come.

It was then she realized the carriage was once more pulling up in front of the depot, and her tears began to flow.

"Oh, Andrew, I am so frightened for you!"

He pulled her into his arms and tried to calm her.

"I have loved you all along," she said, after gaining a bit of control, "and now I fear I may lose you altogether."

"You will not, Liz. I promise," he said softly. He held her until she had control again then gave her one last kiss. "My train leaves first, and I may miss it if I do not go now. I love you, Elizabeth Hudson. Please do not forget that."

Andrew opened the door and stepped out, then helped her down. "Tell Rand that I want his blessing to marry you and that I will try to come to the wedding." He smiled as much as he could then wrapped his arms tightly around her and held her. "Oh, how I love you."

Lizzy gave him one last kiss, tears rolling down her cheeks as he forced himself away, tears in his own eyes. He turned away and after one last longing look and another "I love you," he disappeared between two waiting trains.

Lizzy felt the tears cascade down her cheeks as mixed emotions filled her heart. Love, fear, and longing all pulled at her like tentacles, making her ache inside. Then her heart sank as she remembered. She had not told him about her religion! She was about to pick up the edges of her long skirt and run in the direction he had disappeared when she decided against it. It would not matter. Somehow it would work out, just as her concerns over Andrew's allegiances had done. She would write to him. He was good, and he would understand. As she walked toward her own train, she saw his train pull slowly from the station. Everything would be all right.

Chapter 37

April 10, 1861

RAND SAT IN HIS OFFICE, absorbed with paperwork, when his Uncle Benjamin knocked and stepped in.

"Rand, a fellow is here to see you. He says his name is Jacob Gates, and he has a message for you from Salt Lake City." Benjamin had a wrinkled furrow in his brow. Though things were much better between them, Benjamin still held no love for Mormonism, even though he and Rand had shared several lengthy discussions about its doctrines over the past two months.

Rand smiled. "Do not worry, Uncle. This is not one of Brother Brigham's destroying angels come to wreak havoc on the Hudson family," he said with a wry smile. "It's just an old friend. Send him in."

Benjamin did not smile at the attempt at humor, and as Rand put the papers aside, his uncle ushered in Jacob Gates. Of medium build and wearing a beard that fell to his chest, Gates looked to be about fifty and had bright eyes and a pleasant countenance. He wore a dark waistcoat and pants with a white linen shirt and tie that were well-worn but neat and clean. Though the beard was unfamiliar, Rand recognized him and stepped away from his desk with an outstretched hand.

"Jacob Gates, it has been a long time. Please, have a seat; it is so good to see you."

"Yes, it has been a long time," Jacob said with a warm smile. They shook hands and then hugged one another.

"Jacob, this is my uncle, Benjamin Siddell, my mother's brother."

Jacob stretched out his hand, and Benjamin shook it. "Ah, you have a wonderful sister. Other than my own wife, she is the best woman I've ever known."

"Thank you," Benjamin said a bit uncomfortably. "Uh . . . Rand, I have to meet the *Constitution*. If you gentlemen will excuse me," he said with a nervous smile. He shuffled to the door and closed it behind him.

"Mormons make him nervous, apparently," Jacob said with a wry smile.

Rand laughed. "To say the least—but he will warm to it one day."

"Your mother spoke of him. He . . . well, he seemed to have his share of troubles."

Rand gave a wan smile. "He has changed some since Mother's death."

"Mary passed? I am sorry to hear that," Jacob replied with genuine sympathy in his eyes. "I tried seeing her on my way to England. She would not allow it."

"You tried to visit?"

Jacob smiled. "Yes, President Young asked that I do so, but I wanted to do it as well and welcomed the opportunity. We both promised your father that we would maintain contact with her if she ever left Nauvoo. I believe Brother Brigham sent others to check on her as well, but to my knowledge none were successful."

"It does not surprise me. She was very bitter for reasons she never explained."

Jacob removed an envelope from his pocket and handed it to Rand. "A letter from President Young. Apparently you wrote to him?"

"If you have been in England, how is it that you are delivering this to me?" Rand asked as he broke the seal on the envelope.

"When I arrived in New York, I reported to the mission office. I found a letter giving me a new assignment and asking me to come and see you— first to deliver your letter and then to make a request in the name of the Church. But the letter will probably explain as much."

Rand read the letter. It was of a personal nature at first, telling Rand how glad Brother Brigham was to hear from him and then sharing a few reminiscences about Rand's father and mother. He also wrote of trying to correspond with Rand's mother but without success and that he was sorry to hear of her passing. He said that she was one of the finest women he had ever known.

Then the letter turned to other subjects, telling Rand that the requested copy of the Doctrine and Covenants would be delivered by Elder Gates, who would answer Rand's questions and also make an official request of Hudson Company to aid the Saints in coming west this year. Rand lowered the letter, his gaze on Jacob. The letter concluded with a promise that if Rand ever decided to come to Salt Lake, he would be welcomed as a true friend of the Church. Rand folded the letter and set it aside with respect.

"What is it you need, Jacob?"

Jacob cleared his throat. "Ever since Joseph's prophecy on war, we have known it would come to our country, and though President Young and the rest of the Twelve do not think it to be the end of the world, it is to be the end of slavery—but at a very high cost in life and property. It will also create chaos along the East coast and may even cut off shipping lanes to Europe. This will make travel west much more difficult, so we are making the effort to bring as many Saints to Zion as we can this summer. The Saints have responded even beyond our expectations, and we have thousands who will come to our valley over the next few months. So many, in fact, that the Church will be hard-pressed to meet the demand for transportation across the plains." He leaned forward in his chair. "The first members will arrive from England in only a few weeks. They will come to New York and then take the train to Quincy, Illinois. We will need your help getting them across Iowa to Florence, Nebraska."

Rand took this information in then asked, "Are you in a hurry to get them to Florence?"

"Yes, some will arrive as late as June in New York, and getting them to Florence in time to go west will be difficult. We cannot have a surplus of travelers backing up. That could be disastrous. Our movement must occur as smoothly and uneventfully as possible."

"Then rail travel is your best bet." Rand stood and went to a map on the wall. "There is a new track from Hannibal, Missouri, to St. Joseph's, and I recently moved a steamer to Quincy for the sole purpose of moving people across and down the Mississippi to Hannibal to board those trains. It is much faster than taking them upriver by steamer."

"And at St. Joseph's?"

"I can position a steamer there as well for the two- to three-day journey to Florence."

"But the cost—"

"Both are large ships, and the price received from the other passengers will cover my operating costs. For members of the Church, we will print waivers designating free passage when they reach Quincy. We will authorize such waivers for both the steamer across the Mississippi and the one from St. Joe to Florence."

Gates was speechless, which made Rand smile. He should probably explain.

"The movement west is making me a rich man, Jacob, and I have not paid tithes and offerings for some time. If President Young and the Lord will accept this as a sign of my repentance for past negligence, I will be grateful, and if you will tell me how to make future contributions, I will be even more content." He sat back in his chair. "However, I would ask something of you personally in exchange for this arrangement."

Jacob's curiosity was evident. "I am sure President Young will be most grateful for this contribution, and I can certainly instruct you about how you should send future contributions, but I'm sure you are aware that there is little I can offer you personally."

"You are the only one I know who has what I need at the moment, Jacob," Rand replied seriously. He told Jacob about Ann and their intended marriage and then added, "Ann needs to be baptized."

"She sounds like a wonderful woman. I assume this is her wish as well as your own."

"Very much so. At first she thought her previous baptism as a Southern Baptist would be all right but as I explained the need of authority and its loss, she has been quite concerned that she is no longer in a saved condition and was very disappointed to learn that I had not received the authority to relieve her condition before we left Nauvoo." He smiled. "I have hoped that a missionary might come through, that I would see a group at the docks or on one of the steamers, but if they have come to St. Louis, I have missed them. I believe you are an answer to both our prayers, and she will be very excited."

"We send everyone through New York now. Well then, we must see that she is properly baptized, and you should do it. Are you morally clean?"

"Yes—but as you know, I have not attended my meetings."

"There are no meetings here to attend, so that is not an issue. Do you obey the Ten Commandments? Do you love God and your Savior, and are you honest with others?"

"Yes," Rand said humbly.

"Do you have a testimony of Joseph Smith and the Restoration, of Christ and of His prophets, and will you do whatever the Lord asks of you, and will you honor your priesthood and use it for the benefit of others as the Spirit moves you to do?"

"Yes, if He is willing to share it with me, I will do whatever I can."

"Then sit." He motioned Rand to his own chair as he vacated it.

Rand did as he was told, unsure of what was about to happen. Then Gates laid his hands on Rand's head and proceeded to confer upon him the Melchizedek Priesthood and ordain him an elder. Then followed a blessing Rand would never forget.

When Jacob had finished, the two men embraced, and Jacob finished with some counsel. "Write down the things you remember of this blessing from the Lord and treasure it. My impression is that you have dark days to go through, and the Lord's blessing will be of great comfort to you as well as to others in your life." Jacob smiled. "May I have your permission to put other members in St. Louis in touch with you if they still wish to have contact with the Church?"

Rand cringed when his first thought was worry over others finding out that he was a Mormon, but he quickly put that attitude behind him. After just committing to do more and receiving word of great blessings if he did, he refused to backslide so easily. "Of course, it would be an honor."

"Good, and I will wire President Young and ask permission for you to hold meetings and offer the sacrament."

Rand smiled inwardly. Jacob always considered an idle man the devil's workshop. "I have one other request. If you can get a license in the state, will you perform our wedding ceremony?"

"When is it?"

"In ten days."

"I must go to Council Bluffs, but I will return and perform it for you if you wish," Jacob said. "Now, when can I meet your fiancée?"

"Thank you, Jacob. Ann and I will be at the Riverside Hotel tonight to discuss the reception with hotel officials. It would be an honor to have you join us. She will want very much to meet you and as soon as possible, but be prepared for endless questions. Ann is not shy about such things. We can also talk about her baptism and the wedding."

"I would be delighted. What time?"

"We will have dinner in the hotel dining room at five o'clock."

"I will look forward to it," Jacob smiled." A sudden remembrance prompted him to pick up his traveling bag and remove a book and paper-back pamphlet. "You asked for a copy of the Doctrine and Covenants, and President Young included the pamphlet we call the Pearl of Great Price as well. It contains additional revelations given to Joseph that were too late to be included in the Doctrine and Covenants. I think you will find them interesting."

"Thank you," Rand said, already anxious to read. "I will prize them."

"Now tell me about Elizabeth," Jacob said.

Elizabeth had returned so madly in love that Rand wondered if she would ever survive it. But when she had told him and Ann all of what happened and what Andrew had promised, Rand was both stunned and amazed. He did not believe it all, not at first, but after the first letter had come from Horatio Clay he had accepted that Lizzy had performed that miracle—at least part of it.

He gave Jacob a brief synopsis.

"She is quite amazing, and you say she has remained true to the faith?"

"More than I have. She'll be at dinner tonight. I am sure she will be glad to fill in all the blanks for you."

"I look forward to it." He stood. "I must get my rest before then. It has been a long journey." He extended his hand. "Tonight, then." They shook and Jacob left.

Rand returned to his desk, pulled out pen and paper, and quickly wrote all he could remember of the blessing. When he was finished, he sat back and read it to make sure it was close to what had actually been said before folding the several sheets and putting them in an envelope. He didn't seal the envelope; he would share it with Ann later.

Picking up the Doctrine and Covenants, he thumbed through it until he found Section 20 and searched for the words involved in performing a baptism. His father had asked him to memorize several scriptures when he was young; this was one of them but it had been a long time.

He felt a sudden melancholy come over him. His father. How he missed him, and how things might have been different if his father hadn't left them so soon!

But he could not dwell on that. The past was the past. He was sure Baker Hudson would be pleased with his son's renewed efforts to return to the faith he loved, and that was all that really mattered.

There was another knock on the door. The clerk opened it and ushered in Newton Daines. Rand set the book—and his thoughts—aside for the moment as he nodded toward the chair. Newton sat.

"How are things, Mr. Daines?"

Newton smiled tiredly. The past weeks had been both physically and mentally taxing. "Last load delivered to Mr. Hunter's people early this mornin'," he said. "We did ha' a bit o' trouble, though. Mr. Ridges seems t' 'ave gotten his health back after he was nearly killed in our first run. He nearly caught us as we left the shore at the pickup spot outside Chillichote. He saw the *Constitution* up real close. He'll be watchin' fer us now."

Rand nodded gravely. "We'll be working close to home for the short term, then downriver. Ridges stays close to home now, so you should not have to deal with him for a while." Ridges had not been seen in St. Louis since Hooker had scared the daylights out of him. But Rand hadn't stopped looking over his shoulder. Atchison was still around. "Can you go again this evening? Not far this time. Just to Allenton for three runaways. I told Felix to send you a message before I left the house this morning but now that you are here—"

"I'll arrange it wi' the captain," Newton said. "Mr. Hunter got word tha' Miss Abigail an' 'er children arrived safe in New York. They be workin' on a farm north a tha' city."

"Felix knows?" Rand asked. Rand had been told about the escape, and Felix had been wondering about where Abigail and her family went and how the Underground Railroad worked ever since. Though Rand knew he was in love with Jasmina, Felix thought of Abigail as family—a replacement of sorts for his mother and sister, and he wanted to be sure they were taken care of.

"Yes, sir, 'e knows."

Rand nodded. "How's Mary?"

"Pretty as sunrise," Newton replied with a smile. When Mary wasn't working with him along the Underground Railroad, she still helped Mrs. O'Grady at the boardinghouse. When he'd left this morning, she had been making breakfast for the workers but had seen him off with a healthy kiss and nice cup of coffee along with his lunch.

"You should marry her, Newton."

"I be followin' yer lead, Mr. Hoodsun. Two weeks and we be tyin' the knot."

Rand smiled. He had come to think a great deal of Newton Daines and Mary McConnell. "You know you're invited to our wedding."

"Yes, sir. Mary said Miss Ann brough' an invitation 'erself. Felix said he be comin' as well. 'Tis an honorable thing to be doin', Mr. Hoodsun, seein's most whites, even some o' them tha' calls themselves abolitionists, doan cotton to havin' blacks come t' their shindigs."

"We're inviting all of our true friends, and none of them will think twice about the fact that you or Felix are among us." Turning matters to business, he asked, "What is the latest on the *Elizabeth's* paddle wheel?"

"Good as new by tomorrow night," Newton said. In between runs to Little Dixie, Newton had been busy working on several of the steamers. His expression turned a bit serious now. "I been thinkin' it's time t' be joinin' yer 'Ome Guard, Mr. Hoodsun."

Rand sat back, sobered by the request. Newton hadn't been in the country six months, and already he understood the critical nature of the country's condition better than most citizens. "It would be an honor to have you join us, Newton. They are training this evening at the usual place."

"I'll be comin' then." He stood. Breaking the news to Mary would come next. Though he'd mentioned joining the guard, he hadn't finally decided until last night, after their return from retrieving the runaways. He slapped on his hat and went to the door. "I'll be seein' you this afternoon."

Rand watched the door close and wondered if Newton was a religious man. He had never said anything one way or the other, though Rand figured he was Catholic simply because most Irish were. Maybe it was time to ask.

Chapter 38

CASTLE RIDGES SAT AT A corner table in a saloon on the outskirts of West St. Louis. He had sat alone nursing a whiskey while listening to the jib-jab about the impending siege of Sumter. Arguments were plentiful as to what should be done, but most centered around wanting Beauregard to blast Anderson to kingdom come, and the sooner the better. But then that was why he came to this saloon—its clients were decidedly Southern in their views.

He saw O'Shay come through the door and work his way across the room to his table; he sat as Castle poured him a whiskey. He and O'Shay hadn't seen one another since the humiliation aboard the *National Belle*. Ridges didn't come to St. Louis much, mostly because of Hooker, but he wasn't in a hurry to see Atchison either. His former boss had demanded payment for the loss of the *National Belle* and Ridges had refused, telling Atchison that if he pressed charges he would tell the court just why he had been asked to blow up a steamer and who the original target had been. He hadn't heard from Atchison since, but Castle felt it best to keep a low profile for a while.

"What d' ya find out?" Castle asked. At Chillichote, Castle had finally gotten a glimpse of the superstructure of a steamer that was being used by the Underground Railroad to take escaped slaves out of Little Dixie. And he knew it to be one of Rand Hudson's steamers. He had wired O'Shay to go to the docks and watch for her, then he had caught another steamer to St. Louis.

O'Shay downed his whiskey in one deft swallow. "'Tis the *Constitution* all right. She come in this mornin', an' guess who go' off 'er?" He waited but Ridges was in no mood for guessing games. "Newton Daines. Mary McConnell was wi' him along wi' a big black fella, probably the one you an' Sam lost t' Daines. Ya know, the one wha' escaped—"

"Yeah, Mickey, I remember," Ridges said stiffly. "Yer sure?"

"Ya said ya though' there was a nigra involved in this business. 'Twas 'im as well is me guess."

Castle poured himself another whiskey, his mind mulling over the information he'd just been given. Any amount of concentrated thought took him several minutes, especially with whiskey added to the mix.

"Daines still make his bed in the Patch?" Castle finally asked.

"At Mrs. O'Grady's boardin' 'ouse."

They each downed another small tumbler of whiskey, then another.

"I know wha' yer thinkin', Ridges," O'Shay said.

"And what would I be thinkin', Mickey?" Castle asked dryly.

"Tha' you'll be goin' after Mr. Daines yerself, but O'Brien won't like ya cuttin' in on 'is turf and killin' a son o' Erin." O'Shay recollected sayin' these same words to Sam just before he was killed. He hoped the result would be to his advantage now, just as it had been then.

Castle's jaw hardened. "I don't give a toot fer what O'Brien thinks. If he wants to challenge me over the dyin' of a nigra-lovin' Irishman, I'll clean his clock fer it!" His face was red with rage. He had his mind set on revenge, and Mickey O'Shay knew it.

"All right, all right," O'Shay said. "Keep yer voice down; even this place has big ears. I want Daines dead just as much as you do."

Castle downed another glass of whiskey. "You show me to Mr. Daines, O'Shay, and I'll be doin' the rest."

Mickey moved to pour himself another drink but decided he'd best not. He needed at least some of his wits about him if he was going to pull this off and make a bit of a profit without getting himself caught in the middle of a mess.

He carefully measured his words. "Ya know ya cannot be goin' inta the Patch and killin' someone, so ya need someone t' bring Mr. Daines t' ya."

Castle, a bit inebriated by now and his temper softened as a result, could see the value of staying clear of the Patch, just as he could see the value of staying clear of Mr. Isaac Hooker—but he did not want O'Shay to know that he feared either. "I ain't afraid of gettin' him myself," Ridges said in an attempt to secure his prowess.

"A course ya coul', bu' why take the chance if fer a few coin ya kin avoid any distasteful confrontations wi' O'Brien an' 'is toughs?"

"A few coin?"

"Sam promised me four hundred if I took care o' Daines fer the embarrassment he caused t' yer goo' name. Fer half tha' I'll be seein' ya get t' take care of 'im yerself."

It was only two hundred that Sam Ridges had promised O'Shay in the first place, but this lie would reassure Mr. Castle Ridges that *he* was getting a solid and considerable discount.

Castle glared through squinty eyes. "Then why ain't ya done it?"

"Well, as ya be knowin', Sam is quite dead an' unable to pay, an' killin' a man fer no profit and a good deal o' trouble would be a fool's errand—an' as ya know, I ain't no fool. An' doan forget, instead o' you takin' a chance at rilin' Mr. MacKinnon O'Brien, it be me, an' tha' would be needin' some strong incentive."

Castle pondered for a short moment and apparently bought the proposition hook, line, and sinker. "Two hundred fer Daines and no trouble with O'Brien. . . ." He tried to think, but even without whiskey clouding his brain, this would have been a challenge. With it, he found the task quite impossible. O'Shay, seeing the condition Castle was in and depending on it, quickly went on.

"'Tis a bargain indeed." O'Shay smiled. "Of course, I'll be needin' a hundred up front fer Mr. O'Brien." Mickey O'Shay did not intend to give a cent to O'Brien. It was Ridges who would actually kill Daines, freeing him of enough blame that O'Brien would not deprive him of his life over it, especially since he would also be depriving his sister of her handsome husband.

Castle nodded, then reached into his jacket pocket and retrieved a beat-up leather wallet stuffed with money. He pulled out the bills and slapped them on the table. "Deal."

O'Shay smiled as he picked up the money. "I'll be comin' to yer slave pens this evenin' around seven." He threw back one more solid drink and slammed the glass on the table before standing and taking the bottle with him. "An' be sober, Ridges. I doan wan' t' hafta shoot 'em for ya. That be costin' ya a lot more."

Ridges only nodded as O'Shay walked away. He waited another five minutes before leaving the saloon and climbing into his carriage, showing little sign of drunkenness. He would watch O'Shay, from a distance, but watch him just the same, and if Mickey couldn't handle Daines, he would take care of it himself, whether it was in the Kerry Patch or out of it. He'd had enough of Mr. Newton Daines and his slave running and intended to see it end this night as well as send a powerful message to Rand Hudson about such operations in Little Dixie.

And then he would kill Mickey O'Shay. The fact that O'Shay had done so little the night of the *National Belle* fiasco had become a festering sore in Castle's head. Though even he would be slow to stand up against

Isaac Hooker, Castle felt the circumstances that night had given O'Shay an opportunity he had not taken. And Daines had foiled him and Sam before. To have the little weasel think he could get Castle drunk and take him for a few hundred was infuriating. Besides, he needed someone to take the fall. Hudson was powerful. He would want answers about Daines's death. Mickey would provide them.

* * *

After he had spent hours at the warehouse training the Home Guard, Rand had gone home to pick up Ann and her mother for dinner—but Amanda, not feeling well, had opted to stay at home for the evening, and Lizzy had been out. He left her a note to join them when she returned. Rand and Ann had picked up Jacob Gates at his modest hotel, and they were soon in the dining room of the Riverside Hotel.

"As soon as I left you this morning, Randolph, I sent a wire to President Young and received a reply almost immediately. You are authorized to hold meetings and administer the sacrament as well as see that baptisms are accomplished. President Young is thrilled with your willingness to help the saints in their travels and gratified by your ordination. He considers you the leader of the Church here in St. Louis for now and will be grateful if you will update him on Church affairs here."

"How wonderful, Rand," Ann said.

Rand was about to speak when he saw Lizzy coming across the dining room, a wide smile on her flushed face. He stood, and Jacob quickly got to his feet as well and greeted her with a warm hug.

"Oh, Jacob, it is so good to see you again. You were one of Father's best friends and a good friend of Brother Brigham, if I remember correctly." She leaned across the table. "But how did you find us, and—"

"I wrote a letter to Salt Lake," Rand interjected. He filled her in on the details. "I'm sorry that I kept it a secret from both of you," he said, glancing at Ann, "but I wasn't sure I would get an answer."

"Oh ye of little faith," Ann said teasingly.

Lizzy sat across from Rand and between Ann and Jacob. "Yes, I agree," Lizzy said, showing a stern face, then smiling just as quickly. "But all is forgiven now that Jacob has come. Tell me about Salt Lake City and the migration," she said anxiously.

Jacob spoke on the subject for nearly twenty minutes, stopping long enough only for the waiter to take their orders and then deliver their food a short time later. All three of them listened intently before Lizzy finally spoke.

"And they have begun a temple," she said with admiration and a slow shake of the head. "Another temple. What an amazing people. Does it look like the temple in Nauvoo?"

Jacob smiled. "It's much larger and it will have six spires instead of one. The entire world will flock to it someday—that is the Lord's promise to us."

"And the city—what is it like?"

Jacob tried to explain the wide, straight streets and the endless cabins and new homes that were being built. "We can hardly keep up," he said. "It has been difficult. The soil was so hard that water had to be used to soften it enough even for planting." Jacob recounted frost and described crickets that destroyed crops and caused near starvation one year. "But things are much better now. Our biggest problem is settling everyone, and we are quickly spreading to other locations. It is quite amazing."

They ate as they talked, and all had finished when Rand decided he should fill Lizzy in on why Jacob had come.

"Jacob has come to ask us for help, Lizzy," Rand said. He then explained what he had promised.

"Wonderful!" Lizzy said when he finished. "I want to be involved. I must."

"I am sure that can be arranged," Rand said, smiling at her genuine enthusiasm.

"You haven't heard the best news yet, Lizzy," Ann said with a wide grin. "I am to be baptized. Rand is going to do it. Brother Gates has already given him the priesthood, and he will baptize me first thing in the morning."

"Oh, my!" Lizzy reached for Ann's hand. "Oh, I am so pleased, Ann." She looked at Rand. "And you . . ." Her eyes softened. "You have done it, haven't you?"

"Done it?"

"Decided to commit."

Rand flushed a bit. "Yes, I guess I have. Jacob came at a good time. He has promised to perform our wedding ceremony as well."

"Oh, Jacob Gates, you are an answer to prayer!" Lizzy said.

There was a sudden flurry of excitement near the dining room door as a uniformed man entered and approached their table. Rand recognized him as Sergeant Nathaniel Lyon and received his salute and the note in his hand. He quickly read it as the others looked on.

"Tell General Lyon I will be there shortly," he told the sergeant with a furrowed brow.

"Sir, the city is in disarray. My men and I are to escort you to the arsenal."

"Thank you, Sergeant. I'll be with you in a moment," Rand said, his heart racing.

The sergeant saluted and turned to wait outside the dining room.

"What is it, darling?" Ann held her breath as they waited for what must be alarming news.

"The Confederates have demanded the surrender of Fort Sumter and turned their cannon on our soldiers there. It is the same as a declaration of war. Lyon wants a meeting immediately."

"Then the arsenal could be attacked." Ann was somber. Lizzy grasped Ann's hand to both give and receive comfort.

"Governor Jackson isn't in a position to take the arsenal now. It is just a meeting, Ann, nothing more. I will go with the sergeant; all of you should enjoy the rest of your dinner and then return to the house," Rand said, hoping he sounded reassuring. "Take the river road, away from the city center. It will be less chaotic. Jacob, if you will see Ann and Lizzy home, my driver will take you anywhere you wish to go afterward."

"It would be an honor," Jacob said. "And what about the wedding? When—"

"Nothing will change. Ann can fill you in," Rand noted the look of relief on Ann's face. He actually knew that a good deal might change, but he wanted only to give her comfort, even if just for the moment.

"Andrew is at Sumter," Lizzy said, concern in her eyes.

Rand put his hand on hers. "Do not worry. Anderson cannot resist long, and there will be very little harm done. Andrew is cavalry and will probably not be involved at all."

"They really intend to start a war, don't they?" Ann uttered.

"They are not ready for war anymore than we are. This is meant to force more states to take sides, including ours and Virginia. War, if it comes, will follow." He stood and kissed her quickly on the forehead, but she got to her feet and held him close.

"Be careful, darling," she pleaded.

"Don't worry, Ann. I may be home even before you arrive there. Enjoy the evening, and talk to Jacob." He smiled. "I am sure he has much more to share with you." He turned to his sister, bent down, and kissed her on the forehead. "Take care of her, Lizzy," he said, looking at Ann.

Lizzy nodded, and Rand left the dining hall to join Lyon in a chaotic lobby struggling with the same news. The two men then exited to the street, where the sergeant asked one of his men to dismount. Rand took the horse. The soldier would ride double with another until they arrived at the arsenal.

The scene was relatively peaceful until they neared the center of the city, where crowds had amassed to take sides. Each bellowed their slogans, their defiance, their hatred for whatever and whoever was against their particular views; fists were a part of the conversation as opposing groups came in contact with one another. Police were trying to keep them separate and were caught in the middle. The sergeant led their little party north and through side streets, where chaos was minimal, until they finally reached the gate of the arsenal.

Rand was astounded at the flareup of such sudden violence but he saw clearly that the firing on Sumter was having its intended effect. It would divide the state and the country, destroying peace—not just between nations but also between neighbors, friends, and even families. Rand could see that the anger, hatred, and call for blood would spread like wildfire, igniting the conflagration of war. What frightened him even more was that Southern secessionists intended it. They were fools enough to believe they could divide the country and war would not follow—that they were mighty and powerful enough to control it and force their will on an entire nation, most of whom profoundly disagreed with them! He took a deep breath to control his anger at such stupidity.

The party arrived at the headquarters building of the arsenal, and Rand dismounted to find Hooker waiting for him.

"Captain," Hooker said. "It looks like things are goin' to get a bit nasty."

Rand only nodded, and they went inside, where both Frank Blair and Nathaniel Lyon sat in somber discussion. Rand did not know much about Lyon, having met him the just previous week. Lyon had intended to review the Home Guard in a few days, but events seemed to be proceeding faster than that.

"Randolph," Frank said, his brow creased with concern. "How is Ann?"

"Worried that this mess might prevent a wedding," Rand answered.

"Gentlemen," Lyon said. "Thank you for coming. Because things are moving rather quickly I thought it best to meet and cover our association more carefully. We may need your help much sooner than expected."

"What have you heard?" Hooker asked.

"Davis is intent on taking Sumter as a sign of their resolve. Secretary Cameron sent word that we are to defend the arsenal and keep Missouri in the Union at all costs," Lyon said. Simon Cameron was Secretary of War, and Frank had been communicating for months about the protection of Missouri with him and General Winfield Scott, the country's general-in-chief.

"Is Harney aware of these orders?" Rand asked.

"Not to my knowledge," Lyon answered. "But even if he is he will do nothing about it. He is more convinced than ever that Missouri can remain neutral."

"General Harney will receive a wire asking him to come to Washington immediately. That will leave General Lyon in charge of all federal forces here," Frank clarified. "It will take a few days before Harney actually turns over command, but he will have no other choice. General Scott does not trust him."

They had discussed William S. Harney a number of times. He was commander of all the forces of the West, including Lyon's men at the arsenal. But Harney had questionable relationships with Governor Jackson and Sterling Price, a longtime friend from former years when Price and Harney served together. Harney had already resisted Lyon's appointment, and since Lyon's, arrival he had argued contrary to any views that the Union might need to take action against secessionists in Missouri.

"Lincoln will try to resupply Sumter as soon as possible. The Confederates are starving them out, and we have no choice—but the rebels cannot allow it and will try to take the fort before Union troops arrive," Lyon said. "My guess is Anderson will be forced to surrender Sumter within the next few days."

"And the South will have effectively declared war on the United States," Hooker said somberly.

"Lincoln will call for troops after the traitors in South Carolina fire on our flag, but not before. It is necessary in order to coalesce Northern support for any action that must be taken against Southern traitors." Frank paused. "But once this happens—and most important to us—Lincoln will call for seventy thousand troops, of which four regiments must come from Missouri."

Lyon leaned forward.

"The response of each state will declare the state's position. Senator Blair has it on good authority that Jackson is prepared to refuse, then declare the request an act of aggression against Missouri's Southern brothers. He'll call for secession," Frank said. "He won't have the votes to accomplish it but we do not have the votes to declare for the Union either."

"Then the state remains, officially at least, neutral," Rand said.

"Jackson can't allow that to continue very long. Secretary Cameron has information that Jackson has already promised the new Confederate government that Missouri will provide troops and weapons and leave the Union. Unable to accomplish it by vote, he must do so by force," Lyon said.

"Our sources in Jefferson City tell us that if he does not get a vote of secession, he will ask the General Assembly for military powers to enforce neutrality," Frank said. "Our fear is that he will then call up the militia and use it to take the arsenal, ostensibly to remove federal troops from Missouri territory so that neutrality is maintained, but in effect doing the same thing that South Carolina is doing at Sumter. His action will declare war on the Union and effectively force Missouri into the Confederacy."

There was a moment of silence as each of them pondered the ramifications. Lyon was the first to speak.

"I have only a hundred men here, and the arsenal is poorly fortified, with low walls and easily breached gates. My question to you gentlemen is this: Are you ready to side with the Union, and are you prepared to move your men here to protect this arsenal as soon as I can give that order? And do not forget—you may be fighting the state militia."

Blair looked at Rand and Hooker. "Randolph, Isaac?"

"We are ready, but wouldn't it be unwise to take such an action until Jackson actually calls up the state militia?" Rand asked.

"We will begin slowly. Officers like yourselves and several hundred of your best men will be called up when Sumter falls. They must be men willing to join the Union army so that we are strictly a United States military force. The rest will be called up if Jackson is successful in his effort to activate the militia."

He turned to the map. "When the time comes, your men will billet here, in the center of the arsenal, and will defend the east and west walls and the high ground here. Make your plans accordingly." He picked up some envelopes from the table and handed one each to Hooker and Rand. "Your commissions, gentlemen. Sign them and you will officially be members of the Union Army." He smiled.

Rand and Hooker stepped to the desk and used the general's pen to sign their documents before handing them back to him.

"Excellent, gentlemen. I look forward to our association in defending the United States. If there are no questions, you are dismissed, but stay close to home. I trust that Sumter will fall in the next forty-eight hours."

Frank, Hooker, and Rand stood and left the small office.

"There goes the honeymoon," Hooker said with a grim smile aimed at Rand.

"I will be happy just to have a wedding," Rand said.

Frank turned to Rand and Hooker. "Gentlemen, send word to your best men. Have them here at the first news of Sumter's fall." His carriage pulled up, and once he was inside, it lurched away.

Hooker's horse was led forward, as well as one for Rand. They both mounted.

"Ann sent me instructions about what to wear to the weddin'. I can't say as I'm pleased, but," he took a deep breath, "for her, I guess I'm cornered."

"You are, and thank you. I would hate to be the only one in the room all trussed up like a goose at market," Rand quipped.

They were nearing the gate when Hooker spoke. "Wouldn't it be easier just to ship the weapons held here into Illinois than to try to defend them and start a state civil war in the process?"

Rand smiled. "Yes, it would, and I suggested just such a thing to Frank and Lyon, but it seems to be a matter of territory as much as it is a matter of guns."

Hooker nodded. "Yer sayin' that deserting the arsenal would be the same as deserting Sumter."

"And it would give weight to the argument of both Jackson and the rest of the secessionists that Missouri wants nothing to do with staying in the Union," Rand said.

Hooker's brow was wrinkled as he pondered. "If the South controls Missouri, it controls the western frontier, and the Confederacy practically surrounds the Northern states. They can expand slavery at will and effectively bottle up the North."

"And do not forget the amount of goods that are raised and manufactured here and that controlling the upper reaches of the Mississippi and Missouri rivers is at stake. Whoever controls Missouri controls the western part of the continent and will have a great advantage at winning the war."

Sobered, Hooker only nodded.

They passed through the gate, and Hooker pulled up for a moment. "I ain't much fer tactics and heavy thinkin', Rand, but I want you to know I'm in this fight until it's over. If they call regiments out of Missouri and you have a part in it, I want to be with you."

"I couldn't ask for a better man to fight with, Isaac." Rand smiled. "But that won't get you out of being my best man."

"Nah, I didn't think it would." Hooker nudged his horse forward, and Rand turned his own mount toward home, the dread of war pressing in on him. He wondered how to break the news to Ann. If he was called back before the wedding . . . but he shoved the thought aside. They'd work it out. Nothing would stop him from marrying Ann Alxander. Not even war.

Chapter 39

NEWTON ARRIVED IN THE KERRY PATCH a bit tired and hungry, but there was still the run to Allenton, and he moved quickly toward Mrs. O'Grady's.

He had spent the morning aboard the *Elizabeth* partially fixing the paddle wheel and then at the warehouse getting his assignment in the Home Guard before returning to the steamer to finish the wheel so it would be fully operable.

Among the men of the Home Guard, he had immediately recognized that he was behind everyone else in his training, but he had been impressed by what he saw there. Mr. Hudson and Isaac Hooker were whipping the lot of them into a fine fighting group, and Newton would work extra hard to do his part.

As he neared the busiest part of O'Fallon Street, he found it even more clamorous than usual and stopped to listen to a crowd of men. He immediately heard the word *surrender* and listened more carefully.

"We'll be recruitin' all day, and t'morrow, and the next day and the next. We'll be raisin' a brigade, and we'll be callin' it the Irish brigade, an' anyone who joins up will be gettin' fine pay and a chance to improve 'is life and tha' o' 'is wife an' kids."

"Thirty dollars a month, ya say?" one man asked.

"An' tha' will be guaranteed muny, is tha' it then?" another in the crowd asked.

"Mr. O'Brien 'imself is makin' tha' guarantee," came the answer.

"But we shoul' be fightin' for the North, shouldn't we?" another voice piped in. "Seem's like ol' Lincoln will be wantin' regiments as well, and Malone says—"

"Malone doan run things 'round 'ere, and 'e ain't offerin' no guarantees neither," someone said angrily. "The governor 'ill be callin' fer a vote, and we'll go Southern and be fightin' fer the honor o' the Irish."

"Posh!" said yet another bystander. "We ain't got no reason t' fight. Stay out o' it, tha's wha' I say. North, South, makes no difference. Doan help no Irish get their due. Let 'em bust up one anuther, and then we'll have jobs, and better 'uns too."

"And me folks are still in New York. What'll they be doin'? Lot's o' Irish in the North, and seems to me—"

Newton watched as one of O'Brien's toughs grabbed the man and pulled him away to shut him up. He'd get a good knock to the ears and be sent on his way with his mouth shut. The other protestor saw what had happened and left in silence.

"Doan be listenin' to tha' nonsense," a burly man said. "Any goo' Irish worth 'is keep has the sense to know that fightin' fer the North will bring the freein' o' the blacks, and that'll make yer lives harder when they starts comin' 'ere t' take yer jobs and drive ya out!"

This statement brought a good deal of grumbling agreement, and Newton quickly walked on. As he passed by different assemblies, the talk was all the same: Sumter, war, and the pay for fighting. However, both sides seemed to be recruiting and beating on the drum about the honor it would give the Irish to be fighting for this country. Newton understood the last part. Acceptance came with honor and a show that you were loyal to the country you were trying to adopt. The only difference for Newton was loyalty to human freedom versus loyalty to the bondage of men—and for him it was a big difference.

He spied Mary standing on the edge of a crowd a short distance from Mrs. O'Grady's and quickly pushed through to get to her. She wrapped her arms around him for a hug and a quick kiss before he asked, "What's all this sudden talk o' war? What's goin' on, me love?"

She frowned. "The Confederates 'ave decided to attack Sumter. It's the same as sayin' they want a fight, and these Irish gents are pickin' sides." She raised up on her toes to yell in the direction of one of O'Brien's men. "Ye're dolts if ya listen to 'im! Southerners will be losin' if there's a fight, and you'll be endin' up in the morgue for yer trouble! And don't forget, O'Brien's gettin' money fer recruitin' ya, an' you won' see a cent of it, tha's sure."

A dozen voices were raised against her and only a few in agreement. Two of O'Brien's toughs turned to come after her but stopped short as they saw Newton. "Yer gonna ge' yer ears boxed if yer nah careful, love," Newton cautioned.

"No' chance a' tha' with ya by me side. Look a' them lads; they be thinkin' twice abou' tryin' the man wha' beat Kernlin to a pulp." She chuckled.

"Doan press me luck, lass," Newton answered. "Now, come along afore ya ge' me jaw busted." He pulled her away from the crowd, but it wasn't easy. Mary had become a firm abolitionist since becoming involved with the freeing of slaves and was no longer shy in saying so. She'd had a couple of scrapes with other women for her new feelings, and several men had given her a stiff warning that she should keep her mouth shut, but no one had touched her—not yet.

"You'll be rememberin' wha ya tol' me when I first come t' this fine city," Newton said.

"An' what was tha?"

"That the Irish doan like men talkin abou' freein' the blacks and might ge' their head busted fer it."

She laughed. "I remember."

"We'll be needin' t' get a bite t' eat before we leave," he said.

"Aye, an' Felix sent word. He'll be comin' with the wagon at 'alf past six," she replied. "Said he'll meet us at the bottom of O'Fallon Street."

Newton nodded. Felix had discovered on his first visit to the Patch that colored folks were not welcome, and he had not been back since.

Newton and Mary walked down the middle of the street toward Mrs. O'Grady's in an attempt to stay away from the growing groups of arguing Irish.

"I heard Malone's name used among some o' these folk," Newton said. "I saw 'im today, but he said nuthin' about all this."

"Word just come about Sumter." She stopped, eying Newton carefully. "Ya saw 'im, did ya? An' wha' would be yer business with Mr. Malone?"

Newton blushed a bit. He had intended to discuss his joining with her tonight.

Mary put her hands on her hips. "Ya went an' joined 'em, didn't ya? Fine kettle o' stew when ya doan consider talkin' t' yer fiancée before goin' off t' join the army."

Newton gently took her hand, and the two began walking again. "We'll all be joinin', like it or not, soon or late. I jes' as soon ge' in wi' a crowd I can trust as go off t' fight wi' strangers, and Mr. Hoodsun, he's a fine soldier for tactics and trainin'. Better chance of survivin' with 'im than most others, is my way of thinkin'." He looked at the arguing crowds behind them. "Would ya be havin' me join them folks instead?"

"And if the Southern boys take Sumter, you'll be called up real soon is me guess."

"Maybe, but doan be forgettin' tha' the captain 'as got a weddin' t' see to, an' I doan think Miss Ann will let somethin' as small as a war interfere wi' it." He grinned.

Mary chuckled and put her arm around Newton's waist.

"Speakin' o' weddin's, 'ave ya made arrangements yet fer a priest fer yer own?"

Newton grinned widely. "'Tis on me list of t' dos on the morrow, lass. I promise."

"An' if ya doan, I'll be doin' it meself. Ya ain't gettin' off now, laddy. Me heart has a hold on ya, an' I intend t' have ya e'en if it means puttin' a gun t' yer head."

Newton laughed as they went up the back steps and into the kitchen to find Mrs. O'Grady stirring up a meal for the tenants. He looked at his watch. "Ya must hurry, lass; we be late."

"I'll need only t' change me clothes," Mary said, giving him a peck on the cheek. She had only just stepped away when Mickey O'Shay came through the door, a rifle in his hands. Newton got up slowly, his eyes on the weapon pointed at his midsection.

"Goo' evenin', Newton Daines," O'Shay said in a deceivingly pleasant tone. Though he was seemingly sober, the smell of whiskey cut through the air like sour mash, and Newton felt a sense of foreboding.

"O'Brien will 'ave yer 'ide fer this," Mary said angrily. "Ya know he told ya t' lay off Newton."

"'Tis nah Mr. O'Brien the two o' ya need t' be worryin' abou'," O'Shay said with a dark, inebriated chuckle. "Now ya be getting' o'er there by 'im." He wiggled the rifle barrel toward Newton. "And Mrs. O'Grady, I'll be askin' ya to move away from the drawer where ya be hidin' tha' hand pistol. Do it now."

Mary moved to stand behind Newton, and Mrs. O'Grady, her face flushed with anger, took a step away from the drawer.

"Ya been snoopin' around me kitchen, 'ave ya." She glanced at Newton, a glimmer of hope in her expression at O'Shay having taken his eyes off him, giving him a chance to make a move. But Newton simply shook his head, a sign for her to stay calm.

"An' who would we be needin' to be worryin' about if i' ain't O'Brien?" Newton asked.

Mickey smiled. "I be hearin' ya been helpin' nigras escape outta Little Dixie, Mr. Daines. Foolish o' ya, an' 'avin' Mary here 'elp ya, tha' makes ya even more a fool. Mr. Ridges, he be waitin' for us at—'"

"Ya been drinkin', O'Shay. Put tha' weapon down before ya 'urt someone," Mrs. O'Grady said.

"I'll be 'urtin' someone all righ'," O'Shay said harshly, "an' it'll be Mister High-an'-Mighty 'ere if 'e doan ge' movin'." O'Shay stepped in quickly and jammed the rifle barrel into Newton's stomach, making Newton fold like wet paper. Unable to catch his breath, Newton could not react quickly enough to keep O'Shay from then putting the barrel to his head. "Now, like I said, Mr. Ridges be waitin' fer ya an' yer girlfriend, bu' I be tellin' ya now, I'd just as soon finish it fer 'im right 'ere."

Newton knew he would have only one chance to make his move, and now was the moment. He jammed his hand up hard and into the gun barrel as it went off. The sound was near deafening, but he was shocked to see O'Shay go limp and drop the rifle to the floor, falling to his knees, and finally to his side, his eyes wide and staring, blood pouring from his skull onto the floor.

Newton looked up to see Felix standing over O'Shay, a large cast iron frying pan in his hand. He was breathing heavily, the fear and shock of what had just happened written all over his face.

"I . . . you nevah come, Massa Newton, and I . . ." Felix said, struggling for words, as if to make sense of what he'd just done.

Mrs. O'Grady watched them both, her eyes filled with shock at this unexpected scene. She turned to Mary and reacted with a harrowing cry.

"Oh, dear Lord above!" She stepped quickly past Newton, and he turned to see what had caused such a reaction. It nearly stopped his racing heart to watch Mary melt to the floor, her back against a blood-smeared wall.

"Oh, merciful heaven," Mrs. O'Grady said in anguish as she grabbed for Mary. Newton had already reached her, cradling her as she slid slowly to the hard floor. Mary grabbed his coat by the collar to catch her breath, and he let her head rest in the crook of his arm as his tears spilled onto her flushed cheeks.

"Mary, no!" he said desperately, alert to the growing red stain on the front of her dress. He had never felt such anguish as he realized that his action had caused O'Shay to shoot, and that Mary—his dear Mary—had been hit. "Stay wi' me, girl. Doan be leavin' me now, ya hear," he said, stroking her hair as his tears flowed, his brain muddled with sorrow.

She smiled up at him as if she felt nothing. Mrs. O'Grady got to her feet and ran into the other room, sending one of the boarders for a doctor. Newton heard the door slam as he touched Mary's soft cheeks and begged her to hold on. Mrs. O'Grady returned a moment later and knelt beside Mary, ripping at the cloth around the wound. The shell had gone through her upper stomach below her heart, and Newton nearly fainted at its width and size.

"Newton," Mary said softly, her hand reaching up to touch his face.

"Yes, Mary, I be here," Newton said, trying to force back the despair, to calm himself, to give her comfort.

"I . . . I . . ."

"Doan be tryin' to talk now, girl," Mrs. O'Grady begged while stuffing a clean rag into the wound. Mary grimaced with pain and seemed to go even paler in color as her body stiffened.

Mary blinked, fighting against allowing her eyes to close to escape the pain. "Newton, I . . . I love you."

"And I you, darlin'!' Now, you be fightin', Mary. Please doan leave me. Doan . . ."

Mary's head turned to the side, and her eyes glazed over. Newton shook her lightly as if to wake her, but she did not move. He felt the sobs tear at his chest and could not help the tears or the anguish as they escaped from his throat. He pulled her close, willing her to come back, to live, but still she did not move. He felt Mrs. O'Grady put her arms around him, felt her own sobs, and felt his anguish deepen to bitter anger. How could this be? How could he have lost her now?

Felix stumbled back against the wall, the horror of it all pummeling him. He slid to the floor away from the others in shock. He looked at Newton then at Mary, her eyes wide, and then at the dead man in front of him. It was then that he realized others had come into the room, and he saw one of them run out the back door screaming about a "nigra what killed Mickey O'Shay." It was only then that he realized he must run, but he could not; he could not even move. Another man looked in and said, "Ain't that Mickey O'Shay? O'Brien will kill whoever done this." But Felix still could not move. He did not care. Mary was gone, and he'd done it.

"Newton," Mrs. O'Grady said, realizing herself what was happening around them. She forced back the sobs and gained control of her voice, as she wiped her eyes of tears. "Ya 'ave t' run. Felix . . . they'll hang 'im if y' doan get 'im away."

She tried to shake Newton from the paralyzing grief, tried to get him to listen. "Newton! Please, there is nuthin' ya can do fer her now. I'll handle things 'ere. You 'ave to run. If the coppers . . . if O'Brien. . . ."

Newton caught her words, heard them as if he were in a dream. "O'Shay, he said he was doin' this for Ridges," he said softly. Anger and hate were quickly turning his heart to stone. The only thing he knew for certain right now was that he must avenge Mary and that he must find Castle Ridges. He forced himself to gently lay Mary aside, to get to his knees, then to kiss her tenderly one more time before passing his hand over her eyes to close them. Then he got to his feet, bracing himself against the wall, trying to take it all in. The hall was filled with onlookers all trying to see. Felix was sitting on the floor, and Mrs. O'Grady and Mary—it all seemed like a horrible nightmare, and in his head he screamed to wake up, but nothing changed. Mary was gone. And Felix had killed Mickey O'Shay.

He stiffened. "Felix, get up," he said without emotion. "Now. We have to get you out of here."

Felix didn't move, though he looked up at Newton, his eyes filled with empty sadness. "I did it, Newton. Miss Mary, she be alive if—"

"Nonsense," Newton said brusquely. "Get up, Felix! We've got to go!" He reached down and tugged at Felix's arm. Felix responded, got up, and leaned against the wall as if he did not have the strength to move.

Newton pushed him toward the door once, then again. "Move! They'll 'ang ya, right or wrong," he said hoarsely, "an' ya 'ave a child t' live fer! Now get goin'."

Felix stumbled toward the door as Newton took one last look at Mary, his heart wrenching as he tore himself away. "You take care o' 'er, Mrs. O. Ya see she 'as a nice place, a fine place . . ." His lip quivered, and he could not go on. Mrs. O'Grady could not speak either and simply nodded her head firmly, indicating that she would see it done, then waved him to go on. He threw open the door, his eyes clouded with tears. Half stumbling and half running down the stairs, he pushed Felix on, and they were quickly traveling as fast as their broken hearts could carry them toward the docks. They wouldn't stop until they'd reached the deep hold of the *Constitution*.

* * *

Castle Ridges waited at the top of O'Fallon Street, where he sat on a bench on the boardwalk, his horse tied to a hitching post a few feet away. He checked his pocket watch for the third time in as many minutes. He had seen O'Shay go into the boardinghouse, but had not seen him come out. Then he had heard the shot and figured Daines was probably dead but still saw no sign of O'Shay. Then someone had run out and headed for the *Black Swan*. An uproar in the place had followed, and he watched as O'Brien and his thugs came boiling out of the place, the human contents of the entire saloon right behind them. One of the men broke away and came running Castle's way, so he reached out and brought the man to a sudden and painful stop.

"Hey, wha' d' you think yer do—" the man began. Then he saw that it was Castle Ridges. "Oh, Mr. Ridges . . . wha' can I do fer ya?"

"What's goin' on?" he asked, looking at the crowd disappearing down the street toward the river.

"Mickey O'Shay's been killed. Some nigra done it. They'll hang 'im, sure. Mary McConnell killed too. They say O'Shay shot 'er. Newton Daines, that fella what beat Kernlin, he's in it too. Mac will 'ave their hides on 'is wall, tha's sure."

Ridges shoved the man roughly forward. He stumbled away as Castle stepped off the boardwalk, unhitched his horse, mounted, and headed in the opposite direction of where O'Brien and his men had gone. He wanted nothing to do with the Irish now, not if O'Shay was dead. O'Brien might get the wrong idea, and if he found the darky and Daines and hung them, that was fine with Castle. He'd have what he wanted, and it wouldn't cost him a thing.

Chapter 40

RAND ARRIVED HOME JUST AS Ann, Lizzy, and Jacob Gates pulled up in a carriage. He dismounted and instructed Mose to see that the horse was returned to the arsenal. As he approached to open the carriage door for Ann, she leaned out and smiled at him. "Darling, I've decided to be baptized tonight. Will you do it for me?"

Rand looked at her, taken aback. "Of course, I—"

"Lizzy says she knows a perfect place for it, and everyone we want to be with us is here now. I wish to be clean—and to have your blessing by the laying on of hands. Will you do it?"

"Of course." He smiled. There was never going to be a dull moment living with Ann Alexander. "Jacob, what should the attire be for the occasion?"

"A suit for you will be fine. Ann should wear a white dress if she has one."

"Then we shall meet back here in a few moments," Rand said with a smile.

"While you are changing, I'll gather some blankets and towels," Lizzy said, following all of them into the house.

Rand's heart began beating faster as he thought of what he was about to do. He had never dreamed that such an event would be his privilege. It was very humbling and a bit frightening. As he went upstairs, he tried to remember the baptismal prayer as well as how to confirm Ann. He had neglected to ask Jacob, and now the task was upon him. He gathered an extra shirt and pants and then wondered where he would possibly change. He discarded the clothing on the bed. Lizzy was bringing blankets; that would have to do. But what about shoes and socks? Would he leave them on or take them off, and. . . . He took a deep breath. He was in a suit. The rest did not matter. Entering the hall, he found Amanda pacing and talking to herself.

"Oh dear, oh dear," she was saying over and over.

"Mother Alexander, what is it?"

She looked up a bit dazed. "Oh dear, I am so confused."

"About what?"

"About being baptized," she said impatiently. "If Ann thinks she should have it done again, then it is possible that mine is no good either. And I do want to be sure. I am getting quite old, you know, and something could happen any day, especially with war coming. Here today, gone tomorrow, and having to meet the Lord just after. I do want to be sure."

"Then there should be no question," Rand said. "It can't do a bit of harm, can it? And if the scriptures are right and authority is necessary, and if what Ann and I have been telling you is true—"

"Yes, yes, of course it's true. I quite believe it, but I am a bit nervous about the water. It will surely be cold, and I never could swim—"

"I will be quite careful about it, Mother," Rand said, putting an arm around her shoulder. "Is that the dress you want to wear?"

She looked down at her garb. It was a plain linen dress, white, with small pale blue flowers in it. "I suppose it is good as any other. I will need a change of clothes or a blanket or something, won't I? Of course I will." With that she disappeared into her room as Rand chuckled softly. Jacob Gates came up the stairs at that moment, and Ann exited her room, bonnet in hand.

"Possibly I should give the two of you some instruction," Jacob said.

When Rand nodded gratefully, Jacob went on. "Ann, stand here, next to Rand. No, no, put your blankets on the chair there, both of you. Now, Rand take her right wrist in your left hand. Ann, put your—"

Amanda came out of her room at that moment, her bonnet already in place along with a shawl over her shoulders. She was carrying a blanket as well.

"Mother, what—"

"Rand and I have decided that I should be baptized as well. You will not mind if I join your church, will you, Mr. Gates?" Amanda asked.

Jacob chuckled. "No, Mrs. Alexander. You are quite welcome." He went back to his instruction, and all present paid close attention.

"Yes, that should be quite easy," Ann said when Jacob was finished.

"Easy for you, but not so easy for me," Amanda said, clearly quite confused by which hand went where. "But, never mind. If I drown, I drown—at least the Lord will find me coming to Him a new woman. Let's hurry before I change my mind."

With that they were off down the stairs, where Lizzy waited with towels, Lydijah at her side, holding a stack of blankets.

"I be comin', if ya don't mind, Massa Rand," she said. "And Mose, too. And y'all be needin' someone to dry ya good. 'Sides, been since Nauvoo that I attended a good baptism. Always hep'd me remember my own and dat doan do no harm no how."

"I wouldn't have it any other way," Rand said as they went outside, where Mose waited on the driver's seat of the carriage next to Elliot. Lydijah joined her husband and son, and the rest of them piled in Rand's carriage before Elliot drove down the lane toward the same creek where Newton had been trying to bathe before he came upon Lizzy. Elliot took them to a path above the pond, where they got out; under a lantern's light, they walked down a tree-covered path to the pond. The cover of thick forest muffled the sound; even the birds seemed to be asleep. When they arrived at the pond, Rand and the two Alexander women set down the blankets and towels they had been given by Lizzy and Lydijah, then took off their shoes.

"Ann, you go first," Jacob said. "Rand, help her into the water until you are covered to your waist. That should be sufficient. And Ann, be sure your feet stay down, and tuck your dress in around you so that it doesn't float up. You must be completely immersed."

"Oh dear, so much to remember," Amanda fretted. "Surely I will float to the top like a bloated fish."

"You will be fine, Mother," Ann said with a smile. Ann quickly used a band to pull her hair back so it would not float to the surface so easily.

"Just watch how Rand and I do it. Are you ready, darling?" she said to Rand. There was a childlike look of excitement that lit up her beautiful features, and Rand knew he would remember this moment for the rest of his life.

Lizzy put an arm around a shivering Amanda to watch, and Lydijah and Mose stood directly to the side of them. "Are you cold, Amanda?" Lizzy asked.

"Oh, no, dear. I am quite excited. From the time I first started reading your mother's book and Ann began to explain things to me, I knew I wanted to do this."

Rand and Ann stood in the water, with Rand positioned properly, and they grasped one another's hands as Jacob had taught them. Rand took a deep breath, recalling the words and knowing that he must say them exactly.

"Ann Alexander," he began in a clear, calm voice, "having been commissioned of Jesus Christ, I baptize you in the name of the Father, the Son, and the Holy Ghost. Amen."

Ann sat back in the water, and Rand immersed her. As she came out of the water, Rand looked up at Jacob, who had the lantern held high so that he could see the ordinance clearly. Jacob nodded that everything had been done correctly, and Ann excitedly turned to Rand and wrapped her ams tightly around his waist, causing him to stumble backward, lose his balance, and topple. Ann fell against him, nearly pushing him into deeper water. They both struggled for footing and joined in the chuckles after they finally got their balance. He grabbed hold of her and held her tight.

"Thank you, darling. Thank you so very much," she whispered in his ear before pushing back and looking him in the eye. There were tears streaming down her cheeks, and she hugged him again. They separated a moment later but she held his hand tightly as they walked through the water to the shore, where Jacob helped Ann out onto the bank and Lydijah stepped forward with a towel so Ann could dry her face and hair. Rand noticed that on each face, tears glistened in the lantern light—even on the faces of Elliot and Mose, who stood up the bank a bit. He had to bite his lip against crying as he basked in the warmth of spiritual feelings not unlike those he had experienced so long ago when his father had taken him into a similar pond. "How delightful is the Spirit of the Lord," Baker Hudson had said, and Rand could testify that it was true.

"Come, Amanda, your turn," Jacob said.

"Now, dear boy, you must promise not to fall with me as you did Ann. I would drown if you did," she said firmly.

Rand smiled. "I promise, Mother. Come along." He lifted a hand toward her. Amanda stepped slowly down the bank, and Rand reached out to lead her into the water. He placed her hands correctly on his wrist, then once more said the words of the prayer before lowering her into the water and lifting her up again. Rand once again looked at Jacob, who nodded that all was well. Amanda was wiping the water from her face, a wide grin on her mouth. "How wonderfully warm!" she exclaimed.

"Yes, isn't it?" Rand replied. "Would you mind if I gave you a hug?"

"I would be disappointed if you didn't."

Rand put his arms around her and received a soft-spoken thank-you in his ear. Then he and Jacob helped Amanda get up the bank, where Lydijah handed her a towel and Lizzy offered her a blanket.

Lizzy turned to Rand and hugged him, holding him close. "I am so proud of you, Rand," she said. "I cannot imagine anything Father would be more pleased about than this. Not anything."

"And Mother?" he questioned with a smile.

"By now? She is beaming, I am sure of it."

"Randolph, we can use that log for a seat," Jacob said. "These are the words you must use for the confirmation." He repeated them, and Rand went over them in his mind. "Don't worry," Jacob added. "If you make a mistake, I will be by your side and will gently correct you."

"Thank you," Rand said with some relief.

"Ann, please sit there, and Rand will confirm you," Jacob instructed.

Ann sat down, her hair hanging damp on her shoulders. Rand had rarely seen her hair down, but he liked it very much, even more so given the moment. Rand and Jacob stood behind her; Rand took a deep breath and then performed the confirmation, making no mistake in his words and giving Ann a beautiful blessing. She would have children, see them safe and sound in the gospel, and find true joy in her relationship with her husband. Though hard times were ahead, she would bless the lives of many as she helped them through the struggle, healing spirits as well as bodies. She would receive all the blessings of Abraham, Isaac, and Jacob and stand as a witness for Christ in mansions as well as hovels. When Rand was finished, she stood and hugged him tightly again. "I will remember this forever!"

"I will advise you as I did Randolph about his ordination and blessing. Write down everything you can remember. These are the things the Lord wants most for you to remember," Jacob said. He then asked Amanda to sit. Once more Rand said the words and gave a blessing.

Amanda's blessing was filled with words about her husband and his desire to receive the truth. However, after a moment Rand had words come into his head that made him hesitate, unsure if he should actually say them. The prompting came more firmly though, and he took a breath and spoke.

"You are to see that his work is done for him. If you must go to Utah to accomplish it, the way will be opened for you." He then felt to bless her with comfort concerning her two sons—to tell her that the Lord was cognizant of them and that He would watch over them, but if anything happened to them, Amanda should not be discouraged. She would know of their place before God. Rand then closed the blessing and stepped back, a little apprehensive about the promises he had made.

Amanda looked up at him, her expression peaceful. "I understand what it all means, Randolph. And I am sure it is of God. You could not have known how worried I have been about my husband's place. He was not baptized, you know, and he was so bitter and angry at the end. He never felt the need for religion and felt God had deserted him when his friends took everything. I am sure he sees things quite differently now. Thank you."

Jacob smiled at them all, clearly content. "Now, let's get you back to the house," he said after a moment.

Ann took Rand's arm, and Jacob and Lizzy took Amanda between them as they moved back up the path, Lydijah following behind.

"My, my, Massa Rand, you does handle dat priesthood well," Lydijah said approvingly. "Your pappy, he be pleased, he truly would." Mose smiled in agreement.

Rand had never felt so at peace, so comfortable. There was a warmth to the air that he could not explain, and he wondered if others were present, watching, happy for them, and if they were. . . .

"Do you feel it?" Ann asked.

"Yes," he said softly. "Isn't it wonderful?"

"I know it is probably impossible to hold such a comfort very long, but I hope we can, Rand. I never want to lose it."

He squeezed her hand as she lay her head against his shoulder. "Nor I."

It was quiet as the carriage took them toward home, each of them enjoying the moment. After a few minutes, Elliot pulled through the gate and Jasmina suddenly appeared alongside the wagon, Shaymish in her arms.

"Mr. Rand! Mr. Rand!"

Rand looked out the window to see her running alongside the carriage. He sensed that something horrible had happened and cried for Elliot to stop the carriage.

"What is it, Jasmina? Has something happened to the baby?"

"No, no, Mr. Rand. Poo' Miss Mary has been shot. She dead, Mr. Rand. Oh glory be! She gone!"

A sudden fear descended over all of them, and Ann put her hand over her mouth at the horror of it.

"Jasmina, calm down. How do you know this?" Rand asked as calmly as he could.

"That Mrs. O'Grady, she sent a message. Oh, poo' Mr. Newton, and Felix too, suh! He done killed a white man o'er what he done to Miss Mary! And they's lookin' fo him right now. They's gonna hang 'im if they finds 'im. Oh, I can't bear it if they hangs 'im! Oh dear, what we gonna do, Mr. Rand?"

Rand hopped from the carriage and gave orders to Elliot. "I will be but a moment. Get the carriage turned around. We have to find them before the police do."

"But dey's run, suh! No one knows where dey went," Jasmina cried.

"I know where they will go. If they reach it, they will be safe. Don't worry, Jasmina; he'll be safe." Ann was climbing from the carriage, concern and fear in her eyes. "I will take care of her, Rand; you must hurry."

Rand, shocked at this sudden change in the occasion, did not move. He wanted to hold on to those feelings, but now—

"Go," Ann said again.

Lizzy was already running toward the house and yelled back over her shoulder. "I'm going with you."

Rand looked one last time at Ann then ran after Lizzy, who was already taking the front steps two at time.

* * *

Newton had changed his mind about going directly to the *Consitution*. He and Felix would surely be noticed, and any such sighting would force a search. Instead, Newton took them upriver until he found a small boat tied to a private dock. He did not like to steal, but it was their only way to board the steamer without being seen.

With Felix at the oars, they rowed out into the blackness of the river and approached the docks in the darkness. The steamers were two deep in some places at night, and Newton had a difficult time finding the *Constitution* until they were practically on her. He ordered Felix to row up to the side and then hit the panel that opened the outside door into the hideaway. Both men slithered quickly inside and shut the trap door behind them. Then they lay there in the dark, the heaviness of their feelings so thick it nearly suffocated them.

Newton could not believe she was gone. He had never loved anyone like he had loved Mary, and now they were separated by the most final state he knew: death. He couldn't even begin to comprehend never seeing her again. Surely God was punishing him for something to allow this! There could be no other explanation. What had he done to bring such wrath down upon her—upon them both!

"I's sorry, Massa Newton," Felix said in quiet anguish. "It was my fault. If I hadn't . . ." The sobs came, cutting off his words.

Newton forced himself to his feet and felt around until he found a lantern. Lighting it, he adjusted it to dim and hung it next to them. Near darkness seemed particularly appealing at the moment. Sitting down next to Felix, he put his arm over his friend's wide shoulders as best he could.

"Felix, he was pullin' tha' trigger when I rammed the gun upward. I' was my fault if i' was anyone's, bu' Mickey O'Shay 'ad come to kill or see us killed, all of us, and it's 'is fault Mary's dead—not yours. If he hadn't come . . . if Castle Ridges hadn't sent 'im . . ." Newton bit his lip against the ache and desire for vengeance. "I'll be leavin' ya here for the time bein', Felix. Ya stay put, an' they won' be findin' ya."

Felix did not respond at first, and Newton stepped to the trap door, opened it again and looked out. The small rowboat remained in place just where they had left it.

"Where is you goin', Massa Newton? I don't think youse should be leavin' with them men huntin' fer us," Felix finally said.

"Never mind abou' it, Felix. Mr. Castle Ridges is needin' a visit from the grim reaper, an' I intend to see tha' 'e has it."

Felix sat up straight. "No, suh, ya can't—"

But Newton was out the exit before Felix could get across the room to stop him.

The door slammed shut as Felix reached it, and he slammed a fist against the wall. "Newton! You come back here fo' I comes afta ya. You won't like it if I does. Now you get back here, ya hear!"

Newton heard the muffled sound of his friend's voice but was already rowing away.

* * *

Carrying two suitcases, Rand and Lizzy boarded the *Constitution* but did not go into the hold. They had seen half a dozen of O'Brien's toughs roaming the docks and had no intention of leading them to where Rand thought Newton and Felix were hiding.

Instead, they went up to the wheel deck, then through the deserted captain's quarters and into the hallway between rooms, then down a back set of stairs to the main deck's hold. From there, it was easy to enter the lower hold unseen.

Rand lit a lantern, found the handle, and opened the hideaway door. Entering with lantern in hand, he and Lizzy found Felix sitting wide-eyed on the edge of one of the beds. Newton was nowhere to be seen. Rand found the handle and closed the door behind him, then set the suitcases down.

"Where is he?" Rand asked.

"He done gone afta Mr. Ridges. He got hate in his heart, Massa Rand, and it gonna git him killed." He put his head in his hands. "Dis is all my fault, Mister Rand. I done killed dat O'Shay 'cause he was gonna kill Newton, and that there rifle went off and shot Miss Mary." His voice was filled with anguish. "If I hadn't hit him so hard, if I—"

"Then O'Shay would have killed Newton," Rand said. "You did what you had to, but O'Brien's after you, and so is the law. They're looking for a hanging; we have to get you out of St. Louis." Rand felt a twinge of guilt. He was helping a man escape the law, but he knew what would happen if he didn't. A black man who killed a white man didn't have a chance in almost any state, let alone Missouri. If he didn't help Felix, he was good as dead, and Felix was an innocent man.

"But my baby, and Jasmina—" Felix said.

"When you're safely in Canada, we'll send them to you," Lizzy said. She looked at the suitcases. "All of your personal effects are here. We knew you would want them."

Felix nodded. "Thank you, missus, and you, suh. You been good to Jasmina and me both an' . . . an' Miss Mary, I . . . someone needs to see she's taken care of," Felix said.

"Lizzy will claim the body, and we'll bury her in our family plot on our property," Rand assured him before standing. "I must find Newton now. Lizzy, go for the captain, and tell him to get his crew together and launch as soon as he can. Have him take Felix to Alton, and contact Mr. Hunter to get him on his way to Canada." He extended his hand. "God be with you, Felix."

Felix shook the outstretched hand. "I'll come back someday, Mr. Rand. If'n they let us black folks fight fo' our rights, I'll be doin' it, I promise."

"Let's hope it doesn't come to that, Felix, but if it does, I would be honored to fight alongside you. Now, you marry Miss Jasmina when she gets to Canada with Shaymish," Rand added.

Felix smiled. "Yes, suh, thank you, suh."

Rand and Lizzy turned to the door. "Please write and let us know where you are, Felix. And don't worry, I'll find Newton." He pulled the lever to let the door up, and they stepped through and closed it. Lizzy dabbed at a few tears and quickly followed Rand up the steps, wondering if this might be the last time they would see their friend but knowing that they must get him on his way.

Chapter 41

NEWTON'S ANGER AND RESOLVE GREW as he made his way steadily back to the Kerry Patch and found O'Brien sitting at his usual post, shouting orders to his toughs about finding him and Felix. Newton pushed through the crowd that surrounded the confab with little concern for his own safety and showed himself directly to O'Brien. The man stood, anger etching every wrinkle in his face.

"You!" O'Brien threw the table aside then came at Newton, who pulled a pistol from behind the belt of one of O'Brien's thugs before anyone knew what had happened. He pointed it at O'Brien's chest while he was still three feet away, bringing him up quick. "You'll be dyin' if you take another step."

The room went silent.

"An' me boys will take ya apart fer it," O'Brien replied through gritted teeth.

"Doan much matter t' me. O'Shay 'as killed Mary, and I just soon join 'er as let ya live, bu' it is nah you I be after. It's Ridges."

O'Brien seemed to weigh this statement and decide that Newton meant what he said. He moved his cigar from one side of his mouth to the other, then stepped back a bit.

"Castle? Wha' 'as 'e go' t' do wi' this?"

"He sent O'Shay fer me an' Mary. Mickey said so when he cum t' take us. Now I can pull this trigger an' 'ave me vengeance and die fer it, or ya can tell me where t' find Mr. Ridges, an' I be usin' this bullet on 'im. Bad as I feel right now, it doan really matter much t' me."

O'Brien thought a moment. He knew O'Shay had a history of sidling up to the Ridges, making side deals, but he hadn't cared about it much. Now he could see he should have paid a bit more attention. But there was the matter of Mickey O'Shay's killer.

"And the black fella, I'll be wantin' 'im."

"You can want all ya like, bu' you'll nah be gettin' 'im. O'Shay pulled tha' trigger an' died fer it. Doan matter who did it to 'im, an' if ya think it does, then you'll be wantin' t' kill me 'ere an' now 'cause Felix doan deserve nuthin' but praises fer tryin' to save Mary an' me."

O'Brien chewed on his cigar. "Ya know I won' stop lookin fer 'im."

"Look all ya want, but ya won' be findin' 'im," Newton said firmly. "Now where will I be findin' Mr. Ridges? Or should I pull this trigger an' meet ya at the devil's table?"

O'Brien seemed to relent and said, "He 'as a friend who owns a place in the woods west o' town. He stays there when 'e comes up from Little Dixie. Fond o' the man's woman-slave." Then he gave a few directions.

"Then I'll be leavin' ya." However, Newton remained where he was, waiting for O'Brien to give the word one way or the other. Finally O'Brien nodded to his toughs, and they backed away. "We all be sorry abou' Mary. She was a goo' woman."

Newton's eyes flashed with anger. "Then qui' tryin' to avenge the death o' the man who shot 'er. Doan look goo' fer ya to be doin' it. Brother-in-law or not, O'Shay was murderous scum, an' when ya quit thinkin' otherwise, we Irish will be thinkin' ya be defendin' the meek instead o' the butcher." There was a general murmur of agreement through the group, though O'Brien glared them all into silence.

Newton stuck the gun in his belt. "I'll be returnin' this once me business is finished, an' I be tellin' ya tha' I 'old ya responsible fer breakin' yer word. Ya promised tha' O'Shay wouldn't 'arm Mary, and ya let 'im. There'll come a time, O'Brien, when you an' I will settle on it."

With that he walked between a long row of hushed men. He felt certain that none of them would oppose him now, no matter what O'Brien said, and that some of them would back him if he did return. As far as Newton was concerned, Mac O'Brien's days were numbered.

And Mary would be glad for it.

* * *

Newton arrived at the house of Ridges's friend after midnight, and when he saw the windows still lit, he crept along the fence until he was close enough to get a look at the horses in the corral. He knew Castle Ridges's horse by sight and saw him standing near several others, head down in sleep. Creeping closer to the house, Newton recognized none of the voices and stayed low until he reached a window. Ridges sat with a threesome playing cards and drinking whiskey, and from the slur of their voices they had been drinking for some time. Scanning the room, he noticed a woman sleeping in a bed against the wall, a baby in her arms. A black slave girl sat next to the woman, with her head down, obviously frightened but resigned to whatever fate lay ahead.

Despite his reckless mood, Newton dared not burst in now with gun blazing. The slave girl and the woman and child certainly did not deserve to be hurt by his sudden foolish actions. He would have to be patient. Castle would have to come out sometime, if for no other reason than to relieve himself of the whiskey that would find its way through him. When he did, Newton would deal with him.

Leaving the house, Newton crept to a nearby stand of trees and found a place where he could see the cabin and the outhouse, then planted himself in deep grass to wait. A half hour later, he was startled by a rustle in the brush behind him and whipped around to find himself staring at a rifle barrel.

"Mr. Daines."

"Mr. Hooker," Newton said guardedly. "Ya shoul' nah be 'ere."

"I thought we might be able to help."

Newton recognized this second voice as another dark shadow appeared.

"Mr. Hoodsun. How di' ya find me?"

"I 'ad a man in the *Black Swan* when ya talked t' O'Brien," said a third man as he stepped out of the darkness.

"Mr. Malone. Seem's ya brough' a small army, Mr. Hoodsun."

"Enough to handle Ridges. Come with us, Newton," Rand said. "It's time we talked."

Newton cast a last glance at the house but reluctantly followed them, and the four men worked their way deeper into the woods and down a dry creek bed hidden from view of the house. Rand pulled a match from his pocket and struck it against the handle of his revolver.

"Newton, I understand your desire to put an end to Castle Ridges, but Mr. Hooker here has a better idea. I hope you will listen." He stooped down and put the match to a small stack of brush and kindling he had readied earlier. It quickly caught fire as Malone added a few more small pieces of tinder.

"Me mother give me a goo' set o' ears. She'd be disappointed if I di' nah use 'em," Newton said.

Hooker began to unfold a plan as the four men listened intently, perched on logs around the fire while Malone made a pot of coffee.

Newton did not respond immediately when Hooker had finished; his heart was still wanting revenge but his thoughts turned to Mary. She would not have liked him killing for vengeance, but she would have liked Hooker's plan.

"I'll be goin' along wi' yer idea," Newton acquiesced, "but know tha' if it goes badly I'll nah be flinchin' t' use me pistol on Mr. Ridges."

"Fair enough," Rand agreed. "We have a little time though. Let's get some sleep while we can. I'll take the first watch."

It had been a long walk from town for Newton, and he did not argue. He knew he would need his rest, and he gratefully took the blanket Rand tossed his way and found a dry bit of grass on which to roll up.

But despite his efforts, he did not sleep. Mary filled his thoughts, and he still could not imagine that she was really gone. He ached for her touch, her scent, her laugh, and her wit. He longed for all of it, and the anger and hate swelled until he got up from his blanket and stepped into the dark of night, searching for a place out of earshot. Then he collapsed to his knees and let his emotions go, the tears flowing freely, the sobs wracking his body until he simply could cry no more.

Chapter 42

Isaac Hooker surveyed the old cabin from the cover of low bushes in a stand of thick trees. It was chilly out, but he hardly noticed. He relished the outdoors and had fought in weather twice as cold, with wind swirling snow so fiercely a man couldn't see his fist in front of his face. This task was easy compared to those days and not nearly as dangerous.

Isaac figured there wasn't a man inside that cabin who could fight like the youngest brave of the Plains tribes. And with Malone, Rand, and Newton Daines working together, getting hold of Castle Ridges and putting him in shackles for a few years would be as slick as swallowing raw bacon.

Hooker had watched two men as they worked at chopping and stacking wood under the low-slung lean-to at the end of the cabin, and he had watched another man go to and return from the outhouse behind the cabin. But he hadn't seen Castle Ridges yet, and he wasn't about to give Rand the go-ahead until he did. Rand and the others were out of sight a few hundred feet behind Hooker, waiting for word to move in.

Hooker had readily agreed to the challenge of going after Ridges when he had learned about Mary McConnell. Rand figured it had to do with Newton and Felix freeing slaves out of Little Dixie, and Castle saw it as a way to hit back for Sam's death without getting caught. Hooker had once warned Castle to stay away from anything to do with Hudson, but it seemed that the man needed more than a warning. Isaac intended to see that he got it.

Hooker only wished Rand hadn't decided to take Castle alive. The man was meaner than a mad dog, and putting him away for a few years just didn't seem like enough.

A man stepped out onto the porch, his red flannel long johns visible above the waist of his pants. His suspenders hung at his sides, and he did a mighty stretch in the first rays of the morning sun. It was Ridges.

Hooker quickly signaled Rand and watched as the three men moved to their positions. Then he slithered back into the bushes and quickly caught up with Rand along the shrubbery line to take up a spot with a panoramic view of the cabin.

Peering through thick grass, Hooker could see Castle headed for the outhouse as expected. Catching a man with no weapon and no place to hide was as good as Hooker figured it could get. All they had to do was neutralize Castle's fellow varmints, and they'd have him whisked away before he could take a deep breath.

Rand lifted his rifle, and Hooker did the same. "I'll keep him pinned in the outhouse, you keep the others trapped in the cabin," Rand whispered.

Hooker nodded, then adroitly aimed and fired at the feet of a man who was sitting on the front porch, effectively blowing off a big toe. The man fell off his chair yelping, and another man quickly dragged him inside as Hooker reloaded.

With the first shot a wagon came out of the woods, Newton at the reins and Malone standing in back, braced with one leg against the seat and a rope in his hands, his handlebar moustache blowing in the wind.

The door to the outhouse opened a crack; Rand fired, hitting the top edge of the door. It quickly closed as Castle cursed loudly and screamed for help. Hooker's sharp eye caught the movement of a rifle being poked through a window; he quickly shot at its barrel, causing another curse as the rifle was jammed back into its user's face.

Newton deftly swung the wagon around the outhouse, and Malone threw his rope. It sailed through the air in a large loop that fell over the skinny one-hole structure. Malone jerked hard, and the rope tightened, jamming the door closed. As Rand and Hooker kept Castle's friends engaged, Newton backed the team up to the outhouse, and Malone securely tied the rope to the wagon seat. Newton then moved the team slowly forward, tipping the outhouse into the back of the wagon amid the hefty outcries and curses of Castle Ridges. When the outhouse landed with a thud in the back of the wagon, door up and the bottom third hanging out the back, Newton slapped the reins against the horses' haunches, and they bolted for the road home.

As the wagon passed by the main house, Rand and Hooker stood up, ran into the woods, untied their horses, and raced after the wagon. The first bullets whizzed past them as two of Castle's friends came out on the porch and fired, but the distance denied accuracy and the group rode onto the tree-lined road out of sight and range. As they raced after the wagon, Rand and Hooker eyed one another and grinned widely at the sight ahead of them: Castle's bare feet and trousers were dangling from the outhouse as it bounced and swayed down the road. His cursing burnt their ears as he wrestled with his trousers and the near impossibility of pulling them on inside the jostling, tight quarters.

In another mile the party turned down a side road and came to a stop. Malone and Newton hopped down and helped Rand and Hooker lift the outhouse and dump it out the back of the wagon and onto the grass. The rope slipped to the ground. Rand removed his revolver and invited Ridges out of his penthouse.

"And if you just happen to have a handgun in there, I'd be putting it down, Castle," Hooker said. "My fifty-caliber Sharps will make a mighty big hole in you if I see even the glint of steel in your miserable paw."

The door swung up as he spoke, and Castle's upper body appeared, his face beet red with anger. When he saw the large barrel of Hooker's rifle staring him between the eyes, he slowly and deliberately put his hands through his suspenders and lifted them over his shoulders as he stood straight. His pants in place, he stuck his hands above his head.

"I never done nuthin'," Castle growled. "You got no cause fer this, Hooker."

"Mr. Daines here would disagree," Rand said.

Castle gulped as Newton stepped forward, revolver in hand. "Ya sent O'Shay lookin' fer me. Well, here I be." He handed the gun to Hooker. "And I intend to beat you into a pretty pulp, Mr. Ridges—unless, o' course, ya think ya 'ave better fists tha' the ones I carry."

Castle looked at Hooker, then at Rand. "These boys going to shoot me in the back?"

"No need," Malone said, putting away his revolver. "Mr. Daines can 'andle hisself. Ya best be rememberin' Kernlin."

"I could take Kernlin in my sleep," Ridges said with an evil smile. Without further delay, he stepped out of the confines of the outhouse. He was obviously unarmed and Rand could see he was broad and muscled across the shoulders, thick in the biceps, and half again bigger than Newton—and knew that if he connected, Newton would pay dearly. But he was slow and clumsy, and when he moved in with a hard swing, the agile Newton danced under it, deftly moved right, and was ready with a hard right to Castle's jaw when he turned around. Ridges went to one knee.

After that, Ridges had little chance to even touch Newton. When all was said and done, he lay stretched out on the ground unconscious, his face raw pulp and quickly swelling. Newton rubbed his knuckles, but no other part of him had even been touched. He accepted his revolver back from Hooker.

"Mighty fine fisticuffs, Mr. Daines," Hooker said. "What would you have us do with Mr. Ridges now? Ya know he won't stand trial for what O'Shay done ta Mary." He had the Sharps ready and was itchin' to use it.

Newton stared at Ridges, then said, "'Tis so, but I recollect he's wanted fer blowin' up a steamer and should serve good time a' 'ard labor fer it. As much as I'd like t' stop 'is heart from beatin', Mr. Hooker, we ain't cold-blooded killers like 'im. If ya be takin' 'im t' jail, I'd be satisfied enuf." Newton had worked out his anger during the beating and had come to the realization during the night that Mary would not like him doing something he could not live with.

"Consider it done," Hooker said, lowering the Sharps. "I hope ta see ya back at the training for the Home Guard. We can use a man like you, Mr. Daines."

"I'll be there, but fer now I 'ave to say a proper goodbye t' Mary. Mr. Hoodsun, will tha' horse ride double?"

"No need," Hooker said. "Take mine. I'll ride with Malone in the wagon."

Newton nodded. He was bone weary, and after one last glance at Ridges, he mounted Hooker's blue roan and accompanied Rand back to the city.

They had gone nearly a mile before Newton spoke. "Mr. Hoodsun, ya spoke t' me once about religion. If there be a God I wish to know it, and I wish to know what be the future o' Miss Mary McConnell." The tears erupted once more, and Newton quietly sobbed out his grief.

Rand took a deep breath, pulled his horse closer to Newton's, and put a hand on his friend's nearest shoulder. He gave his best comfort, his own tears blocking any ability to speak. In his heart and mind, he said a prayer. Newton Daines needed understanding and he needed a blessing, and Rand intended to see that he got both.

Chapter 43

April 13, 1861

CAPTAIN ANDREW CLAY WATCHED FROM the shoreline nearly half a mile from Fort Moultrie as another cannon fired, this one from the direction of Cummings Point. The blast hit the walls of Fort Sumter and blew away additional stone and rock. Fire glowing from Sumter lit up the overcast sky like a torch in a dark room. Returning shots from Sumter had stopped; the wooden roof was now in flames, the walls crumbling from the incessant bombardment of nearly three thousand cannon shells over the last two days. Through his glass piece, Andrew watched Union men setting up a bucket brigade from the burning gate to the harbor, frantically passing buckets of ocean water inside to douse the flames.

Andrew then turned the glass to take in the three Confederate forts and floating battery that had done the damage. The Union had fired back when the Confederates had attacked, and each of the three forts had been hit; two had small fires burning, and Moultrie had two cannons knocked out, a good portion of her aging walls down. Win or lose, Robert Anderson had caused significant damage to Charleston Harbor's defenses.

"Let me take a look." Andrew handed the glass piece to his friend Campbell Owens, "Campy" for short. They had become friends in the time since Andrew had resigned his commission from the Union and joined the South Carolina militia. Both he and Campy served under Colonel Johnston Pettigrew of the First Carolina Rifles. Fortunately for Andrew, his unit was not directly involved in the fighting. He had friends at Sumter, and he did not relish the thought of their deaths in Davis's attempt to start a war. However, these were thoughts that he kept mostly to himself.

"Surely they can't last much longer," Campy said.

Andrew gave a wan smile. "But what will we have left when this battle is finished? Anderson knows what he's about. He'll make us work our tails off to get that place, then again repairing it, along with the rest of the lot he has managed to ruin. He might not win this battle but he will certainly make us miserable for inducing it."

It had been an interesting but mostly wretched two days. The people of Charleston, South Carolina, had lined the road along the shore to watch the affair as if it were some sort of sideshow. This had angered General Beauregard, but what could be done about it? Finally God had seemed to take the matter into His own hands, giving them a strong and hard rain for several hours that discouraged such onlookers and drove them into the dining halls to celebrate the Southern victory they were sure would come. It all seemed macabre to Andrew; for people to come to such a place to watch men die was surely an ungodly thing. He hoped he had seen the last of such sickness but deep down he doubted it. This was all a lark to most—a passing fancy. He wondered how many would look back on this time as a pleasant picnic if both sides didn't come to their senses before real war and destruction broke out.

"The place is nothing but flames. They'll have to come off that island soon," Campy said. "If they don't . . ."

Andrew took the glass piece from Campy and scanned toward Fort Moultrie, finding a small, twelve-man steamer just leaving its dock and heading to Sumter. "That's them in the steamer."

"Who?" Campy asked.

"Beauregard organized a peace commission this morning. They'll give Anderson one last chance to surrender." Andrew looked for the flagstaff over Sumter. "Flag's still up."

"Then he's still not ready to surrender," Campy grumbled.

"Oh, he's ready, but that flag won't come down until he gets the terms he wants." He put down the glass piece. "They'd have to knock those walls to dust to get Anderson out of there unless he was ordered out."

"You think Lincoln called this off?"

"Why not? He got what he wanted. The South just declared war on the United States. He can declare us in rebellion against the Constitution, stamp us all as traitors. Can you think of anything that would rally the North behind him in greater numbers than our actions here? And our aggression will keep Britain and France out of this matter as well. How can they justify helping traitors conquer a constitutional government?"

"We ain't traitors," Campy insisted gruffly.

"Yeah, but we ain't heroes either," Andrew said.

"You sound like you don't want war," Campy said, giving him a frustrated look.

"I don't. Lincoln gave us a chance to avoid this. We just slapped him in the face for it."

"Careful, Andy. Those words could get you put in the stockade."

Andrew nodded in reluctant agreement. The peace commission had reached Sumter's docking steps at the fort's gate, and Andrew trained his eyepiece on them. He scanned the Union officers who were now greeting the Confederates; all were accounted for—and except for a few bandages, soot-covered uniforms, and what looked to be near exhaustion, they had all survived without serious injury. Even from his view, however, he could see that the fort had not fared nearly as well. The main gates and wood-planked windows were smoldering embers, and the walls were completely torn out in several places and badly damaged in all others. None of the roof was left, and Andrew could only imagine that the wood walls of the barracks were gone as well. Most of the barbette guns had been hit; the rest were likely warped from the fire's heat. It would take months to repair the place and ready it for service.

"We had better get back," Campy said.

Andrew nodded. They had a regimental meeting awaiting them. The Union would assuredly attempt to retake Sumter, and the Confederate war department would have to protect against it.

Andrew had returned from his quick visit to see Lizzy in high hopes that all this wouldn't happen—that the so-called Confederate government would back down and avert this war—but when he'd arrived, the cataclysm had already broken, and now the South was plummeting into a war that Andrew figured it could not win. His only hope was that the North would back down or that some kind of treaty and negotiation would take place, but his gut told him it wouldn't. And he was trapped like a caged rabbit. He could not desert—he would not. But to fight his friends—to fight against his country. . . .

He shoved the thoughts aside even as he shoved his eyepiece into its case, and he and Campy started back the short distance to their horses. They reached the horses as a crowd of citizens passed along the street that fronted the harbor. Everyone was in full celebration with chaotic hurrahs and prideful chants that denounced the country they were still technically a part of. Charlestonians were pouring into the roadways, ballyhooing like they had just won the war. It was an affront, and Andrew wondered how many of the men and women dancing and patting each other on the back at this "great triumph" would be willing to sacrifice their blood when the Union army came south to reclaim their territory.

The two men rode quickly back to their encampment, avoiding the crowds and the celebrations. With every passing moment, Andrew worked to brace himself against thoughts of real war. There was still hope. There could be a compromise. He would trust that. He must trust it.

Andrew and Campy dismounted and stepped inside the headquarters building then waited nearly an hour before Colonel Pettigrew joined them. Pettigrew apologized but said he had been called to a meeting with General Beauregard. He then brought them up-to-date on what he called the "Sumter affair." The terms set forth by Anderson and his men had been honored, and they and all their arms and personal property were even now being placed aboard a federal ship waiting outside the harbor. They would be taken back to the North. Sumter was now in the hands of the Confederacy. There were no celebrations among the officers, some of whom, like Andrew, had been members of the Union army until only a few weeks earlier.

Pettigrew paused, his hands clasped behind him. "By confiscating federal property, we have effectively declared war on the Union. Telegrams from our friends in Washington tell us that Lincoln will call for seventy thousand troops to come and take Sumter, along with every other fort they say we have illegally removed from the United States. The response from the Northern states is sure to be overwhelming." He stood up straight. "Gentlemen, they will outnumber us three to one by the end of the month. President Davis has asked that we move north immediately to stop any Union army from marching into the South. We will prepare to leave in seven days' time."

"Doesn't that mean marching across Virginia?" Andrew asked.

"If they secede, yes. If not, our border will be just south of that state and we will defend it there."

"But there is a good chance they will secede," one of the officers said with hope in his voice.

"Very good," Pettigrew said.

"Then we should march across her and take Washington," said another.

Pettigrew smiled. "In good time, gentlemen. In good time."

The room was filled with eager comments before Pettigrew's aid called them all to order again and Pettigrew, his brow wrinkled at the interruption, continued speaking. "Gentlemen, we are no longer playing games or waiting on a political solution; we are preparing to defend borders. Make sure your companies are supplied and ready to move at a moment's notice. General Beauregard will expect us to rise up and fight forces larger and better trained than our own, but the survival of our infant Confederacy will hang on how we defend our new country." He forced a smile and leaned forward across the table behind which he stood. "They will come, but if we are successful in beating them back, gentlemen, Washington will sue for peace!"

The room was electric with excitement as Pettigrew dismissed them. Andrew and Campy said their good-byes then and mounted to return to their own companies. Andrew felt queasy with excitement and foreboding. Pettigrew had not mentioned war, only defense. Possibly if the South showed that it was willing to go to war to defend its borders and its sovereignty, the North would let it go. He would cling to that hope. He did not want to think about how much a war would change everything.

He moved his horse to a gallop and quickly arrived at his tent, where a private took the reins, allowing him to go inside and catch his breath before sending orders for his officers to join him. His eyes scanned the desk, where several letters awaited him; he sorted them quickly until he found the one he wanted. It was from Lizzy. His day suddenly became much brighter.

Chapter 44

RAND AND ANN HAD JUST finished breakfast in the hotel dining room when Lyon's adjutant walked up and handed Rand a message. Rand opened the envelope and quickly read it.

"I have transport waiting outside, Captain," the adjutant said. Rand nodded and saluted. The lieutenant left the way he had come.

"Sumter has fallen, hasn't it," Ann said softly.

Rand nodded.

"Lyon wants us at the arsenal immediately."

Rand had told her about his conversation with Lyon and his new commission, but both had hoped that Sumter would somehow survive, that the South would withdraw. Deep down, though, they knew the South would not surrender, and the wedding was still a week away.

"And Governor Jackson? What has happened in Jefferson City?" she said, trying to hide her disappointment.

"Not exactly as we anticipated. He is calling for a state constitutional convention on secession instead of a special session of the legislature."

"But what does that mean?" Ann said.

"It means he is buying time. Feelings are running high, even trending against the secessionists, because of Sumter. He is hoping that feelings will settle some before he asks for a vote on secession." Rand paused.

"But he will not get it, will he?" she asked.

"No, but we won't get a vote of support for the Union either. Neutrality will remain in place, and Jackson will insist that he will need the militia to enforce it."

"How long will that take?" Ann asked.

"A week at least." He forced a smile. "Don't worry, the wedding is still on. Unfortunately, I will be at the arsenal until then. We have a lot to do to prepare for Jackson's next move." The arsenal was poorly protected, and until now they had no reason to fortify it. The attack on Sumter had given Lyon an excuse, and he would take it.

Ann only nodded. Rand sensed her concern and put his arm around her, pulling her close.

"I am sorry, darling. I wish—"

She forced a smile. She knew she must not make things worse with pouting. He needed her support now more than ever. It occurred to her at that moment that there would be endless days of such need ahead of them and she must be up to it.

"My dear Rand, I am marrying you because of your integrity as well as your uncommon good looks. We will manage this, and we will do it together."

She put her arm through his and guided him toward the door and the carriage that waited beyond. "What will you need?"

He squeezed her hand, knowing she was hiding her feelings in the same way he was. He was scared at what this meant for them, and it was wrenching, but he knew he must control his emotions. "Tell Lizzy what is going on, and have Mose bring Samson to the arsenal along with my army uniform and a week's change of clothing. Send my scriptures as well."

"I will send everything you need," she said. As they reached the carriage, she turned into him and they kissed, long and tenderly. "I love you, Ann," he said.

She put a finger to his lips. "And I love you. It is what will get us through this." She climbed into the carriage, and as it pulled away, Ann leaned out and threw him a kiss. Then she fell back in her seat and let the tears flow.

* * *

The four hundred men Rand and Hooker had selected for the first call responded to the news within a few hours of hearing it. They had hastened to the arsenal and were given tents and gear, then bivouacd on the arsenal's parade ground, which had been designated days earlier. By five that evening, four hundred had signed up and were members of the regular army. That same day Jackson's request for secession was voted down in the assembly.

The next morning Lyon saw that the new men were all given the best weapons at the armory, and orders were issued for its complete defense. Two days later they were well entrenched and prepared fully to defend the arsenal. That same day Lincoln asked for seventy-five thousand troops, with five thousand of them to come from Missouri. Jackson's answer fully revealed his sentiment. Claiming Lincoln's request was "illegal, unconstitutional, and revolutionary in its objects," as well as "inhuman and diabolical," he refused to comply.

Jackson and other secessionists privately ranted against Lyon's fortification of the arsenal. They were even more inflamed when Lyon issued a statement declaring that with the attack on Sumter and other federal forts—and the governor's obvious Southern sympathies—he had no choice. The defense of the Union was ordered by the president, and he intended to protect federal property at any cost.

By the evening of the third day, a building just outside the confines of the arsenal had a dozen Minutemen soldiers on its roof, all watching the army build fortifications. As Rand and Hooker watched the place, they figured a good fifty men were housed inside. Word was that Jackson had ordered Atchison and others to begin uisng the secessionist Minutemen to keep a close eye on the arsenal and to make sure that the weapons did not leave the premises.

By the end of the fifth day, a dozen patrols of Minutemen were seen in the streets that ran along the low walls of the arsenal on three sides. The river flowed along the fourth, and no patrols were seen there, but Lyon wisely ordered some of Rand's men to build fortifications to defend it just the same.

By April 18, the forces under Lyon's command were dug in and had finished a half dozen cannon emplacements. They were ready for what might come.

Rand hadn't slept much. He missed Ann horribly and though he sent notes each day, he had not seen her since coming to the arsenal. He had talked to Lyon about the wedding and had been assured he would be able to be there, but he also knew that could change at any minute. Torn between his duty and Ann, his nights had been torture.

Rand was called to a meeting at about eight that evening, and as he entered the outer reception room of the headquarters building, he heard the voice of Frank Blair coming from the adjoining office. Lyon's aid stood and saluted Rand then ushered him into the room where Frank, Hooker, and a few of Lyon's staff had already gathered.

"Captain," Lyon said, returning Rand's salute. "Please, sit." Lyon pointed to a chair. Rand took his seat while nodding at Frank. Something wasn't quite right.

Frank turned to face Rand, who sat to his right. "Rand, it looks like the legislature will give Jackson permission to raise the militia. They are already gathering at Lindell's Grove, just a few miles from here. It will take them at least a week, maybe longer, to gather enough men to be of any concern to us. But we have learned that the Confederacy is amassing an army on our southern border and will send some of them secretly into the state to join Jackson's forces." He looked at Lyon, who cleared his throat before speaking.

"The army on our southern border is preparing to come into the state as soon as Jackson is ready. We can no longer afford to remain here, defending the weapons. We have to become mobile if we intend to keep Missouri in the Union."

"If you do, we will have a civil war of our own," Hooker said.

"There is no longer a choice. If that army joins up with Jackson's militia, we will lose the state, and the Union will be surrounded by the Confederacy. It is a dire circumstance, and we must respond. We can no longer remain tied to the arsenal," Lyon said.

"What you are saying is that we have to get rid of the weapons, then move inland to protect the state," Rand said.

"That is correct," Lyon said. "We will keep what we need for our growing force and send the rest to Illinois."

"If you are looking for our support, you have it," Rand said.

Lyon looked at Frank, who seemed a bit nervous. "The weapons will not go to Illinois alone. As you know, I have promised that we will send troops for the defense of Washington. We are sure now that Virginia will secede, and there is deep concern that Confederate troops will move against the capital. They need every man we can provide," Blair said, pausing as if to muster strength. "Though we cannot send as many as he asked, now they must have at least four hundred in Washington as fast as we can get them there." Frank leaned forward. "But they must be our best men."

Rand realized what was coming and felt sick inside. Washington was a long distrance from Ann Hudson.

"General Lyon and I want you to lead them. Hooker and Malone will go with you," Frank rushed on. "I know what we are asking, Randolph, but we need someone of your ability, strength, and personality to lead these men. You will be taken into an eastern regiment with men and leadership unfamiliar to our men—soldiers who may not be all that willing to readily accept Missourians. A strong leader who can hold his own with such men will be absolutely necessary." Frank put a hand on Rand's shoulder, his eyes tearing up. "I consider you family, Randolph, and I have agonized in coming to this decision, but you are the only one we feel we can trust with this. Will you go?"

Rand felt weak, overwhelmed. Leaving Ann, now? It was like someone had hit him in the stomach. But what other choice was there? How could he stay behind, after everything he had said and asked of others? He looked at Hooker, who only shrugged and gave a slight nod, which meant it was Rand's call but he was with him whatever he decided.

Rand took a deep breath and said, "We'll need Rosenthal as well, and we will accept only volunteers from members of the Home Guard who I know have the heart and preparation for a fight."

"I would send federal troops if I could, Captain," Lyon said.

"Your men are needed here," Rand replied. "After all, we'll need homes to come back to when this is finished."

"I will have papers drawn up that will introduce you to the appropriate leaders in the capital," Frank said with obvious relief. "We will also give you vouchers you can present to the treasury for any costs incurred getting you and your men to Washington. You will be given uniforms all of the same kind even if some of the other men have to give theirs up, and those who go with you should be encouraged to pack a good deal of extra clothing and personal items. I fear they will be gone for some time. We will send tents, wagons, and other supplies with you. You will take a steamer to Alton, catch the train to Chicago, and then travel on to Washington."

"And you want us to go when the arsenal weapons are sent to Illinois. How soon?"

"Now. Within a day or two at most." Lyon stroked his reddish hair back and away from his high forehead.

Rand felt weak, even queasy. How was he going to tell Ann all this?

Seeing the look on his face, Hooker spoke. "Three days. We can't get them ready in less," Hooker said.

Lyon nodded agreement. "The only question that remains, then, is how to get you and those weapons out of here without the opposition gaining knowledge of it—at least until you are well on your way. Not an easy task, to say the least."

Rand only half listened to them discuss options while his mind reeled from what was being asked of him. Three days. Only three days. He leaned forward, trying to shake it off and catch up with the conversation. As he did, he realized he had a solution. He cleared his mind and his throat to speak. "May I offer a suggestion?"

Lyon was standing behind his desk, eyeing a map; he turned to face Rand. "You may."

Rand laid out his plan over the next fifteen minutes, answering questions and making clarifications.

"It should work," Hooker said when he was finished.

"Captain, you know your tactics," Lyon said with a smile. "You have the order to see it done." He pulled a cigar from a box on the desk, and both Rand and Hooker got to their feet. "Gentlemen," he said, looking at Rand, then Hooker. "Begin your recruitment; Captain Hudson, see to your plan for the removal of the weapons."

They saluted one another, and Rand and Hooker left the office.

"Well, we've stepped in it now," Hooker said with a grim smile.

Rand felt only numb. "You know the best men, Isaac. Talk to them and talk to Malone and Rosenthal."

"What are you going to do about the wedding, Rand?"

"I don't know, Isaac; I don't know."

Hooker only nodded as he walked away to take care of his orders.

Rand stood where he was for a moment simply because he was too petrified to move. It wasn't just about Ann, either. Though he had no doubt that the three men he selected wouldn't do anything other than accept and be as true to him as men could be, and even though he had no fear of a poor response in recruitment, he completely feared his own inadequacies. He had never been in combat, and the fight was sure to come to Washington. His men would rely on him for their very lives. How could he possibly be all that they needed?

After another few seconds of paralysis, he finally forced himself to turn right and head into the armory building. The guard stood outside the door, the key hanging from his belt.

"Soldier, I'd like to go inside," Rand said, saluting.

The soldier saluted back, then used his key to open the door.

Rand went inside, and the door shut behind him. The sound of his boots pacing the floor echoed off the walls as he tried to think things through; to gain some sort of confidence in his ability to accomplish this mission; to calm his fears about leaving Ann, Lizzy, and everything else—but to little avail. He found himself as confused on all points as when he had first entered the room. Finally, he knew he must pray. Finding a shadowed corner, he knelt and bowed his uncovered head, pouring out his heart for help.

Rand prayed every day now, sometimes many times, but not always in any formal fashion and not very often with the deep need he felt now. He knew he must find help far beyond himself, and he had come to know in recent months that there was only one place where that need could be met.

Rand did not leave the armory for nearly an hour. He prayed, paced, and prayed again. Finally he felt peace and felt that he had some direction. He got to his feet and put on his hat before leaving the Armory. He must trust the Lord to take care of things that were too far away to see clearly, and he himself needed to focus on the things that needed his attention now.

As he turned around the corner of the Armory, he nearly ran over Newton Daines, who was pacing in front of Lyon's offices. He could see Newton had something on his mind.

Newton had been on his list of those he could trust and the first to walk through the gates and enlist in the regular army when Sumter fell. They had spent two nights talking about Newton's questions, but mostly Newton had just kept to himself and done his duty.

"Mr. Daines," Rand said. "What can I do for you?"

"Rumor is that you be takin' some men to Washington. I'd like t' be goin' wi' ya, if ya doan mind."

Word had gotten around quickly. "I'd be honored." Rand still felt a keen ache for Newton and could see that he needed this assignment—and needed it badly.

"I have something for you, but I will need you in your old civilian clothes for a few days. Do you have them here?"

"Yes, sir."

"Get changed into them, and then find a horse. Meet me here in fifteen minutes."

Newton saluted and was about to leave when he turned back. "Just though' you'd like t' know, sir. Castle Ridges was found t' be guilty and will be sent off t' prison today."

"Too bad they didn't hang him," Rand said.

"'Tis true, but he'll be learnin' first 'and wha' he did t' men like Felix o'er th' years. Tha's goo' fer somethin'." Newton walked toward the neatly formed rows of tents in the middle of the arsenal's parade ground. Rand figured having Castle Ridges punished helped Newton only a little, but even that counted.

Rand went to where Samson was tied; he saddled and bridled the horse, then went inside and asked Lyon for permission to leave the arsenal for the night. He received it without question, and by the time he was mounted on Samson, Newton had returned, an army horse in tow. They mounted and rode to the gate and out of the arsenal.

After riding to the docks, they dismounted in front of the slip where the *City of Alton* was docked. Rand asked Newton to wait, then went inside and visited with the captain. When he was finished, they mounted again and rode farther south to the slip where the *Elizabeth* was just returning from her voyage upriver. Rand and Newton tied their horses to a hitching post and walked to the ramp now being set in place from ship to shore. They found Captain Welltrain and pulled him out onto the second-deck walkway.

"Mr. Daines and every other carpenter working for us who is loyal to the Union will begin to refit this ship for armor," Rand told him, then turned to Newton. "I want you to go and see Mr. Eads at Eads's shipyard. He'll give you a crash course on making a good beginning."

"You are going to armor her here, at this dock, right in plain view?" the captain asked in amazement.

Rand smiled. "We are."

"Nothing like thumbing yer nose at the Southies," the captain replied with a shrug.

"That is our intent, Captain Welltrain. I want every secessionist in St. Louis to see what we are doing, but I want armed guards around the steamer night and day. A show of force. The Minutemen might take offense to our armoring this steamer and might try to burn her down to the watermark."

"You've got somethin' up yer sleeve, Randolph," Welltrain guessed.

"I can't tell you any more, but your assignment is important. I'm trusting the two of you to make this look good." He turned to Newton. "Are you up to the task?"

"Yes, sir," Newton said.

"All right. Go see Eads, Corporal. And Captain, keep the steam up. We'll need her under full power in two days."

Newton was already mounted as Rand reached Samson. He watched as Newton rode away, then mounted and headed home. Ann had to be told.

Chapter 45

During the next two days, aside from occasional trips to check on the *Elizabeth*, Rand spent his days and nights at the arsenal. As word thundered around the city that the militia would be called up and camp at Lindell's Grove, only a mile from the arsenal, Lyon and Blair pushed training at a fevered pace. Rand was heavily involved.

He had gone to see Ann with the news of what had happened, then held her as she cried. They had read and prayed together. He promised before leaving that he would be there for the wedding—a wedding that was to take place in just two days. He longed to be with her.

In midafternoon the next day, Rand dressed in regular street clothes and mounted Samson to ride to the *Elizabeth,* where he wanted to check in with Newton on the progress and preparations for the night's transfer of weapons to Illinois. Tension was rising on both sides, and now was no time to confront men of a Confederate mind, alone and in uniform.

As he and Samson approached, he could see the superstructure of the *Elizabeth* and was amazed by the progress of the armoring. He also noted the growing crowd along the pier, an unfriendly dark cloud hanging over them. His plan was working.

Seeing he would have to go through a hostile crowd to get to the *Elizabeth* this way, he turned Samson around to come in from the south, where there seemed to be an opening along the dock strewn with crates ready for shipping.

The mob near the steamer had begun to gather on the first day as lumber had been stacked on the pier and the armoring had begun. Newton had made no attempt to conceal the operation, and as they had worked, the mob had grown drastically in size. Shouts and denunciations had followed, and the captain soon saw that the guards he had armed would not be enough. He had since called on the local police to protect the *Elizabeth*. Fortunately, the head of the city police was a friend of the Union and had responded quickly, placing his men in such a way as to prevent anyone from boarding the *Elizabeth*.

Rand tied Samson to a post, worked his way around a dozen crates, and boarded the *Elizabeth* to the sound of raucous name-calling from the crowd. He hid his smile and approached Newton and the captain.

"Gentlemen," he said, "congratulations. Our little deception is working quite well."

"Too well, if'n you want the truth," Welltrain said uneasily. "Ya could lose this steamer if we wait much longer."

"We move early tomorrow." He laid out the plan for the two men and asked if either had any questions; both said no, wide grins on their faces at last.

Rand then quickly left the steamer, mounted Samson, and returned through the city to the arsenal. As he traveled, he noted growing numbers of Minutemen and militia in the streets near the arsenal. Their numbers had been multiplying in the city, and the building they occupied to keep an eye on Lyon's force was growing. Rand figured there were a hundred men on the premises watching the arsenal both day and night. Rand was glad of it. He needed them to see every move he made.

Passing quickly through the well-guarded gate at the arsenal, Rand returned to the administration building. He went inside the headquarters office and was highly surprised to find Ann and Lizzy present. He could not help his grin as Ann ran to him and threw her arms around his neck.

Rand glanced at the other officers in the room, all of whom were smiling expectantly. As Ann pulled him in for a kiss, he heard the chuckles until Lyon cleared his throat and Ann pulled away, her face flushed and her hand trying to put her hat in place—something she always seemed to have to do after kissing Rand. But Rand was sure that the bright red color of his soon-to-be bride's face could not come close to matching the color of his own scarlet flesh.

"Captain, your wife and sister have been kind enough to deliver a few victuals for our use this evening," Lyon said, glancing at a long table nearby. Rand saw that it was heavily loaded with cooked ham, baked pies, loaves of fresh-baked bread, and endless other items.

"Obviously they know how to reach the hearts of us all," Rand said, smiling at Ann and Lizzy.

"Yes. They will be joining us for this fine meal, along with General Blair and his lovely wife and some other folks your wife has invited. It seems she would like to have a wedding," he grinned. "But only if you're agreeable, of course."

Rand wasn't sure he had heard correctly until Hooker stepped forward dressed and ready to be best man.

"Gentlemen, let's bring a little order to these proceedings," Lyon said. He looked at Rand over the top of his reading glasses. "Captain, I think you should find your uniform."

As the men in the room moved about to set up chairs, Ann pulled Rand into the back room and threw her arms around him, kissing him passionately. Then she pulled back and smiled up at him. "After you left the other night, I decided I could not stand by only to have you whisked away to Washington on the evening of our wedding. I hope you do not mind."

"Mind? My darling, I am elated, but how did you get Lyon to agree?"

"As you can see, it took a rather large bribe. I fear your larders are temporaily emptied but I hope," she blushed slightly, "that as the evening wears on you will feel the sacrifice is worth all of it."

"I have no doubt. What about your mother and Lydijah and—"

"All the important guests will be present." She gave him a hug and then pulled him toward the kitchen. "Come and see."

Rand found the entire household family present, and each stepped forward with a wide grin to give him their congratulations.

"Jacob," Rand said as his friend stepped out of the crowd.

"I just arrived and glad to be in time." Amanda stepped to his side and smiled at Rand. "Isn't this wonderful? Far better than we had planned! Mr. Gates, I need your help with some lifting. Do you mind?" The two of them went to the task, and Lydijah and Mose replaced them, tears in their eyes as they hugged him. "Now you go on," Lydijah said. "Get ready for dat weddin.' We's got work to do to prepare all dis food."

The chatter and bustle were happy and warm, and Rand had to choke back his tears as Ann pulled him back to a side room where Lizzy waited. "I have to dress, and so do you. A half hour, Rand."

Rand pulled her to him for one last kiss, but Lizzy put an arm between them.

"Oh, no. I'll never get you two apart. Off with you, Rand." Lizzy grinned as she opened the door and pulled a reluctant but smiling Ann inside and closed the door behind them.

Rand left by a side door and went to his own building. Hooker intercepted him halfway across the lawn.

"The things we do for the cause of freedom," he said with a wry smile.

Rand laughed. "Not exactly the setting I had in mind but it will certainly do."

"And think of the logistical value."

Rand looked stumped.

"It should make the Minutemen assigned to watch us very jealous to see us having such a feast. Possibly some will slip across lines and change their loyalties," Hooker said.

Rand chuckled again. "Yes, I suppose that could be a plus, but I am not exactly sure where Ann and I are to . . . uh—"

"Elliot will have your chariot waiting just outside the office door. After the I do's and the rush back down the aisle with rice stinging your handsome face, he will take you two lovers to a hideaway only he and I will actually know about. You will have your privacy until duty calls early tomorrow."

"Thank you," Rand said.

"Now, off with you. You have a wedding to dress for," Hooker said. He watched his friend disappear through the door to his quarters, then turned and went back the way he had come. Somehow it just didn't seem good enough.

Chapter 46

THE EIGHTEEN-YEAR-OLD MILITIA recruit watched the arsenal grounds from a nearby rooftop. The smells of roasted meat and good food still hung in the air, making him salivate, but the meat was gone and the Union fires were but dying embers. Except for a few stragglers walking around the compound, most men had gone off to their tents to sleep, and the arsenal no longer had the air of feasting and celebration.

It had been a revelry at the arsenal, but there had been no drinking—something that was mystifying. The recruit could not understand such a party. He had been fed moonshine since the day he stopped nursing at his mother's breast, and a party without it just didn't seem right.

But he had still enjoyed the sounds and smells for some three hours before men and music went to bed. Then he had watched as wagons and several carriages had left the compound before settling in for the rest of his watch.

Yawning, he looked up at the stars. From their position he knew it was after midnight. He dozed a bit until he heard the sound of several wagons moving into the arsenal compound. He quickly got to his knees, squinting into the darkness, where he could see the outline of the wagons as they pulled up outside one of the buildings. He narrowed his eyes even further and noted that there seemed to be a good deal of sudden movement, with doors swinging open and lanterns lighting up crates being packed by soldiers to be put in the back of wagons. He immediately nudged the man sitting next to him; he did not wake. He nudged the man again, speaking in a loud whisper and telling him to get up. He was answered with nothing but a moan and a slap at his hand. Finally he slapped his friend hard on the side of the head.

"Get up, idiot."

"Ouch!" the groggy man said. "What'd ya do that fer?"

"Quiet! They're movin' them rifles and all that other stuff! Look!"

The man got to his knees and looked over the edge of the building. He blinked, tried to focus, then rubbed his eyes. "Holy cow! Yer right!" He scrambled across the roof, keeping low, and went to the door. Taking the steps two at a time, he was quickly downstairs and bursting into an office where a dozen men wrapped in blankets slept on the hard floors.

"Hey! They're movin' them guns!" He started shaking one of the men. "Sergeant! Hey, Uncle Bradford! Wake up!"

Bradford King rolled over and looked into the eyes of his nephew, the words only beginning to register. When he realized what was happening, he scrambled to his feet, ordering everyone else up. He then ordered his nephew to run to the Bernholdt Mansion and tell those at headquarters. The young man ran from the room, the clamor of his boots on the brick pavement echoing in the street.

King had arrived at Lindell's Grove only this morning and had been sent to command this unready bunch of Minutemen to watch the arsenal. Now he considered it his good fortune to have gotten here just in time, as he was militia and had the governor's authority to act and gain control of the arsenal's weapons.

Going immediately to the roof, King looked at the wagons that were loading in the distance. It was dark enough that he could see only their outlines against the whitewashed buildings, but he could hear voices and see the movement of large crates being put in the back of each large hauler. He called for all men still on the roof to join him, and as they went downstairs, he opened several doors and ordered more men into the street. By the time he had his boots on the paved brick, there were nearly a hundred men stumbling after him, eyes wide despite their sleepiness, trying to figure out the fuss. He called them to order and told them to be ready to march. He then moved between buildings to a covert position he had located earlier where he could watch the arsenal at ground level. The loading of the wagons continued for another fifteen minutes; with each passing second, Bradford King became more convinced that Blair and Lyon were moving the weapons out of the arsenal. They had to be stopped.

"Bradford, what is going on?" King turned to see David Atchison behind him with several other soldiers.

"Well . . . near as I can tell, they're moving the weapons, sir," King said.

Atchison stepped to a vantage point, pulled out his field glass and took a closer look. "Ten wagons, all loaded to the hilt." He put down the field glass and turned to the Sergeant who had come with him. "What's going on with Hudson's steamer?"

Rand's lack of effort to hide his work on the *Elizabeth* had not failed to attract Atchison's attention. He had assigned his own men to keep an eye on the *Elizabeth* and had even gone to see the steamer himself. Rand Hudson still stuck in Atchison's craw and pained him worse than a bad tooth, but Hooker's rather direct warning had kept him at bay thus far. But this was different. Atchison and King had the governor's authority now, and Hooker could do nothing about him keeping those weapons from going aboard Hudson's steamer.

"Half hour ago she was still in dock, sir," the sergeant replied. "But we think she took on cannon this morning. Two big crates. They sat 'em in those reinforced positions at the stern we've been watching 'em build."

"Did you see the cannon?"

"No, sir, just crates, but they showed up on a steamer that came from Washington and were transferred immediately to the *Elizabeth*. They're armoring her, sir, and it seems likely they'd need cannon before they send her to war, sir," the sergeant said.

"Was she still holding steam?" When a ship was being repaired, her boilers were usually shut down, but the captain of the *Elizabeth* had kept hers going.

"Yes, sir," came the reply.

Atchison smiled. "Mr. Hudson has prepared a ship for the delivery of those weapons to the Union. Mr. King, get your men down to that steamer. If those wagons get anywhere near her, I want them stopped. If they get the weapons aboard her, we'll lose them."

* * *

Rand watched from the upper deck as the wagons turned from Fourth Street onto Chestnut Street and headed down to the docks. The *Elizabeth* was taking on a whole new look as the carpenters threw up a superstructure and built cannon emplacements at the back of the main deck. After tonight's activity she'd be taken to Eads's boatyard for the rest of her plating.

"Corporal Daines, the wagons are coming. You know what to do," Rand said.

Newton, standing on the first deck near the front of the steamer, positioned the men across her from side to side. There were a dozen of them, all armed and well instructed.

Rand descended the steps and stood on the ramp connecting the ship to the dock. He watched as the wagons drew close and a group of men ran out of Market Street in his direction. They were rather excited and well armed; most were dressed in the uniform of the Minutemen. And they looked determined.

The first wagon reached him and was about to pull onboard when the apparent commander of the armed mob stepped up and demanded that the wagon be stopped. Daines and his men hesitantly drew back at the sudden demand, and Rand put up a hand to the teamster as the horses came to a halt. It was then that he recognized Bradford King.

"Bradford. What seems to be the problem?"

"Those guns are not leaving this city." King seemed determined, sure of his position.

"Guns?" Rand said as if confused.

"These wagons came from the arsenal. We watched them loaded and followed them here. We know what is in them, and we will not allow them to leave this city," King said adamantly.

"Mr. King, even if you are correct—which you are not—you would be a fool to interfere with the transfer of federal property. These men could shoot you if you tried to stop those wagons."

King glanced at Daines and his scant group of soldiers, then gave a hard smile. "We outnumber your men five to one."

Rand did his best to look disturbed at this apparent revelation. "Any attack on these men would be an act of war. Is that what you're looking for?"

King hesitated and seemed a bit confused, as would any man confronted with such a question. His hesitation caused a good deal of murmuring in his command as well until a second fellow stepped from among them and came to Bradford King's side. Rand was actually delighted to see him but kept a straight face.

"Mr. Atchison, you might want to attempt to convince Mr. King to reconsider any attempt to take federal property."

Atchison sneered. "The arsenal sits inside the state and is housed on state property. That makes the weapons state property as well, and the governor has asked that we confiscate them as such."

"Has he? Then he is a bigger fool than either you or Mr. King, which is saying a good deal," Rand said.

"Listen you . . . you nigra-lovin' abolitionist; we are taking those crates, and if you fire on us for it, I swear that every man here will drink your blood." He turned to his men. "Unload those crates, immediately!"

No one moved, and Atchison became even more irate, causing Rand to stifle a laugh.

"You idiots! Move!" Atchison screamed. He stepped to the wagon himself and started pulling at one of the crates. The others, seeing that Newton and his men did not fire, joined him and began unloading.

"Mr. Atchison, you realize you are declaring war with this action," Rand said firmly.

Atchison hesitated only a moment, then scoffed, "That's already done, Hudson. At Sumter. You foolishly think you can keep Missouri from seceding. With these weapons and ammunition, we'll chase every Union-loving sympathizer out of this state, and that includes you and Frank Blair. You just as well pack yer bags. You're finished in Missouri."

Several cases were unloaded from the first wagon and stacked on the dock as another steamer in the midst of the river passed by, blowing its whistle. Rand smiled.

"Mr. Daines, it looks like we've done what was necessary. Get those wagons on board as soon as they're empty, and let's move away from the docks before Mr. Atchison decides he can butcher us as well as steal crates belonging to the federal government."

Newton waved the wagon onboard when it was unloaded and did the same for each succeeding one. After all were loaded, Rand ordered Captain Welltrain to cast off.

Newton watched as Atchison gloated and King finally got his composure back. Then he smiled at both of them as the last rope was pulled on deck and the *Elizabeth's* paddle wheels turned and moved her away from shore. "I hope the South is pinning their hopes on the two of you," he called. "It will be a short war if they do, and that is best for all concerned. Good day, gentlemen."

Atchison turned away without bothering to reply, then called, "We've done it, men. We've got 'em!"

The men gave a loud hurrah and began shaking their weapons in the direction of the steamer as a sign of victory and bravado. Rand watched with a wide grin as Atchison grabbed a big knife from King's scabbard and pried up the lid of one of the crates. The *Elizabeth* was a good hundred feet offshore when he lifted the first lid and began flinging out packing material.

Rand heard the curse, then the quiet of the men as Atchison lifted a large stone from the crate. He tossed it aside with even greater curses. He fumbled through the packing material only to find another, and another. King joined him as they continued their frenzied search for the absent firearms.

"Mr. Atchison," Rand yelled. "Sorry to disappoint you, but we thank you for being a part of this necessary diversion. We are much obliged for your cooperation."

The short-lived celebration turned to a sudden realization of what had happened; then a frenzy of angry cursing erupted. Atchison ordered his men to fire on the *Elizabeth*, but King quickly countermanded.

"Don't be a fool," King said loudly. "That's exactly what Hudson wants. He can call federal troops into the state if you fire on a civilian target, and that will cost us everything!"

A fuming Atchison glared at Rand from across the water. He then turned and pushed his way through the crowd and disappeared.

Rand turned to the others onboard the *Elizabeth*. "Thanks for following orders. You did manage to look frightened."

"It t'wern't easy," one man said. "Came mighty close to putting a bullet into the arrogant traitor just to see how many would stand and fight 'cause I done it."

Rand laughed and watched as a distraught group of Minutemen left the docks. The first skirmish over Missouri had been won.

* * *

Lizzy watched from her carriage parked in the shadows of a side street as the *Elizabeth* distanced herself from the docks. It gave her a good deal of satisfaction to see Atchison's reaction and then watch the men drag themselves off the docks with their horns sawed off. She told Elliot to take her home, and the carriage began to move.

It was probably the last time she would see the *Elizabeth*. She had signed the papers to sell their largest carrier to the government, and once the steamer returned to St. Louis to drop its last passengers, including Ann, the steamer would be on its way to Eads's boatyard to finish refitting. It had been a grand vessel and their most profitable steamer. Elizabeth only hoped her namesake would prove as successful in the field of war.

She removed a small hand lamp, lit a match, and fired its oil into flame. Pulling a folded wire from her purse, she opened it and read it once more in the dim light of the lamp. It was from Andrew and was received only last night.

"Sumter has fallen. Going north to defend new borders. Send new address soon. I still trust in a quick end. Pray for me. I will write soon. Love, Andrew."

She blew out the lamp and put it in its metal box on the carriage wall, but she held the wire from Andrew a little longer, a concerned wrinkle to her brow. He had said nothing one way or the other about the declaration of faith she had painstakingly written in her last letter. But the wire was signed with his love, asked for her prayers, and said he would write soon. That certainly was a postive.

But would it even matter? The South was already on the march, and Rand was headed for Washington to defend the Union against just such an action. The one thing she had dreaded since falling in love with Andrew was about to happen—the two men she loved most would face off in the killing fields of war. The thought was paralyzing.

But she could not let it be. Surely even rabid politicians would come to their senses before blood was spilt. They must. This country had a much higher purpose and could not be destroyed even by devils incarnate. She must plan for their return—both of them. She must keep the business operating for Rand, and she must keep her heart strong for Andrew. They would all survive, and her efforts would help determine what they would come home to.

Despite her attempt to be positive, Lizzy felt suddenly overwhelmed, and her shoulders sagged in near despair. How could she do it all? How could she?

She could not. She needed help. More than Ann or her uncle or a dozen clerks like William Dickson. She needed God. She fell to her knees and bent over the seat, her elbows pressed against the warm leather. She would not rise until the carriage pulled up to the step of her own home. It was an act she would duplicate hundreds of times as the storms of war gathered and poured forth their deluge in the months and years to come.

She wiped away her tears and put on a smile, telling Elliot to get something to eat before they left again. She still had a trip to Illnois of her own to make. It was time to send Jasmina and Shaymish to Felix in Canada.

* * *

The *Elizabeth* made her way upstream, her two powerful paddles dipping deep into the dark water as she hastily glided on the surface of the Mississippi toward Illinois. Rand could see the lights of the steamer *City of Alton* a half mile ahead of them. When she docked, a small contingent of Lyon's federal troops would offload the weapons she had received under cover of dark at the arsenal's landing, put them in the wagons the *Elizabeth* now carried, and accompany them to Springfield, Illinois, where they would be turned over to the Union army. They would end up in the hands of the gathering numbers of Union troops preparing for war.

Rand and his men would board the late train to Chicago. Frank Blair had arranged for several extra cars to be added to accommodate their numbers. In a few days they'd be in Baltimore.

"What are you thinking, Darling?" Ann was standing next to him, her arm through his. He turned into her and put his arms around her waist, holding her close while looking into her eyes. "How much I will miss you."

Ann lay her head on his shoulder. They did not have much time. Rand would disembark at Alton, and she would return to St. Louis on the *Elizabeth*.

Fear and anguish at parting were about to overwhelm her when she remembered the blessing Jacob had given Rand—a blessing she had nearly memorized over the last two days as she sought some solace for their separation.

Randolph Hudson, the Lord promises to bring you through the great storm of wrath and destruction that lies ahead. Trust in Him, listen to Him, heed His commandments, and He will bless you, keep you, and bring you home.

Ann took a deep breath and pulled her husband closer, basking in his warmth. She knew he would do his part—he would trust, he would listen, he would keep the commandments.

And she would hold the Lord to His word.

About the Author

Robert Marcum is a retired member of the BYU–Idaho religion faculty and is presently serving as a stake president in the Rexburg Idaho Henry's Fork Stake. He is married to Janene Andreasen, formerly of Grace, Idaho, and they have eight children and twenty grandchildren. He graduated from BYU in 1972 and received a master's degree from Idaho State in 1982. He taught for seminaries and institutes for seventeen years before receiving a position at Ricks College/BYU–Idaho, where he taught for another seventeen years. There, he served as chairman of the Religion Department for five years. During that time, he led student and adult tours to Israel, Egypt, Greece, Turkey, Italy, France, and England, and he, his wife, and four children lived in the Ukraine while he taught a semester of religious studies at a university in Donetsk. He has written ten additional novels for the LDS market in action, adventure, and historical fiction.